ACCIDENTALLY

Engaged

ACCIDENTALLY Engaged

FARAH HERON

FOREVER

New York   Boston

Forever
Hachette Book Group
1290 Avenue of the Americas, New York, NY 10104
read-forever.com
twitter.com/readforeverpub

First Edition: March 2021

Forever is an imprint of Grand Central Publishing. The Forever name and logo are trademarks of Hachette Book Group, Inc.

The publisher is not responsible for websites (or their content) that are not owned by the publisher.

The Hachette Speakers Bureau provides a wide range of authors for speaking events. To find out more, go to www.hachettespeakersbureau.com or call (866) 376-6591.

Library of Congress Cataloging-in-Publication Data

Names: Heron, Farah, author.
Title: Accidentally engaged / Farah Heron.
Description: First edition. | New York : Forever, 2021.
Identifiers: LCCN 2020042919 | ISBN 9781538734988 (trade paperback) | ISBN 9781538734964 (ebook)
Subjects: GSAFD: Love stories.
Classification: LCC PR9199.4.H4695 A63 2021 | DDC 813/.6--dc23
LC record available at https://lccn.loc.gov/2020042919

ISBNs: 978-1-5387-3498-8 (trade paperback), 978-1-5387-3496-4 (ebook)

Printed in the United States of America

LSC-C

Printing 1, 2021

To my parents.
Thank you for teaching me to hope, to love, and
to always be empathetic. And most importantly,
thank you for teaching me to laugh.

ACCIDENTALLY

Engaged

CHAPTER ONE

For most urban dwellers, Sundays were a day of rest and relaxation. Not for Reena Manji. For her, Sundays required vigilance and a thick skin. She had long ago learned that the only way to survive the so-called fun-day was to erect a proverbial steel wall around herself. But today's wall hadn't prevented her deep sense of disappointment when she woke up to see Brian's betrayal. She approached him slowly in her kitchen. Three days of headway meant nothing. Today, Brian the Rye, her temperamental sourdough starter, hadn't risen at all.

Her shoulders fell. "Seriously, Bri?"

Her first mistake had been naming the starter after a man. After a dozen failed relationships, Reena felt confident that she knew next to nothing about the male segment of the species, except maybe that they sometimes needed tender coaxing to get them to behave. But she didn't have the time or energy to coddle Brian through his histrionics now.

So she parked him in the fridge, dressed quickly, and downed a cup of cold brew coffee. Sunday brunch with her family was nonnegotiable and would start in less than half an hour. A slight hangover from last night's nachos and rosé wine upstairs had Reena hitting snooze on her alarm one too many times, and she was now dangerously close to being late.

As she dropped her keys into her purse to head out, she noticed an unfamiliar man lugging a bike backward up the exterior stairs to her building, while struggling with a six-pack of what looked to be imported beer.

Her head tilted as the mystery man reached the top of the stairs and attempted to wedge the bike on the narrow porch before opening the door into the building. He wore shiny black athletic shorts and a gray muscle shirt. No dreaded Lycra, which told Reena either he didn't take riding too seriously or had enough fashion sense to avoid those sorts of monstrosities. As he bent to put the beer on the porch she was treated to a peek of toned thighs and…*yum*, a spectacular ass. Ripped arm muscles flexed as he lifted the bike to rest it on the railing around the porch.

A brown Captain America. *Nice.*

She stepped closer to the door—outwardly to help the man, but really to get a better look. Plus, Reena had questions.

How did he ride a bike while holding a six-pack?

Did he live here, or (perish the thought) was he just visiting someone?

And most importantly, did his front come anywhere close to matching that fine back view?

Reena pushed the door open for him and finally got a glimpse of his face: smallish eyes, thick brows, and dark, floppy hair. Plus, a meticulously trimmed douche-beard a touch too trendy for her tastes. What a shame. He did have that nice sweaty-man smell, though. God, it had been too long.

"Thank you," he said as he passed through the door into the tiny hallway, leaving his bike outside. "I'm not sure I could have managed that on my own."

Mystery man had a British accent! And a deep, almost aristocratic voice. Totally unexpected. He put down the case of beer in front of the door across from hers and took a key out of his pocket before turning to Reena. He stared wide-eyed for several seconds before speaking.

"Oh, shit. It's you. You're my neighbor. You live here?" he said, pointing toward her door.

"Yes...why?"

"You're the one." Dark brows raised as his mouth widened to a grin. "The goddess who makes my apartment smell like a bloody French boulangerie!"

Reena's eyes widened. Goddess? She'd been called elfish, pixie, and even a sprite once by a Renaissance fair-type boyfriend, but Reena Manji was never a goddess.

"It's driving me fucking mad!" Sexy-voice continued, tilting his head and winking. Kind of flirty, this one.

Reena reassessed her first impression of his face. When he was smiling, his dark eyes sparkled under the fluorescent lights of the narrow hallway, and his lips looked wide and expressive. And that voice? Kind of swoony. Couple that with the impressive physique, and Reena started to think today was looking better. Nothing like a little British Isles to spice up this building. Some fun, flirty banter with a sexy Brit to boost her self-esteem each day. Plus, he liked the smell of her bread. Double swoon. And, she glanced at his hand resting casually on his doorknob, he appeared single—no ring.

"Thank you." Reena beamed. "Baking bread is my hobby. I'll bring you some one day. I have to head out now, but nice meeting you, neighbor."

"The pleasure's all mine." That charming smile again. White, straight teeth. And...a dimple on his left cheek? Mr. Uninspiring quickly advanced to Mr. Pretty Damn Hot. He should never stop talking with that voice. Or smiling with those teeth. Thankfully, he hadn't yet. "I'd love to take you out for a pint if you'll share any extra baked goods lying around. Are you free tonight? I'm Nadim." He held out his right hand to shake.

Ooh, did he just ask her out? "I'm Reena." She shook his hand, taking note of his firm, confident grip. Nothing worse than a weak handshake.

A moment into their handshake, however, Nadim's face fell. His smile dissolved and furrowed lines appeared on his forehead. What the hell?

Eyeing her intently, he snatched back his hand and ran it through his sweaty hair. "Bollocks," he whispered. "You're Reena Manji?"

She spoke slowly. "Yes."

"Aziz Manji's daughter?"

Obviously. "Yes...why?"

"Fuck. You live here?" He tugged at the back of his neck. Finally meeting her eyes again, he smiled sheepishly. "I've made a terrible first impression. Any chance we could start over?"

Her eyes widened.

"Forget all my swearing, and pretend I'm showered and dressed respectably. I had this suit picked out for our first meeting," he continued. "And my hair was supposed to be clean. Also, you didn't see that beer. And I didn't call you a goddess...although I meant it..." His voice trailed off, losing power as he seemed to shrink in the hallway.

"Why? How do you know my father?"

He smiled again, but this time the smile looked forced. It

didn't quite reach his eyes. "I am here in Canada to work for him." He sighed. "Your father and my father just entered a business partnership together. And apparently...you and I are to be married." He shrugged, one side of his lip raising slightly. "Surprise?"

CHAPTER TWO

Reena closed her eyes and took a deep breath. Crap. Not this again. Her captivating stranger turned out to be just the same as the countless other men her parents had dug out of the *Muslim Bachelors "R" Us* warehouse. She met his sheepish smile with a blank gaze for several seconds before mumbling something about being late and rushing down the stairs. Cute smile, sexy voice, and strong legs could not even come close to overriding this monstrous problem with the new hottie across the hall: Nadim worked for her father, and his presence in her life had been orchestrated by her parents. That was a great, big *no*. Yet another thing she couldn't have because of them.

～

There were two things Reena could always count on during her weekly brunches at home. One, there would be soft puri. Puffy, pillowy rounds of fried flatbread ready to sop up spicy channa and yogurt. And two, her overinvolved parents would attempt to insert themselves into every aspect of her life, all while her younger sister, Saira, managed the impossible feat of being both passive-aggressive and self-involved in the same breath. Reena attended these brunches religiously for the puri, not for the quality time with her family.

And, as expected, the heady scent of strong chai and spices eased her annoyance as she walked into the house after driving the ten minutes while fantasizing about being an orphan. She inhaled deeply as she removed her shoes. *This.* This was why she decided to come today. Nothing like her mother's cooking to ease stress, even stress induced by her parents themselves.

Of course, Reena knew she was deluding herself. She hadn't *decided* to come to brunch for the puri any more than she had *decided* to come for the family judgments disguised as scintillating conversation. The word *decided* implied free will. And when it came to family, free will was nothing but a convenient illusion Reena created for her own sanity.

She operated under the assumption that giving in to these insignificant demands on her life would trick them into leaving her alone with the big stuff. It sort of worked. She'd stood her ground on *some* big decisions. Like her decision *not* to work in the family real-estate development business. Her decision *not* to live at home, despite being single. And her controversial decision several months ago to insist her sister move out of her apartment. But it was becoming harder to make her parents understand that she had no interest in any of the approved Muslim men they had been parading in front of her since she reached the age of twenty-five. Including this new overseas model.

But at least the puri helped make up for this emotional torture. She took another from the platter and added it to her plate heaped full of channa masala.

"Reena," her father said, pouring himself more chai, "I don't know if I told you, but my friend Shiroz from Tanzania is investing in the Diamond building project. His son Nadim has come from Dar es Salaam to work with me. I've put him in your building."

Dar es Salaam, Reena's parents' hometown, was the largest city in Tanzania, a country with an active and vibrant minority Gujarati-Indian population. The Diamond project was her father's biggest real-estate development to date—a large retail/ residential building north of Toronto. She knew there were foreign investors from Africa involved but hadn't heard about the involvement of any flirty beefcakes who sounded more British than Tanzanian.

"I hope you will make Nadim feel welcome. He's a very smart man. Graduated from the London School of Economics. He's religious and well-mannered, and has a promising future ahead of him. You two have much in common."

Proof that Dad knew nothing about his middle child. No one who really knew Reena would call her well-mannered. Her sweetness ran surface-level only. And clearly, her father didn't know Nadim too well either. The man swore like a Manchester United hooligan and invited her out for a pint upon first meeting, all while holding a six-pack of beer. Reena had nothing against drinking, as evidenced by her low-key hangover most Sunday brunches, but in her religious Muslim father's opinion, *well-mannered* and *respectful* meant no alcohol.

Also, Nadim seemed a bit of a player—winking at her, calling her a goddess, and asking her out before even knowing her name. Reena enjoyed players for a good time every now and then, so long as she recognized what they were. But it was troubling that Nadim asked her out when he knew he was supposed to marry his boss's daughter (the fact that he unknowingly flirted with his fiancée seemed beside the point).

Saira smirked across the table while stirring a green smoothie. "Sounds a little ambitious a match for Reena, don't you think? He's probably completely bald, like that architect guy you dug out for her."

"Saira!" Dad said, his hand up to quiet his youngest daughter. Wow. Was Dad standing up for Reena?

Reena herself didn't bother glaring at Saira. Didn't even glance at her. Just mopped up her channa with that last bit of puri before licking the masala off her fingers. It wasn't worth it.

Saira was currently smack-dab in the middle of a year from hell, and her coping strategy of taking subtle jabs at her older sister seemed to be working for her, so Reena kept her mouth shut. It was the least she could do after Saira lost her job and came home to cry to her fiancé Joran, only to get an eyeful of Joran's naked ass above his cousin visiting from his hometown in Holland, or something. Saira wasn't Reena's favorite person, but she wouldn't wish that sequence of events on her worst enemy.

"Reena, I know you will be on your best behavior with Nadim, and make the *man* feel comfortable at *home*," Mum said, smiling. "Your father has known Shiroz Uncle since primary school. They are already like family."

Reena tensed. It was impressive the way Mum could say *marry this man*, without actually saying *marry this man*. Even if the proposed groom himself hadn't leaked her parents' intentions himself, she would have known what they were up to.

"Mum..." Reena groaned. "I just—"

"Na!" Mum snapped. "No more excuses. You're *thirty-one*, beti. No more single in the city...it's time for you to settle down! Look at Khizar! He's having twins! Even Saira was engaged, and when that didn't work, she found Ashraf!"

"Seriously, Mum? What do you mean, *even*?" Saira snapped.

Mum smiled, patting Saira's hand. "Shush. Reena is older than you. It's her turn to find someone successful." Mum looked at Reena with a proud smile. "Ashraf is management!"

Technically. Reena was happy that her sister had put her life back together and was dating again, but managing a mall kiosk selling prepaid cell phone plans hardly made Ashraf upwardly mobile.

"We're getting older," Mum continued. "I don't want to worry about my children anymore. Who will take care of you when we're gone?"

Reena had no idea if Mum realized how ridiculous she sounded. This wasn't Regency England and she was no Mrs. Bennett, desperate to marry her children off well to prevent financial ruin. How the hell could a beer-drinking, douche-bearded, bicycle-dragging flirt be the answer to avoiding spinsterhood?

"Promise me, Reena. Don't be like with the other ones. Promise me you will make an effort with Nadim," Mum pleaded.

Reena forced a smile. "Anything else going on?" she asked. Deflect and distract. Reena wouldn't make promises she had no intention of keeping.

"I heard on the Facebook site that Salim Shah lost a small fortune on a hotel deal gone bad," Dad said.

Holy crap, *the* Facebook site?

"Dad, since when are you on Facebook?" Reena made a mental note to update her profile's privacy settings.

"I've joined a new group there. Ismaili business networking group." Keeping tabs on his professional rivals was Dad's favorite pastime.

But Reena was trying very hard not to be as judgmental as her parents. Time to change the subject again. "What's that?" She pointed to a glossy black bag on the sideboard.

"Oh, it's for you." Mum reached behind her to get the bag and handed it to Reena. "I was in Zipporah yesterday and they had these lovely rollerball perfumes. I bought you a langi langi one." She handed the bag to Reena.

"Sephora, I'm assuming." Reena took it and peeked at the small glass bottle in it. It was ylang-ylang essential oil fragrance. Langi langi was the name used for ylang-ylang flowers in Dar es Salaam, and Mum knew Reena had always loved the scent. It was a generous gesture…but Reena had to wonder…

"You know in the summertime all of Dar es Salaam smells like langi langi. There is even a big tree in the courtyard of the Jamatkhana in town. I'm sure the smell will remind Nadim of home."

There it was. The gift was to lure the man in with a siren scent. Reena opened the bottle. It did smell amazing. She'd been to the Dar es Salaam Jamatkhana, the Ismaili Muslim place of worship, and the entire courtyard was filled with huge trees with fragrant blooms. This scent totally reminded her of the warm tropical breezes there. She sighed, closing it and putting it in her bag. "Thanks, Mum."

"Now tell me, Reena," Dad said, "is there any more news

about your company hiring a director of finance? It's high time you took a management role. If not at Railside, I am sure we can find a company with more growth opportunities."

Reena finished chewing her channa before answering. "I'll definitely inquire, Dad, but I have no interest in leaving Railside right now. I love it there," she said, an enthusiastic smile plastered to her face. It was a lie. She hated her job. In fact, she hated working in finance altogether. But if Dad knew that, she'd once again get grief for insisting on this line of work instead of working in the family business. She wanted that like she wanted to lick a metal pole in January.

Reena had enough of a life outside of work that she didn't care that she didn't find her work fulfilling. But Dad would never ask her about that life—in his eyes, only work mattered. Not hobbies. Not bread. She couldn't let on she'd been seriously thinking of enrolling in a night school program in artisan bread baking, hoping it would temper the monotony of the day job. That conversation would be weird—*hey, Mum and Dad, my finance job is sucking out my soul every day, so I'm draining my savings to take an insanely expensive class to learn to make better baguettes and a really good pain de campagne.*

"Well, I'd hate to hear that your career is stagnated," Dad said. "You know, at your age I had—"

"Saira has news," Mum interrupted as she passed the dish of channa to Reena to refill her plate.

Saira smiled. "Mum, I wasn't going to tell Reena yet! It's still not confirmed."

Reena prepared herself to hear Saira's fabulous news. It would be fabulous—in the Manji house bad news came whispered in hushed voices in darkened rooms, not told at the brunch table.

If told at all. Maryam Aunty had been admitted to hospice before anyone told Reena she had cancer.

Straightening her spine, Reena took the bait. "What's going on, Saira?"

Saira's brows shot up as her smile widened. "Remember Janice? From high school? She works PR for publishers, now. She saw my posts on the Nourish blog and thought I should write a cookbook. She's helping me with a book proposal!"

Reena blinked. Her sister was aiming to get published? A cookbook?

"Clean living is so big now, and Janice thinks I can sell my Indian take on it."

Reena took another puri and squeezed the whole flatbread in her mouth at once, cheeks expanding like a hamster eating a burrito.

"Careful, Reena," Saira said. "That's how many puri now? You don't need all that refined wheat."

Sage advice from her sister. The puri was now a gummy, doughy ball in her mouth. She took a long gulp of lukewarm chai to wash down the bread before speaking. "That's great, Saira. Good luck."

"Yeah, isn't it amazing! My therapist thinks it will be healing for me."

Reena drained her chai, wishing for whiskey in it. Healing. That was why she couldn't be angry at Saira. Saira needed this more than Reena did. And technically, no one in the family knew it was Reena's almost lifelong fantasy to write her own cookbook. And they didn't know just how close she'd come. That a small independent publisher had approached her and asked her to pitch a project when her cooking blog was still going strong. But the book deal fell through thanks, in part, to Saira. Reena wasn't over her dream crashing and burning, and having the very person who lit the match now rub it in her face felt a bit much.

She ate another puri, chewing until the gummy mass almost choked her.

"Reena, you should be proud of your sister. Look how well her life has turned around," Mum said.

After hitting some serious rock bottom, Reena *was* glad Saira had a job at Nourish, her favorite health food store. Was glad her depression was being managed with professional help. Even glad Saira had a new relationship. But being glad about her sister writing a cookbook? She tried to be a good person, but Reena wasn't Mother Teresa.

"Reena, did you hear Khizar is being considered for junior partner in his firm?" Dad asked. No surprise he changed the subject—a cookbook project couldn't come close to the prestige of his eldest child being promoted in one of the capital's biggest accounting firms.

And that's when Reena decided she had done her filial duty for the week. Time to get the hell out of this house. She had already heard about Khizar's likely promotion—he'd texted her about it before he'd even told their parents. But any conversation with Mum and Dad about her brother's success would very quickly delve into the type of firstborn hero worship that usually left Saira in tears and Reena wondering if a thirty-one-year-old could emancipate from her parents. True, Khizar always outshined his younger sisters, with a great job, a loving wife, and not one, but *two* babies on the way (trust Khizar to take overachievement way too far). But Khizar also had the distinction of being the nicest of the three of them. Reena tried to avoid the sibling rivalry her parents seemed to want to instill, lest she start to resent the only member of her family she really trusted. She knew her limits—she already felt mighty small because of Saira's cookbook news. Khizar's absolute winning at adulting might be a bit too much to pile on top of that heap of self-loathing.

Reena mopped up the final puddle of channa on her plate with the last bit of her puri. "I didn't notice the time." She took her plate to the kitchen, rinsed it, and placed it in the dishwasher. "I have to feed…Brian." Crap. That was a terrible excuse.

"Brian? You got a dog?" Saira asked.

Mum snapped her head toward the kitchen. "Keeping dogs is haram in Islam. You can't have a dog."

"I don't have a dog." Reena sighed. "Brian is a sourdough starter. A rye bread one. Get it? Bri the rye?"

Mum's nose wrinkled. Reena needed to get out of this house before Dad and Saira joined in voicing their displeasure about Reena's obsession with bread.

Saira's face puckered in the exact expression Mum had just sported. Uncanny, really. "I guess rye flour is better than all that refined wheat, but maybe you're taking this little hobby too far?"

"Noted, Saira. Thanks for brunch, Mum and Dad. See ya later." Reena rushed out before someone else could drag her through the mud. And she really did need to feed Brian.

CHAPTER THREE

Twenty minutes later Reena stood in her kitchen, thinking about how to save poor Brian. She lifted the jar and held it up to the midday sun. Some minuscule bubbles dotted his grayish surface, but those were probably just regular bacteria fermentation—not yeast development. Sue, her other starter, tripled last night, with large airy bubbles and a pleasant acidic smell when Reena lifted it to her nose. Sue always behaved. Brian had always been tricky. Her first rye starter, he preferred spring water instead of filtered. Organic rye flour instead of regular bulk-store stuff. And even then, like this morning, sometimes he still refused to do what Reena expected of him. She wasn't going to give up on him yet, though—she'd try increasing his feedings before taking drastic efforts.

After carefully weighing equal amounts of rye flour and spring water, she stirred them into the jar. As she fastened a rubber band around it, her phone rang and the screen lit up with the knowing scowl of her best friend holding a blackberry-lavender cupcake. Reena had snapped the picture months ago, when Amira had been ranting about sexism in cupcake shops. Her expression had been so quintessentially *Amira* that Reena wanted to preserve it for eternity.

"Meer," Reena said instead of hello, "remind me again why

distancing myself from my toxic family means still going to family brunch?"

"You're supposed to distance yourself *emotionally*, Ree. We're Indian, it's impossible to distance physically. What'd they do this time?"

"The usual. Dad found me yet another husband prospect. I left as they started their ode: *Khizar the Perfect and His Auspicious Promotion*."

"Khizar's not really perfect, you know. Remember the time he tried to make a salad and burned the lettuce?"

Reena snorted. She'd forgotten that one. Smiling, she closed the jar of sourdough.

Amira had been Reena's best friend since grade two, and their friendship lasted through tween drama and high school fights over cute boys and loaned makeup. Amira had left town a few times over the years, twice for university, and again about two months ago for a job and to live with her boyfriend, and Reena had not forgiven her friend for abandoning her yet again. They still spoke daily, though, and probably always would.

"How was Saira?" Amira asked.

Reena sighed. "She's pitching a cookbook to publishers."

"She's not."

"She is. A clean-eating cookbook." Reena cringed as she placed Brian on his perch on the windowsill.

"The woman who wrote a manifesto against gluttony in food blogs that directly attacked her own sister's livelihood shouldn't get to make money writing recipes."

Reena didn't want to get into this again with Amira—who would no doubt use it as proof that it was time for Reena to revive her old blog. Uncharacteristically, though, Amira did what Reena usually did—she changed the subject. "Who'd your dad try to set you up with this time?"

"Actually, this is pretty funny. He's my new neighbor." Reena told her friend about the brown Captain America (Captain Tanzania?).

"So, your dad moves a buff Tanzanian guy with a British accent and a love of bread next door, and this is a problem for you?" She paused. "Your parents would never force you to marry this guy, would they?"

"No. Not force, but yes, strongly encourage. And then I'd never hear the end of it from them. Mum still claims she found Nafissa for Khizar, remember?"

"Yes, and Khizar and Nafissa have a beautiful love that transcends time and space! Why wouldn't you want that?"

Reena rolled her eyes as she put away the rye flour. Her previously cynical friend had gone all rainbows and butterflies since she fell in love with a small-town lumberjack-type musician.

"I don't want what Khizar and Nafissa have," Reena said. "They had to leave town to get away from the gloating and intrusion from Mum and Dad. I know my parents will intrude no matter who I'm with, but I'd like to minimize their role in my relationships." Reena shuddered. "They've been looking for a suitable match for me for years. Clearly, they have no faith I'm capable of finding someone on my own. Believe me, it's for their best interests, not mine."

"What's a suitable match? Someone in your tax bracket?"

"No. Someone in theirs."

"Okay maybe giving in to your parents' matchmaking isn't the best idea, but I do think it's time you got back on the dating horse. In fact, that's why I called. Duncan and I have decided to have a housewarming party two Saturdays from now. It will be full of sexy male musicians."

Reena groaned. Not her best friend, too? Why the hell did everyone insist on throwing men her way lately? Amira knew Reena was on a dating break.

Reena's twelve ex-boyfriends and countless hookups and casual dates were not a source of shame for her. But her sister's engagement implosion had felt like a wake-up call.

In the last three months, Reena had been there to watch several friends fall stupidly in love with men who were so perfect for them that bluebirds practically followed the happy couples wherever they went. One friend was even proposed to by his boyfriend in a tearful serenade in front of an audience of hundreds. Reena wanted that. All of that. Not necessarily the huge, singing spectacle or to be followed by woodland creatures, but she wanted the *certainty* that their feelings were *real*. And *real* feelings could not start with meddling parents, or friends, for that matter.

Unwanted man-buffet aside, a weekend with her best friend did sound lovely. "Can I come early?"

"Yeah, come Friday. You can help cook."

Reena finished the call with a smile. She loved having something to look forward to, and a weekend in the country sounded perfect. The fact that she could use it as a reason to skip Sunday brunch also helped. She'd play her deflect-and-distract game with any matchmaking attempts, and just engage in a bit of light flirting and admiring of Duncan's friends. Because although she knew her Amira meant well, Reena felt positive she was not ready to ride any horses anytime soon.

Reena's heavy limbs and pounding head slowed her as she walked up to her building Monday evening. It had been yet another brutal day at the office. All day, just numbers. Reports. Spreadsheets. Sales data. Numbers, Numbers, Numbers.

Letting herself into the building, she noticed her friend Shayne on the stairs heading to the second floor. A Black man with the most enviable sense of style of all Reena's friends, he was wearing a stunning purple brocade vest with ripped jeans and a T-shirt today. An outfit only Shayne could pull off.

"Reena! Haven't seen you in a bit." He stepped back down and hugged her. "Come catch up at Marley's. I picked up this amazing barrel-aged saison beer and triple crème Brie. We're celebrating." Marley, aka Mahreen, was Reena's cousin, and Shayne was Marley's best friend. Marley lived in one of the top-floor units, and Shayne officially lived in a nearby basement apartment with roommates, but he preferred Marley's couch most nights.

Reena smiled. "What are we celebrating?"

He raised one manicured eyebrow. "That Monday is over? I don't even know. Today felt like a day and a half, and I need a drink. Plus, it's always a good time for cheese."

Good point. "Let me change and I'll come up. I have some bread and plums I can contribute."

Ten minutes later, Reena was curled up on Marley's oversize white couch with a glass of craft beer in one hand and a slice of her own sourdough topped with Brie, thinly sliced golden plums, and a light drizzle of honey in the other. Heaven. Like Shayne, she needed this drink.

"Reena, who is the new haircut on your floor?" Marley asked from her perch on a massive round armchair.

"Nadim. He's working for my dad."

Marley sipped her beer. Reena had spent most of her life intimidated by the beautiful cousin with the Victoria Beckham smile. Tall, with large brown eyes, high cheekbones, full lips, and thick, long, straight brown hair, she looked polar opposite to Reena's short-and-cute vibe. Marley worked in the fashion industry, selling high-end designer clothes to desperate city-wives, and she'd mastered aspirational flaw-lessness. But Reena had learned that beneath Marley's cool perfection lay a sweet shyness with people she didn't know too well.

Shayne also worked in the fashion industry—as a part-time menswear sales associate, while he built up his portfolio as a fashion photographer. He had been a huge help to Reena with her blog and taught her how to capture and edit the pictures that took it to the next level.

"Shayne's been stalking the guy since he first heard him speak. He has a thing for accents," Marley said, narrowing her eyes at Shayne.

Shayne nodded. "He's quite striking. Very intense eyes. And that voice... I wonder if he'd let me take his picture. Do you know if he's into men?"

Reena curled her legs under her. "Shayne, did you invite me up here to get me to dish up on the new neighbor?"

"Yes." He smiled. "But I brought beer and cheese, so I know you're fine with it."

Reena laughed. Her friends knew her well. She took another slice of bread and topped it with the cheese and plums. "I don't know if Nadim is into men. I hope he's not *only* into men. It would be a bit of an issue, since he's supposed to marry me."

"What?" Marley said, laughing.

"Yep. My father and his father are hoping we'll marry and combine the families and business interests. I'm assuming my hand in marriage was a bargaining chip in their deal."

"Jesus, Reena!" Shayne said, his expressive eyebrows reaching unparalleled heights. "An arranged marriage!"

"No," Reena said. "A *facilitated* marriage. They won't force me to marry him, but they will lean on me heavily. Mum may have already bought a mother-of-the-bride sari."

"Still, though..." Shayne shook his head. "But it could be worse. Maybe you should take one for the team? Can you imagine that voice in the bedroom?"

Reena rolled her eyes. "I'm not marrying anyone my parents choose, no matter how sexy his accent. They're already way too involved in my life as is! I'd very much like to pick my *own* husband. Plus, the man's a mystery! He's not even from England, but only went to university there. I think he's a player. All flirty and charming—"

"You have an issue with him flirting with the woman he is supposed to marry?" Marley asked.

"Yes, because he didn't know who I was then. He practically cheated on me. With me!"

Marley laughed. "I met him yesterday when I took out my recycling," she said. "He seemed perfectly respectable. Nice suit, too. Topshop, I think."

Reena poked a fingernail into the crust of her bread. She didn't want to talk about Nadim anymore. She wanted to ignore the awkward fact that he lived too close to avoid. She took a bite, relishing the sensation of the acidic fruit cutting through the creamy cheese. The sourdough flavor was there, but this wasn't her best bread. She had been distracted and overproofed the loaf last night, resulting in less caramelization on the crust. Oh well, lesson learned—don't get sucked down the rabbit hole of looking at bread-baking courses online while actually baking bread.

"What's going on with you? You still seeing that Celeste girl?" Reena asked Marley.

"Technically," she said. "but not really. She's been working nights all week and I'm on the early shift."

"They've mastered simultaneous orgasms on the phone, though. So, there's that," Shayne said matter-of-factly before sipping his drink.

"Shayne!" Marley said, before falling back on her seat in a fit of giggles. Beer always affected Marley this way, and Reena found it adorable. She couldn't believe she had once found her cousin cold and distant.

"Hey, this is a no-secrets zone." Shayne smiled. "I also have some promising prospects for regular simultaneous orgasms. I hooked up last night. Anderson Lin. What a name, right? And he always goes by Anderson, never Andy. Oh, and Reena, you'll love this, he works at FoodTV."

Reena sat up straight. "Really? Can he introduce me to the Barefoot Contessa?"

Shayne laughed. "Unlikely. He's a mere production assistant, and this isn't the Hamptons. Anderson is *young*." Shayne sighed happily. "I love them fresh out of college. So pure."

"You shouldn't just be meeting TV chefs, Reena, you should *be* one," Marley said. "I can't get over how good your stuff is. And you teach so well—my aloo gobi would be nothing without you."

Shayne smiled. "Anderson did mention a search or contest or something they're doing for new talent. I didn't get the details because that's when I noticed he had the tiniest earlobes I'd ever seen. Seriously, they were like little Tic Tacs attached to his ears. I half expected them to be peppermint flavored, but sadly...no."

Reena snort-laughed before taking a long sip of beer. "You're a doll, Shayne, and I'm happy you have some tasty lobes to suck on, but I have no interest in cooking on TV."

"Why not? This is perfect for you," Marley said. "At least get the details. Shayne, call him now."

Shayne recoiled. "Oh, my god, I can't do that!"

"Why not?" Marley asked.

"I called him first thing this morning, I couldn't resist—I *love* sexy, sleepy voices. So now"—he checked his watch—"I can't call him for at least thirty-six hours. Minimum. Forty would be better, but I absolutely cannot go past forty-two."

"What?" Reena frowned. "Why?"

Shayne tilted his head knowingly. "Seriously, Reena? I know you've sworn off dating, but it hasn't been *that* long. I'm in the most delicate time. Going from hookup to relationship is the hardest maneuver in modern love."

"I've had twelve boyfriends and I never followed such strict rules."

Shayne raised one brow. "Exactly. Twelve *ex*-boyfriends."

Reena winced. It was true, but she didn't need it pointed out.

Marley picked up Shayne's phone from the coffee table and thrust it at him. "Shayne, you're being ridiculous. Just call him."

Shayne rolled his eyes at Marley. "Fine. But if I get friend-zoned, your vintage McQueen scarf is mine. I'm doing this privately."

He took the phone into Marley's room and shut the door.

Marley chuckled. "Honestly, I've never seen him like this. He's so smitten with this guy that he's talking out of his ass."

"Well, I hope we don't mess up his chances. I'm pretty sure I don't want to do this FoodTV thing anyway."

"Why not? You'd be great at this. You've done other contests, haven't you?"

"Not for a while."

"Well, let's hear what Shayne has to say before you make a decision."

Reena smiled blandly, but she couldn't imagine any more information that would tempt her. After everything that had happened to her blog, she did not want to be put in the spotlight again in the food world.

Ten minutes later, Shayne wordlessly sat back down on the couch, eyes glistening with excitement.

"Well?" Marley asked, leaning forward.

"Anderson..." Shayne sighed and fanned his face with his hand. "I just absolutely can't with him. You know what he just told me? He said I was the first person who'd ever—"

"Shayne, the contest!"

He seemed to snap out of his daze. "Right. Yes." He scanned the room, then grabbed a pad of paper from the coffee table. "Here...this is complicated, you'll want to take notes." He tossed the paper and a pen at Reena. "So, this is the most *Reena* thing that I've ever heard about, and if you don't do it, I will no longer be able to gloat that my friend is the savviest blogger out there. This thing is made for you."

"Yes...but Shayne, I'm not actually a blogger anymore. I—"

"Ah!" He put his hand out to stop her. "Just listen and trust, Reena. So, it's called the FoodTV *Home Cooking Showdown*.

It's not a search for a new network host, per se, but the winners get a one-off special. The buzz is they don't want to commit to promising a show, but are using the contest as an unofficial open call for new talent."

Shayne frowned and poked the still-blank paper in Reena's hand. "You're not writing!"

She rolled her eyes, but wrote *FoodTV Home Cooking Showdown* on the sheet.

"How do you apply?" Marley asked.

"You do an audition video to get in. They pick, like, eight contestants or something out of the auditions. Then the contestants make two more videos by themselves from home. And I think they get to go to the FoodTV studios? I kinda zoned out then because I was imagining Anderson wearing one of those headset things on set…I want to play director and innocent ingenue with him…"

"Shayne," Marley said, laughing.

"Right. So, it's public voting, not expert judges. Because really, it's about the personality and what the food looks like, not the taste, or anything."

"This sounds like a reality show, Shayne." Reena had no interest in that. None.

He nodded enthusiastically. "Yes!"

"I don't—"

Shayne grinned. "Here's the inside scoop that only someone who is *intimately* acquainted with someone on the production team would know—they are really hoping for a bit of diversity in the contestants. They want to showcase all the different food cultures in Canada. They are not going to pick any run-of-the-mill Mike and Michelle McBasic. I think you'd be a shoo-in."

Her eyes narrowed. "Because I'm brown?"

Shayne nodded. "Yeah, and because you're the best cook I know. And you're cute as shit, too. Marley can fluff up your hair a bit and put you in something sexy. And believe me, you *want* the grand prize."

The more he said, the more Reena was sure that she didn't want to do this, but Shayne's expression was so annoyingly smug, she wanted to wipe it off his face. "Okay, fine. I'll bite. What's the grand prize?"

He smiled broadly. "Get your pen ready . . . the *Home Cooking Showdown* is in conjunction with the Asler Institute of Culinary Arts. The winner gets a ten thousand-dollar scholarship."

Damn.

Reena stilled. That changed everything. The artisan bread course was at the Asler Institute. With that scholarship, she could finally enroll. Hell, she could take the whole baking and pastry arts program.

She bit her lip. Soooo tempting.

"You have to do it, Reena," Marley said. "Seriously. We'll help. Shayne can film it, and I'll help with your hair and clothes. You don't need help with the cooking part. We'll make sure you get this. No one deserves—"

"Cool your jets, Marl," Shayne interrupted with one hand up. "There is one glitch. There is something Reena doesn't have that she would need as a contestant."

"Oh? And what's that?" Reena asked.

Shayne smiled his knowing, mischievous grin, which Reena knew not to trust. She wasn't going to like whatever he had to say, and he relished it.

"What you need, my dear friend, is a husband."

CHAPTER FOUR

For the love of god, why did everyone want Reena to have a husband? This was getting absurd. She stared blankly at Shayne.

"A husband?" Marley asked. "What kind of puritanical drivel are they producing?"

Shayne's lips curled into a tiny smile. "Not puritanical. Culturally diverse, remember? But this contest is about home cooking. *Family* cooking. It's okay if you don't have kids, but they want the contestants to work in couples. Same-sex couples are okay. But since you only like dudes, you'll need a husband. A fiancé would also work."

Reena exhaled. Goddamn Shayne. He could have started with that. For all of two minutes, she'd been convinced this could make her longtime dream come true. She could practically smell the country loaves baking.

But once again, life kicked her when she was already down. She'd lost a dream only two minutes old, but Reena felt almost as disappointed as when she'd lost her cookbook deal.

"Well, that bites." She slumped, tossing the paper and pen on the couch.

Marley sat up straight. "This doesn't mean you can't audition.

Just find a husband! Or a boyfriend. Or a wife! Pretend! Nothing on TV is real anyway."

"I'm a terrible liar," Reena said. "And who the hell would pretend to be my boyfriend or girlfriend on TV?"

"Well, on a website at least. I'd do it for you," Shayne said. "But I think my dalliance with Anderson will get in the way. Or at least I hope it will. Actually, no...I'm using guided visualization. I *will* be with Anderson then, so I cannot be your fiancé."

"Seriously, guys, I am not doing this. I can't. Even if by some miracle I can manage to find someone who would pretend to be my fiancé for this thing, what will happen when my parents see it?"

And there was another reason that she didn't say aloud. At this point in her life Reena didn't think she could face pretending to be in a happy relationship. She knew her limits. That was way, way beyond what she could handle.

Tuesday night, after an evening spent tinkering with a new bread recipe, Reena found herself with too much fougasse and a craving for nonfinance conversation. A quick text to Marley told her Shayne would be over soon, and they would love to help with the abundance-of-bread problem and talk about anything except numbers.

She checked the time—six fifteen. She'd have to hurry if she wanted to avoid seeing Nadim in the hallway. She was not in the mood for awkward conversation. Forgoing shoes and socks, she packed the crusty breads into a canvas bag, grabbed her purse, and pulled the door open when her phone rang. Struggling with her heavy door and the overladen bag of bread resulted in her dropping the bag as she answered the phone.

"Hello?" she said while retrieving the bag. Thankfully, all the fougasse remained safely enclosed in the canvas.

"Reena, why do you sound out of breath?" her sister asked, sounding annoyed and clipped. Not out of the ordinary. Saira usually sounded annoyed and clipped.

"Just about to head out. What's up?"

"I need you to show me how you make that eggplant dip you always do. I think it might be good for the cookbook pitch."

"Okay, um…" She leaned against her door. Figures. She considered her smoked eggplant dish—loosely based on an East African eggplant curry—to be one of her signature dishes. It had won awards. It would have been in her *own* cookbook. She couldn't let it end up in Saira's.

"I'm at home tomorrow night. We can do it then," Saira continued.

"I'm busy," Reena said. "I'm…"—damn it, she couldn't think of an excuse—"going out."

"Really? Where?"

"I have a date."

Saira exhaled with exaggeration. "What about Friday? I'm working until six—"

"Can't. I'm helping Marley with—" She sneezed. Good. Must be finally developing an allergy to her sister demands.

"Seriously, Reena. I don't even know why I asked. I would have thought that you would be more supportive about this project, but—"

Reena's text tone rang on her phone. She said a silent thank-you to herself for the drawn-out bagpipe jig she had chosen as a text notification, as it muted her sister for the rest of that statement.

"Gotcha, Saira. Anyway, I'll call you next week and we'll set something up." Reena disconnected the call before Saira could finish. Bullet dodged. She had no intention of helping her sister with this cookbook project. She leaned her head back against the door of her apartment, closing her eyes.

This shouldn't bother Reena so much anymore—Saira's betrayal was months ago, and it wasn't intentional. Or mostly not intentional, at least. It all started when Saira had written a viral diatribe outlining everything wrong with the hero worship of food stars online, claiming their artery-clogging recipes were contributing to the decline of all of society. Saira didn't know the fallout from that post would lead to sponsors pulling out from many food blogs, including Reena's. Reena lost her cookbook deal when the publisher felt the market was shifting toward more health-conscious cooking. Reena's indulgent brand wasn't in demand anymore. Story of her life.

But it was fine. Saira could have a cookbook now, and Reena could just avoid the cooking section of the bookstore when it came out. Problem solved.

❧

Reena sneezed again as she pushed herself off her door to head upstairs. Damn her cubicle mate, Theresa. She'd been sneezing for two days and apparently passed her germs on.

When Reena knocked on Marley's door there was no answer. She knocked again. Still nothing. What the heck? Marley's last text was fifteen minutes ago, and she had told Reena to come right over. She checked her phone and noticed that the message that had come while talking to Saira had been from Marley. A group text to both her and Shayne.

Marley: Something came up and I have to run. Will call you guys later.

Reena texted Shayne as she walked back downstairs.

Reena: What's going on with Marley?

Shayne: No idea. She's been a bit flaky for a few weeks but won't talk about it.

Reena: Weird. I'll call her later.

Reena reached her door when she realized she had no keys.

Crap. She forgot to grab them when she left the apartment. Her overprotective father had of course insisted on doors that locked automatically for his precious girl. Reena locked herself out pretty often, so she left several spare keys among friends and family. One with Amira, who now lived an hour and a half away. One with Marley, who, while normally convenient, right now was MIA. And the last at her parents' house. Where Saira lived. Who Reena just pissed off over eggplant.

She called Marley anyway. No answer.

Reena groaned as she slid down against the wall, landing with her butt on the cold floor near Nadim's door. Her bag sat next to her, a golden brown fougasse peeking out the top.

At least she had bread if she got hungry. Or hangry. Scratch that, she was already hangry. She'd missed dinner.

Closing her eyes, Reena contemplated the merits of either

walking forty minutes to her parents' house or climbing up the fire escape and breaking Marley's window. And probably breaking a leg, too.

"Funny, I don't remember ordering a woman. And I'm surprised they leave deliveries by the door here even when no one's home. Anyone could have walked by and taken her."

Damnit. Nadim. So much for avoiding him. Reena opened her eyes and raised her eyebrows. "Oh, hello. Was that supposed to be funny?"

"Apparently not. Sorry," he said, smiling. "But I didn't expect to see you sitting in front of my door. Next time give me some warning and I'll write a better quip." He looked down. "Nice feet."

She tucked her bare feet under her. He looked much cleaner today. And his hair was styled upward. Reena now understood why Marley had called him a haircut. "I'm locked out. Left my key inside."

He pulled his key out of his suit jacket. "No spare?"

"No. My cousin isn't answering her phone."

He turned back to his door and unlocked it, opening it widely before looking down at Reena again.

"Well, come on then." He motioned her into the apartment.

"It's fine. I'll wait for my cousin."

"I'm not leaving you on the floor. Come inside, I won't bite."

She stared blankly.

"I won't even make jokes about wanting to bite you. Or you to bite me. Or…"

Reena scrambled up quickly, before this conversation could go any further.

"Marley will be home soon. I left her a message."

He tossed his keys on the kitchen counter and dropped his bag on a chair. "Marley. That's the tall one upstairs, right?"

Reena stepped around his dining chair and put her purse and tote bag on the table. "Yeah, the breathtaking woman upstairs. Don't feel you have to hold back on my account. You can sing Marley's praises. Everyone drools after meeting her."

He looked at Reena for a full three seconds before his gaze shifted to the ground in front of her as he removed his suit jacket and tossed it on the chair. "She's not my type. It's been a long day. You mind if I have a beer?"

Reena watched his back as he walked toward the fridge. He was wearing a suit today instead of athletic gear, so his impressive physique was a little more hidden. The suit looked good, though. Went well with that upper-crust Brit voice. Was this the image he had wanted her to see for their first meeting?

"Go ahead," she said.

"I don't have much to offer you. Water? I have some soda water, too, but it's not cold."

Reena removed Nadim's jacket from the dining chair and folded it, before planting her own butt on the chair. "Beer is fine."

He turned and stared at her. "You drink?"

"Yeah. I love beer. Why?"

"Your father..." He shook his head with amazement. "I've had to hide my evening pub habit since I started working for him. Does he know you drink?"

Reena laughed. "Yes. He doesn't approve."

Nadim smirked as he joined her at his table, two tall cans of beer in one hand and two pint glasses in the other. He opened one can. "This is an English special bitter. My favorite type of beer in the UK, and this local craft brewery does a bang-up job of it. Shall I pour?"

She nodded. The matte black can had an artfully drawn elephant on the front of it. He poured the beer slowly down the side of the glass, eyes glued on the copper brew. She could see why Shayne said Nadim had intense eyes. He had a way of zoning in with razor focus that left her a little breathless.

He *really* was handsome. She didn't know how she ever thought of him as less than impressive. She felt her body flush.

Ugh. No. She couldn't let her libido win.

To break the spell of his beer-pouring mastery, Reena looked around his apartment. Since the layout of his place mirrored her own, she expected it to be spacious, with low ceilings and simple midcentury moldings, but she didn't expect its emptiness. Save for the old kitchen table and chairs they were sitting on, Nadim had only three pieces of furniture in his living area: a purple sofa, a strangely familiar olive-green armchair, and an ancient dining-room sideboard that held his electronics. No paintings or pictures on the walls, no cozy throw on the sofa, not even any books or magazines. Only one decorative element adorned the room—an ebony wood-carved African elephant on the sideboard next to the TV. The elephant wasn't entirely unexpected—the man was from Tanzania, and most East Africans had at least one carved animal in their home. She herself was partial to giraffes and had a few in her bedroom.

"Love the minimalism in this place," she said.

"Shush," he said, grinning and holding out a glass for her. "It's a work in progress. I just moved in, you know."

She lifted the glass to her nose, and scents of smoky burnt sugar and mature grains mingled with a slight fruitiness. The taste exploded in her mouth when she sipped—rich molasses, caramel, and a slight bitterness that coated her tongue. This beer was exquisite. She closed her eyes as she took a second sip, stifling a moan.

"Like it?" he asked.

"Love it. Would be amazing with…" She thought for a moment. "Cheese. Maybe a sharp cheddar. Or smoked meat…short ribs. And definitely salty bread—pretzels, maybe."

He grinned. "I am going to bloody love living across from you."

Reena tensed, feeling exposed. She scanned the room and her eyes caught that puke-green chair. "Where'd you get that chair?"

"Your parents. They gave me a bedroom set, too."

Of course! That chair had been in the storage room at her parents' house for years. Along with other furniture no one needed anymore, like her old…

"Wait, what bedroom set?"

He tilted his head toward the bedroom, clearly visible from this vantage in the dining room. She glanced in his room. His clothes lay strewn around the floor and his pink bed was unmade. Scratch that, *her* pink bed. Because apparently, her intended fiancé had already been sleeping in her bed.

"They gave you my little-girl bedroom set?"

He huffed defensively. "I'm planning on painting it. It's got nice workmanship. Solid wood and all that. Is this a problem? Your father said you didn't want it."

Reena looked into his room again. So bizarre to see her four-poster bed unmade, with a crumpled flannel blanket and a balled-up pillow. Like the poor thing had been held hostage at a frat house. She leaned closer. Definitely dirty socks hanging off the end of it.

He was right, though, she hadn't wanted her old bedroom set when she moved out of her parents' house six years ago. She'd been adamant she wanted to stand on her own two feet and not bring any of her old life with her, resulting in her spending way too much on poor-quality (but fabulously styled) furniture. Unfortunately, the new slatted platform bed she had bought hadn't been up to the task of supporting Reena and her ex-boyfriend Carlos's nighttime fun. The bed crashing to the ground at a climactic point had been hilarious to Reena, but poor Carlos had been mortified, thinking of it as a commentary on his body shape. The relationship never recovered. A shame, really. She had been quite fond of Carlos. And that bed. Her mattress directly on the floor was a bit depressing.

Her pink bed was solid—it would have held up to rigorous entertainment, not that she'd ever dreamed of bringing anyone back to her parents' home when she lived there. But now there was finally a naked man in her strong bed and she couldn't enjoy it.

Not that she wanted to see Nadim naked in her bed. She watched his bare forearm beneath his rolled-up white shirt as he took a sip of his beer. Damnit. She loved a firm forearm. In actuality, she *did* want to see him naked, but she didn't *want* to want to see him naked.

Maybe.

Wait, what were they talking about? Reena needed to get a grip before the undercurrent of attraction took her down.

New strategy: focus on his negatives. "I see you haven't hired a maid yet either."

He snorted before getting up and closing the door to his bedroom. "So, how is it you ended up locked out of your apartment and on the floor beside my door with bare toes and a bag of baguettes? I'm not exactly sure how you figured out my exact fantasies, but since you appear to hate me, I doubt you were there as a housewarming gift."

"I don't hate you."

"Oh, come on, you bolted faster than a gazelle catching a whiff of lion when we met."

"Nice. An African metaphor."

He beamed. "Thank you. It sounds better in Swahili."

"Anyway, how can I hate you? I don't know you. At all. I guess... I hate what you represent. My parents butting into my life again."

He watched her hands for several seconds, his thick brows in a straight line on his forehead. This was awkward. Eventually, one of them would have to say something about the fact that they were supposed to get married, despite him thinking she hated him, all while she was imagining him naked in her bed.

No. No one needed to talk about the naked part. That could be her secret.

"So, should we acknowledge the elephant in the room?" he finally asked.

She turned to the carved animal on the TV stand. "It's a nice piece. I have a giraffe in my bedroom. Did you get it in Dar es Salaam?"

He laughed, head tilting backward as his shiny teeth reflected the overhead light. Reena flushed as her eyes darted around the room. Was there another elephant around? The beer?

"You're precious," he said. "And no, I didn't mean that

elephant. It's an expression. The obvious thing we are reluctant to talk about."

Reena felt herself turning red but giggled. Man, this guy had thrown her completely off-kilter. "Yeah, I get it now." She raised her knees, hugging them to her chest. "I've told my parents to stop introducing me to eligible men, but they're persistent."

He rubbed the back of his hand in a nervous gesture before turning to look out the window. "Yeah, that. I've been meaning to thank you."

Thank her for what? Bolting midconversation the last time they spoke? Insulting his decorating and cleanliness? Reena exhaled. She was usually better mannered than this. "Why? I haven't exactly been a great neighbor or anything…"

"You have. You obviously didn't tell your father that we met on the weekend. And you didn't tell him about my, you know, less-than-model-son-in-law behavior."

"About your rakish flirting?"

He raised one brow. "Rakish?"

"Yes, rakish. What are you afraid of, that he'll rescind my hand in marriage? Wait, you do get that I am not *actually* going to marry you, don't you?"

He snorted. "Yeah, marriage seems a bit of a long shot at this point. But he *is* my boss."

"Well, I have no intention of blabbing to your *boss* about anything you do in your personal life, and, as your neighbor, I would expect the same courtesy from you. Hell, we can pretend neither of us have ever met my parents. Lord knows I've had that fantasy before." She tried to smile, but another string of sneezes started. She covered her face with one hand as she banged the table in time with her eruptions.

Nadim's eyes were wide when her nose calmed. "Bless you. You have an adorable sneeze."

Yes, yes, tiny girl with the bouncy curls and the high-pitched sneeze. She was a damn pixie. She'd heard it so many times and it never failed to piss her off. She usually smiled and said thank you, but with this guy, she said what she usually only thought when someone called her sneeze cute. "Fuck adorable. I feel like shit."

He chuckled. "You're nothing like the Reena your father described."

She snorted. "I thought we were going to pretend we don't know my parents?"

He winked, smiling. Still a flirt. She needed to figure out how to snuff that out before her inconvenient attraction got out of hand. "Fine," he said. "You're a tragic orphan with over-bearing parents. A millennial Oliver Twist. But seriously, I owe you for not telling him. Massively. You ever need a neighborly favor, I'm your man."

What could she possibly need from a man content to live in her father's pocket, utterly terrified of disappointing him? She dragged the bag of bread closer. "Anyway, they're fougasse, not baguettes," she informed him.

"*Fou* what?"

"Fougasse," she said, pulling a few of the flat crusty breads out of the bag. "They're a flatbread originating from Provence, France."

For a new recipe, she was pleased at how the oval breads had turned out. The lean dough had no fat in it, and deep cuts made the finished crisp, yet chewy bread loosely resembled fall leaves.

Nadim's eyes widened. "You didn't seriously make those, did you?"

"Yes. I told you, bread baking is my hobby."

He leaned a little closer to her, eyes still on the olive fougasse in Reena's hand. "Are those black olives?"

"Yes. This one is olive and Stilton." Specifically, tiny black Niçoise olives that she painstakingly pitted before gently folding into the dough so they would stay whole.

"And the other..." He peeked into the bag.

"Roasted red pepper and Ementaal."

He frowned. "And they're seriously not for me?"

She couldn't help but smile at his hungry eyes as he ogled the bread. She really did have way too much fougasse. What harm could come from sharing bread with a neighbor?

"Help yourself. I made a lot. I was on my way up to Marley's for wine, but something came up and she left."

"I don't have wine but there's a full case of this special bitter. Is beer and bread appropriate?"

"Why not? The olives will pair well with the bitter brew."

He smiled widely, a small dribble of beer leaking from his mouth. As he wiped it with his left forearm, Reena noticed a small tattoo just past his wrist. Looked like an African baobab tree.

He stood and went to the fridge. "I've got some beef sausages and a block of cheese. And a couple of apples—oh, and I forgot. My boss's wife, who you definitely *don't* know, sent some dhokla for me. It's a strange dinner, but shall we feast?"

Reena smirked as she curled one leg under her. She had nowhere else to go, so why shouldn't she get to know Nadim? She did have to live across the hall from him. They could be friends. She could pretend he didn't work for her father.

And she damn well didn't have to marry the man.

But eating fougasse and cheese of questionable origin with a new neighbor while enjoying some of his delightful microbrew couldn't hurt. And looking at those arms while listening to that voice certainly wasn't torture either. And if she found herself growing too attracted to the mystery English/East African man, she could just eat a bite of her mother's dhokla as a reminder that any involvement with this man would *always* include her parents. Whether she wanted it to or not.

CHAPTER FIVE

Reena woke Wednesday morning with a serious case of the sniffles and a massive sinus headache. Figured. All that sneezing yesterday had blossomed to a full-on head cold. She had reports due by the end of the workday, so she didn't want to call in sick. She phoned her boss, Tina, to ask if she could work from home.

"There's an important meeting I need you for this afternoon." Tina sounded annoyed.

"I can videoconference in—I don't want to get anyone sick." She would have thought Tina would be more enthusiastic about Reena putting the health of the team first while still getting the reports in.

"Okay," Tina said. "I'll email you the link."

After taking two twelve-hour sinus pills, Reena booted up her laptop.

The pills worked their magic, and she was chin deep in numbers all morning, making progress on the sales reports. It was almost the end of the day when she logged into Tina's "important" meeting, and Reena knew the moment the camera turned on that something was amiss at Railside Clothing Inc.

The meeting was strangely in the executive boardroom. Tina was there, looking exhausted and maybe...sad? Next to her was the normally stoic HR rep, except her smile was unnaturally chipper and most definitely fake. There were two strangers there, too, both wearing the easy-wear, yet formal clothing of a consultant. And a large stack of cardboard file boxes in the corner—the kind they give you to clean out your cubicle. Those were presumably for the unlucky sods who had to attend these meetings in person.

Reena didn't need to see the pink slips; she knew what was happening here. Layoffs.

Shit.

She had seen this three times before. Most recently here at Railside last year, when the fast fashion trend had forced the midrange basics company to reduce 8 percent of its workforce. She'd been spared. She hadn't been so lucky at her two previous jobs: first Pharmamart, where she'd worked as a clerk in their payroll department for only six months before the business downsized, and more recently at Avenue, the discount department store that opened a Canadian division with great fanfare, only to fold eighteen months later.

She wasn't that surprised. Railside was a long-standing company that sold work-appropriate basics in stores located in most mid- to high-end malls. Three years ago, they'd opened a hip new spinoff store called Sidecar. But no midrange clothing company could compete with American fast fashion.

This was this first time Reena had lost a job over a video-conference call, though. It was a shame she wouldn't have the chance to empty her favorite office supplies into her purse before being led out, but at least she was spared the walk of shame out of the building.

Small blessings, she supposed.

The first thing Reena did after disconnecting from the call was scream into a pillow. Then she called Amira.

"Third time's the charm?" she asked while she unplugged her godforsaken webcam and tried not to throw it across the floor.

"Hi, Reena! Third time for what?" Amira sounded upbeat this afternoon. True love agreed with her.

Reena fell dramatically onto the sofa. "Downsizing."

"Oh, shit. *No*. Not again."

"Yes, again. Standalone Sidecar stores are closing, and Railside corporate just let go of fifteen percent of its workforce."

"And you...?"

"Got a very generous package."

"Oh, Ree, I'm sorry."

A sharp twitch in her eye made Reena blink a few times. She squeezed her eyelids shut, glad no one could see her break down. "I guess I'm used to it now."

"I know but, ugh. What are you going to do?"

"What can I do? Wallow in self-pity for no more than two days, then call the recruiting agency the bubbly 'organizational change consultant' gave me the number for. It's a brutal market, but I have great references and hopefully will have something new before my severance runs out."

"I hate that you have to do this shit all over again," Amira said. "Do you think maybe it's time to try a new industry?"

"I don't know, Meer. I've been working in retail corporate offices since college. It's what I know."

Reena heard Amira sigh. "What are you going to tell your parents?"

She had considered this. "Nothing. I'm not telling them. I can't deal with Dad pressuring me to work in the family business right now. And I can't handle Mum's insinuating that I'm to blame. I'll find something new, then tell them I was recruited for a better position."

"You're going to keep this from them?"

"I cannot deal with their crap right now. Khizar makes partner and I get let go. Dad's still on me that I'm not a manager. I can't tell them I'm unemployed." She sat up and wiped her eyes. "It'll be fine. It's always fine. I can brush myself off and get back up again."

"Yeah, you can," Amira said softly. "You're the strongest person I know. But this is blatantly unfair."

Unfair. When had her life ever been fair? She inhaled deeply. "Ugh. I need comfort food. Why don't I have any samosas?"

"Go buy some."

"I'm not wearing any pants."

"What? You went to work without pants? And you're surprised you were let go?"

Reena rolled onto her back. "I was sneezing, so I worked from home. I videoconferenced into my layoff meeting. I have a blazer and blouse on, but below the waist is underwear only."

"*They let you go in a videoconference?* What's wrong with the world these days?"

"I know. And the clincher is I'm not even sneezing anymore." She sat up. "I can put pants on. Samosas are worth pants. Meer, I wish you were here to take me to the Sparrow."

The Sparrow was Amira and Reena's favorite dive bar. They had spent countless hours drowning away their fucks over bourbon, beer, or gin, depending on the number of fucks they had to kill on a given day. Today felt like a gin night.

"I know, sweetie. I wish I could come, but I have a really early meeting tomorrow. Go without me. Don't forget to wallow the next few days. Eat crap and drink whatever. Pick yourself up later."

Reena nodded to herself. "Yeah. I could go alone."

After hanging up with Amira, Reena looked out the window. It was pretty warm for early September, and the leaves were still vibrant and green. It didn't seem right for it to look so cheery outside. But when had her life ever felt right? She peeled herself off the couch, slipped on a pair of yoga pants and flip-flops, and headed to her car.

At the Indian grocery store, she bought a half-dozen samosas, a bag of gram flour, and some starchy potatoes. Samosas were great, but when she was upset Reena craved potato bhajias the way others craved French fries. She suspected that later tonight, once this news really sunk in, she'd feel even worse than she did right now, and right now was pretty low. She'd need the bhajias. She dropped her groceries and her car home before walking to the Sparrow, since she was planning to take Amira's advice and drink. Maybe heavily.

⁓

Reena believed strongly that everyone deserved a dive bar, and the Sparrow managed the unlikely balance between boneless comfort and indifferent hospitality that suited her perfectly. With walls covered in signs, stickers, graffiti, and knickknacks customers brought from their travels, the Sparrow made it easy for Reena to blend into the cluttered decor.

She sat alone at the bar, her forehead in one hand, her second gin gimlet in the other, and contemplated the cosmic purpose behind the cruel pranks the universe had been pulling on her since birth. Someone tapped her shoulder. She turned.

"Okay, so I guess you probably don't hate me because you appear to be stalking me," Nadim said.

Reena tilted her head in confusion. What the hell was he doing in *her* bar? She narrowed her eyes.

"If looks could kill," he said, sitting heavily on the stool next to her. "You alone?" After she nodded, he put his elbows on the bar, making himself comfortable. He motioned to Steve, the longtime bartender, who immediately started pulling a draft beer, seeming to know what Nadim wanted. "Well, whether you hate me or not, I'm joining you. I need to keep a close eye to see if you're glaring or scowling at me."

She was doing neither, but she could bet her expression wasn't all that welcoming. She was in no mood for forced niceties today.

His mood didn't seem too hot, either. His suit was rumpled, and his tie was not just loosened but hanging off his neck undone. Doubtful his day had been as bad as hers, but Nadim looked and sounded as miserable as she felt.

"What are you doing here?" she asked.

"I should ask you that. You following me? I told you I go to the pub after work."

"But this is my bar."

He glanced around at the busy decor. "There is a lot on the walls here, but I don't see the words 'this pub belongs to Reena Manji' anywhere." He turned back to her. "I've been coming here regularly for weeks and have never seen you here."

"I know," she agreed, dejected. "Amira left."

"Who is Ami... never mind." He took a long sip of his beer, almost emptying the glass before turning back to her. "Tough day at work?"

Reena bit her lip. She no longer had a work, but she couldn't tell this man that. She didn't trust him not to tell Dad. Especially since every third thing out of his mouth seemed to be *does your father know?*

Deflect and distract. *"You* look like *you've* had a rough day."

"The utter worst." He took another long sip of beer, then wiped his mouth with his sleeve. "But I can't talk about it. Especially to you."

Well. That would almost be offensive if she hadn't just thought the same thing about him.

Reena drained her glass. How serendipitous. A drinking buddy who didn't want to talk about what was bothering him. She didn't care if he had a secret. She had enough secrets to fill all the beer kegs in the Sparrow.

She smiled. "Shall we drown our private sorrows together then?"

He nodded. "Steve?" Nadim called out. "Bring my neighbor here another..." He lifted her empty glass and sniffed it, then looked at her appreciatively. "Gin? Nice. Make that two. On my tab."

"Tanqueray gimlet on the rocks," she added, resting her head back down on the bar.

Once Steve placed the two goblets in front of them, Nadim grabbed her arm and pulled. "C'mon."

She picked up her drink and let him drag her toward the back. When they reached a table, his eyes swept over her body.

"Interesting outfit. You're all investment banker upstairs and yoga mom downstairs." His gaze trailed lower as his eyebrow raised. "Are you mocking me?" he asked.

"What?"

"Why no socks? It's September."

"It's warm. I hate socks." She slid into the seat.

"You know, Sunshine, you just might be my soul mate."

Reena squeezed her cold drink as a lump formed in her throat. "I'm not marrying you."

"Yeah. So, you said." He lifted his glass. "To finding this fine antidote to misery." He hummed with appreciation after sipping the drink. "I always forget how much I love gin. I rarely drink it when out, but I always had a bottle of Beefeater in my flat in London." He took another sip. "This tastes like another."

The room had spun slightly after her first two drinks, and with a third already in hand, a fourth sounded ill-advised to Reena. But maybe this was all part of his plan. Maybe he hoped the gimlets would render her more pliable for...what, exactly? Reena hiccupped and waved a finger at him. "Don't think you can pour drinks into me to make me more acquiescent. I'm still not going to marry you, no matter what my parents want."

His eyes crinkled in mirth. "You can say *acquiescent* while drinking? You, my dear, are a woman of many talents. And anyway, after today, don't be so sure what your parents want anymore."

Could there be trouble in this business relationship between their respective families? She leaned a little closer to Nadim, ready to dig out the dirt.

But…wait. Ugh. She slumped in her seat. If she wasn't willing to come clean about her job, she couldn't expect him to tell his secrets.

"I thought we weren't going to talk about our problems. Or about our parents."

He nodded, still frowning. "I'm all for that." He sipped his cocktail. "And I'm all for this drink."

Reena swirled hers around in her hand, watching the lime wedge crash against the ice cubes. "Can I ask you something? No obligation to answer me."

"Um…"

Reena patted his hand reassuringly. Ooh, that skin was soft. She patted him again. Hand cream maybe? He laughed as he inched his hand away.

Right. Questions. Gin on the brain had distracted her from the topic at hand. And the topic at hand was not Nadim's hands.

"Okay," she said, straightening. "Why is your British accent so strong? My father said you were from Dar es Salaam, but you said you had a flat in London?"

A small smile appeared. "Yes. I *am* technically from Dar es Salaam. I attended a British private school there and transferred to a boarding school in England at age twelve. I went to the London School of Economics for both undergraduate and graduate degrees. Afterward, I moved back to Africa but ended up in London again a few years ago. And now"—he grinned widely—"I'm here."

"So, do you consider yourself English or Tanzanian?"

"Tanzanian, one hundred percent." He lifted his sleeve to show her the tattoo of the African tree on his forearm, smiling fondly at it. "I've moved a lot, but my soul knows when I'm home." He chuckled as he pushed his sleeve back down. "I tend to pick up dialects and accents easily wherever I am, though. Give me a month in Canada and I will match your *eh's* and *aboots*."

"I don't aboot!"

"Yes, Reena, you do. What *about* you. Were you born here?"

"Yup. Toronto girl, through and through. Both Mum and Dad are from Tanzania, though. And going further back, my great-grandparents are all from India. I've been to Tanzania a few times. Pretty country."

"I love it." He looked wistfully sad at that thought. "I'd like to move back one day. I've lived in a lot of places, but it's hard to really feel at home, you know? Tanzania did that for me. I am surprised at how much I like Toronto, though."

"Remind me, one day I'll take you out to see all the under-rated sights."

Reena bit her lip. She shouldn't have said that. She should be distancing herself from him, not offering to be his Toronto tour guide. "Why do you want to go back to Africa?"

"I don't know. I feel the most...me, there. I told you I pick up dialects easy, right? I think I'm a little too adaptable. I acclimate to environments so easily that I forget who I am, sometimes. I think I've only felt like me, really me, at home in Tanzania." He looked down. "I'm not making sense. Ignore me." He sipped his drink.

Reena smiled sadly. She understood exactly what he meant. She was also the adaptable one. The amiable one. The one who made friends easily whenever she changed jobs. Adapted her interests to whoever she was dating. Cosplay, hockey, barbecue, tabletop gaming. She even played in an axe-throwing league once with a boyfriend. She never faked interest—she honestly enjoyed those things. But she understood what Nadim meant when he said he didn't feel like himself. She only felt like herself when baking bread.

She felt for him. But at the same time, his revelation raised new questions. Like: Why did he move here if he wanted to be in Africa? And more importantly, did her parents know that this potential husband wanted to return to Africa at some point? Was this their way of shipping Reena off the continent?

She took a gulp of her gin. *Can't ask those questions.* She closed her eyes, feeling a sharp prickle behind them.

She. Fucking. Lost. Her job today. She *could* move to Africa, and no one would care.

A squeeze of her hand jolted her eyes open. "Hey," Nadim said, concerned. "You okay?"

"Yeah…just really crappy day. Let's talk about something else." She gently removed her hand from under his.

"Okay." He grinned. "Can I ask questions then? Don't feel you *have* to answer them."

"Deal."

"Why do you make so much bread?"

She shrugged. "I love bread. Always have. There is nothing like the feeling of creating something so complex with my own hands. Sourdough bread is pretty much three ingredients—flour, water, and salt. But when you play with the other variables: hydration, fermentation, wild yeasts, temperature, or flour types, you can create something that tastes nothing like—and is nutritiously nothing like—the original ingredients. Bread is truly magic."

"I fully support and enable your habits, so long as you share." She smiled.

His hand waved in the direction of her head. "Another question: How long does it take you to do that with your hair?"

"Do what?"

"Make it so perfectly curly."

She wrinkled her nose. "I don't do anything. Just a bit of hair product. It grows out of my head this way."

"Bullshit. My ex used to curl her hair with this weird hot cone-shaped thing."

Reena laughed. "I assure you, my curls are natural. I don't need a curling iron."

"But yours are like, *perfect*. They're like little springs. Like bungee cords."

Well, that was a new one. "Bungee cords?"

"Yeah. Look." He picked up the bottom of a ringlet near her face and held it on the top of her head. "You could bungee jump with your hair." Still holding the end of the curl, he mimicked bungee-jumping by launching the hair up and then down, pulling it taut before letting go and watching the curl spring back in place.

Reena frowned. "Anyone ever tell you that you're very strange?"

"It's been mentioned, yes." He sipped his drink.

"You asked two questions. My turn. Why are you so buff?"

He laughed, head falling down to his arm on the table. Clearly, he was as drunk as she was. Also, he had thick hair. It looked soft. As did the skin on the back of his neck. She was resisting the urge to touch when he finally raised his head and leered openly before answering, flexing his biceps to give her a show. "Glad you approve. I try to lift every day at lunch and on most mornings. I love the rush of weight lifting."

"Oh, god, you're one of those '*do you even lift, bruh?*' guys, aren't you?"

"I have no idea what you mean."

She waved her hand in the direction of his body. "I mean, like, what's even the point? You work out just to look good? You do anything else physical with that body?"

She squeezed her lips shut. *Must stop drinking gin. Must stop saying things he can construe as an intentional innuendo.* "That's not what I meant," she said before he could even consider a side-eyed smirk or eyebrow waggle.

He laughed again. "You are fantastic at cheering me up. And, as a matter of fact, yes. I bike, I run, and I played football in London. Need to find a team here."

"Ah, so a jock, then. I assume you mean soccer."

He waved a finger at her. "Just because I live in North America now doesn't mean I have to bastardize the name of the world's most popular sport like you people do."

Wrong. She tried to explain to him that *soccer-football* was the original name of the sport, and in North America they shortened to it to soccer, while the rest of the world shortened it to football, thus forever confusing it with *rugby-football*. But the crystal-clear thoughts in her head weren't translating to coherent statements from her mouth.

She blew out a puff of air before draining her glass.

"You really are a lightweight, aren't you? How many of those did you drink before I showed up?" he asked.

"Two. But I missed dinner. I think," she slurred, frowning. Her tolerance should be better than this. "Shit…sinus pills."

He shook his head, disappointed, before turning back to the bar and calling out, "Steve? You have any more of your lentil soup? Could we get a couple of bowls? And some of your mixed pickles?"

"This isn't 1952, bud. I can order my own meal," Reena snapped.

"Sorry. Hey, Steve? Only one soup. Lightweight's going to have..." He looked at her.

Reena sighed. "Lentil soup. Extra bread."

Nadim laughed so hard he nearly fell off his seat. Who was he calling a lightweight?

Reena had always loved the lentil soup at the Sparrow. Even better, the country bread from the bakery up the street they served it with, complete with cultured butter. But the soup did nothing for her lost sobriety. The room still spun when she finished eating. Nadim paid and led her out of the bar.

"C'mon, sunshine, fresh air will do you good. I'll walk you home."

"No need." She stumbled, wondering if the sidewalk was always so far from her head.

"Relax, Reena. I'm going there anyway. This isn't unwarranted patriarchal chivalry."

His hand on her elbow, he guided her along the busy main road. The dark sky looked clear, spotted with more stars than she expected to see so early in the evening. But maybe it wasn't early—how long had they been in there, anyway?

As they got to the building, she felt herself waver a bit on the stairs up to the front door. "Put your arms around me, sunshine," Nadim said.

She looped her arms around him and rested her face in

his neck as he unlocked the door. He felt warm and solid, grounding her as the world spun. Mm...he smelled good.

"Have you eaten anything other than the soup today?" he asked once the door was opened and they were entering the building.

"A samosa. Wait, no. I forgot to eat the samosas."

"Do you have any homemade bread right now?"

She blinked. "You don't know me that well, do you?"

He laughed, pulling her toward her door instead of his. "C'mon, I'll make you some toast."

She let him into her apartment. A part of her realized just how terrible an idea it was to bring a man she was seriously attracted to into her place at this hour, but considering the effects of both cold medication and gin were still coursing through her veins, she wasn't able to make the leap from realizing the danger to doing anything about it.

He walked in, looking around with a huge grin. "Ah, nice to see what my place could look like if I shopped somewhere other than...well, nowhere."

"My parents' basement."

"Yeah, but we're not supposed to mention them, right? Cozy in here."

Reena looked around, frowning. Her apartment was fine— a bit of a mess right now, and her furniture may look comfortable, but it wasn't anything but cheap box-store stuff. She fell onto her couch, resting her head on the soft cushion.

Okay, so maybe he had a point. This was cozy. She closed her eyes.

"So, you don't want toast?" Nadim asked.

She sat back up. "I do. Just..." She rubbed her face. "Give

me a second, and I'll show you where to find the bread and the bread knife."

"I can get it," he said.

No, he couldn't. Reena might be intoxicated, and Nadim may be a bit of a foodie himself, but there was no way she was going to let someone she barely knew be unaccompanied in her kitchen.

He was suddenly sitting next to her on the couch. "You really feeling that drunk?"

"No." She sighed. "I think I'm sobering. This is more of an emotional crash than an alcohol crash. It's been a hell of a day."

He didn't say anything, so she closed her eyes again. Maybe she should just go to bed. Maybe asleep, she wouldn't feel so worthless.

"What's this? *Home Cooking Showdown*? Did you enter this?"

Nadim had that damn piece of paper from Marley's apartment in his hand. Why had she let Shayne force it on her?

"No, ignore that."

"This looks fun! You should do it. Says here the deadline is tomorrow. A five-minute cooking video is no big deal."

"I'm not doing it." Reena snatched the paper from his hand and tossed it back on the coffee table.

Nadim shrugged and stood up. He headed to the cabinet that held Reena's liquor bottles. "May I?" he asked, his hand on a bottle of gin.

She nodded. "There's soda in the fridge. Make me one, too, please." Another gin was as good as sleeping.

He pressed a glass into her hand a few moments later. When she took it, she noticed he had the paper again. "I don't get why you won't do this, Reena. I just googled the Asler Institute—they're a big deal."

"Yeah, I know, but . . ." She then realized that she couldn't tell him the reasons why she had no intention of entering Shayne's contest. Like the fact that her focus right now should be on getting a job. Or, that the contest was for couples and families, and she was much too alone to have someone to enter with. She sipped the gin.

"Not really into cooking contests?"

"I used to be." She hiccupped. "I actually won a bunch of blogger ones. In fifth grade I was a finalist on *Mini-Chef*. And I was in a Muslim competition barbecue team once. We won first place."

He laughed. "Reena Manji, you might just be the most fascinating person I have ever met. You should enter this."

She took another sip, then stood. Deflect and distract. "C'mon. I'll show you where my bread knife is. Let's see how your toast-making skills measure up."

But when they were in Reena's small kitchen, the box of samosas on the counter distracted him. "Are these the samosas you forgot to eat? Samosas might be better than bread."

"Hold your tongue." Nothing was better than bread. "I needed comfort food. Help yourself."

He took a large bite out of a samosa. "Nylon bhajias are my favorite comfort food."

Nylon bhajias was another name for the potato bhajias Reena had planned to make later. She laughed. "Me too. I literally bought potatoes and gram flour to make bhajias."

His eyes rolled back in his head with pleasure. "You make them yourself? Like, homemade? Not from a shop?"

"Yeah, I'll probably make them tomorrow."

"Make them for me now."

She raised a brow. "Excuse me?"

"Sorry. Can you please make me bhajias? I'll help...actually, teach me how, and I'll make you nylon bhajias every day for the rest of your life." He solemnly put his hand on his chest. "Swear to god."

"You're drunk."

He nodded happily. "And hungry." He opened the fridge. "And I would kill someone for fresh bhajias right now. Where are the potatoes? Yay! You have cilantro!"

"You really want me to give you a cooking lesson at"—she checked the time on the microwave—"twelve thirty a.m.?"

"Yes! This will be fun."

He pulled out random other things from her fridge. None of them were ingredients needed for bhajias.

Reena cringed. "Ketchup?"

"No ketchup?"

She put the ketchup back in the fridge and took out some tomatoes and onions. "Fine. But we'll make a tomato chutney, too. And I'm only doing this because I'm drunk and want to eat bhajias." She giggled. God bless gin.

"First, you need to peel and slice your potatoes," she said, pulling one out from the bin in her pantry. He grinned and held up his phone in front of her.

"Are you recording me?" she asked.

He nodded. "Since you're doing it anyway, you can enter that contest!"

"Nadim! I thought I told you I'm not doing that video! Besides..." She frowned.

"Besides what?"

She should keep her mouth shut. "It's not supposed to be one person. The video is supposed to be...pairs."

He beamed. "I have a tripod! C'mon, grab everything you need." He started filling his arms with the stuff on the counter: the potatoes, bag of gram flour, cilantro, tomatoes, and garlic/ginger paste. Also, the box of samosas and the bottle of gin, of course.

Reena had no idea why she was going along with this, but his infectious enthusiasm was irresistible. She grabbed some onions and chilis, her cutting board and knife, a jug of oil and some spices, and followed him to his apartment.

They dropped it all in his much cleaner kitchen, and he connected his phone to a large tripod.

"Okay," he said, eyes twinkling with excitement. And probably a healthy dose of gin. "Just need a second to set this up."

While he fiddled with camera placement and turned on a bunch of lights in his apartment, Reena poured oil in a pot and started heating it. She then peeled and sliced the potatoes, and diced the onion and tomatoes for the chutney.

"All set up. I can start recording using this remote."

Reena laughed at the ridiculousness of it all. "This is preposterous."

"Don't say that in front of the camera!" He rushed to stand next to her. "You'll never win without confidence. Okay...action!"

She looked up at him, struggling not to laugh, and having no idea what to say.

"What are you showing me how to make, oh brilliant one?" he asked.

"Brilliant one?"

He nodded enthusiastically. "You and I both know you're a culinary genius. So, tell me what we're making."

"Potato bhajias." She turned and looked at the camera instead of at him. "These are similar to pakoras and are also called nylon bhajias in East Africa. This recipe is my mother's—she grew up in Dar es Salaam."

Nadim grinned. "Which is where I grew up. I used to get these at food stalls late at night. My favorite shop back home would make a fresh batch every five minutes. They put chopped green chilis in the batter."

Reena raised a brow. "Can you take that kind of heat?"

He narrowed his eyes seductively. "Oh, I think you know I like it hot. Scorching hot."

Reena laughed so hard at his corny line that her forehead fell on his chest. Mmm…firm. Warm. Smelled good.

"Uh, Reena…the potatoes?"

"Right." She lifted her head. While describing what she was doing, she made a batter with gram flour, onion/garlic paste, turmeric, cilantro, red chili powder, and, just to see how much heat he could take, a whole, finely diced green chili.

Nadim helped her dip the potato slices in the batter and deep fry them. She made the chutney next—sautéing onions and tomatoes with dried chilis and spices before pureeing.

"Utterly brilliant," Nadim said, picking up a crisp bhajia.

"Wait!" She took the bhajia out of his hand and coated it with the chutney. A lot of chutney. She gave him back the slice, but instead of eating it himself, he held it up to Reena's mouth. "Let's see how hot *you* can take it."

Reena could take the heat. She opened her mouth and let him feed her the bhajia.

It was delicious. Spicy, perfectly crispy, and with the acidic chutney cutting right through the richness of the deep-fried potato. She dipped another one into the chutney and held it up for him.

He wasn't as graceful with his bite, immediately hopping up and down and waving his mouth. Maybe she'd put in too much chili? She erupted in laughter as he fell into her arms. He finally said "cut," and turned off the phone camera. She'd forgotten they were filming this.

That was the last thing Reena remembered that night. The next thing she knew she was waking up in Nadim's bed with terrible heartburn. Thankfully, alone.

CHAPTER SIX

Waking after passing out in a drunken stupor should include at least a moment of blissful ignorance of all the events of the night before. An innocence before the wave of humiliation crashed in. But despite rousing in her familiar childhood bed, Reena experienced no such luxury. She remembered everything that had happened yesterday—losing her job, her asinine mixing of gin gimlets and sinus meds, letting Nadim film her making bhajias...and...

They'd made the contest video. Together. Shit.

She quickly looked through the videos on the phone. Yup. It looked like he'd sent her the five-minute clip. She had no intention of actually entering it on the FoodTV site. She wasn't even going to watch the thing.

Head pounding and muscles aching, she sat up in bed. To add insult to an already abysmal situation, her cold had intensified. She sneezed, covering her nose to muffle the sound.

Quietly padding out of his bedroom, she found Nadim out cold on his purple sofa, a thin bedsheet covering his lower half and a yellow T-shirt covering his upper half. Thank the lord. She didn't need an eyeful of toned chest and shapely biceps now. She crept closer. He looked younger asleep, with his expressive brows relaxed and that world-weary yet amused expression missing. How old was this man, anyway? She'd assumed about her age, but from what he told her yesterday, he'd achieved so much more in his life than she had. An undergraduate *and* graduate degree from the London School of Economics. Lived in Dar es Salaam *and* London, before moving here to Toronto. He was miles ahead of Reena, with her community college diploma and no job. She sighed. Nadim Remtulla *was* an ambitious match for her. She didn't know if she should be pissed at her parents for setting her up to fail, or happy they thought her worthy of this man.

A wave of nausea overcame her. She needed to get out of here before he woke.

It truly was a walk of shame as Reena snuck out of Nadim's apartment with her cutting board and chef's knife in one hand and flip-flops in the other. She'd buy new spices and vegetables. It wasn't worth the embarrassment.

She needed to put that whole night out of her mind.

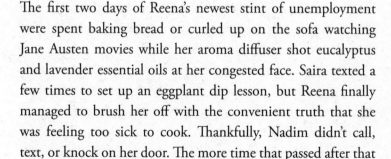

The first two days of Reena's newest stint of unemployment were spent baking bread or curled up on the sofa watching Jane Austen movies while her aroma diffuser shot eucalyptus and lavender essential oils at her congested face. Saira texted a few times to set up an eggplant dip lesson, but Reena finally managed to brush her off with the convenient truth that she was feeling too sick to cook. Thankfully, Nadim didn't call, text, or knock on her door. The more time that passed after that gin night, the less mortifying it would be when she inevitably saw her neighbor again.

By Friday evening, her cold had eased somewhat. Her misery? Not so much. Running out of Austen movies without Gwyneth Paltrow in them meant she had no escape from the mind-numbing self-loathing that inched into her consciousness whenever her mind stilled. She needed distraction. And thankfully, distraction came in the form of a dainty knock on her door at dinnertime. Marley stood on the threshold, oblivious to Reena's troubles, with a glimmer in her eye and a bottle of sangria in her hand.

"Hey, Reena. I just got home, but Shayne's upstairs with a ton of his grandmother's jerk chicken and that pumpkin rice you like. Apparently, he needs to talk to you. Can you come for dinner?"

She took a deep breath. Being around people sounded good. Being around people meant not being inside her own head anymore. "You're my savior, Marley."

She followed Marley up to her apartment to find Shayne carefully transferring Jamaican rice and chicken from the microwave to the dining table. It smelled amazing. Shayne's grandmother came from Jamaica and always sent Shayne home with a freezerful of food whenever he visited. Reena greeted Shayne before plopping herself at the table, watching Marley pour their drinks into tall glasses.

"They had this new sangria at the liquor store," Marley said. "No aspartame. I will never understand why every food or drink company assumes anything *girly* has to be sugar free or low fat. Fake sugar tastes like—"

"Despair," Reena interrupted. Even without Marley's stellar metabolism, Reena wouldn't let "substitutes" touch her lips. No fake sugar, no fake butter, or, *shudder*, fake meat.

She lifted the glass and took a sip. The fruity wine tasted surprisingly rich and complex. Full-bodied and almost voluptuous in flavor. The taste a perfect antidote to her mood. She sighed with pleasure.

What would it be like to share something like this wine with someone every day? To feel this warm comfort of companionship instead of having to wait for a friend to invite her out?

"You okay, Reena?" Marley eyed her as she scooped rice onto her own plate.

"Yeah, fine. Getting over a cold and a little stuffy." Forcing a smile, she took another sip. She hadn't told them about losing her job. She didn't want to be the one who brought a dark cloud to their carefree get-togethers. Plus, Marley was family—and she couldn't let her unemployment get back to her parents.

"Great. Now, Shayne, tell us what's going on," Marley said. "He's been practically vibrating with this secret news."

"Give me a minute, Grams forgot the pepper sauce." Shayne stood. "You have any more of that habanero hot sauce, Marley?"

"Yeah, in the cupboard over the stove," she said as Shayne walked away.

Reena took a bite of her chicken, the smoky, spicy flavor clearing her lingering sinus congestion in one bite. "Oh, man, your grams makes the best jerk chicken." She made a happy moan as she kept eating.

"This news has something to do with Anderson, right?" Marley called out.

Anderson, Anderson. Reena wracked her brain. She grinned when she remembered. "Tic Tac ears!"

Shayne laughed, returning to the table. "I've seen him three times this week. And not just booty calls either. We had lunch today. *Lunch.* A brightly lit, fully clothed date at one of those corporate grain-bowl situations downtown." Shayne sighed happily. "He is the absolute sweetest man I have ever met. He's like saltwater taffy, all sweet and innocent, and...squishy. I hate corrupting him, but he is starved for a little corruption." Shayne smiled wistfully. "Anyway, at lunch he told me something very interesting, Reena."

Crap. About the contest, no doubt. Maybe the deadline was extended. Reena had no intention of telling them that she and Nadim had made a video while drunk. She had done a great job of putting that whole episode out of her mind. "Yes, about that contest, it's just not something I'm interested in doing."

"No interest at all?"

"None."

Shayne smiled. "Okay, then maybe you can explain to me how your name ended up on the list of finalists?"

Holy shit. Reena's hand shot to her mouth.

Marley grabbed her arm. "You entered? Why didn't you tell us?"

"I didn't enter!" Reena said.

"Then how are you a finalist?" Shayne asked. "Cooking videos don't just make themselves."

Reena winced. "I'm not a finalist! Tic Tac Ears is mistaken."

Shayne shook his head. "Nope. At lunch Anderson told me he saw the name Reena on the list of finalists. He remembered your first name from when I asked him about it. I got him to double-check the last name when he was back at work, and yup. Reena Manji. Of course, I swore to him I wouldn't tell you, but here we are."

Reena cringed. "There's no way... We didn't enter the video..."

Shayne looked at her with a wide grin. "So, you did make a video then? We need details. Who was your husband?"

The sound of bagpipes filled the room. Reena had a text. She put down her chicken and wiped her hands before checking it.

Nadim: I've been sneezing all week. Thank you.

Crap. He *did* remember she existed. She ignored the message and put her phone facedown near her plate.

"Honestly, Shayne," Reena said, "it was silly. I was drunk when we made the video. But I can't be a finalist. I didn't actually enter it..." Then again, she didn't remember much from the end of the evening.

Another text. She flipped the phone over to look.

Nadim: And I have a newfound love of gin gimlets. You are rubbing off on me.

Reena couldn't let this go. "One minute, guys, I need to answer this."

Reena: World consumption of gin has risen steadily for the last couple of years. It is predicted it will surpass bourbon as the hipster's drink of choice. So, not my fault.

Nadim: And the cold? You going to take responsibility for that?

Reena: It's cold and flu season in Canada, and your African/ British immunity is not prepared for hard-ass germs. Also not my fault.

"Excuse me..." Shayne said, voice clipped. "I assume, based on you looking all doe-eyed at those texts, that you're talking to this British boy toy of yours. Is that who you made the video with?"

"I do *not* have a boy toy."

"I saw you leaving his room at six a.m. with your shoes in your hands. Don't tell me you were there to borrow a cup of sugar."

Bagpipes sounded again.

Nadim: You calling me a hipster?

Reena: With that tall hipster hair and precision beard, yeah, I am. You, sir, are a hipster.

She heard a snort behind her. She looked up to see Shayne standing there reading her texts over her shoulder. "She *is* texting that British dude. About his *hair*."

She put her phone facedown again and glared until Shayne went back to his seat. "Okay, fine. Yes, I made the video with Nadim. But it was a middle-of-the-night, drunken mistake, and it won't be repeated."

Shayne had his hand out and was about to say something when Reena shot him down. "And if anyone points out that sounds like most of my relationships, then no more rye bread for either of you."

Marley tilted her head sympathetically. "So, you did enter then?"

Reena sighed. "We may have. I don't remember much from the end of the night."

"*Did* you hook up with him?"

"No! Nothing happened! I'd remember that. I bumped into him at the Sparrow and we started drinking. And then drank more at home. And recorded a video of us making potato bhajias together. Perfectly innocent, calorie count notwithstanding. I had no intention of entering the thing."

"Well, seems either he did without telling you, or you two

did some drinking and contesting. You're finalists, so the drunk video must have worked," Shayne said. "I would advise you to do the next one sober, though."

No. There wouldn't be a next one. She absolutely couldn't spend her time making cutesy cooking videos for a web contest now. She needed to be job hunting. Her severance wouldn't last forever. It ran out months before she found a job last time. She couldn't let that happen to herself again.

"Reena, are you okay?" Marley said, voice laced with concern.

Reena wiped a rogue tear that escaped her left eye. "Yes... No." She sighed. "Just my cold. And...life is just really heavy. I can't do this right now. Honestly."

Shayne smiled warmly. "You can. You deserve this. I'll do the camera work, and Marley will help you look your best. I know you want that scholarship. You're doing it."

The bagpipe melody filled the room again.

"Jesus, Reena, can you change that? Unless there's a man in a kilt somewhere, the Highland pipes are a bit much," Shayne said.

Reena checked the phone.

Nadim: I googled hipster for the North American definition. I don't think you meant it as a compliment.

"Tell him you made the contest," Shayne said. "We need to all get together and plan the next video."

"I'm not telling him," Reena said, turning the ringer off the phone. "Why would he do this with me?"

"Didn't he already do it with you?" Marley asked.

"No. Well, sort of. He didn't know we were supposed to be a...you know...a couple. Engaged. I just told him it was supposed to be two people."

"Of course he'll do it!" Shayne said. "You spent the entire night with him, and don't tell me that the only cooking you two were doing was in the kitchen. You're totally into each other. Drinking together, making midnight snacks. Not to mention he won't stop texting you! You're already as good as engaged, according to your parents. He has both the face and the voice for TV. Wouldn't mind him in a kilt at all."

Reena tucked her phone between her thigh and the seat. "He did me a one-time favor. That's it. We're not into each other."

Marley and Shayne stared at her. Reena considered turning the ringer on her phone back on so the sound of bagpipes would cut the tension.

"Maybe you could ask him if he's willing to do more videos?" Marley finally said. "I agree with Shayne. Nadim would be perfect for this. You can pretend to be engaged."

Reena threw her hands up in exasperation. "I can't exactly pretend to be marrying the man that my parents have arranged my marriage to, can I?"

Shayne slowly shook his head. "I don't think I fully understand Indian culture."

Her phone vibrated under her leg. Ugh. She lifted it and took a look.

Nadim: You calling me a hipster may be a case of the pot calling the kettle black, little Miss Hipster Scratch Cooking and Baking Bread like it's 1890.

Nadim: Not that I want you to stop baking bread. Ever. And you must let me try more than just your fougasse.

Nadim: I could smell something you were baking today. If you have any extra . . . I'm just saying.

Reena sighed as she shoveled a bite of rice in her mouth. God, she needed this comfort food. Life had become uncomfortably complicated.

"Let's at least see the video," Shayne said, putting his hand out for the phone. "Whether you continue or not, I need to see how a couple of drunk boneheads managed to end up as finalists in a contest with hundreds of entries."

Reena sighed. To be honest, she wanted the answer to that question, too. She moved to the other side of the table so the three of them could watch together and started the video.

And holy crap. Nadim looked good. Reena barely even noticed herself, but Nadim was charming, charismatic, and enthusiastic on-screen. His attention was completely on her, but still somehow it was all about the food. She shivered when screen Reena buried her face in his chest, and when they both nearly fell over laughing at the end, she understood why they were picked. They were magnetic.

"Wow," Marley said. "That's what I call chemistry."

"Seriously. He's spectacular. Like a brown Jamie Oliver." Shayne fanned himself. "You sure you didn't hook up after that? Because that was cooking-show foreplay."

"Shayne!"

"Fine, fine. I understand now," Shayne said. "Obviously it's your decision, but Anderson told me a lot of people entered. The fact that you managed to do that while drunk off your ass is pretty impressive. Seems a waste not to continue. That scholarship could be yours."

"I know. I know. I just..." She turned off her phone. "I have a lot of shit going on right now, and I don't want to add to my stress. But...let me think about it."

Shayne shrugged. "Fine. Then I'll leave it be. Anyway, there might be a conflict of interest if you do it, since I was planning to help you with your videos and I'm dating a production assistant at FoodTV."

Marley grinned. "So, you and Anderson are officially a couple?"

Shayne groaned. "I have no idea. I wish I knew."

~

Reena left Marley's soon after dinner, went straight to her kitchen, and sliced several thick slices of her Sue loaf, a country sourdough made with unbleached white flour, and her Brian loaf, a Swedish dark rye with caraway, molasses, and orange peel. She wrapped them up first in brown paper, then in a plastic bag, and walked across the hall to Nadim's. She'd been rude when texting him during dinner and felt the need to make amends.

And she felt a little guilty for giving him her cold.

Nadim opened his door, and she stared. He looked... different. A red nose, watery eyes, flat hair, and a grin wider than a Cheshire cat. It was a strange contradiction, looking both miserable and elated consecutively.

"Reena!"

She gathered her composure, shooing away the fluttering in her stomach, and handed him the bag. "A sampling of my efforts today. A peace offering, and a thank-you for...obliging me and taking care of me the other night. I'm sorry for being such a mess. And I'm sorry I gave you my cold."

He took the bag. "It wasn't my most put-together moment

either. I feel like I should be thanking you for cheering me up that night. I had a great time."

"Glad I could help." Reena smiled, turned, and returned to her apartment. She had no intention of spending more time with him than necessary, not when seeing him appeared to make her skin pebble with goosebumps. Annoying.

~

Saturday felt wrong. Saturdays were supposed to be about spending time with friends, relaxing, and unwinding after the work week. But with no job, there wasn't much to unwind. Reena felt restless. What she needed was to make bread. But today wasn't a day for her usual crusty, sourdough-leavened country breads. Reena's mood needed something more sumptuous. But which recipe? Brioche would be lovely, but the loose dough really needed an electric mixer to make it work. She had a professional-grade KitchenAid, but she used it rarely, preferring to knead by hand most of the time. She finally decided on challah, the traditional Jewish celebration bread fortified with eggs and oil. Reena gathered her ingredients.

She was tying her apron around her waist when there was a knock on the door. She answered, expecting Marley popping down for coffee. But no. It was Saira.

Damnit. So much for brushing her sister off. Saira was looking altogether too chipper for nine a.m. on a Saturday, and was carrying a large plastic container.

"I'm on my way to work," she said, dropping the container on the kitchen counter. She approached and put her hand on Reena's forehead. "You said you had the flu."

"I had a cold. I'm feeling better."

Saira raised one brow, looking at the ingredients laid out on the counter, eyeing the jar of yeast especially. "What are you making?"

"Challah bread."

She picked up the jar of instant yeast. "You know, long-fermented breads are much better for you. I read an article about the molecular changes wheat flour undergoes during sourdough fermentation."

Now Saira approved of Reena's starters? "You didn't seem to like sourdough when you threw Bob out the window."

"I apologized for that. And you made new ones. No harm done." Saira smiled, white teeth gleaming under the kitchen lights.

Saira honestly looked amazing these days. A few inches taller than Reena, she had brown skin a shade lighter, and brown hair a shade darker. She'd been a cute, chubby child and continued to carry more weight in her teens, but her healthy-living kick and career as a dietician left Saira strong with toned muscles. After Joran's cheating, though, Saira had started to lose weight rapidly. Lately, she seemed to be more into healthy balance than depriving herself. And she looked so much better now that she was back to herself.

Saira opened the container she had deposited on the counter. An overwhelming scent of black pepper wafted over. "I woke up early to make you bone broth in the pressure cooker. This is like super-food when you have a cold. Do you know how many minerals and nutrients are in bones? The broth is rich in amino acids, and all that collagen will do wonders for your skin. I put extra black pepper to help loosen all the phlegm in your throat."

"You cooked. For me?" Reena was skeptical. Was this to weaken her resolve over the eggplant dip?

But Saira just smiled. "Don't put it in the microwave. The radiation will zap out all the antioxidants. A gentle heat on the stove is good. This is still warm, but the natural gelatin might thicken it when it's cold. Do you know how good that gelatin is for your joints? It's never too early to start preventing arthritis." Saira patted Reena's shoulder before plopping herself on a dining chair. "I have a few minutes before I need to leave for work. What's new, sis?"

Reena raised a brow. Was Saira expecting...small talk?

"Um, nothing interesting. You know, same old. What's going on with you?" This was weird.

"Things are great. Ashraf and I are thinking of going south for Christmas. You should come."

"Well, I probably have to work...you—"

"Oh, you'll love this, I heard the best news from Rish yesterday," Saira said, grinning. Ashraf's sister Rish was the apparent town crier when it came to gossip within their community. "Get this—Jasmine Shah was just *abandoned* in Egypt by her fiancé. She had to get an emergency visa to get out and everything."

Reena cringed. Though she didn't know her personally, Jasmine Shah was the daughter of her father's former classmate. The Shahs were her parents' favorite family to dig up dirt on. And although Reena tried to stay out of it, judging them was a longtime family pastime. "Holy crap. Did you tell Dad?"

"Yeah, Dad's schadenfreude was pretty epic. And speaking of schadenfreude, did you hear—"

"Saira wait—is that why you came over? To gossip?"

"No, I came to bring you soup. But"—she checked the time on her phone—"I should go. I need to bring Ashraf his lunch before my shift." She got up and headed toward the door. "Feel better, sis!"

She left. Reena stood blinking at the closed door for a few seconds. What the hell was that? Since when did Saira make hot soup for anyone?

Shaking her head at the strange visit, Reena went back to her counter and started combining ingredients for the challah.

This was a good idea. Mixing the soft, almost silky dough managed to feel both comforting and cathartic. She took out her frustrations, squishing the pale-yellow blob around the enormous bowl. But the dough was still a loose, shaggy mess when another knock on her door interrupted her Zen-like kneading.

Now what? Maybe Mum with *her* favorite cold remedy, haldi jo dudh? God, she hoped not. One Manji visitor a day was more than enough.

She carefully turned the doorknob with her elbows, a talent she had long ago perfected, since she usually had her hands deep in some cooking project or another.

Thankfully, it wasn't family, but Nadim at her door. Maybe. Or…was that Nadim? She tilted her head. Yes, definitely her neighbor, but again, he looked different. Eyes and nose back to normal after last night's weeping clown look. But…clean-shaven? And hair trimmed close enough to his scalp that she half expected him to tell her he joined the Marines after she saw him last night.

Did Canada have Marines? Could Tanzanians join?

"What happened to your hair?" she asked in lieu of a greeting.

He ran his hand through the short strands, as if he'd forgotten about it. "Oh. Uh, I cut it this morning." He took a deep breath. "Reena, we need to talk. Can I come in?"

She blinked, annoyed at this interruption. The weird pang of attraction she had felt last night seemed to have left the building along with the man's hair. Maybe the douche-beard had magical, magnetic qualities?

And anyway, *we need to talk* never went well, so more bad news seemed inevitable. She motioned him in and went straight back to the kitchen and dumped the dough onto her big butcher-block board for heavy kneading. He stood opposite her in front of the breakfast bar.

"What's that?" He nodded to the dough as she formed the blob into a big ball and started working it.

"It's going to be challah. What's up?"

"Are you standing on a stool?"

"Yes. I'm too short to knead well otherwise. You look… healthier."

"I'm on cold pills. Why does it smell like a pepper mill in here?" He looked around, trying to find the source of the overwhelming scent.

Reena rolled her eyes and closed the container of her sister's soup. "Is this twenty questions, or are you going to tell me what we have to talk about?"

His eyes shifted to the door. Why did he seem nervous? Had something happened with her father? Had Dad found out about Reena's job? Crap, did Nadim discover they'd made the finals in the contest? She hadn't planned on telling him about it—since she wasn't sure what to do about it yet. She squeezed the dough against the worn wood surface.

"Okay," he said as he sat on the barstool. He took a long breath. "I don't know if you know this, but I got here to Toronto a couple of weeks before moving into this building."

She didn't know that.

"I stayed with this distant friend of the family. Some aunty and uncle I'd never met. Anyway, I went out a lot because they were a little...cold...and..." He paused, mesmerized by her hands on the dough.

"And what?" she said, hoping he would get to the point. If the point would be particularly sharp for her, she'd like to get it over with as soon as possible.

"And I met someone. At a bar. And we...well...met up several times that week."

Reena squeezed the dough. Why the hell was he telling her this? She didn't even know he existed back then. Why would it matter if he hooked up with someone before they met? She'd already pegged him as a player, and she had no intention of going along with this blasted arranged marriage anyway...

She slapped the dough on the counter, glad to have an outlet for her frustration. This couldn't be jealousy, could it?

Nadim continued. "Sharon. She's a kindergarten teacher. And...camp counselor. It was casual. I haven't seen her since I moved to this building and didn't expect to hear from her. But she called me late last night. She had to tell me..."

Holy shit. Nadim had knocked up this kindie teacher and now he had to marry her, which meant he couldn't marry Reena. Dumped by the fiancé she didn't even want. Figures. Could this week get any worse?

Nadim continued. "She needed to let anyone who could be

exposed know. And I have to tell you now, since you are at risk, too..."

Reena froze. She'd seen this after-school special before. Kindie teacher gave Nadim some STD, and he exposed Reena to it. She'd need blood tests and antibiotics and...wait. She hadn't even kissed the guy...

What the hell was he going on about?

"Nadim, can you get to the point sometime soon?"

He took a deep breath, before running his hand through that cropped hair again. She'd liked his hair better last night. Long enough to fall into his eyes when not styled within an inch of perfection. But she couldn't deny that this new velvety head looked deliciously touchable now.

"I have head lice," he said.

Okay, maybe not so touchable. *Lice?* Ew. But at least not pregnancy or an STD...yay for blood-sucking parasites?

She wrinkled her nose. "Gross."

"I know. I didn't even realize it, but Sharon said she may have given it to me, so I googled it, and then looked, but I couldn't really tell."

"That's what this new hairstyle is about?"

He nodded. "I figured I'd rather be safe than sorry and shave everything. I found a twenty-four-hour drugstore and got hair clippers. But..." He looked at her face, eyes wide. "I'll have to check your hair. You may have picked up some bugs when you slept in my bed." He sighed. "I'm very sorry, Reena."

She said nothing. Her dough felt smooth and pliant now with the gluten fully developed, so she dropped it in a greased bowl, covered it with plastic wrap, and placed it on top of her fridge to rise. Washing her hands and the counter, she considered this new blow to her life. Head lice. She didn't know whether to laugh or cry at this one.

"I'm not shaving my head," she told him, not meeting his eyes.

"No," he assured. "I won't let you...I'll help you. I bought special shampoo and a comb. I just want to check your hair..." His voice trailed off, hopefully as he realized how utterly ridiculous their relationship had become.

"Nadim, I—"

"Please," he pleaded. "Let me help. I feel terrible, Reena. I know I messed up again. Your father's going to—"

She put her hand up to stop him from continuing that statement and moved around the kitchen to sit on the barstool next to him. "I have no intention of telling my father this."

"You don't?"

"Of course not! Can you imagine how that conversation would go? *So, Dad, I needed to drown my sorrows, so I went to a bar and had way too much gin while taking sinus medication. But don't worry, your employee also had a shitty day, so we drank together. But then I slept in his bed, and he gave me lice.*"

He frowned. "We don't know if you even have them. Let me at least check..."

There was rock bottom, and then this. "Okay. Fine. I don't have a whole lot of shame left to lose, anyway." She let her head fall into her arms on the breakfast bar, needing the solid countertop under her to hold her up.

She definitely thought this situation warranted a cry, not a laugh.

"Okay," he said softly, "I'm going to put my hands in your hair. Tell me if you want me to stop."

She nodded into her arms. The room fell silent a moment. Two moments. Finally, she sensed a whisper of a touch on her neck. Feathery light fingers that trailed upward into her loose curls. She shivered as he raked through the hairs on the back of her head slowly. It was like nothing existed but her head and his hands parting through her hair. She fell into a sleepy trance, more relaxed than she had been all week.

As he reached the sensitive patch behind her ear, he stroked the soft skin there. The soft skin where no hair grew. That was a caress. She should put a stop to this. Now.

But as he continued to the top of her head, warmth enveloped her whole body, all while his touch, barely there, reminded her exactly what was happening, and who was making her feel this good. This was heaven. The deep serenity eased her mind and calmed her soul.

"I'm sorry," he murmured.

"You found some?"

"I don't know for sure, but I think so. You should use the treatment shampoo and let me comb out your hair, just in case."

She closed her eyes again, leaving her head in her arms. Another blow to her battered life. It didn't seem fair that this one came with boneless tranquility and soft fingers stroking the back of her neck.

CHAPTER SEVEN

Reena had endured much in her thirty-one years on the planet. As a short, middle-born, socially awkward visible minority, she'd had birthdays forgotten, been bullied at school, been dumped on the subway, and even once had an ex-boyfriend post a picture of her sated, after-sex face on social media—with a self-congratulating caption. But having insecticide shampoo thoroughly applied to her hair by a brown Captain America type felt like a new level of humiliation. She managed only with her eyes squeezed shut—because this stuff apparently stung like the dickens if it came into contact with eyes, and so she wouldn't catch a glimpse of this in her bathroom mirror.

Surprisingly, though, sitting on the sofa with a man close behind her carefully dragging a narrow comb through her hair turned out to be an oddly intimate experience. Intimate, but not sexual. The comb was hard metal, and Nadim's enthusiasm about the process of looking for bugs in her hair didn't do much for the sensual allure of the experience.

"Don't you find that gross?" she asked after he wiped the comb on a damp paper towel.

"Not at all. I grew up in Africa, remember? I have nothing against creepy-crawlies, unless they carry malaria. Lice are annoying but harmless."

Reena shuddered, closing her eyes. Only way to survive this was to pretend to be in Tahiti. Or Siberia. Anywhere but here.

"We're never going to speak to anyone about this, right?" she asked.

He moved her head to get behind her left ear. "I have no intention of telling the world I picked up lice from a hookup. Or that I may have passed them to you, of all people. I don't even think *we* should talk to each other about this again."

Add it to the list of things they wouldn't speak about, right after the drunken cooking video. "What do you mean *me of all people*."

"The boss's daughter. The woman I'm supposed to impress, but who I've already made a fool of myself to."

She lowered her head so he could reach the back. "You don't need to impress me. I told you, I'm not going to marry you. Think of me like any other neighbor."

He didn't respond. With her head down, she felt brave enough to ask the question she'd wondered since the beginning. "Nadim. Did you *really* agree to marry a complete stranger?"

He took a while to answer, silently working through her scalp. "I agreed to come here and get to know Aziz Manji's daughter with the intention of seeing if we could be compatible as husband and wife."

"Then what? I'm supposed to drop everything, marry you, and move to Africa?"

He sighed. "I hadn't thought that far ahead." He unclipped a section of her hair and started combing it. "If you aren't interested, that's obviously okay. But they told me you were willing."

There were so many more questions. Why did he sleep with that teacher if he'd already resigned himself to marrying Reena? And why did he care so much about what Reena thought of him, even after she told him she wasn't going to marry him? "Is that all I am? Aziz Manji's daughter?"

He stilled for a moment. "No. No, you're not. You're… unexpected. You know that night at the Sparrow? I was having a monumentally shitty day. I was one step away from saying screw it all and leaving town. But"—he stroked behind her ear—"you were there for me. With your flip-flops, and your gin, and your even worse mood. I had the most fun I've had in a very long time, on the night that was supposed to be the worst. You were a great friend exactly when I needed it."

Reena squeezed her eyes shut. She felt the same way. She'd told her friends that she had regrets after that night, but it wasn't true. On what should have been the worst night ever, she'd laughed, she'd cooked, and she'd forgotten about it all.

"But at the end of the day," he said, "I work for your father, and if I upset you, my job is at stake."

And there it was. Any relationship between them, even a simple friendship, sat in the shadow of her family. Could she ever truly trust a man employed by her father?

He worked a little longer at the back of her head before speaking again. "Done," he finally said, putting the comb down. "We have to do the whole thing again in a week, to be sure."

Reena lifted her head and stood up, stretching her tired legs. She turned to look at Nadim. "I'm not sure if you figured this out yet, but I don't have the best relationship with my parents.

We can't be friends if you're always worried about what my father will say and...and I'd like it if we could be friends."

Reena bit the side of her lip, realizing how pathetic she sounded. Was this grade two? Asking him to be her friend?

He smiled, though. Wide enough for her to see that dimple for the first time without the concealment of facial hair. She had an urge to stick her pinky finger into the deep crevice. "I'd like that, Reena. Friends." His smile was infectious.

She could do it, be his friend. She could put aside her attraction, her parents' interference, and his secrecy, and just get support from the man who lived across the hall, and who needed a friend as much as she did. "Deal."

He beamed. "Okay, then, friend. Be back in a second. I just got a pumpkin porter that you have to try. We can toast this friendship." He grinned and left her apartment.

Reena smiled to herself as she checked her phone. And a perfectly timed message from the foodie gods themselves was waiting for her in her inbox.

To Reena Manji,

Congratulations! Among hundreds of entries, yours has been chosen to participate in the FoodTV *Home Cooking Showdown!* The winning couple of this talent search will be awarded a ten-thousand-dollar scholarship for the Asler Institute, Canada's premier cooking school with locations in every major city across the country. Winners may also be showcased in a FoodTV holiday special, sharing their unique home-cooked cuisine!

Reena skimmed the rest of the email outlining the rules while her heart beat heavily in her ears. Shayne's inside information was right. She was in.

And at that moment, Reena decided that she wanted to do it. Cooking with Nadim had saved her the night she lost her job—she needed, *deserved* more of that.

Her kitchen timer went off before Nadim returned, so by the time he was back in her kitchen pouring the dark beer into glasses, she was at her counter getting ready to form the challah dough into loaves.

"Pull up a stool," she told Nadim after he handed her the beer. "I need to ask you something. No pressure, just an idea, okay?"

He grinned as he sat opposite her at the breakfast bar. "I'm all ears. Go ahead."

"Okay." She took a breath. "First, a question. Do you remember that video we made for that FoodTV contest?"

"Of course."

"One of us sent in the application." She paused. "I was too drunk. I don't remember who did it."

He cringed. "Yeah, I should apologize. We applied together, but I talked you into it. I may have been a bit persuasive."

"We got in."

His eyes widened. "Shit. *Really?*"

She nodded. "And...I want to do the contest. But I'll need your help to continue."

Pulling off a six-strand braid of bread dough while explaining to an attractive man that she wanted him to pretend to be her fiancé to compete in an online cooking contest was no easy feat, but she'd made challah enough times that she managed.

And the smirk on Nadim's face told her the idea didn't turn him off. Amused him, though.

"We were supposed to be a couple in that video?" he asked. "You told me it was just supposed to be pairs."

"It's a family cooking challenge. We were supposed to be family."

"I thought you *didn't* want to marry me," he said, laughing.

"I don't. It's just for the contest. I may not have wanted to enter, but we did. And we're finalists."

"So now you want me to do it?"

"I'll do all the cooking, and you would be like my sidekick. I really want this scholarship. The Asler Institute has the most amazing artisan bread baking program. I've wanted to take it for years."

"I don't think you need a course, Reena," he said, watching her hands again. "That bread you gave me last night was divine. And that"—he pointed to the thick, plaited loaf that was forming from the six snakes of dough—"how are you doing that?"

"Practice," she said, finishing the braid and tucking the ends under. "Look, you don't have to do it if you don't want to. I just...I wanted something fun to keep me occupied right now. Things have been...but you don't have to." She turned to fetch the beaten egg white she had saved after adding the yolk to the dough and started to brush it over the bread.

"No, of course I'll do it. I pushed you to enter. I'm not going to bail on you now. What exactly am I saying yes to? More videos?"

"Yes." She opened the email. "There are four rounds, and it starts with eight couples. Two couples are eliminated through online voting after each round. Rounds one and two are videos that we produce and submit. If we make it to round three, they fly us to Toronto—or I guess we'll just take the subway. The four couples tape that round in the FoodTV studio and get a tour. Finally the last round will have only two couples, and they send a camera crew to tape it in our own homes."

"Okay, that's a lot."

"I know. And we'll be pretending to be engaged the whole time. And we have to keep it from my parents. They're not really into the FoodTV scene and it won't be on TV, just the website, so I don't think they'd find out, but it might mean lying to your boss. Would you be okay with all that?"

He nodded. "I gave you lice, Reena. I owe you majorly. But I'd do it anyway. Sounds like a lot of fun." He paused, watching her again. "Hell, I'd do it if only to watch you cook again."

"I'm baking now, not cooking." She smiled. "But I will be cooking for the contest. Home cooking. So, you're in?"

He grinned. "Yes. Apparently, we'll be engaged after all."

CHAPTER EIGHT

The balancing act of résumé writing and job searching while hiding her unemployment from her neighbors and family turned out to be no problem whatsoever. Reena just dressed in her usual business casual on Monday and headed to the library with her laptop in hand. She'd worked part-time shelving books in college and was well aware of what some people got up to while using public computers. Ew.

So far, job searching had gone better than expected—after a cursory scan of positions in her field, Reena found several she miraculously felt both qualified for and interested in. Well, sort-of interested. After all, these were still finance jobs, but the companies seemed up her alley and the locations good. She made a list of suitable options for when Amira finished helping her polish up her résumé. She also made an appointment with the employment agency Railside contracted to help laid-off employees. And she made an appointment for a mani/pedi. Job searching felt like a scorching walk through the hot bowels of hell, so may as well walk with painted toenails.

Her meeting with Abigail, the employment counselor, on Tuesday morning was exhausting, but fine. She subjected Reena to countless online tests to determine her proficiency with various computer programs and interviewed her so thoroughly Reena half expected to be asked what brand of peanut butter she preferred. Abigail was almost comically optimistic and believed she would have no problem placing Reena in a full-time position before the end of the month. She said she had several leads, including a top secret posting that hadn't gone public yet for a position in the food-services industry. Between chirpy Abigail's infectious optimism, and the sparkly purple polish on her fingers and toes, Reena had an honest spring in her step as she climbed the stairs to her apartment at the end of the day. Shayne, Marley, and Nadim were joining her for dinner to discuss plans for the next video in the contest. She had some chicken thighs marinating in Thai curry paste and planned to wrap them in pandan leaves and roast them to serve with cucumber salad and sticky rice.

But her hope for a pleasant evening with friends crashed into the sun when she got to her apartment door. Standing there was a five-foot, zero-inch tracksuit-wearing woman carrying a stack of foil pans, along with a spaced-out-looking woman drinking muddy green sludge.

"Mum. Saira. What are you doing here?" Reena asked as she pulled out her key from her bag.

"What, a mother can't visit her daughter? Why are you wearing flip-flops? It's September."

Strangely, she'd heard this question a lot lately. The flip-flops, of course, were to protect her newly painted nails from smudges. But if she told Mum that, she'd have to admit she'd had a pedicure and was not at work.

"It's warm. I don't like driving in heels," she said before unlocking her door. "And of course you guys can visit me.

I'm just surprised." She motioned her mother in first, before dropping her bag on the kitchen counter. She gestured toward the foil pans, which her mum was placing near the stove. "What's that?"

"Dinner. Kebob jo shaak and rice."

"I just got off work or I would have made you something, too," Saira added. "Did the bone broth help with your cold? I'm not sure the pressure cooker extracts the nutrients as well as a long simmer."

Reena hadn't subjected herself to Saira's weird soup. It was still sitting in her fridge, the jellied mass mocking her whenever she opened the fridge looking for real food.

She opened the top foil tray. The rich tomato broth with spicy kofta meatballs and potatoes smelled heavenly, but her mother showing up at her door with one of her favorite dishes was not unconditional parental care. She doubted the woman knew a thing about unconditional anything. Mum and Saira wanted something.

"There's lots. I thought you could invite Nadim to share dinner with you." Mum grinned.

Aha. Mystery solved. In Mum's opinion, a home-cooked meal was just the thing to make him fall head over heels in love with Reena. Food being the way into a man's heart and all. It was a laughable attempt.

If Reena wanted his heart (or any other part of him), she would have cooked herself—and made something more show-stopping, like the duck and shallots au vin she made for Amira's going-away dinner. Ooh, maybe with smoked salt focaccia, and star anise-cardamom crème brûlée for dessert. And to drink, maybe...wait. Mum was still talking.

"I didn't make any maani," Mum said. "But I bought you some frozen ones."

Reena's nose wrinkled. "Ugh, Mum. Frozen bread?"

"You know what you should try, Reena?" Saira said. "Serving the kebobs with lettuce cups."

Reena tried so hard not to snort. Lettuce cups wouldn't win a man's heart, any more than frozen bread. But since she didn't want to win Nadim's heart, it was a moot point. She'd serve the kebob jo shaak, but with her own sourdough bread, and save her Thai for another day.

But she didn't want Mum to know that—Mum would see it as a victory.

"Maybe tomorrow. I'm eating with Marley and Shayne today. Thank you for the food, though." Reena smiled, hoping Mum wouldn't push.

"Mahreen? We never see her anymore. We don't even see Amin and Shaila that much since her sister died."

Amin and Shaila were Marley's parents. Shaila's younger sister had passed away from ovarian cancer a few years ago, and it was true, Shaila Aunty had taken her sister's death hard. But it was understandable, they were very close.

"Mahreen's not still doing that stuff, is she?" her mother asked.

Saira rolled her eyes and plopped herself on the barstool at the breakfast bar. "Really, Mum? *That stuff*? You can just say she's bisexual. Nobody cares."

Saira had a point. When Marley came out to her parents last year, the news caused barely a blip on anyone's radar in the extended family gossip. Really, there had been more judgment when Marley dyed her hair blond for about six months than when she started dating women. But, of course, Mum judged.

Deflect and distract time.

"Thank you for the food..." Crap. She'd already said that. Reena raked her brain to think of something suitable to say...

"You must ask Nadim to come another time," Mum said. "Alone. I invited him for brunch next Sunday, too."

Wow. Family brunch? Bold move. Nafissa hadn't been invited until she and Khizar were engaged. "I thought I told you last Sunday, I'm missing next week. I'm going to Amira's for the weekend. She's having a housewarming."

"Reena! This is important! You can come back for Sunday brunch. Ask Nadim what kind of daal he likes."

"I can't come back early. Amira's party is Saturday night and will probably go late. I'll be too tired to drive home early Sunday. And also"—she took a deep breath—"please stop setting me up with men."

Saira snorted loudly. Reena raised a brow at her sister. She still had no idea why Saira was here. Maybe for the eggplant recipe?

"Reena, please. I'm not *setting you up*," Mum huffed. Did Mum not know the definition of *setting up*?

Mum bit her lip slightly and looked at the door before turning back to her daughter. "Is it wrong to want my daughter to be happy? I want you to find a nice man and settle down. But..." Mum sighed. "This time isn't like the others. The family needs you now."

What the everlasting hell? Had she stumbled into *The God-father*? The *family needs* her? Other than the fact Nadim worked for Dad, he was exactly like the others: educated, from a parent-approved, good family, and a complete stranger to Reena.

Except for his toned legs and firm biceps. Okay, that was not like the others.

"Mum, tell me what's going on. Why do you need me all of a sudden?"

Mum sat heavily on the barstool next to Saira and rubbed her face—an unfamiliar gesture from her mother.

"Girls, please don't tell your father I told you this, but he's in trouble."

Finally! Honesty! So refreshing. But…why was Dad in trouble?

"The Diamond project is at risk. Your father was swindled. The first architect he hired turned out to be a crook. I never trusted the man. In fact, I told your father that from the beginning. I can just look at someone and know they're lying. But your father—"

"He took Dad's money?" Reena froze. Her father worked with a lot of people on a lot of projects, and she worried that one day someone would take advantage of his trustworthiness.

Mum nodded. "Yes. Cash flow is empty."

"Wait, isn't this the last guy you tried to set Reena up with?" Saira asked.

Actually, about three potential husbands ago, not that she was keeping track or anything. "Can't you guys go to the cops?"

"What, and let everyone know he was cheated?" Mum said. "People will laugh at our misfortune!"

Reena didn't doubt others would enjoy watching the mighty Manjis fail publicly. Just like Dad enjoyed watching his rivals', like the Shahs', downfall.

Mum sighed. "Shiroz Remtulla's investment is essential to keep the project going. But he will only invest after his son finishes a three-month probation period. I would never have agreed to this plan... What do we know about this boy? To tie up the business in this—"

"Wait, Mum, you don't trust Nadim when it comes to the business, but you expect me to marry him?"

"Reena! I'm not forcing anything," she said. "But it's time you settled down anyway. And we need to keep Shiroz happy."

"By *marrying* his son?"

"I have said this before, and I will say it again, we ask that you meet him and get to know him. That is all we want."

"Didn't anyone think to ask me or Nadim what we want?"

"I don't understand why you are not willing to even talk to the man. This business is our family—it's yours as much as it is ours."

Reena glared. This was a new low. As the middle child in her household, being an afterthought felt more familiar. Not as smart as Khizar, not as needy as Saira. Her parents had finally found a use for her—as a bargaining chip in a business deal. It almost made her feel valued for a change. Almost.

"Wow," Saira said, shaking her head at Mum. "I can't believe you sold Reena. What year is this, anyway?"

"We have done no such thing," Mum said firmly. "This is a good match. Similar families, same religion, both families even from Dar es Salaam! That means a lot more than what OK Cherub or whatever will give you."

"Cupid," Saira corrected.

"Have dinner with him, Reena. That's a start."

Someone knocked on her door.

"Marley's already here?" Saira asked.

Mum stood immediately and headed to the door. "I would love to say hello..."

Reena was behind Mum when she opened the door, so she didn't see her mother's expression when she opened it to Nadim's smiling face and ever-present six-pack of beer.

"Rosmin Aunty! This is a surprise!" he said, quickly putting the beer down in the hallway next to the door before Mum noticed it.

Mum hugged him and motioned him into the living room. "Nadim! What happened to your hair? Come, come. We were just talking about you. Come meet Saira, my younger daughter. I brought kebob jo shaak for Reena. You can join her for dinner."

"Hey," Saira said, raising a hand but not getting up from her seat.

Nadim stood, hesitating, and looked from one to the other before focusing on the floor in front of him again. Reena tried to get his attention to wordlessly let him know not to admit they already had dinner plans. He seemed to get the hint, eventually.

He looked at Mum. "Oh, I don't want to intrude. I just, I'm here to borrow, some, um..." He looked down again. "Nail varnish."

Reena fought back a laugh.

"Nail polish?" Saira asked.

His eyes widened as he looked up at Reena. "Um, yeah, sorry, I just..."

Okay, this was adorable. His hesitations and mumblings... her normally confident-bordering-on-cocky neighbor completely flustered. But, of course, Mum was the wife of his boss. She decided to help the guy out.

"You're welcome to join us for dinner. My cousin and her friend are coming. Why don't you come back in half an hour?" Reena said. "And did you want the nail polish to help label your keys, like I showed you when we bumped into each other leaving for work this morning?"

"Yes. That's totally why." His eyes flashed gratitude. "I'll just go...now. Thank you for the dinner invitation, and good to see you, Aunty. Nice to meet you, Saira."

"Later," Saira said, waving. "And don't worry—I'm a pretty low-maintenance sister-in-law!" Saira laughed loudly at her own terrible joke (that was a joke, right?) as Reena gently pushed Nadim out of the room. She hoped he remembered to take his six-pack out of the hallway—and bring it back in half an hour. She definitely was going to need that.

CHAPTER NINE

Mum's phone chimed loudly the minute Nadim left. Reena picked it up from the counter and glanced at it.

"Mum, who's Giovanna, and why is she asking if you're coming tonight?"

Mum snatched her phone. "Nah! Don't look at my phone!" She walked to the far side of the living room, presumably to respond to her text.

"Mum has a secret?" Reena asked her sister. "Mum has no life. She can't have a secret."

Saira shrugged, noisily slurping the end of her mystery drink. "I try not to pay too much attention to what they're up to."

"Why exactly did you come here with her?" Reena asked.

"She was loading that stuff in her car when I got home from work. I thought you might need backup while you were ambushed. No one needs a surprise visit from parents. Anyway, I'm glad I came. I had no idea that Mum and Dad sold your hand in marriage for cold hard cash. This is juicy..."

"I'm not going to marry the man."

"Obviously. Although"—she looked at the door—"I was right about him being bald, but he's hotter than I expected. Doesn't talk much, though. Anyway—"

Mum was back at their side, giving Saira a stern look. "This isn't gossip, Saira. I don't want to hear that you're telling anyone the family's personal business."

"Give me some credit, Mum," Saira said.

"We have to go." Mum put on her shoes and coat. "You need to prepare yourself for your dinner with Nadim."

Saira handed Reena her empty cup. "Toss this for me, will you? Later, Reena." She followed Mum out the door.

And with that, Reena was left with two mysteries: one, what was Saira's real motive in coming over again, and two, what in God's name did Mum mean when she said *prepare herself*? Actually, she shook the thought from her mind. She didn't want to know.

Nadim reappeared at her door about three seconds after her mother left. "That was awkward," he said as Reena let him back in. He placed the six-pack on the kitchen counter and held a bottle out to her. She nodded, so he took a glass out of her cupboard for it.

"Why did you tell them you wanted to borrow nail polish?" she asked.

He snorted. "I was so worried I'd spill about the contest that I spewed nonsense. You have varnish on your toes. It threw me. Why did you invite me to dinner?"

"Weren't you here for dinner?"

"Of course. But now your mother knows that. Which means tomorrow your father will ask me how dinner went, and I will have to pretend things are going well and that you haven't been saying you have no plan to marry me at least once per night." He handed her the beer. "Your sister's a little..."

Reena cringed as she sat on the barstool. "Sorry about her. She's a lot."

"Is she telling everyone we're engaged?"

"Doubt it. Saira's a huge gossip but doesn't air our own family laundry. She's more radio receiver than broadcaster."

"You sure you two are sisters?"

"I've often wondered the same thing. I still can't figure out why she was here today. My guess is it has to do with eggplant." She sipped her beer.

Nadim's hand shot to his mouth, stifling a laugh.

"That's not a euphemism. I actually mean eggplant."

"With your family, I believe it. Just to confirm, I can't let her know about the contest, either, but your cousin knows, right? I'm having trouble keeping up with who knows what. Hard enough to come up with a story for why I shaved my head."

True. This had become ridiculous. She considered whether a spreadsheet could make things easier. She couldn't let her parents know about her friendship with Nadim, and couldn't tell him about her father's business troubles. And, of course, no one could find out that she'd lost her job. The only secret easy to keep here was the head lice.

She took a long sip of the beer. "Just follow my lead. Why are you early, anyway? I told you Marley won't make it until six thirty, at least."

"I know. I wanted to watch you cook dinner. Since we're supposed to be fake-engaged, I figured I should see you cook more than once before we film."

She laughed. "Sorry, I'm not going to cook after all. Not when I have all this stuff Mum made. You okay with Indian food?"

"I *am* Indian, Reena. More than okay with it." He sighed. "I miss my real food, the stuff I grew up on in Africa. Indian food in restaurants is nothing like the Gujarati–East African stuff we were raised on, right?"

"There are a few decent East African restaurants in town. I'll take you one day. But, yeah, I know what you mean. Restaurant Indian food isn't the same."

"The joys of being a double-migrant."

Reena hadn't heard that term before but liked it. She smiled. "Double-migrant because our families first migrated from India to Tanzania, then Tanzania to Canada?"

"Yup. Of course, for me it's India to Tanzania to UK then to Canada. Triple-migrant."

But he didn't want to stay here.

"That's why I learned to cook," Reena said. "I wanted to be able to eat the good stuff without relying on my mother."

"The little bit of your mum's food I've had has been great. I think you're the better cook, though."

"You're sweet. You really going to Sunday brunch this week?"

"Yes. They invited me, so I must go."

She smiled as she patted his shoulder. "Well, have fun. I'll be up north with friends."

"What? You're leaving me to face the den of wolves alone?"

She laughed. "Yup. You'll do fine. They're more bark than bite. Well, usually, at least."

At dinner, Reena found it hard to pay attention to the conversation around her. Confirmation that her parents *did* sell her in a business deal had soured her mood.

She poked at her kebob, moving it around with her spoon.

"This is good," Nadim said, eyeing her plate.

Reena tried to smile. "It is."

"So, like," Shayne said, helping himself to more kebob,

"for the first video, you're going to do Indian-fusion food, right? Like...I don't know...curried shepherd's pie, or butter chicken poutine?"

"No," Reena and Nadim both said simultaneously. He looked at her and laughed.

"Sorry," he said. "It's up to Reena, she's the expert, but personally, *fusion* just means dumbed down. We don't have to conform our food to the tastes of the majority."

A small smile pushed through her sour mood. She'd been thinking the same thing, albeit she would have said it a bit differently. The point of this contest was to showcase *home-cooked* food. Fusion had its time and place, but with all the crap minorities were facing in the world, she didn't feel much like making the food she grew up on more palatable to mainstream tastes.

"They want home cooking, so let's give them the kind of food we grew up on," Reena said, sitting straighter. "What was your favorite after-school snack when you were little?"

Nadim frowned. "At boarding school, they gave us tea and two biscuits. No more, no less."

"Poor little rich boy." Shayne laughed.

Marley's forehead furrowed as she tapped her nails on the table. "Probably celery and peanut butter for me. Or Oreos."

Reena chuckled. "Indian food, Marl..."

"I didn't really eat Indian food after school. Oh, if there was leftover maani from dinner, I sometimes ate it with jam."

Reena smiled widely, remembering her favorite snack. "Yes. Leftover maani with strawberry jam. Or, even better, with butter and sugar." Her mouth started to water.

"Maani is like roti, right?" Shayne asked.

Reena nodded. "Roti, chapatti, rotli, maani, it's all pretty much the same thing."

"Forget leftover," Nadim said, his eyes glazing with pleasure. "*Fresh*. My housekeeper used to make fresh maani after school for me. I'd eat them with ripe mangoes."

Reena rolled her eyes with exaggeration. "Well, we peasants had to make do with leftovers." She squeezed her lips together in thought. Mum had kicked little-girl Reena out of the kitchen so many times while she cooked, but the smell of fresh maani roasting over the stove felt like home.

"Maani is the homiest food we have, right?" Reena said, reaching for a slice of sourdough. "We should make it for the first video."

"Just maani?" Nadim asked.

Reena grinned widely now. "Maybe something simple like aloo gobi to go with it, but the maani will be the star. Nothing represents Indian home cooking better, whatever they call it."

They continued to plan for the video while eating. It needed to be sent in by Sunday, so they were on a bit of a time crunch. The plan was for Marley to dig through their closets on Wednesday to decide on their wardrobe, then film Thursday evening. Shayne would have plenty of time to edit it on the weekend, and they could submit it Sunday night.

~

Thursday came, and the four of them were crowded in Reena's kitchen. Marley fluffed Reena's curls while Shayne placed LED lights on long black poles. They'd already been waiting an hour for Shayne to finish setting up, and Reena was getting a little impatient with his constant "almost got its." Especially since Marley had rejected the sensible business casual and yoga pants in Reena's closet, instead squeezing her into skinny jeans about two sizes too tight and black high-heeled ankle booties a size too small. Nadim fared better, as Marley had found appropriate clothes in his own closet—dark wash jeans and a blue V-neck sweater. The royal blue looked amazing against his warm skin, and thankfully, Marley insisted he keep his douche beard shaved off.

"How come I don't get an apron?" Nadim asked, tugging on the pale blue apron tied around Reena's waist.

"I'll do the cooking. You're here for amusing banter and endless admiration." Reena glanced at the items she had laid out on the counter. Whole wheat durum atta flour, canola oil, salt, and warm water. She'd insisted on using locally grown canola oil and flour, as it would give her an interesting fact to talk about during the clip. The video needed to be five minutes long, and when they'd rehearsed it yesterday, filling the time with something other than just rolling out maani proved to be a challenge. Closer to the stove, precut cauliflower and potatoes waited for her, along with a bowl of peas and a gleaming new polished stainless-steel masala dabba holding little round pots of fragrant spices.

"Okay, guys, almost there," Shayne said.

"Finally." Reena moved into position. "These shoes are killing me. Why do I have to wear them? No one will see my feet behind the counter."

"Needed you a touch taller," Marley said.

"Not making much of a difference," Reena muttered. "Still too short."

Nadim looked down at her. "I like you pocket-size. Hey, is that our engagement ring?" He pointed at the wide, silver-toned ring with clear rhinestones channel-set throughout.

"Yep. And it's already turning my finger green. Shayne swears he didn't get it from a gumball machine, but I don't know."

"Okay, I'm ready," Shayne said.

A few seconds of getting into position, and Shayne yelled, "Action!"

Reena froze, staring at the camera. This had been easier with gin. Nadim poked her hip.

"Hello! I'm Reena! And this is my..." She looked up at Nadim, unsure if she could say the word.

"...fiancé, Nadim." He smiled that charming camera-ready smile "Today we're making—"

"Maani. Also called Chapatti," Reena interrupted. "And aloo gobi matar."

"Cut!" Shayne said, shaking his head. "Stop with the finishing each other's sentences. You sound like Tweedledee and Tweedledum."

Why had she agreed to this? Reena wanted to rub her face, but Marley had contoured her within an inch of humanity. Her feet hurt. The lights were in her eyes. Laughing and making a drunken midnight snack was one thing, but this felt so much more real.

Nadim rubbed her upper arm. "We're doing fine, Reena. Don't be nervous. Pretend no one else is here. It's just you and me."

She looked into his dark eyes. Warm and so kind. She nodded.

"All right, take it from the top," Shayne said.

They got through the intro sounding less like cartoon characters this time. And Reena managed to get the flour, salt, and oil in the bowl without freezing again.

"What's the point of this step?" Nadim asked as he rubbed the oil into the flour.

"We're coating each grain of flour in oil. It helps with tenderness."

He wagged his eyebrows. "I agree. Lubrication always helps with . . . tenderness."

Reena's head fell forward in laughter. "I can't believe you said that. Here, I'll add water. Keep squishing it with your fingers."

She poured warm water into the flour mixture as he mixed with his hands.

He hummed with pleasure. "This is surprisingly sensual. I'm not sure I'll be able to watch you knead bread again without blushing like a schoolgirl."

She giggled. It appeared Nadim didn't need to be drunk to be comfortable and flirty on camera.

While the dough rested, she showed him the simple curry. First they lightly fried mustard seeds, cumin seeds, and curry leaves before adding onions, crushed garlic and ginger, and tomatoes. Finally, the diced potatoes, cauliflower, and peas.

"Cauliflower is a weird vegetable, isn't it?" Nadim said as he stirred the pan. "Did you know that it comes in four colors, but similar to people, white is considered standard."

Reena tried hard not to snort with laughter again while his bubbly morning show host-type banter continued. "It's a flower, isn't it? You should totally carry a head of cauliflower as your bouquet at the wedding. Purple, green, and orange, though. No boring white."

Shayne had been spot-on—Nadim *was* like a brown Jamie Oliver, with a genuine enthusiasm that felt downright infectious. And he was affectionate—he repeatedly touched her arm or put his hand on the small of her back. His playfulness helped her fight through the stage fright. Their final sequence, as they rehearsed, had Reena tearing off a piece of the round flatbread, scooping up some curry with it, and feeding it to Nadim with her fingers.

"Mmm...Tastes like home. But also tastes like new beginnings," he said.

"Beginnings?" she asked. He hadn't said that in their rehearsal.

He grinned widely and turned to the camera. "As you can tell from my accent, I'm new here. I was worried about being comfortable in this country, but I quickly learned that our common food can make any beginning can feel like home." He planted a quick kiss on Reena's lips before Shayne yelled "cut."

CHAPTER TEN

Good lord. If their drunken potato bhajias video managed to beat hundreds to get a spot in the contest, the maani/aloo gobi matar video was going to win it.

With Nadim's heartfelt enthusiasm, his affectionate gazes, and that off-script speech about food and home, getting through round one seemed inevitable. Reena didn't have to see the footage to know that her fake fiancé had the ability to turn the insides of anyone watching into mush.

She wanted to win, but... *ugh*. Her emotions were tied up in knots she couldn't come close to untangling. Gratitude. Euphoria.

Fear.

She'd been pushing down her growing attraction pretty well so far, but faking an engagement added a new layer of complication to their already bizarre relationship. She couldn't let herself forget he was acting. He didn't mean those loving gazes, and subtle brushes on the hand. The firm, warm weight on the small of her back.

That kiss.

"Wow," Shayne said, turning off the bright lights. "You were fantastic. Both of you. But seriously, Nadim, you were born to be in front of a camera. You two are going to rock this."

Reena forced a smile in gratitude and quietly started cleaning up, hoping to hide how off-kilter she felt. The sun had set, and with the powerful LED lights off, the dim room seemed to revert back to the real world. The loving fiancé was just her neighbor, pretending. The skinny designer jeans were cutting off circulation and giving her an epic muffin top under a borrowed silk blouse. She bit the inside of her lip. She shouldn't be doing this. This creative and fun project to distract her from her problems was only amplifying them. She hadn't anticipated the crushing low after coming down from the dazzling high.

Marley rushed out to meet her date while Shayne finished packing his equipment.

"So, I'll cut and edit as fast as I can," Shayne said as he opened the door, "and upload the video to the cloud for you to look at on the weekend."

"Take your time. We're not submitting until Sunday night after I get back from Amira's," Reena said, following him into the hallway. She held open the exterior door for him.

Shayne smiled at her before climbing down the stairs. "You okay, Reena?"

"Yeah. These shoes are just killing me. Can't wait to get out of them. Thanks again, Shayne."

He nodded, taking his equipment to his car. Reena headed back into the hallway, where Nadim was unlocking his door.

"Hey, thanks again for doing that," she said.

He smiled. "I had fun. And thanks for letting me have the leftover food."

"No problem." She leaned her head back against the wall next to her door.

"Why don't you come inside for a bit," he said. "You look beat. I think you need a cup of tea or something."

Smart man. Reena smiled and followed him into the apartment. She fell on the old green armchair immediately and removed the too-tight boots. She wanted to remove the too-tight jeans, too, but decided it best to save that for her own apartment.

Nadim went straight to the kitchen, put the leftover food away, then filled his kettle. "So," he said, once he'd joined her in the living room. "You think that went okay?"

She sighed. "Yeah. Really well, actually. You were a natural. And I know Shayne will do an amazing job editing it."

"Yeah. I'm excited to see it. The production value will at least be better than what we did alone." He sat on the sofa across from her, watching her face intently. "Reena, why do you seem, I don't know, sad? We have it in the bag, right?"

She bit her lower lip. She couldn't explain her moodiness, at least not to him. She couldn't explain how things going well in one part of her life had always coincided with things going spectacularly wrong in others.

The other shoe always dropped. No good came without a crushing bad to chase it away.

"No, I'm fine." She smiled. "Just sore feet."

He raised a brow. "I'd offer to massage them for you, but, well, I'm not sure you'd want that. What with my...you know."

She sat up straight. "Your what?"

"You know. My thing."

Their arranged marriage? Their fake engagement? Why would any of those mean he couldn't give her a foot massage?

"What thing?" she asked again.

He ran his hand through his cropped hair. "I told you, remember? This is awkward."

Yes, *awkward* was the right word to describe this conversation. Was there another big-bad thing Nadim hadn't told her? Worse than when he told her their parents had arranged their marriage, or that he had slept with the kindie teacher? Worse than telling her he might have given her lice? At this point she didn't just expect the other shoe to drop, she expected the whole blasted shoe museum downtown to fall on her head. What the hell was he trying to tell her?

Her shoulders fell, resigned to the pain that would no doubt come. "Nadim, just tell me."

He sighed. "I told you this. I . . . I have a thing for, you know, a thing for, er . . . feet."

She blinked. "Feet."

"Yes."

Reena's eyes widened. Feet? Really? "Is that why you're always looking down at your feet?"

"It's not my feet I'm looking at—it's yours. You have lovely arches," he said.

Reena stared at him for several long seconds before bursting out into full-body laughter. "You have a foot fetish?"

His brow furrowed. "It's not a fetish. I just think women's feet are . . . sexy."

"Dude, that's the definition of a fetish!" She valiantly tried to stop laughing, but another wave overcame her, and she slid right off her parents' armchair onto the floor.

"Are you seriously laughing at my preferences?"

She waved her hand. "No, no. I've known enough people

with unique tastes, I don't kink-shame...it's just that it's so totally *not* what I expected you to say! I thought you were going to reveal some deep, dark secret you've hidden that would ruin everything. I literally at that moment thought the next shoe was going to drop and—"

He smiled. "I dropped a foot on you." He chuckled. "What did you think I was going to say?"

"I don't know. Last time you had that look you told me you had li—"

"Don't say it," he warned.

"Sorry." She got back onto her seat. "I thought you were going to say you had a secret girlfriend or an incurable disease or something. Not that you enjoy the odd foot job."

His nose wrinkled. "I didn't say I—"

"Shh..." She waved her hands again. "Don't even worry about it. I don't care what floats your boat." Especially since she had no intention of floating that boat in any manner herself, she didn't judge an adult's sexual predilections, so long as they were legal and consensual. Still, this was too funny. She burst out laughing again. "Now I get why you said nail polish when you were telling my mum why you came over. You were staring at my pedicure!" She nearly fell off the chair again.

"I said nail *varnish*, and glad I'm so amusing," he muttered.

"No one has ever complimented my feet before. So much makes sense now—a foot fetish!"

"You can stop laughing anytime now..."

His brown skin tinged with pink, and his body seemed to have folded in on itself. Big, confident Nadim was embarrassed. She stopped laughing. Smiling at him, she got up from the green armchair and joined him on the sofa. "If I give you my foot to massage, you're not going to like, rub up against it or anything, are you?"

He laughed, but he still looked embarrassed. "No, it's not like that. And I'm not into fishnets or stilettos or anything. I just like bare feet. They are soft and vulnerable but strong enough to carry your weight all day. They are private and hidden most of the time, but then women adorn them with colorful nails and sometimes jewelry. They're sensitive and ticklish . . . and I'm going to shut up now." He lifted his eyebrows and squeezed his lips shut.

Well. When he put it that way, Reena could see the appeal of the humble foot. She slowly leaned down and removed the thin cotton sock on her right foot. Her toes inside were red, still angry after being squeezed in Marley's boots for so long. She placed her foot on his lap.

"As long as we stay G-rated, this can be a symbiotic exchange for us. I get a foot rub, while you get to admire my lovely arches."

He laughed as he picked up her foot in his hands. "I can handle that."

She shouldn't have been surprised that he was rather spectacular at foot rubs. Those hands, which had been so firm yet gentle on her scalp, would of course be amazing on her feet. She hummed with appreciation as his thumbs kneaded her arch. "You're good at that."

He chuckled but continued rubbing.

"One thing I don't get," she said. "Why'd you think you told me about this foot thing? You didn't."

"I *did* tell you. The second time we met. You were sitting

outside my door barefoot with a bag of bread and I said that you managed to hit all my fantasies. I like feet, and I like bread."

She giggled. "Well, I bake bread. And I have feet." Match made in heaven. Except... *no*. "You also accused me of hating you that night."

He laughed as those talented fingers moved on to gently squeezing and pulling on her toes. Ahhh... it felt amazing. "Considering you have gifted me with this remarkable foot," he said, "I'm pretty sure you don't hate me anymore. We're friends, right?"

"Yes. Even though you gave me lice. But you also brought my drunk ass home safely, even if you demanded I make you bhajias in the middle of the night. So, friends." Jesus, they'd been through a lot in the two weeks they'd lived across from each other.

"True." He laughed. "That reminds me, I'm sure you're fine, but you have to do the final lice treatment Sunday. I'll comb out your hair again."

"Let's do it Monday. We have to do the contest application Sunday, and I'll be home late from my friend's place."

He focused silently for a while, rubbing all the tension out of her sore foot. "It's all pretty funny," he said. "This is not what I expected when I moved to Toronto."

She giggled. "Yes, yes, I know I'm not the good-girl wife you wanted me to be. No need to keep reminding me."

He pinched the arch of her foot lightly, making her giggle. "I'm starting to think the good-girl wife concept may be overrated."

She smiled. "I still have no intention of marrying you."

He chuckled as he lifted her other foot onto his lap, peeled off her sock, and gently started massaging. God, he was too good at this. "I think my favorite thing about you is that you keep telling me you won't marry me."

She laughed softly as that boneless calm she'd last felt when he had massaged her scalp overcame her. She closed her eyes, sinking into the couch. He managed to release the tension she knew she had, and about a truckload more tension waiting in the wings. "Mmm..." she groaned. "I like your hands best."

"So, you agree that I'm better than your other parent-approved husband prospects?"

She chuckled, nodding. "Seems so. You don't have a comb-over or a secret after-dinner paan habit, and you know how to make chai." She sunk lower until almost reclined on the sofa, both her feet on Nadim's lap. Her third parental setup had been a man addicted to paan—a type of Indian chew which sometimes had psychedelic effects. The man's teeth were permanently stained red. Nasty. "Then again, I don't know you that well. If I wanted to know more I could ask around. The Ismaili community is small, wouldn't take much."

He stilled, hands clutching the arch of her foot. She opened her eyes and looked at him. His expression looked strange. Oddly frightened and vulnerable. Maybe he *did* have a secret addiction to legal Indian narcotics. "Don't," he said.

"What?"

"Don't ask around about me."

She smiled warmly, hoping to wipe that look of insecurity off his face. "Don't worry, I was just kidding. I'm not much of a gossip."

He looked back down at her feet, resuming the massage.

"It's just...I came here to start a new life. I didn't expect to make a good friend here. I don't want to let our pasts color this friendship, okay? That goes both ways."

This time Reena stilled. Of course, she hadn't expected or planned on this friendship when she met him. Back then she was thinking he would be eye candy in a conveniently close location. And once she found out about her parents' intentions, she tried valiantly to avoid him. But now, they were friends. And she couldn't deny he had a way of calming her like few could. She needed his friendship to cope with life right now.

But friendships were based on honesty and open communication. And she hid things from him, too. The loss of her job for one, but also her crippling self-doubt. And her past. What would he think if he knew about that scary time when she failed so miserably at life that she was drunk more than sober? Hell, she wasn't even sure she wanted him to know her romantic history.

Her curiosity had piqued about what he was hiding, but unless she was willing to be open about her own past, she couldn't expect to know everything about his.

"I like that. No past, no future. Our friendship is in the present, only," she said, sinking back into the couch.

"Perfect," he murmured, digging his thumbs into the ball of her foot. "I just...I'm really glad to have you as a friend."

"Because I refuse to marry you, or because of my feet and bread?"

His hands kneaded as he winked at her.

She sighed in pleasure. "Don't answer that," she said. "I don't care. Just keep doing what you're doing."

CHAPTER ELEVEN

Reena woke up way too early Friday morning. She had planned to sleep in after her late-night foot rub, but her body hadn't quite accustomed itself to unemployment yet. She got out of bed, figuring she'd get a head start on the drive north to Amira's. But first, she needed to feed the starters.

Brian had been doing much better this week. She had reduced his feedings to one a day, and he had doubled in size like a trouper each time. But, of course, like Murphy's Law, today he acted up again. He'd barely risen since yesterday's feeding, in contrast to Sue, who'd tripled in size. Crap. She'd intended to feed the starters, then park them in the fridge for the weekend, where their growth would stay in stasis until Monday. But now that Brian was misbehaving again, she worried that missing a few days of feedings would mean the end of him forever.

But who could she trust to feed him for two days on such short notice?

She grabbed her last loaf of rye bread—this one a classic dark rye—and deliberately refrained from putting on shoes, socks, or slippers before knocking loudly on Nadim's door.

He answered, wearing dress pants and a dress shirt, no tie, and a startled expression on his face.

"Reena. What's wrong…"

"Sorry to bug you so early, but...you said we were friends, right?"

He looked down at the loaf of bread in her hand. He may have sneaked a glance lower at her feet, but she couldn't be sure. "Of course."

"Well, here." She handed him the bread. "I'm not going to get through this, since I'm going away for the weekend. And...I have a favor to ask you. You'll think it's strange, but—"

He took the bread, and one eyebrow shot up. "Is it kinky?"

"No!" She shook her head in disbelief. "Jesus, do you have any social boundaries?"

He laughed. "No, not with my friends. What do you need?"

"I need someone to feed Brian while I'm away."

"You have a pet? And his name is Brian?"

"No, Brian's not a pet...He's my...he's a sourdough. Well, one of them."

"He's a what?"

She sighed. "He's a sourdough starter."

"A sourdough starter."

"Yes, it's a mixture of flour and water that contains natural yeast. It needs to be fed so the yeast can leaven my bread. C'mon, you've had my bread before, how did you think I made it?"

"It just never occurred to me that people raised their own starters. People who aren't pioneer homesteaders."

Reena frowned. Maybe this wasn't such a good idea. "Look, can you help me or not? It's not that big a job."

"No, of course. If you need me to feed your sourdough, I will. I'm just finding this to be the oddest favor a friend has ever asked of me."

She rolled her eyes as she motioned him into her apartment.

She took Brian down from the windowsill and placed him on the counter. "This is Brian. He's pretty young. A rye starter... Why are you looking at me like that?"

"I'm seeing a whole different side of you. So nurturing. How many kids should we have?" There was way too much mischief in his voice for this hour.

"I'm not marrying you. And I told you there's more to me than bread and feet."

He laughed. "Clearly..." He deliberately leered at her bare toes and waggled his eyebrows. "Those are your strongest assets, though."

She rolled her eyes.

"Fine, fine. I'll behave," he said. "Teach me how to take care of Brian."

She showed him the steps of feeding the starter: discarding half, then mixing in equal amounts by weight of flour and water.

"Why'd you throw away half?" he asked.

"Because you need it to double each time you feed it. If you don't toss half, you'll end up with too much starter. It'd grow exponentially, forever."

"What a waste! What you *should* do is—"

"Don't *should* on me, buddy. I don't normally throw it away. I make bread with it, that's the point. And you're this close to never getting any of that bread again."

He smiled that charming smile. "I'm just kidding. This will be fun. Nice to have someone to keep me company while you'll be gone. Does Brian prefer quiet nights at home or long walks on the beach?"

"Ha-ha. Smart-ass."

After leaving Brian, a bag of flour, a bottle of spring water, and her kitchen scale with Nadim, she changed and packed for the weekend. Her phone rang just as she zipped the bag. She glanced at the call display.

Her father. Her father never called her.

"Hi, Dad. What's going on?" She sat on her bed, body tensed in preparation for bad news.

"Your mother tells me you are going north for the weekend."

"Yes, I took the day off work so I could head to Amira's early."

"Can we speak before you leave? I'm at the project site all day."

"Today?" she asked. Also, alone?

"Yes. We can go for coffee. Nadim is at an off-site meeting with a restaurant developer this morning."

Hmm. Why did Dad bring up Nadim?

Reena took a deep breath. She should be good at keeping secrets by now but was actually terrible at it. It seemed a wonder her parents didn't thrust her into speech therapy as a kid with how often she hesitated and said *um*...

She really had no choice here. "Um...okay. I can be there in about an hour."

After Reena finished packing her hair products and makeup, she downed a quick cup of coffee before taking her bags to her car. It was a twenty-minute drive to Dad's worksite. When she got there, she parked in the gravel lot and went looking for him.

Reena hadn't been to the Diamond project in a while, and she couldn't help but be impressed at the progress since then. A medium-size low-rise building, it was loosely modeled after European mixed-use structures, with space at the bottom for stores and restaurants and four levels of condos and rental units facing into a large center courtyard. The building stood on the edge of a big residential subdivision in the city of Markham, filled with cookie-cutter single-family homes. It had been a major challenge to get zoning approval, but Reena had never been prouder of her father than when he won it, and seeing the project now, in the last stages of construction, the pride swelled in her heart even more.

And to think, he'd almost lost all this thanks to that architect guy. Reena tensed a bit as she peeked into the building. She didn't want to think about how, in a way, the success of this project was resting on her and Nadim's shoulders.

She found her father outside the building, talking to a man who looked like a construction foreman. "Reena," he said. "This is Igor. I'm sorry I don't have time to show you around—I have a meeting in an hour—but after we have coffee, Igor can show you our progress. We'll have to drive. There is nothing around here."

She followed him to his car. Aziz Manji was an imposing man. Tall, at least tall by Indian standards, and with a full head of black hair even in his fifties. His appearance reflected his intelligence and his respectability in the community, where he was revered and admired for his philanthropy as well as for the modest empire he had grown from the bottom up. None of the Manji children had inherited his stature or dignity.

They went to a Tim Hortons doughnut shop a decent distance from the project. "There's nothing closer," he said. "I don't understand why the neighborhood fought against the development. Who wants to go so far for tea?"

"You guys putting a coffee shop in the building?"

"Yes." He pulled into the parking lot. "In the corner unit. Nadim is negotiating with developers."

Dad bought some doughnuts, a coffee for her, and a tea for himself. "Shh," he said with a smile. "Don't tell Saira I'm eating doughnuts. Or maybe we'll tell her they're made with kelp and kale?"

Reena laughed before suddenly stilling. She couldn't remember the last time her father cracked a joke. She blew gently on her coffee.

"I wanted to speak to you about Nadim," Dad said.

"Okay…" she responded, raking her brain to sort through which parts of their friendship she could reveal. The contest, the shared beers, the lice…definitely not. The foot rub? Most definitely not.

"I know your mother has hopes for you and him," Dad said, seemingly oblivious to Reena's distraction. "An eligible man around your age with a master's degree from LSE? It is a blessing he has come into our lives and is eager to join our family."

Ugh. Nadim was nothing but the letters after his name. She sighed. On the surface, Dad cared a lot about "young people starting out," as he put it. The goal of this project was to provide affordable home ownership to millennials who had been priced out of the city. But when it came to his own children, he just spewed orders and expected them to obey. Or used them as bait to lure investors.

"I understand you have had the opportunity to get to know the man?" he asked.

She bit the inside of her cheek. "Um, yes. A little."

"What are your thoughts?"

Reena blinked. Her thoughts? What could she say? Bit of a

rake, a definite flirt, and in the possession of a weirdly charming foot fetish? A man who had very, very talented hands…

She swallowed. "He seems…interesting. Well-rounded. Smart, too."

"Have you met any of his friends?"

Friends? Did he have any? She couldn't recall Nadim mentioning friends to Reena. Ever.

Dad's eyes narrowed. "I don't believe there is any value to listening to this kind of chatter, but I heard rumors about Nadim's past. I hoped you would help me confirm they aren't true."

Reena stilled. "What rumors?"

"Just some rumblings that he may have been involved with some underhanded people. I don't know much about his life in London. Has he told you anything?"

"No. Honestly, he hasn't mentioned anything." In fact, he specifically expressed a desire to keep his past hidden, so maybe there was something to Dad's rumors.

"Could you keep an eye out for anything that looks amiss about the man? I want to preserve the reputation of the business."

"You want me to spy on him?" This was rich. Not two minutes ago he was encouraging her to marry the man because of his MBA.

Dad shook his head. "I didn't say spy."

"But that is what you're asking."

Dad frowned. "I have to protect this project and the family's good name. I trust your judgment, maybe more than anyone's." He sighed. "Find out more about him. Who does he have associations with? Who is important to him? Both here and overseas. You'll know if you hear something that doesn't sound right."

Amazing. Her mother wanted her to find out what kind of daal the man liked, and her father wanted to know who his friends were. Why didn't they just ask him? Reena picked at her doughnut, scraping a fingernail full of the maple icing and sucking it off her finger. And besides, Dad trusted her? Bullshit. He only said that now because he wanted intel on his protégé.

She knew little about Nadim and his life before he moved to Toronto, and she knew he was hiding things from her. A hollowness formed in her core. She trusted Nadim. Maybe too much?

"Can I count on you to be *honest* with me, Reena?"

And that was the crux of it. Reena had *never* been honest with her father. Not at sixteen, when she snuck out of her bedroom window to meet boys, not when she happily told him how much she loved working in finance, and certainly not now, out of work, and making cooking videos for a national contest. Did her father realize she never told the whole truth? Probably. After all these years, he had to know.

But the stakes were higher now. And this little heart-to-heart was his way of reminding her of that. Asking her to meet him specifically at the building so she could see its progress. Buying her a doughnut and making a joke about their alliance against Saira. And finally telling her, for the first time, that he trusted her judgment. These confessions were intentional. All the family finances were tied up in this project. Even if Reena didn't care too much about her parents' opinion of her, she didn't want to see them lose everything. This was her family.

And Dad wanted her to decide if she had their back. Did she? She had a lot to think about while up north this weekend.

CHAPTER TWELVE

I s this some sort of intervention? And why did Duncan leave
to feed turkey to chickens?"

The calming view of the river across the street from Amira's
house framed by trees dappled with shades of orange, red, and
yellow did nothing to soften the effect of the unique torture
that Reena just endured. For the last ten minutes, her best
friend in the whole world had been listing everything wrong in
Reena's life with the thorough accuracy and attention to detail
one would expect from a brilliant industrial engineer.

Reena curled her feet under her on the soft couch on the
porch, hugging her warm chai close. It still felt strange that
this beautiful century house belonged to her best friend. Up
until this siege of misery, it had been a lovely weekend. Well,
it had been lovely only *after* Duncan's absolutely mortifying
lice check as soon as Reena got there. He was a teacher and
practically raised his niece, so he claimed to be an expert. Once
he was sure Reena was bug-free, he made a crack about Nadim
not knowing a louse from a mouse, and welcomed Reena
into his home. Reena was relieved there were no bugs, but
maybe life would be less embarrassing if she didn't tell Amira
absolutely everything that happened to her. Now she felt like

she was under a magnifying glass again, this time with Amira inspecting her instead of Duncan.

"It's *not* an intervention. And Duncan left to go feed his *parents'* chickens, since they are *in* Turkey. I told you about the Galahads' new fascination with Islamic architecture," Amira said, before blowing gently on her mug. "Besides, isn't an intervention supposed to be a roomful of judging people pretending to be concerned? This is just you and me."

Another shovel of shit to add to the steaming pile. Even if she did need an intervention, who would come? Mum, Dad, or Saira? Laughable. Khizar maybe, but with two babies and a promotion coming, his middle sister wasn't high on his list of concerns right now.

"I'm fine, Amira," Reena assured her friend.

"Screw fine, Ree!" Amira threw her arms in the air, causing a small spurt of chai to erupt from her mug. "You're always *fine*. The fucking house is on fire, and you're that idiotic dog with a cup of coffee saying *this is fine*. It's not fine. You've been downsized, *again*. Your father has all but traded you in a business deal and is now asking you to spy on the man he wants you to marry. A man who slept with a flea-ridden kindergarten teacher!"

Reena blinked at Amira. She really didn't need this mirror held up in front of her life. Deflect and distract time. "Meer, why is there a couch on your front porch?"

"Don't you play that deflection game on me." Amira clenched her teeth. Reena knew her friend was currently counting under her breath to calm herself. "I know what happened when you were out of work before. You barely left your apartment and subsisted on bourbon and baguettes for weeks. You need people—wallowing a little bit is okay, but you can't stay like that. When's the last time you went on a date?"

Reena's phone erupted in a Highland jig, and since Reena understood exactly how the universe worked, she had a good idea who the text would be from.

Nadim: I'm hiding my phone under the table so they don't notice me texting you. Am I supposed to mention that your sister is only eating what looks like seaweed when your mum made daal, eggs, and paratha?

"Who's that?" Amira asked.

"Nadim. He's brunching with the fam and judging Saira's food choices."

Amira snorted. "Haven't we all? But why's he texting you?"

"He texts me a lot. We're friends."

Another text.

Nadim: She's offering me seaweed. She isn't flirting, is she? I'm still a little frightened of your sister.

Reena wrote back.

Reena: Rule number one when dealing with Saira. Never accept the seaweed.

Nadim: Noted.

At that moment Duncan's truck pulled into the driveway. Amira didn't even look up as her boyfriend got out and walked up the porch stairs.

"You sure, Ree?" Amira asked.

"She sure about what?" Duncan asked as he wedged himself on the couch between them. Reena shifted to make room for him.

Amira pointed at Reena. "Is she sure she doesn't have a thing going on with her intended on the down-low."

"I'd hope she'd notice if she was," Duncan responded.

Another text came through.

Nadim: I asked your mother why she made three kinds of daal, and she said it was your fault.

Reena snorted.

Reena: You going to blame me or thank me for that?

Nadim: Thank you, of course.

Reena smiled, putting her phone away. "I'm not involved with Nadim."

Amira, amazingly, sat quietly for a few moments before turning to Reena again. "Is he still all flirty? You think he's into you?"

She bit her lip, thinking. "Don't think so. I do think he'd still marry me if I agreed, though. Although, not because he likes me, or anything, but because of Dad."

Amira frowned. "He'd marry you, but you don't think he's into you? That's weird. This is all weird."

The bagpipes rang again, but this time, when Reena checked her phone, it was Shayne texting that he was done editing the video.

He sent a password-protected link to take a look at it on a shared drive. Amira grabbed an iPad so they all could watch it together on the porch.

Despite the embarrassment of seeing herself all dolled up on the screen, curiosity kept Reena's eyes glued to it. Would the edited clip be as great as it seemed when they'd filmed it?

Immediate answer: yes. And then some. This was night and day compared to the audition video. Shayne's videography skills were more than above average, and Marley's clothing, hair, and makeup took Reena's usual look up several notches. And this time? It wasn't just Nadim's magnetic on-screen persona coming through, but both of theirs. Nadim and Reena. They matched. They looked like a team. A real couple, or at least the best of friends.

"That's Nadim?" Amira asked, surprised.

"Yeah," Reena said. "Why? What's wrong with him?"

Amira's eyes narrowed at the screen. "I don't know. He's not what I expected. You said he talked like he went to an English private school?"

"He did. He does."

Amira frowned. "I guess I expected him to be more formal, or something. Stuffy. This guy...I don't know. He's hot. I'd do him."

"Hey!" Duncan said, glaring at his girlfriend. Duncan hadn't quite gotten used to the fact that Amira and Reena pretty much had no filter with each other.

Amira rolled her eyes. "I meant I'd do him if I was *her*."

"I told you he was hot, didn't I?" Reena asked.

"You said he had an okay face and a hot body. But this guy, he's easygoing, friendly, charming. Not the kind of person who needs to resort to an arranged marriage at the age of...how old is he?"

"Thirty-two," Reena said.

"I see why you like him. He reminds me of Jamie Oliver," Duncan added, head tilted in concentration. As if that was a selling point. Nigella Lawson and Heston Blumenthal were Reena's preferred British celebrity chefs.

"Actually," Duncan continued, "Jamie Oliver has that estuary English thing going. This guy sounds like Tom Hiddleston."

Amira laughed. "Don't mind him, Duncan's high school

students are putting on *My Fair Lady* and he's been studying English dialects."

They watched in silence a little longer, as on-screen Reena took on-screen Nadim's hands in hers to show him the right amount of pressure to use when rolling out maani. He mouthed a moan as he leaned in close to her. She didn't remember him doing that.

"He's sniffing your hair," Duncan said. "You sure this is fake?"

Amira laughed. "Maybe he was looking for bugs?"

Reena rolled her eyes. It was possible to have friends who knew too much about your life.

The video finally ended with that kiss, which looked longer on screen than she'd remembered. Duncan turned off the iPad without a word. The silence stretched for several seconds before Reena gave in. "What did you guys think?"

That was the moment Reena's text-tone rang again. She should have turned the ringer off.

Nadim: Your mother just asked me what I liked best about you. You should be proud of me, I didn't say your feet.

She put her phone facedown on her leg before Amira or Duncan could see it.

Amira took a breath. "I have three thoughts. One, if I worked at FoodTV and got that video, I'd cancel the whole competition and just give you the prize. You guys were amazing. Two, my worries about you are needless, because the woman in that video is most definitely *not* alone. I'm glad you have such a good friend nearby right now. And three, you're going to have to figure out exactly what's going on between you and that man. Because either that was an Oscar-worthy performance, or your fake fiancé is completely smitten with you. Be careful, Ree."

CHAPTER THIRTEEN

By the time Reena made it through Toronto's seemingly never-ending traffic Sunday evening, she was tired and wanted nothing but her bed. Her mind had spun like her stand mixer on high the whole way home—as Amira's comment about Nadim being smitten with her whipped through her head. Could it be possible?

In her experience, men like Nadim—handsome, charismatic, educated, and worldly—usually only wanted a surefire hookup or an easy fling from someone like her—an unassuming woman with little higher education and whose obsession with bread left her with a body that looked like it belonged to someone obsessed with bread.

By the time she walked up the stairs to their building, she felt sure of one thing only—that she had no idea what went on in Nadim's head. Maybe his screen presence really was that good. But the off-screen moments of tenderness couldn't be forgotten—that spectacular foot massage and the nonstop texting all weekend. Was he just a player? Or was this just friendship and loyalty to the boss's daughter? Or was there more?

As much as she wanted to avoid him in hopes her unease would disappear on its own, Nadim still had Brian, and her curiosity about how he fared with the temperamental starter had her knocking on his door as soon as she dropped off her bag.

He answered wearing jeans and a T-shirt with the London Underground logo emblazoned on it.

"You're back already? I thought you'd be late," he said. His eyes shifted up then down.

"It is late. And we need to send in the contest video, remember? Everything okay? How's Brian?"

"Yeah. He's fine. Give me a minute. I'll bring over your sourdough. He's...great." His eyes shifted again.

She'd seen that face before. Nadim was hiding something and doing a terrible job of it. "What's wrong with Brian?"

"Nothing's wrong with Brian. He doubled in size after each feeding. He's fine, I'll bring him by to your place."

"Why can't I get him now then? It's just a jar, I can carry it."

"No, it's okay. Give me ten minutes."

"Did something happen to Brian?" Her voice was sharper than she'd intended. Why had she trusted anyone with something she valued?

Nadim's eyes widened as he reached out and grabbed her arm. "Reena, stop." He sighed with resignation and let go. "Fine. Come in and see for yourself. Brian is absolutely fine. Thriving, even."

Annoyed, she followed him into his kitchen, where he pointed at his windowsill. He had been truthful. Brian looked fine. In his regular swing-top jar, his volume easily doubled from the level of the rubber band. Brian did appear to be thriving.

But Brian was not alone.

Because also on the windowsill, and on the counter near the windowsill, sat more jars. They were standard screw-top mason jars, each with a rubber band around them marking un-risen volume. And each had doubled in volume. Reena took a quick count.

Nadim had sixteen sourdough starters.

"What the hell?" she asked.

"I, um..." He rubbed his palm.

She squeezed her lips to stifle a laugh. "Brian had puppies? Didn't I tell you not to let him out without tying him up?"

Nadim threw his arms in the air. "Your bread is so good! This stuff is precious gold! I couldn't throw away half each time...so I bought some jars and just kept it all. But then I had to feed those ones, too, and..." His shoulders slumped.

Reena stood frozen a few seconds before finally bursting out in giggles. "Were you planning to hide all this starter from me? What were you going to do with it? At this rate, you'll have thirty-two jars tomorrow morning!"

He shrugged. "I know, I know. I didn't think this through. I thought I could hide it and get you to teach me to make bread and then I could use it up. But I get that this isn't sustainable." He looked down and rubbed the back of his neck.

She giggled again.

"Stop laughing at me," Nadim said.

"Stop being adorable then. If you didn't want to throw away the discard, you didn't have to put it all in separate jars, you could have put it all in a big bowl. And there are a lot of ways to use up discard starter. Tons of recipes online."

His brows furrowed. "That was my next step."

This was too funny. If she hadn't come home his entire

apartment would have been nothing but jars of sourdough. Eventually the bubbling starter would've eaten him. She frowned. Wasn't that a horror book?

"So, will you teach me? I did well with the maani, right? I think I can make sourdough," he said.

She smiled. So much for deflect and distract. She couldn't abandon him now, after he'd hilariously kept sixteen distinct sourdough starters. He looked at her, those brown eyes a little sheepish. Not a trace of the confident rake. This Nadim was rather endearing.

"Tell you what," she said. "Give me Brian and toss the rest of the starter into a plastic container in the fridge."

"Why? What do I do with it?"

"It'll be fine for a week. Next weekend, we'll make sourdough pancakes, or rye English muffins, or something that doesn't need active starter. And I'm happy to teach you to make sourdough bread in the meantime."

He grinned widely, that unexpected dimple transforming his face. "Yeah? Brilliant." He took one of Brian's progeny and clutched the jar to his chest. "Can I keep one, though? I could use a pet."

She smiled. He was just so cute sometimes. "Of course. Can we finish up with the video now? I'm beat."

They watched the video one more time together before submitting it. Reena carefully avoided looking at Nadim's reaction while watching. She didn't want to know if seeing their on-screen chemistry gave him goosebumps like it did for her. She was nervous about all of this. True, this wasn't the first cooking video they'd put out in the world. But she'd been too drunk and had no memory of submitting that last one, so it was hard to compare. This video was different. They openly said they were engaged in it. And this would be seen by the public.

She knew the chances of her parents paying the slightest attention to the FoodTV website were slim to none, but what if someone else saw it and told them? What if Saira saw it?

Maybe it wasn't that big a deal if her family found out—she could admit they were only pretending. It would be a bigger disaster if they found out about Reena's job. But it was just easier when her parents didn't know about her life.

Nadim high-fived her once the video was sent. "We totally got this. Don't forget me when you're a rich and famous food personality and I'm just the project manager you exploited to get your way."

She laughed. "I don't want to be rich or famous. I just want to take that course."

Nadim tilted his head and smiled warmly. Which prompted Reena to grab Brian, say goodbye, and get the hell out of there. Because that look on his face just made it even harder for her to figure out exactly how he felt about her.

~

Reena's phone rang early Monday morning. Well, not really *that* early. She'd finally learned to enjoy some of the perks of unemployment. But despite knowing the rest of the world was awake and bringing home the bacon (or for her fellow Muslims, chicken bacon), confusion still washed over her when she heard that shrill ringtone before nine a.m. Who would call her at this hour?

She grabbed the phone and checked the call display. Crap. Saira.

"Hey, sis, what's up?" Reena asked, schooling her voice to sound as if she'd been awake and getting ready for work.

"Reena, I'm coming over."

Jesus. Why was her sister dropping by so much all of a sudden? "But, Saira—"

"Look, Reena. I figured out you're not working, so no need to make up a story."

Damnit. Saira knew?

"Do you have a job interview or something to do? If you're home, I'm coming over," her sister informed her.

Reena sighed. Apparently today her carefully constructed wall of secrets would be tumbling down. She rolled out of bed. She should've been afraid but instead just felt numb.

"I'm home," she said. "Come on over."

Saira arrived twenty minutes later, two vibrant green smoothies in hand. Reena tried to conceal her unease as she let her in.

"Relax, Reena," her sister said, handing both smoothies to Reena. "You look tense. Do some yoga, or something. I haven't told anyone you lost your job." Saira bent to take off her boots.

So much for hiding her feelings.

"Um, okay...let's sit." Reena took the armchair in the living room, letting her sister sit alone on the sofa.

"So, Railside laid you off."

"How did you find out?" Reena asked, putting the almost luminous green smoothie on the coffee table.

"Did you think I wouldn't notice that Sidecar stores are closing? Ashraf's phone store is right near a Sidecar. They're having a big clearance sale. I got a bunch of sweatshirts and leggings."

Crap. She'd forgotten Saira's boyfriend worked in the mall. "But how did you know they let me go? Railside is still open."

"The cashier told me about layoffs. And your work email address bounced back."

Reena's hands fisted. This deception wasn't sustainable.

"I'm not going to tell Mum and Dad, if that's what you're worried about. Drink your smoothie, Reena. You're looking a little peaked. You should watch your blood sugar in the morning, you'll find a power smoothie like this will boost your energy all day."

"Why?"

"Oh, it has a combination of both complex and simple carbohydrates, plus a time-released—"

"No, Saira. Why won't you tell Mum and Dad?"

"Really? Give me some credit. You're my sister. You obviously don't want them to know, so I won't say anything."

Reena squinted at her sister, suspicious. "You told them when I snuck out of the house when I was dating Eddie."

"That was a long time ago! I was a kid!"

"You were twenty-two. I was twenty-four." Which was why Reena felt no guilt about sneaking out then. A curfew at that age? Ridiculous. The fight with Mum and Dad after Saira blabbered eventually led to Dad agreeing to rent one of the units in this building to her, so maybe Saira's loose lips proved useful. That time.

This time, though? Reena couldn't let them find out about her unemployment. Not now. The last thing she needed was pressure to work with Dad.

"This isn't so I'll share that eggplant recipe with you, is it?" Reena asked.

"Why are you so obsessed with eggplant?"

Reena snorted. "I'm just not used to you being nice to me."

"I made you soup when you were sick, I came to run interference when Mum was being all...*in-your-face* like. I'm trying, here, Reena." Saira frowned. "We have such an effed-up relationship. We should be more like sisters."

Reena glared suspiciously again. They'd never had a close relationship, even as kids. Their personalities were too different. Not even complementary. Reena had been a shy child, and Saira's anxious histrionics had always been too much.

Saira exhaled. "Are you still mad because of that blog thing?"

She shouldn't be. It was months ago. Saira hadn't meant that post against Reena specifically. And her sister had gone through such a hard time.

But it was a hard time for Reena then, too. And Reena had lost so much.

"Saira, why are you here?"

"Well first, to see how you're doing. You looking for a new job?"

"Yes. I have two interviews this week. My employment counselor thinks I will find something quickly."

"Oh, that's good. They're looking for a part-timer at Nourish, if you're interested." A job at Nourish would be torture for Reena. Surrounded by chia seeds, kombucha, and Saira all day? No.

"Anyway, let me know if you want me to put in a good word. The employee discount is really good," Saira said.

"Sure. Will do."

Saira smiled, seeming to be pleased with herself. "I also had some dirt to share. I know you hate gossip, but this might concern you. That guy, what's his name... the one Mum wants you to marry. Nadir?"

"Nadim. What about him?"

"You going to marry him?"

"No! Of course not. I keep telling Mum to stop setting me up with men, but she won't give—"

"So, there's nothing going on between you?"

"No! We're friends. Why?"

"At brunch he said a bunch of ass-kissing stuff about you. I think just to suck up to Dad, but just in case there's more, I thought you should know."

"Know what?"

Saira smiled as she curled her legs under her on the sofa. "I thought the guy looked familiar when I came by that day, but yesterday he said he used to have a beard, and I remembered I'd seen pictures of him on Rish's Facebook."

"What? How does Ashraf's sister know Nadim?"

"She doesn't. She was posting some pictures of her cousin in London, and Nadim was in them. With that whole posh crowd out there. You know the ones. The swanky, trust fund kids? I heard at least three of them have been bailed out of some mess or another by their rich daddies. These people are shady. Look." She handed Reena her phone with a picture on the screen.

There were three people standing together on a boat, each holding drinks out, as if toasting the camera. And yup, one of them was Nadim. With his longer hair and precision-trimmed beard. He wore white pants, white deck shoes, and a lavender polo shirt with the collar popped up. The two people he stood near seemed to be a couple, with their arms around each other's waists. The woman squinted at the sun, and the man mugged for the camera in a pose reminiscent of those boys on the Jersey shore. Yuck. Behind them were several other people, talking and holding drinks.

It was the douchiest picture she'd ever seen. What the hell was Nadim—her foot-rubbing, bread-eating neighbor—doing with the likes of these people?

"Where is this?"

"Probably somewhere in Europe. There are loads of these pictures. I think that chick next to him is Rish's cousin. Oh, and you'll love this." She pulled up another picture, similar to the first. Douchey Nadim and about ten other people. "That skinny one there?" She pointed to the woman standing next to him. "That's *Jasmine Shah*. Remember how she had to be rescued by her father when her fiancé stranded her in Egypt? Can you imagine if Dad knew his new employee was partying with his rival's daughter?"

Reena looked at the woman in question. Ridiculously leggy, with perfect highlighted hair in loose curls cascading halfway down her back. She wore a short flowy caftan and rose-gold aviator glasses, and looked exactly like she belonged on this golden yacht over turquoise waters. Reena tried not to judge based on appearances, but it was kind of hard not to when her father had been low-key blasting the entire Shah family for as long as Reena could remember. Okay, maybe low-key was a bit understated.

"You haven't shown this to Dad, have you?"

"Nah, I wanted to show you first."

Reena squinted at the picture. This wasn't really the damning gossip Saira seemed to think it was. Reena knew Nadim had lived in London and came from a wealthy family. Hanging out with other wealthy people was expected.

But Dad wouldn't see it that way. Partying like this? With the notorious playboy gang? Conspicuous displays of money? Drinking? Dad wouldn't approve of anything he saw happening on this yacht, no matter how harmless it actually was.

She wasn't going to tell her father. This was Nadim. Her friend. The man who'd kept sixteen sourdough starters instead of throwing any out. She couldn't throw him under the bus before she understood what she was looking at.

But clearly she did need to find out what he was hiding from her. She was relying on him so much. And her family's business was at stake. She needed to know if he could be trusted. "Saira, don't tell Dad, but ask Rish for more information. Was Nadim into shady stuff, too?"

Saira nodded. "Okay, fine. Let me dig a little deeper."

CHAPTER FOURTEEN

Reena studied the pictures again once Saira had left. Nadim looked like a self-absorbed dimwit surrounded by other self-absorbed dimwits. Not the responsible project manager her father had hired. One eyebrow raised in mirth and lips ever so lightly pursed. Duck-face. Her new friend had duck-face on a yacht.

Her phone rang. Of course, Nadim's name flashed on her screen. She answered it.

"I'll come straight by after work," he said when she answered. "Want me to pick up some takeout?"

He was coming by? She'd hoped she would have a little more time to process all this before she had to face him again. "Um, that's okay. Thanks, though. I planned a quiet night at home. I did too much socializing on the weekend."

"Reena, did you forget?" His voice lowered. "We have to do the lice treatment tonight."

Her shoulders slumped. Yeah. Even if Duncan said she was lice-free, she'd still rather do the treatment again to be sure, and it needed to be Nadim who did it. As mortifying as it was to have her sexy neighbor shampoo and check her hair, she couldn't let another person witness her shame.

Wait, sexy? Where did that come from? She'd just been

worried he had deep dark secrets and now he's sexy? Stupid libido...Reena wondered if it was time to get laid, so she could really focus on this issue with Nadim.

That did not make sense.

"Reena, you there? Will you let me do this for you?"

"What?"

"Are you okay? You seem a little spacey."

"I'm fine."

"I'm asking if I can bring you dinner tonight. Maybe that Thai place you told me about?"

Reena needed to get a grip as soon as possible. She sighed. "Yeah, sounds fine." She let him know which dishes she liked and hung up.

~

Once Reena was done unpacking, she started cleaning to calm her nerves. Deep cleaning. Starting with the kitchen, she scrubbed, scoured, and polished until her fingers were numb and her mind was clear enough to make a decision: It was high time she and Nadim talked. Really talked. No more skirting any serious topics, no more pretending their pasts didn't exist. She was going to ask him about his life in London and see if he mentioned the yacht people. She wouldn't wait for Saira's gossip train. No more deflecting.

She finished deep cleaning by midafternoon, but her low-level anxiety (okay, honestly not that low) about confronting Nadim hadn't eased. Breathing deeply to slow her rising heart rate, she grabbed her iPad and logged into a few job search boards while her email loaded. And...crap. An email from

Abigail, the employment counselor. She didn't get the job she had interviewed for last week. They went with another applicant.

Because of course they did.

Reena threw her iPad on the couch. She had let her hopes sail a little too high there. She took a deep, long breath, but it didn't help. She needed to cook something.

Since she didn't feel like making a yeast bread, she decided on pie. Mixing the pastry and cutting the fruit would distract her from that stupid job she didn't realize she had wanted so much. Eating the pie later, with a scoop of the crème brûlée ice cream in the freezer, would be just the thing to soothe the crushing rejection. And finally, feeding Nadim the pie would soften the impact of the personal questions she planned to spring on him.

She went with her favorite: sour cream apple pie. Rich, buttery pastry filled with tart apples nestled in a sour cream custard and topped with a brown sugar crumble. No one could hold secrets when faced with the scent of that pie, let alone the taste.

Nadim arrived on time, armed with a plastic bag and a huge paper bag of takeout in one hand, and a six-pack in the other. He had grabbed Thai beer to go with the Thai food. Nice choice. His jeans were worn and faded, and his T-shirt carried the emblem of her favorite brand of sriracha hot sauce.

"God, it smells good in here." He grinned as he dropped his things on the breakfast bar. "Sometimes I still have to pinch myself that I get to live near these smells."

Reena started opening the paper bag of take-out containers. "Thanks. And thanks for grabbing dinner."

"No problem at all. I'm looking forward to trying that chicken mint salad…" He wandered over to the counter, near the stove. "I found the smell." He leaned forward, nose inches from the cooling pie. When he stood straight his face looked luminescent with pleasure.

"Did you make the pie for me?" he asked.

"Yeah, um, for us. Dessert."

He groaned. "You're killing me, Ree."

She bit her lip. Few people called her Ree, and only one person did it consistently, Amira. Hearing the nickname said from his lips with that accent made her shiver up her spine. "Where'd you get that shirt?"

He grinned as he pulled two plates down from her kitchen cabinet. "From a thrift store, if you'd believe it. There was one near a meeting I had with a restaurant developer, and I had time to kill. Here." He went to the breakfast bar and took something out of the plastic bag and handed it to her. "I found this and *had* to get it for you."

It was an old ceramic crock, probably from the seventies or older. Beige with a brown lid and the word SOURDOUGH stamped across it. An old starter jar. He bought her this?

"I don't know why I've never been in a thrift store before, but you have to see all the stuff I got for my apartment! It won't be so bare anymore. And I love that the stuff has, you know, history. Personality."

"You're a trust fund kid. Of course you've never been to a thrift store."

His expression was incredulous. "I am not a trust fund kid!"

"Did you have a trust fund?" she asked.

He frowned. "Technically…But anyway, I cleaned out the

jar for you. Although now I wonder if it had decades' old traces of sourdough in it. Personality, right?"

She smiled, letting her finger trace the letters on the crock. She wasn't sure she'd ever received such a casually thoughtful gift.

"Thank you for this," she said, putting the crock on the counter. "I've actually always wanted one of these. I still can't see you in a thrift store, though."

"I've been missing out. But new life, new Nadim. Shall we eat?"

"Yes, let's."

Nadim made up for her terrible mood by being especially chipper and charming. He called her "goddess" no less than three times over their khao soi and made a suggestive comment when she said she preferred tom kha gai to tom yum soup. He couldn't have picked a worse time to be all rakish again.

"You're quiet today," he said, twirling egg noodles on his chopsticks. "Nervous about the video going live? It's up in four days."

She shrugged. She hadn't really thought much about the video, to be honest. Unemployment and the unearthed dirt about her fake fiancé was actually a pretty good distraction from stage fright. She should tell Hollywood.

"No. Not really nervous."

"Worried about your parents finding out what we're up to?"

She shrugged. Their finding out about her job and the yacht would be worse. "Nah. I mean, I'm not telling them, but they're the ones who want us engaged, so what's the big deal if we tell a national TV station that we are?"

"Then what's bothering you, Ree?"

"Just a rough day."

"Did you leave work early? That pie was warm."

Crap. Of course, he noticed the pie was fresh. Ugh…she felt like an idiot.

She considered telling him the pie came from her freezer, when she sank in her seat. She planned this whole evening to get some honesty out of him. She couldn't start by lying. He bought her a starter jar, for god's sake. He deserved the truth.

"If I tell you something, can I trust you not to tell my parents? Actually, not to tell anyone. At all. No one knows this, except Amira and Saira."

"Of course. You know you can trust me. What's wrong?"

Could trust him? The man on the gold yacht? She took a long breath. "I didn't go to work today. I was laid off two weeks ago."

He looked up at her, his eyes warm with concern. "Oh, shit, Reena, I'm so sorry. Did this happen that day I found you at the Sparrow?"

She nodded, not trusting her voice not to crack.

"Why didn't you tell me?"

She bit her lip. "I didn't want you to tell my father. I don't want my parents to know until I have another job."

"Why? Your dad can probably help you find one. He knows so many people."

Reena fidgeted with her chopsticks, scraping the rough wood with her fingernails. "This isn't my first…I've been downsized twice. Last time Mum kept saying 'how could you let this happen to you?' And Dad kept saying 'now's the time to join the family business.'"

"And you don't want to do that."

"No." She pressed her eyes closed a moment. "I'm thirty-one. I can afford to live alone only because my parents own this building and charge me a fraction of what the average Toronto rent is. It's still hard to stay afloat. As soon as things start going well and I start to think, *there, I've done it, I am an adult now*, boom. Downsized again. Don't get me wrong, I know it could be worse, but I wish their help didn't come with so many damn strings. Telling me where to work. What to eat. Where to live. Who to marry."

Nadim sat silently for a while. Reena wondered if she had said too much. Delved too deep into serious talk. Not to mention that the marriage comment didn't shine too brightly on him.

He finally spoke. "I'm sorry, Reena. I...I'm sorry you're going through this. A part of me wants to say you should be happy your parents care enough to interfere. But that's not right, either. There should be a middle ground, yeah?"

His parents didn't care enough to interfere? Reena tensed. "I'm sure your parents care."

He smiled sadly. "Let's just say my father didn't send me to school in England only for the quality of education. Out of sight, out of mind."

"Nadim, that's...I'm sorry. That's messed."

He sighed. "Yeah. Messed. I was such a cliché...screwing up to get noticed. And when he had no choice but to notice my mistakes, I wasn't left with many options." He absently glanced out the window.

There it was. A little hint he had a past he regretted. But how exactly had he screwed up? Should she ask now?

No. Not now. Not while he looked at her with warm,

concerned eyes. He put his hand over hers, which were still clutching her chopsticks. "Enough about me and my past, though. I am *so* sorry about your job. If you need any help at all with your search, please count on me. I can look at your CV or practice interviews. I'll keep your secret for as long as you need. Have you found any good job leads?"

"Yeah, some. My employment counselor is optimistic. I'll be okay."

"Keep your chin up, yeah? Let me clean up dinner, and then maybe a cup of tea? Or something stronger?"

She sighed. "I have to wash my hair. The lice stuff."

"Right. I'll make tea while you're in the shower. You can drink it while I'm combing you."

"Okay." She got up from the table slowly, straining not to meet his eyes. She couldn't bear to see pity in them.

"Reena." He held her arm as she started to walk away. "I'm glad you told me. I won't tell your parents, you have my word."

Later, after he helped her rub the noxious chemicals into her scalp, she sat alone on the edge of her tub, letting the bug killer do its thing. She decided then that this could very well be the absolute lowest point in her life.

CHAPTER FIFTEEN

I'm definitely not finding anything," Nadim said. They were both on the couch in her living room, sitting sideways. Her wet hair was pulled into sections, which he combed through.

Hallelujah. Duncan was right. "Yay." She deadpanned, before sipping the tea Nadim had spiked with bourbon. Good man, this one.

"Sorry again to have to put you through this," he said.

She chuckled. "You're coming along nicely in your Canadian assimilation. Step up your apologies a bit more, and start ordering your coffee double-double and you're there."

He laughed. "I'm doing my best. Eh."

He combed silently for a while as Reena considered how to get the conversation to steer toward his past again.

"You know," he said, doing her work for her, "years ago, I had a dream of moving to Canada. It's a little surprising it's actually happened."

"Really? When?"

"As a boy. Before England. Once I got there, I figured I'd end up staying in London."

"Then why *did* you come to Canada?"

He didn't answer right away, but without being able to see his face, she couldn't guess what he was thinking. "I told you.

My father invested with your father and arranged this opportunity for me to learn from him." He paused. "I'd admired your father's reputation as a successful real estate developer. I'd heard he was like the Muslim Donald Tr—"

"Don't you *dare* finish that sentence."

"Okay." He snorted. "But, like, not really, because your father's reputation is that he's *good*. That he's ethical as well as shrewd. A good, stable man with a brilliant mind for business."

"You said your father doesn't usually get involved in your life?"

He exhaled. "No. Not *usually*." He sighed as he ran the comb through her hair again. "My mother died when I was six, and my father never remarried. A series of housekeepers pretty much raised me until Dad sent me to boarding school. I was a *problem* child."

"I'm sorry. That doesn't sound like a fun childhood."

"It didn't seem terrible at the time. I mean, I had so many friends and we always had fun, but…yeah. I had these two classmates when I was kid—Joseph and Jabari. We used to prank our teachers—you know, like hot sauce in their food, switch the sugar and salt. Harmless stuff." Nadim laughed. "One time we moved the teachers' bicycle rack ten centimeters a day for a few weeks. They didn't notice until the rack was two meters across the field. We were *always* in trouble. And my father was always punishing me. He had very high expectations for my character but left me on my own to develop that character. I stopped trying to please him a long time ago. And the older I grew, the less he seemed to care about how I was doing." He shrugged.

"But he cares now, right? He sent you here." Not to mention planning his son's marriage.

"Yes, but only because I screwed up. Badly, this time. I take full ownership of my mistakes and am grateful he's helping me find my footing."

Typical desi parents. Always taking things to extremes—years of neglect, and then way too much interference. His father's idea of helping him seemed to not only be planning his entire life for him, but also shipping him off again, this time to Canada instead of England. Why would Nadim even care to please this man?

"So, he sent you off to marry a *good girl* because you messed up?"

"Reena, I'm thirty-two. I wanted to do this. We both decided it would be a fresh start for me."

"What was your big mistake, anyway?"

Nadim stilled.

This was it. The reason for the bailout. Maybe the truth?

"It sounds ridiculous, and I feel all of fifteen years old, but I fell in with a bad crowd. A situation snowballed, and I needed my father's help to get out of it."

Father's help. Wrong crowd. He *was* one of those troubled *daddy needs to bail me out* kids. What had he done?

Nadim knew what she was thinking. "Don't worry, Reena, it wasn't illegal or anything. Just a lapse in judgment. Anyway, I promised my father I'd put it behind me," he continued. "And he helped me do that."

Reena closed her eyes as the comb scraped behind her ear, causing her to shiver. She didn't know what to say next. Nadim seemed to have no desire to talk about the details, and maybe for good reason. She could bet his father told him not to tell anyone, especially not *her* father. And why should Nadim trust Reena? After all, as Dad said, the business was a *family* business—and she was a Manji.

But she wouldn't betray him. She didn't work for her father and had no obligation to carry out his corporate espionage. Dad would judge Nadim for his past. Just like he judged Reena for every mistake she made. She couldn't subject Nadim to that.

"I think I get it," she said quietly. "I know I've made mistakes, before. Lapses in judgment."

He silently took the hair tie out of the next segment of hair and started combing. They were both silent for a bit while he worked through her hair. As he gently tilted her head to get behind her other ear, he asked, "Reena, are you glad I moved here?"

What a question. Yesterday, she would have said maybe. Probably. But now? After hearing him tell the truth about why he was here? "Yes. I'm glad you're here. I'm sorry things went badly for you in London, but I'm glad you're getting a second chance." Her voice quieted. "And I'm glad to have you for company when my life is complete shit."

"I'm glad I'm here, too." She heard the smile in his voice. After a few more runs of the comb, he straightened her head and ran it down the middle of her now fully loose hair. "You have such soft hair," he murmured, letting his fingers trail down her neck and behind her ear. She shivered again.

"Thank you."

"It's a lot longer wet. I guess because the curls are stretched out. No more bungee jumping." He scraped the comb through the top of her head with his right hand while his left hand dug into the back, raking his fingers through the wet strands.

The touch made her insides melt. It felt charged somehow. "I thought you had a foot fetish? What's with the scalp love?"

"I think I may be developing a taste for wet curls, too." He placed the comb on the coffee table but did not remove his left hand from her hair. Soon his right hand joined in the party, lightly fingering the wet ends. "I think I'm done combing," he murmured. He leaned closer and brushed his face in her hair.

"Nadim?"

"Hmm?"

"Are you coming on to me?"

"Maybe." He leaned even closer, his warm breath tickling her neck. It was getting harder to breathe in her living room.

"I..." She shuddered as he pushed her hair to one side. What were they talking about?

He dipped his head and soft lips starting to graze her sensitized skin. Barely making contact, but with a promise of so much more.

Reena's internal alert system blared: *Mayday!* He was going to kiss her neck. And if he did that, her asshole libido would let him, and she would lean into him and turn around, and then there would be kissing and writhing and clothes thrown to the floor, and she was pretty sure there were unexpired condoms in her bathroom, but maybe they could go to his place because his bed was better, even though it was technically her bed and... *ungh*. She closed her eyes and leaned into him.

There were thousands of valid reasons not to do this. And maybe just as many to do it. But with lips on her neck, it was hard to weigh the pros and cons right now.

Her upper body reclined on him as one of his hands moved to her hip and the other gently pushed her shoulder down to expose more of her neck. He kissed, licked, and sucked gently, turning her spine to goo.

His mouth was on her with intention. Maybe she was just imagining it, but there was a deliberateness in his actions. It had been months since she'd been touched by a man. Even longer since she'd felt completely wanted. Not just the convenient girl, not the party girl. *She* was the one he wanted to be with right now. It was *her* neck he wanted to kiss, *her* hair he wanted his hands in.

That thought was more intoxicating than the bourbon in her tea, so she let her brain turn off. Let it not worry about what a terrible idea this was. It didn't matter. All that mattered were those soft lips closing the circuit that had been open since they met.

Somehow she ended up facing him. Legs draped over his, his hand still on her hip and his lips still feasting on her neck. Her chin. Her cheek.

And finally, her lips. The kiss wasn't the frantic meeting with writhing and gripping she was expecting, but a slow, sensual awakening that curled Reena's toes. It was immersive. The strong, confident body under her. The scruff of his jaw on her live-wire skin. The heady scent of his amber beer and...him. She pressed closer. He kissed her like he ate her bread—savoring each taste like he'd been gifted a rare delicacy. She could kiss this man forever, making her life bearable as she let everything else blur away. It was frightening how right this felt.

Because it was wrong.

"Stop," she said, loudly. Okay, that was maybe a little too loud. Startled, he disentangled himself, and she shifted six inches away.

"Stop?" he asked.

"Yeah. Sorry." She took a deep breath and turned to face him.

"Don't apologize. I should apologize. Sorry." He blinked a few times, seeming as off-kilter as she was.

They stared at each other. Heart racing, she tried to put on a casual face. His lips were pursed slightly for a second, before he smiled wide enough for that damn dimple to emerge. God, that perfect little indent was going to be the death of her—she felt sure of it.

"Appears we both have this Canadian apology thing down pat," he said.

"Yeah." Breathe in. Breathe out. "Give me a sec, I have to collect my thoughts."

Thoughts. Thoughts. What were they, anyway? Not surprise, she'd seen this coming. They had been carefully inching over that line of appropriate behavior for a while now. Reena got that "just friends" didn't give innuendo-laced foot rubs. Or agree to go on a national cooking contest as a couple. Or spend almost every evening together for the last week. Denial wasn't just a river in Africa. After two weeks of insisting she wouldn't marry the man, she'd let this current between them take her closer to something even more dangerous. She'd developed feelings for him. Real ones, not just the physical lust expected for a man who looked like...him.

She inhaled sharply before speaking. "I'm just trying to make sense of you and this weird relationship. We're getting closer...as friends, I mean..." She exhaled. "You confided in me, and I confided in you, and we're here for each other, but..."

"I'm sorry, Reena. Really. Don't freak out. I won't cross the line again. You can trust me."

Could she trust him? She squeezed her lips together. With her body, yes. She did trust him. Even with her feet. But with her heart? Could she trust him to be honest about his true feelings?

"I don't..." she started. "I mean, if we'd done that yesterday, I'd be...receptive...I mean, I wouldn't have stopped. But after what you just told me..."

He tensed slightly. Any other person may not notice it, but she could read this man like she could read the bubbles on the surface of her starter. She saw when it was sour.

Nadim came to Toronto to marry the girl his father had chosen to make up for some big bad mistake he made. And despite the number of times Reena told him she would not marry him, he came on to her tonight. He kissed her, with a clear intention that he wanted to do much more. And she almost let him.

Was it really *her* he wanted? Or to placate his father? Or to please her father, the man he respected so much?

Reena bit her lip. "Do you really want *me*? I've told you I wouldn't marry you, but it's what both our fathers want. And now...I just told you about my job. I'm upset. Vulnerable. It's a good time to soften me, right? What's riding on our marriage anyway?"

"No! Reena, I—"

She put her hand up to stop him. "I have no way of knowing what you think of me. Honestly. No matter what you say or do, we're tangled in our parents' web, and our own actions can't be separated from them. I don't know what you promised your father, or what he will do if things don't go the way he wants. And since I can't know how you actually feel about me, all I can look at is my own track record."

Reena stood. "I've been laid off three times." She walked over to the kitchen and put her empty mug in the sink, carefully avoiding Nadim's gaze. "I've had twelve boyfriends in the last fifteen years," she continued. "Four were relationships that lasted over a year. Not one man said he loved me. The relationships didn't end with a bang, they just kind of fizzled when the convenient sex and home-cooked meals lost their novelty. I'm the middle kid. My older brother, Khizar, is perfect. Kind, brilliant, successful. My little sister is brash and high-maintenance. I'm just there. Unmemorable. Weird hobbies and boring career. Easygoing, but not particularly good at anything." She stood near her bedroom door. "I don't know what deal our fathers made, but your father was definitely sold a lame horse." She smiled sadly. "And despite that depressing pity party, I *do* have self-respect. Those twelve guys may not have been in it for the long haul, but at least they were into me for *me*. Not to impress their father or mine. They *chose* me. Good night, Nadim. The door locks automatically."

She walked into her bedroom and closed the door. Had she been harsh there? Yeah, probably. She hadn't even given the man a chance to defend himself. She knew what he'd say—that he cared for her. That she was a good friend when he needed it. That she could trust him.

But what good was trust really? It made no difference in the end—the people she trusted still left. Her brother, her best friend. Hell, even her job. And probably Nadim. She'd trusted him, and he'd only cared about obeying his father's demands. She'd lost his friendship, if she ever really had it at all.

Reena didn't even change. She just turned off her light and climbed into bed.

This whole fucking day could go shove itself.

CHAPTER SIXTEEN

Three days, four cartons of rocky road, and a full bottle of vodka (she was *so* done with gin) didn't do crap for Reena's foul mood after that night. And nothing intervened to cheer her up. She didn't hear about any new jobs and didn't hear from any of the ones she'd applied for. She *did* have the new luxury of no longer giving a shit if anyone in the building discovered her unemployed state, but since she saw no one, it felt like a hollow benefit.

And she literally saw *no one*. Not even Nadim. It wasn't that she wanted to see him. After hearing how hard he worked to please his father she now questioned every flirty wink, every concerned look, every friendly touch. The competition video told her how well he could perform. How great he was at faking affection. She couldn't believe she'd fallen for it. If they made it to the next round, how could she continue with this charade?

And if she was wrong about him, if all this wasn't about fulfilling some promise to his father or hers, then she had to see it for what it really was.

A fucking pity-kiss.

Pity for poor unemployed Reena. Unlucky in love, and with parents forcing an arranged marriage on her because she couldn't manage to figure out how to make a dozen previous guys stick around long enough for an "I love you," let alone a proposal.

Either option—the calculating Nadim or the pitying Nadim—didn't make Reena feel all that great about herself.

She looked around her messy room. Plates strewn about. Empty bowls of ice cream and glasses. She was clearheaded enough to realize that after a full bottle of the best vodka thirty Canadian dollars could buy (honestly, not that good), she should probably stop using isolation and liquid mood enhancers to cope. Or full-fat ice cream for that matter.

She pulled a sweatshirt over her T-shirt and slipped on her flip-flops, glad this time no one could criticize her footwear, and headed out the door.

She went straight to the back deck. This was a mostly unused space that was technically for all the tenants, but no one came here. It held a few chairs and an old bistro table. After climbing the few stairs up, she noticed the deck looked different. A grouping of aluminum lawn chairs, the type popular in the eighties with wide woven straps in brilliant colors, now surrounded a yellow Formica table. And lights encased in translucent white balls had been wrapped around the railing—off now, but Reena could imagine their ethereal glow illuminating the quirky decor here. It felt like stepping into some sort of bubbly oasis behind the graying brick building. A cheerful hipster paradise.

As she was taking in the improvements, she heard someone walking down the steep stairs from the fire escape on the second floor. It was Marley, holding a tall rainbow-striped melamine glass and smiling at Reena.

"Oh, hey, Reena. I didn't know you were here."

"I didn't know anyone was ever here. What happened to this place? You've been decorating?"

Marley shrugged as she placed her glass on the table. "Shayne's been decorating. He wants to start doing photo shoots here. And I like having an outdoor space."

"What kind of photo shoots?"

Marley shrugged. "He's got a ridiculous new idea to start a new Instagram and fashion blog. Want some tea? I picked up this super-smooth oolong. It's fantastic iced."

Reena smiled and nodded, and sat on the purple lawn chair. Marley went back upstairs to her apartment. Once she was back with a second glass of iced tea, Marley sat on the yellow chair. "I'm completely wiped."

Reena looked at her cousin. Something in Marley's expression told Reena that her cousin's exhaustion was more than just because of a busy work schedule. "You know, Marl, I know I've been a little self-absorbed lately, but if you ever needed to talk, I'm here for you."

Marley squeezed her lips together a moment, before smiling again. "Eh, everyone is dealing with their own shit. It's such a nice afternoon, I'm glad to have someone to hang out with. Did you take a vacation day?"

Reena closed her eyes a moment and debated whether to lie. But...fuck it. Marley was her cousin, yes, but her friend, too, right?

Reena tried to paint on an unaffected smile. "Nah. Got laid off a couple of weeks ago."

Marley tilted her head sympathetically. "Ah. I'd wondered. I heard about the Railside layoffs."

Of course. Marley worked in fashion retail. Reena had frankly been a bit deluded when she thought she could keep this secret. Mum and Dad would probably find out soon.

"I'll be okay. I'll find something else," Reena said. Her four-day pity party hadn't completely zapped her optimism about finding a new job. Her fear was more what would happen to her between now and getting that job.

Marley nodded. "I can ask around to see if anyone I know is hiring."

"Thanks. And…"

"Don't tell anyone, right?"

"Yeah. Mainly my parents. I don't want them to know."

"Of course." Marley glanced out over the tiny parking lot behind them, the sun highlighting her high cheekbones in perfect relief. She sighed. "You know, it's kinda ridiculous. Our parents force us to be so secretive because we'll never meet their expectations. And then they tell us to keep *their* secrets to save face. We're all suppressing deep feelings and traumas, and no one can support each other like a family should." She paused, scrunching her nose.

"This family is completely fueled by secrets."

"Yup." Marley sipped her iced tea. "Hey, when's your FoodTV thing going live?"

"I don't know for sure. Tomorrow, I think?"

"I saw Nadim in the store yesterday. I waved to him, but I was with a customer so couldn't chat."

"I haven't seen him in a few days."

"He was buying dress shirts, I think. Probably for those fancy meetings your dad keeps sending him on."

Logically, Reena knew that Nadim's life had continued after

that night when they had kissed. He still went to work every day, and apparently shopped on his lunch hour. He probably went to the Sparrow after work and laughed with Steve. He wasn't sitting at home in three-day-old pajamas and dipping sourdough bread into melted rocky road. Life just kept going for him.

And it would keep going. She had no doubt Nadim would be successful. In her father's company and even in his love life. He was smart, charismatic, and so handsome. And she would still be just Reena, watching all that from the sidelines.

She was used to looking in from the outskirts of success. A memory flashed through her mind. Years ago, their community had organized a kids' trip to an amusement park. Reena couldn't deal with roller coasters, not unless she was okay with wearing regurgitated funnel cake and fudge all day, but Amira and Khizar loved them. Reena still spent the whole day with them, in line for hours for extreme rides, each one bigger and more stomach churning than the last. And each time they got to the front of the line, Reena would step aside, watching her best friend and her brother squeeze into the hard seats and buckle themselves in. They'd still be spinning and laughing when they exited the ride, and Reena would join in the mirth, drunk on their pleasure and thrill.

And that's what life felt like. Everyone taking a deliberate step onto a roller coaster while Reena stood by happily, anticipating their highs with them. But after the ride rolled off leaving Reena in a cloud of dust and happy smiles, who did she have left? Not Amira, the friend who'd left to live her own life. Not Khizar, four hours away and about to become a father of twins. Not even Saira, who was recovering well on her own.

Now she could add another name, Nadim, to the list of people who she needed more than they needed her.

It was a sobering thought.

"You okay, Reena? Something happen between you and Nadim?" Marley asked.

"No." Another lie.

"He's a cool guy. Even if you're not interested, you should thank your parents for setting you up with him." She giggled. "Clearly they've been taking notes when we talk about our favorite Bollywood stars in from of them."

Reena chuckled. "Nah. They didn't pick him for his 'Shah Rukh Khan meets Shahid Kapoor' looks, they picked him for his father. Believe me, there is no goodwill to me in this arrangement."

"Well, I'd say it worked out. If nothing else, you have a new friend and a new fake fiancé to enter contests with." She shrugged. "It's more than you had before."

Maybe. But considering how empty she felt after only a few days apart from this new friend, she wondered if maybe she would have been better off without Nadim Remtulla in her life.

CHAPTER SEVENTEEN

Reena had had a Google Alert set up for her name for years—harking back to her blogging days when it was important to know when she was mentioned online. It had been silent for months. But after checking her email once back in her apartment, she saw several new alerts—the first of which linked to the main landing page of the FoodTV *Home Cooking Showdown*.

The contest had officially opened.

She took a deep breath as she skimmed the other alerts. They came from blogs and forums where internet foodies were already talking about the contest. After a few minutes of looking at all the links, she noticed that no one seemed to make a connection between her old blog and this. That was good, she supposed.

But still. Seeing her and Nadim's names together turned her stomach upside down.

Reena Manji and fiancé, Nadim Remtulla.

She went back to the FoodTV site. The other contestants' videos were all there. Should she watch them?

Her text rang. It was Nadim. Contest went live.

It was now too late to back out. Was that what he wanted?

She bit her lip and texted him a response: I know. I saw it. Do you want me to pull out?

He didn't answer.

After Reena stared at her phone for about two minutes, the three little dots started flashing. She rubbed her sweaty palms on her leggings and waited.

Nadim: You wanted this so much. I am willing to continue. As your friend.

Why had he added that last sentence? To remind her or himself that they were only friends?

Also, why was this so complicated?

After seeing her name on the website, she realized that she *did* want it. Not just the prize, but also the recognition. The prestige. She wanted proof that even though her life was a steaming pile of turd, she was still a great cook worthy of a national contest. She just wasn't sure how wise it was to do this with Nadim.

He wrote again before she could respond.

Nadim: Come for dinner tomorrow. I owe you a home-cooked meal. We can talk. Total honesty.

Reena finally exhaled.

Reena: OK. What can I bring?

Nadim: Just you is all I need.

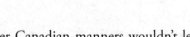

Her Canadian manners wouldn't let her go to a dinner party without bringing something, so despite the flock of butterflies using her stomach for flight practice, she still went to a local microbrewery on Friday afternoon to grab some craft beer. When she returned, the most unexpected smell overcame her as she entered the first-floor hallway.

Bread. Home-baked bread. And there was only one place it could be coming from.

Nerves be damned, she knocked on Nadim's door, despite being two hours early for dinner. The smell couldn't be from him, though. He should still be at work.

But he answered the door, eyes wide, wearing a red plaid apron.

"You're early," he said, quickly untying the apron and pulling it over his head. He tossed it on the couch.

She handed him the six-pack. "What's that smell? Sourdough? What bakery is it from?"

"I made it." His shoulders fell. "But I messed it up. I was just about to go out and buy another loaf. I should've waited for you to teach me."

"You made bread?"

"I tried. It's to go with dinner."

"How? With what? Where'd you learn?"

He raised an eyebrow, one side of his mouth barely curling up in a smile. "Have you heard of this new thing, Ree? It's called the internet. There's so much information there—"

"Let me see," she said, still disbelieving.

She followed him into the kitchen. And sure enough, cooling on the kitchen counter was a golden, flat, sourdough loaf.

"I made it with Al," he said, "but something went wrong. It didn't rise like yours."

Reena pressed her finger into the crusty loaf. Good spring back. Crisp crust. True, it *was* a little flat, but it had some lift. She lowered her nose to smell the crust. Nice, slightly sour, nutty scent. Not bad for a first time.

"You made it with what?"

"Al. My all-purpose starter. Remember, the puppy from Brian's litter you let me keep?"

"You kept that starter? And you named him *Al*?"

"Yes, I told you I planned to keep it. I wanted a pet. I've been feeding him every day. Al's quite robust."

Reena tilted her head. This man. She'd spent the last four days wallowing in self-loathing, mind swirling with doubts about how he felt about her. And he'd spent it...figuring out how to make bread.

He was so strange. In all the same ways she was. They were a set. And, for now, at least, they should stay that way. She had to find a way to salvage this friendship. She opened her mouth to apologize for everything, when he interrupted her.

"I'm glad you came early. Before I say or do something else stupid, I wanted to say I'm sorry," he said. "I shouldn't have, I mean. I know everything I told you Monday came out wrong. I hate that I upset you. We had this boundary between us, and I overstepped it when I kissed you, and I'm sorry. I didn't come on to you because of my dad. Or yours. You were warm and smelled so good and I just forgot everything and..." He sighed.

He looked upset. And so weary. "Wait here," he said. "I have to do this before I lose my nerve."

He went into the living room, took a small white gift bag from the coffee table, and pulled a black velvet jewelry box out of the bag. Leaving the bag on the kitchen counter, he walked around until he stood in front of Reena.

He took a deep breath. "I took today off work and went shopping." And then he did the unthinkable. Slowly, remarkably, eyes only on Reena's, he lowered himself to one knee, and opened the box.

Inside, nestled in black velour, sat a beautiful, glimmering ring. A large, clear stone in the center, with several thin bands of rose gold and white gold dotted with tiny stones on each side of it. Reena's eyes widened.

What. The. Hell. Reena tried to speak, but her tongue seemed to have grown three sizes.

"Ree, I know I haven't known you that long, but I…I *really* like you. And that is completely because of who *you* are. You're funny, and competent, and generous, and…I can't lose this friendship. Remember when I told you that I don't know who I am most of the time? I'm not like that with you. I feel like me with you. This…connection we have, it's completely separate from our families. I would never, *ever* want something from you that you didn't want, too." He took a deep breath and held out the box. "This ring cost me thirty dollars, but it won't turn your finger green. Will you keep it as a promise to *never* marry me?"

CHAPTER EIGHTEEN

S he blinked. "You're giving me an engagement ring?"

He smiled nervously and raised one eyebrow. "No. It's an *un*-gagement ring. I called my father and told him things were going well at work and with your father, but you and I will not be getting married. The deal with your dad will still go on. I bought this ring because... I thought you'd need a better ring for the contest, and..." He bit his lip. "I don't know... I just..."

That look on his face. He thought he'd screwed up again. But he hadn't. This ring was... it was lovely. The first thing Reena needed to do was to wipe that look off his face. She let a small smile reassure him. "It's a beautiful ring."

But inside, her mind was spinning faster than a food processor blade. An un-gagement ring? Who ever heard of such a thing?

Only Nadim. The man who'd made her laugh, both intentionally and unintentionally every time the walls closed in on her since the day they'd met. Who shared gin gimlets in her local dive bar when she lost her job. Who rubbed her feet after several hours under bright lights for a cooking contest she wanted to enter. And now, when faced with the terrifying prospect of facing this lonely life alone again, he bought her a fake ring to prove his real feelings.

It couldn't be more perfect. Reena didn't want to hide the truth anymore—she was coping and surviving thanks to this man.

Fuck it. Salvaging the friendship was one thing, but this ring, this remarkable, extraordinary symbol, didn't mean commitment, family, tradition, or *forever*, but only meant he *cared* for her. Just her. Whatever this thing between them was, it was as real as this diamond was fake, and maybe it was time for Reena to trust the feelings that were threatening to consume her whole.

Reena grinned widely and pushed his shoulders down. He fell back on the living room floor with an *umph*, legs stretched out in front of him. He still held the ring.

Chuckling, she lowered herself on his lap, straddling his firm thighs. She leaned in to kiss him softly on the neck before presenting her left hand to him. "You're so weird," she said, "but yes, I'll accept your un-gagement ring."

His eyes widened with her kiss, but he quickly laughed as he put the ring on her finger and tossed the box behind him. A warm smile on his face, he rested his hands on her hips. "It's a perfect fit. And you're weird, too," he said.

"Is that all you can say about me? Competent, generous, and weird?"

"Hey." He laughed, pulling her a little closer by the hips. "I love competence. I could watch you knead bread all day. But"—he leaned over and spoke into her neck—"I missed some other descriptors. You're sexy. You always smell fantastic, and you have the most amazing curly hair I've ever seen. You're so cute when you're thinking hard and you bite your lip and I just want to pull it out with my teeth. And don't even get me started on your feet. I'll never understand how anyone could think you're unmemorable."

Reena blushed. For a split second, her traitorous insecurities wondered if he only said these things to please her father. But when he lifted his head and she saw the sincerity in those intense eyes, she trusted him. She trusted this. She looped her arms behind his neck and steadied herself. "Shut up, Nadim," she said, before lowering her lips to his.

This kiss wasn't like their last one. It felt more like a question—an intentional action instead of getting caught in a moment. Because though she had enough confidence to kiss him, her self-doubt prevented her from showing him exactly how much she wanted him.

He apparently had no such reservations. He growled from deep in his throat before lifting his knees to slide her even closer, eliminating all space between them. His hands trailed up from her hips to her waist as his most rakish smile yet transformed his face.

"You kissed me," he said.

"I did." She smiled.

His arms raised, one to the small of her back and the other behind her neck as he leaned in closely, but didn't touch. He just stared for a few moments as the air around them seemed to crackle with electricity. She bit her lip.

"So, it's open season? I can kiss you, too?" he asked.

She nodded.

Slowly, he lifted his hand to her mouth and pulled her lip out from between her teeth. "I didn't think you wanted this. It's not why I bought you the ring," he whispered, his hand lightly stroking her cheek. He breathed a sigh. "I bought it to *apologize* for thinking of you this way... This is complicated, yeah? And I really don't want to mess it up, but..." He leaned in close again, his hands stroking the skin on the back of her neck. "I dreamed you wanted me. Tell me that you do."

She did, but she preferred actions to words. "Kiss me."

His smile widened seconds before his lips claimed hers. And this kiss was like the one on Monday—completely enveloping. She didn't know why she'd waited—she should have come here and kissed him every night since that first kiss. Actually, they should have done this weeks ago. Intense and enthusiastic, he had one hand on the back of her neck and the other rested on her cheek as he all but devoured her whole. She wrapped her legs around his waist and finally ran her fingers over that velvety cropped hair. He moaned in appreciation.

Out of breath and needing some air, she pulled back and looked at him.

His lips were swollen and curved into a smile. Pupils dilated. Skin flushed. He leaned forward, chasing the connection she'd broken. She grinned.

"Fucking hell," he murmured. "I should have promised to never make an honest woman out of you a long time ago. Are you sure, Ree?" He rested his head on hers.

She nodded, tilting her chin up to kiss him again.

"I haven't been able to think straight all week," he said, once they broke free again. "I want you. All of you, in every way. I want you in my home. I want you with me in my kitchen. I want you in my bed." He let his hands fall back to her hips. "But I'm okay if you want to go slow here. Or stop altogether."

She considered it for about two seconds before she giggled. "I've already slept in your bed. You've searched for bugs in my hair. We've managed to have both an arranged and a fake engagement. Not to mention the things you did with my feet. I'm not sure *slow* is possible." She leaned forward and nipped at his neck.

He laughed. Grinning, she finally took the opportunity to get her tongue into that dimple. She nibbled and licked her way back to his lips.

His hands tightened. "So, you're saying…"

"Do you have condoms?"

His smile nearly split his face in two. "Yes."

"Then take me to bed, Nadim."

He beamed. "Gladly." In one smooth movement, he grasped her bottom and stood, barely letting go of her lips as he walked her over to the pink four-poster bed.

It turned out that talent while making out on her couch or his living room floor easily predicted talent in a bed, too. Granted it had been a long time, but twelve boyfriends and a handful of casual hookups had left Reena feeling pretty confident at judging sexual prowess. She tended to categorize first times as either: wow, potential to become wow, awkward, or nope. For Nadim, she needed a new category. Something between wow and holy crap *wow*.

"Sweet mother of God…" he said, collapsing on top of her afterward, arms straining to keep his weight off her.

She laughed, pushing him off her. "I'll take that as a compliment."

"It was fully intended as one," he said into his pillow.

"I'll be back." She hopped out of bed to use his bathroom because she wanted a UTI like she wanted a nuclear winter. While in the bathroom, she looked at her face in the mirror.

Hair a mess. Neck reddened with friction irritation. And a goofy smile plastered on her face. Not a trace of regret.

He got up after she returned, presumably to clean up and dispose of the condom, before they settled back in his bed.

She smiled, nuzzling her cheek in his satiny sheets. "You have excellent sheets, by the way."

"They're Egyptian cotton. Is that why you wanted to sleep with me?"

She giggled. "Maybe. I've always had a soft spot for Egypt. I want to see the Pyramids one day."

"They're on my bucket list, too."

"What else is on your bucket list?" she asked.

"Would you call me weird if I said it was to eat fresh bread in bed?"

She laughed as she shifted to rest her head on his chest. Mmm... nicer than the sheets. She rubbed her cheek against him.

He chuckled before checking the time. "Ha! It's not even five. Going to have to kick you out soon. I'm making dinner for this chick I'm really into."

She grinned. "Oh really? What are you making her?"

"It needs to be spectacular to impress her—she's a fantastic cook. I'm doing shrimp and scallop linguine with a white wine sauce."

Reena twisted onto her side and ran her hand down his side, resting it on his solid hip bone.

"I'm sure she'll be impressed. And I'm sure she'll be willing to help you cook, if it means we can spend more time in bed together."

He laughed out loud and pinched her bottom. "Have I mentioned you have a rather amazing ass?"

She laughed harder as he grasped her hips and pulled her on top of him, kissing her soundly. She took that to mean they weren't going to get out of bed quite yet.

Later, Reena was resting her head on his chest again, her hand drifting across one of his hip bones to the other. It still felt unreal that this was happening, that she had access to touch the body she'd been admiring for weeks. "Can I ask you something? Actually, two things."

"Of course."

"Your stomach…" Her hands skimmed over his belly. "You have those big arms but no…six-pack. And…don't take this badly but…do you even lift anymore?"

He laughed at her bro-dude impression. "Nah, not much. Not at all, really. And you keep feeding me bread…You mind if I lose the biceps?"

She readjusted herself so her head rested on his arm instead of on his chest. "Nope. Not at all." She knew better than to ever say it out loud, but she didn't care one bit if he was squishy or built like a tank. Both had their benefits. And right now, during after-sex snuggles, a layer of squish covering the hard muscles would be welcome.

"Okay. Second question. You keep saying that I'm not what you expected. What exactly did your father tell you about me?"

"Well, he said you were *good*. Not that you're not good"— he squeezed her—"but you know what I mean. Wholesome. They told me you worked in finance and were still single because you'd been focusing on your career. I thought you were a devoted daughter who lived with your parents. That's why I was shocked to see you across the hall."

"You didn't know what I looked like?"

"I did see a picture in your dad's office. But it didn't really look like you. You were wearing this purple salwar kameez and standing with your parents. And your hair was straight. I could tell you were cute, but—"

"I know that picture. From my brother's wedding. Mum's makeup artist totally overdid it." She chuckled, remembering the ridiculous high heels she'd been forced to wear. No wonder he didn't recognize her. She'd felt like an illusion that day. In fact, the whole day had been a charade. Despite Khizar and Nafissa being so madly in love, both their parents' interference on the wedding day ruined any chance of them enjoying any of it. Mum even hired that makeup artist, despite Nafissa *being* a makeup artist and wanting to hire one of her friends. Reena decided then not to have the big Indian wedding her parents would insist on, and to never even consider one of the arranged introductions they forced on her.

And now she'd slept with one of them.

She pushed away the feeling of impending doom and squeezed him playfully. "And now that you know I'm not what they sold you, you don't want to marry me anymore?"

His other arm snaked around her and pulled her on top of him again. "No. I don't." He buried his head in her neck and inhaled. "I've been restless for a long time," he said. "Actually, *restless* is the wrong word. I was too busy to realize how bored I was. Too many people around to realize how lonely I felt. But then you came along and turned everything upside down." He smiled. "I'm not sure about the future. But I *am* sure about the present." He pulled her head up and kissed her gently. "And all I want right now is to make you happy." He kissed her again, deeper this time. Reena lost herself in the perfect embrace. He pulled back again. "You're unexpected, Reena Manji. Never unmemorable." He kissed her again, before murmuring against her lips. "Twelve boyfriends?" he asked, smiling. "Is it too unlucky to try for a thirteenth? Am I doomed to fail?"

She shook her head. "Thirteen is a baker's dozen. The extra one always tastes the sweetest." She kissed him again.

"We still can't tell our families," she said as they broke apart again. Not when Mum wanted to start wedding planning and Dad wanted her to report back everything she learned about his new mentee. They wouldn't understand simply dating Nadim with no plans for a future. There was a reason why Reena stopped telling them about her dating life by the time she was twenty-seven—that was the arbitrary age when every conversation about men turned into interrogations about his marriage prospects. Reena couldn't see where this would go naturally without keeping her families out of it.

"We'll create a bubble in this place, just you and me," he said.

She kissed him again, letting herself sink into a replay of their earlier entertainments, but a thought invaded her mind at the same time. As a bread baker, she knew a thing or two about bubbles. The glorious pockets of air captured in bread dough that made it rise were not as delicate as they looked, so long as the dough had a well-developed gluten foundation. Without the foundation, the bubbles would deflate when exposed to the heat of an oven.

She really hoped their foundation was strong enough to keep their bubble.

CHAPTER NINETEEN

After finally emerging from his bedroom, Reena was delighted to learn that her new boyfriend was a pretty good cook. The shrimp was perfectly cooked, even if the pasta wasn't quite as al dente as she usually preferred. And as she suspected, the bread was good, too. After they ate, they sat on his couch to watch the *Home Cooking Showdown* videos together.

They'd seen their own clip, of course. But watching it with the other seven couples' videos confirmed three things to Reena. One, as a fake couple they had more chemistry than most of these real couples. Two, FoodTV wasn't kidding when they said they were looking for diverse contestants. There were three same-sex married couples, including one where both men were unfortunately named Jeff, and half the pairings had one or two people of color in them. Reena and Nadim weren't even the only Muslim pairing. And three, Shayne and Marley were geniuses. Because Nadim and Reena were lit better, dressed better, and edited better than all the other videos.

There was no question in Reena's mind, with only two contestants being eliminated this round, that they had a definite shot at moving on. And now that they were a real couple instead of a fake one (although not engaged), their chemistry might be even better in round two. Reena could practically hear the crack of the baguette crust she'd be making in that course.

"How do we know how we're doing?" Nadim asked after they had voted for themselves. Because who else would they vote for?

"We don't. They'll show the number of votes next week. And if we're not eliminated, we'll have a few days to upload the next video."

He snorted. "We won't be eliminated. My money for the next round is on us, the hijabi woman and her daughter, that couple from Hamilton, the Jeffs, and the Jamaicans."

Reena giggled. "Six groups move on. That's only five."

"And that's why we have this in the bag. There is no way we're in the bottom two. I would tell everyone I know to vote for us, but we don't need the help. Not with you cooking, anyway."

Reena grinned. He was right. They had this round. No question about it.

⁓

Reena was surprised to see her father at her door Saturday morning, a scant half hour after Nadim had left her apartment for yet another meeting with a restaurant developer.

She had assumed that after Nadim told his father he wouldn't be marrying Reena, Shiroz Remtulla would call her father about their children's abject failure at uniting the families. And, of course, Dad would want to confront her on it. But she wasn't expecting a parental house call.

"Dad. This is a surprise."

"Why would you be surprised? I am your father." Dad strolled in and stood near the breakfast bar like he owned the place. Which was fair—he did.

"Would you like some…coffee? Chai? Breakfast?"

"Just coffee." He sat at the high stool.

"It's cold brew, but I can heat it up."

Dad's forehead wrinkled. "Cold brew? Why don't you just use a coffeemaker? You make things more difficult than they need to be, Reena."

Reena sighed as she pulled her old French press from the top shelf of the cabinet. Her father's mood was nothing like their last meeting, when Dad had been all compliments and jokes. She filled the kettle.

"I had a disappointing phone call yesterday," he said.

"Shiroz Remtulla. You're upset because I refused to marry Nadim."

"Yes, Shiroz was the call, but no, Reena, that is not what upsets me. I believe our role as parents is to facilitate an introduction, but of course I allow you to make your own choice."

"*Allow?* Dad, I'm thirty-one. I don't need your permission to make a choice."

He exhaled. "If you've discovered so early that you and Nadim are incompatible, then I am happy. No harm done."

She stifled a snort. Multiple simultaneous orgasms, the last one being a mere hour ago, did not lead Reena's thoughts to *incompatibility.*

She poured hot water from the kettle over the coffee grounds. "So, then what, Dad? Why are you angry?"

"I am not *angry*, just confused. Shiroz said you and Nadim have become close friends."

"And? If I won't marry him, I'm not allowed to be friends with him?"

"Of course you can be friends, Reena. But I was under the impression, from both of you, mind you, that you barely knew each other. Have you forgotten what I asked you that day?"

"You asked me to spy on him."

Dad put his hand down on the counter heavily. "I asked no such thing. But this is our business! I can't ignore the rumors I heard. All I want to know is who his friends are. Who is he in regular contact with?"

"I'll tell you who his friend is. Me. Why would you want me to betray my friend by telling his boss about his personal life?"

"I had hoped my children would show a bit more loyalty to the family."

Reena pinched her lips shut while pushing down the plunger of the French press. She pulled out a mug and poured the coffee. Where were her loyalties, anyway? She *did* know information about Nadim, albeit not directly from him. And while the intel she had was worthy of a little raised eyebrow on the gossip train, it was hardly worth risking Nadim's job and his father's investment.

So what if Nadim used to hang with a bad crowd? And how rational was her father's dislike of Salim Shah and his ilk anyway? Her father was condemning these people while barely knowing a thing about them.

She placed his coffee on the bar in front of his seat. "How is Nadim working out at the Diamond project? Do you have any reason to be concerned?"

"No. I am still very impressed with him. I told Shiroz that yesterday. He doesn't have a lot of faith in his son. It's a shame, really. Nadim is a remarkable worker." He took a sip of his coffee, then smiled warmly at Reena. "I hope I never underappreciate my children."

Part of Reena wanted to say that the first step in appreciating his children would be to take a real interest in their lives, but he was only doing what he knew. His father, and the men in his life, had modeled only unconditional filial piety. They probably spent even less time with their children. Why did she expect more? And besides, she should be more sympathetic. All this was because he had been swindled. Cheated by a business associate he trusted.

She took out a box of cookies that he loved but Saira wouldn't allow in the house and put some on a plate.

"Here's the truth, Dad. Yes, Nadim and I have become close friends. And yes, I told him I would not marry him. He told me a bit about his troubled past, but really, it's nothing unexpected, considering he lost his mother at a young age and his father doesn't appreciate him. As far as I know, he has no close friends outside of his coworkers, and me and Marley in the building. And I will not attempt to extract any more information out of my friend. I trust him, and you should, too."

Everything she had said was true. It just wasn't *all* the truths.

But it seemed to satisfy Dad. "He's lucky to have you." Dad smiled. "Now, how is work going? Did you ask for a promotion like we discussed?"

Reena groaned internally as she seamlessly transitioned into telling lies instead of truths.

CHAPTER TWENTY

It took Reena about fifteen minutes to regret calling Amira Monday morning after Nadim left for work, as it felt a little early in the day for an interrogation by her best friend. She should have known better—Amira's reaction to Reena's relationship upgrade wasn't exactly unexpected. "So, you don't return my calls for two days and only send cryptic texts, and now you tell me you're sleeping with Nadim?"

"Dating."

"So, you're not sleeping with him?" Amira asked. She was on her speakerphone in the car and was very loud.

"No, I am sleeping with him, but we're *dating*. We're exclusive."

"You're *dating* the guy you're pretending to be engaged to for a cooking contest and who your parents want you to marry?"

"Yes. But our parents don't know," Reena explained. It made sense to her.

"And, you haven't told them so they won't buy jalebi and saris." Amira paused. "Actually, not telling your parents is probably the only intelligent thing you've told me today."

"Amira, really? Did I judge when you forgave Duncan despite all the crap with his family?"

"Yes, you did judge, Ree." Amira's voice rose. "That's what

we do. We advocate for the devil with each other. It's our shtick. It has been for over—"

"Amira, please." Reena was in no mood for this blunt investigation of the pitfalls of her new boyfriend, not when she could still feel the lingering echo of his touch on her body. "Give me some time to enjoy him before you pounce on the negatives. Believe me, my eyes are open. We're getting to know each other." Reena smiled as she stretched her sore limbs over her cheap sheets. Good lord, had they ever gotten to know each other over the weekend. They'd spent most of Saturday together after his meeting, and most of Sunday, too, save for the few hours Reena took off for family brunch. She now knew her neighbor well. Very well. He liked his eggs sunny side up, his TV comedies British and dry, and his hands were spectacularly talented on more than just her scalp and feet. She squirmed as the warm memory washed over her.

"But what about Saira's picture?" Crap. Amira was still going on about this? "You had all these pressing questions, but one sparkly rock and you fall into his bed? Did he tell you about his friends in London? I asked my mum about—"

Reena sat up. "Amira, that sparkly rock, as you put it, was fake, and a symbol of us *not* committing to anything big right now." She bit her lip. How to make Amira understand this? "I'm unemployed, and my family is a bunch of whack jobs who will probably evict me and force me to move home and join the business when they find out I'm out of work. My head is *not* in the clouds. I know Nadim's keeping secrets. I'm keeping secrets from him, too. But…" She squeezed her eyes closed and fell back into the bed. She hadn't been able to stop her voice from cracking, and her oldest friend would catch it.

Amira was silent while Reena squeezed her eyes shut. "You like him. A lot," Amira finally said.

"I do. I hate the way we were forced together, and I hate my parents' interference and Dad asking me to dig up dirt and Saira listening to gossip...but I like *him*. He makes me laugh. And he's sweet. Our pasts will unfold slowly, like they are supposed to in a normal relationship."

"Okay, Ree. Okay. But you know I'm only saying all this because I love you, right? I judge because I care."

"I know." And did she ever know. One could not be best friends with the likes of Amira Khan for so many years without understanding that behind those judgments was a fierce protectiveness that no one could match. She knew Amira would get her objections off her chest now, and then stand by Reena and support her no matter what she chose to do. And Amira would never, ever resort to "I told you so" if things went sour with Nadim.

But sometimes getting through the judgments could be trying.

There was a bit more silence as she heard Amira park and turn off her car. "I've said my piece and will let it go. Oh, and by the way, Duncan has all of his students voting for your video, so don't get confused if you see an uptick in votes in the fourteen-to-nineteen age range from the Peterborough area."

Reena laughed. "I'm not sure they'll tell me where the votes come from, but thank you."

"Will do. He voted for you even though he was quite taken with that Syrian mother and daughter. Any chance you can get their muhammarah recipe?"

"I don't know. I can try."

"Oh, I forgot, I'm supposed to ask you if you want any fresh eggs or goat milk?"

"What?" That was not a question Reena expected.

"Doug and Shirley insisted I call my *cooking friend*. They got a few more chickens, and of course Belle and Ariel are way too productive and—"

"What are you talking about, Amira?"

"*Doug and Shirley*. Duncan's parents."

Reena chuckled. "Are they still treating you like their little Muslim pet?"

Amira snorted. "Yup. Shirley even eats beef bacon when I'm not there. Anyway, they have an abundance of eggs, since they can't seem to say no when their granddaughter wants a new chicken."

"And Belle and Ariel..."

"Their goats. Who produce way too much milk." Amira said it like it was the most normal thing in the world to have goats named after princesses. "They asked me to ask you if you wanted any. They said you're welcome to come to the farm any-time. They also have a bunch of fresh vegetables. I told them it wasn't likely you'd drive over an hour for some free eggs and milk, but I said I'd ask."

Actually, Reena probably would drive that long for farm-fresh ingredients. "How fresh are we talking here?" Unpasteurized goat milk was in high demand. She could get good money for it on the food blogger black market.

"I need to get into work. Call me later and let me know what to tell them. And sorry for nagging on you earlier. I just want you to be happy, but you know that. Love ya, babe."

"Bye, Meer." She disconnected the call.

Reena closed her eyes. Amira didn't understand Reena's new relationship. She didn't get that this thing with Nadim meant a hell of a lot more than convenient and spectacular sex. Reena needed him right now. And she didn't want to think about how needing someone so much after such a short time was the very definition of a bad idea.

CHAPTER TWENTY-ONE

After recovering from the call with Amira, Reena finally rolled out of bed and grabbed a quick shower before setting up on her dining table with a latte and toast to look at the job boards. But the moment she logged on, a knock on her door interrupted her.

"Saira. I wasn't expecting you," she said as she opened the door.

Saira rolled her eyes in the most Saira-specific expression that Reena nearly laughed.

"You asked me to dig up dirt for you, and then you're surprised when I show up?" Saira strolled past Reena and began unloading tote bags on the breakfast bar.

Had Reena asked Saira to dig up dirt? Crap. Nadim. She had asked Saira for more info about that blasted yacht picture. Reena wrinkled her nose. She shouldn't have done that. Especially after telling Dad so empathetically that she trusted Nadim. So much for letting their pasts unfold organically.

Reena snapped out of her crisis of conscience when she noticed her sister had taken out a series of identical plastic food containers from her tote and was lining them up on the breakfast bar. "What is all that?"

Saira wrinkled her nose as she pointed. "Green pea dip,

masala hummus, and lemongrass white bean dip. And these"—
she pulled some large Ziploc bags from the second tote—"are
spelt cumin seed crackers, and semolina mustard seed. I'm not
sure about the crackers, the mustard seed flavor didn't really
come out. But I don't know how to fix them." She opened
a bag and shoved it under Reena's nose. The crackers smelled
good, with a nice toasty fresh smell, but not much mustard
seed aroma.

Saira opened the other bag and moved it toward Reena's
nose when Reena put her hand out to stop her. "Where'd all
this come from?"

"Oh my God, Reena, I told you about the cookbook thing!
Do you even listen?" She opened one of the plastic containers,
revealing a muddy green paste.

"You made all these?"

Saira rolled her eyes again. "No, Dad did. Of course I made
them! But you need to tell me what's missing here." She thrust
the container under Reena's nose.

Reena's hand reflexively shot up to prevent her nose from
being caked in army-green gruel. "Saira, chill! I'm trying to
understand what you're doing!"

"I'm trying to get help with these recipes! You wouldn't give
me the eggplant dip, so I had to develop other ones. You're still
the best cook I know. How can I get the mustard seed flavor
stronger? I tried—"

Reena put her hand out again, stopping her sister from
continuing. "Did you just compliment me?" Was this the
twilight zone?

"Reena!" Saira sat heavily on the barstool. "I don't see why
we can't be, like, *normal* sisters."

This clearly *was* the twilight zone. Reena could write a novel of all the reasons why she and Saira couldn't be normal sisters.

Reena looked carefully at her sister's dejected face. Maybe it was thanks to the bliss of her new relationship, but she saw her sister differently today. It couldn't have been easy to be excluded by her older sister repeatedly. Always being told she was too young or too emotional to play with Reena and Khizar. And for months now, Reena had been resenting Saira for something without even really explaining to her sister why.

What would have happened if she'd told Saira about her own cookbook deal? And a bigger question, what would have happened if she'd included her sister back when Reena was blogging? Saira was a registered dietician—she could have been helpful to Reena's blog. Maybe really supporting her sister should have meant more than just offering her the sofa bed.

She pulled out a mustard seed cracker from the bag and took a bite. Chewing, she analyzed the flavor. "Did you fry the seeds at all?"

Saira frowned. "No."

Reena smiled as she moved around the breakfast bar and pulled her apron from its hook. "Come, Saira. Let's see if we can bump up the intensity of these flavors. And while we're at it, I think it's time we talked...for real."

⁓

Reena couldn't remember cooking with her sister, not since they were knee-high arguing about who got to stick her thumb in food coloring to decorate nan khatai cookies with Mum. But inexplicably, they spent the rest of the afternoon tweaking

Saira's recipes for crackers. Toasting the spices in oil jacked up the flavor in both cracker recipes, and Reena's suggestion of adding fresh curry leaves to the mustard seeds while they fried in the grape-seed oil brought a new aroma that made the crackers sing.

Reena had ideas for the dips, too. Adding mint to barely blanched frozen peas before pureeing them in the food processor resulted in a fresher dip, both in color and in complexity. And adding pomegranate molasses to the hummus created the perfect balance of sweet, savory, and acidic. She left the lemongrass white bean dip alone—it tasted so good she found herself in the unlikely position of asking her sister for a recipe.

"This is good. I'm impressed," Reena said, dipping a spelt cracker into the creamy white dip again.

Saira smiled widely, taking a hot cracker off the tray. "See! Healthy food is tasty!" She crunched loudly on the cracker. "Mum says I have to stop with this diet food or Ashraf is never going to propose. But he loves my bird food, as Mum calls it."

"You think Ashraf will propose?"

Saira shrugged. "Don't know. Probably. Neither of us are getting any younger. It's about time to settle down if we want a family."

Reena cringed. Saira was two years younger than her, and if she recalled correctly, Ashraf was a year younger than that. Any other day, Reena would have immediately chalked that comment up to another dose of passive aggression—an off-hand quip about being thirty-one with no husband on the horizon? Textbook Saira. But Saira looked so focused on cutting out crackers with a pizza wheel, Reena doubted insults were anywhere near the front of her mind. Reena bit her lip. Had she misinterpreted her sister?

Maybe Saira was just selfishly clueless and not actually evil?

"Is that what you want?" Reena asked. "After everything that happened with Joran, is it wise to dive in again?" Despite everything, Reena's big-sister protectiveness was still on high alert.

Saira sighed as put the cut crackers on the tray. "Yeah, it is what I want. At first it was about proving to myself that I could get a man who would treat me better." She laughed sadly. "Janeya, my therapist, helped me figure that out. She's like you and thinks I should stay single for a while. But Ashraf is not Joran. Joran and I...we were never good for each other. He brought out the worst in me. My relationship with Ashraf is not the same. He would never do what Joran did."

This conversation felt so strange. Reena couldn't remember talking to her sister before. Really talking, without Mum or Dad butting in with their own two hundred cents.

Twilight zone was getting creepy.

"Anyway," Saira continued, "let's talk about you messing around with Dad's mentee on the down-low."

What? "How the hell did you know that?"

Saira laughed, slapping Reena on the arm. "Reena, c'mon! I'm your sister! You have a tell...I always know when you have a new man. Your eyes glazed over when Dad was talking about him yesterday at brunch. Don't worry, they didn't seem to notice."

Jesus, was she really that transparent?

It had been a weird brunch yesterday. Nadim hadn't been there in person, but apparently his echo lived in the secrets they all kept. Dad didn't mention he'd been to see Reena only a day earlier to gather information about him. Saira didn't mention she had been tasked with digging up dirt on him. And, of course, Reena didn't mention she'd left him naked in her bed. "Are you going to tell Mum and Dad I'm seeing him?"

That question prompted another slap from her darling sister. Enough of these playful whacks, and Reena was sure Saira would leave a mark. "Of course not! What kind of sister do you think I am?"

She shrugged.

"Well," Saira said, "you going to ask me about the dirt I dug up on that picture?" She held up the yacht picture on her phone.

"Fine. What did you learn?"

"Well, first of all, the cousin is apparently—"

"Wait, Saira, back up. What cousin?"

Saira rolled her eyes again. "Rish and Ashraf's. We talked about this, didn't we? Their cousin is the one in the picture with Nadim. Anyway, I asked Rish to ask her cousin if Nadim had a shady past. But Rish couldn't give me an answer because apparently she and her cousin had this huge fight."

"Why?"

"Because Rish called her cousin out on their family WhatsApp for being obsessed with this socialite wannabe and her thirst traps. Rish is a bit dramatic sometimes. God, I'm glad Mum hasn't learned how to use WhatsApp yet. Can you imagine—"

"Wait," Reena interrupted. "Whose thirst traps? The cousin's?"

"No, someone else's. Rish says her cousin is obsessed with her."

This was why Reena usually avoided gossip. She had no clue what the hell was going on. "Does any of this mean you found out something about Nadim?"

"No, I got nothing at all about him. But I did learn that Rish is even pettier than I thought she was. I don't know how Ashraf lives with her."

Fuck. All that, and nothing?

She looked at the picture again. Nadim, with that terrible beard, artfully disheveled hair, and popped-collar lavender shirt. It was so incongruous with the man she had spent most of the weekend with. The man who loved Monty Python and kissed her neck while she kneaded bread. How could it be the same person?

But if he really wanted to put that lifestyle behind him, she was happy to play a part in this transformation. She was doing the world a service and ridding it of one more bro-flake.

"You haven't told Dad about all this, have you?"

"Of course not, Reena. No one needs Dad's lectures about *the face you show the world.*"

Hallelujah for that.

"So," Saira said, putting her phone down, "I'm only doing the appetizer section now to pitch to the publishing people, but if they bite, can you help with my mains? I don't want to go completely meat-free, but primarily plant-based—"

Reena put her hand up. "Saira, wait." They'd been pretty honest with each other today, probably more than they ever had. Maybe now while Saira's lips were loose, it was time to ask the question that Reena had been avoiding for months.

"One question. Is this wise? I mean with your problems, with you know, your—"

Saira cut her off before she could finish the sentence. "My mental health?"

"Yeah. Sorry."

"Why are you sorry? I'm not hiding anything. I'm not ashamed of my diagnosis."

Reena tilted her head. "I don't actually know what your diagnosis was." How weird was it that they'd never talked about it?

Saira shrugged. "When I was in the outpatient program I was diagnosed with depression and an unspecified eating disorder. I was obsessed with the *healthiness* of what I was eating, not depriving myself for weight loss. Did you know mental illness runs in our family?"

"No. I didn't know that." She took a breath. "Did you know I used to take antidepressants?" Reena couldn't believe she'd told her sister that. No one in her family knew.

Saira tilted her head sympathetically. "No. You should have told me."

"It's been a while." Reena shrugged. "Are you okay now? I mean, you're still kinda food obsessed."

"I'm a lot better. Reena, you don't know how bad it was in my head. All food felt evil to me then. But now it's about a healthy balance. And finding the joy in food again. Doing this cookbook and developing recipes is helping me with that. I have a good relationship with food and wellness, instead of an obsession." Maybe to prove her point, she took a cracker from the baking tray and popped it in her mouth. And, true, old Saira would never eat crackers. Even homemade ones.

It was interesting to learn that Saira also looked for joy in food when her mood was bad. Reena had always baked bread when her mood was low. She even started her old blog when her life was in the shits.

The blog that Reena folded indirectly because of Saira.

But it was fine. Saira had been sick. And Reena was proud of how far her sister had come. Proud of how open and unashamed she was, and proud of her finding healthy ways to change her life for the better.

What happened to Reena was no big deal.

No.

It *was* a big deal. A big deal that no one in this family ever actually talked about what was going on. Saira never telling Reena about her relationship problems with Joran or about her diagnoses. And Reena never telling any of them about her own struggles. Or her dreams and how hurt she was when she lost them. She was tired of everyone hiding their feelings under the rugs, hoping no one noticed they were far from smooth on the floor.

"I need to tell you something." She took a deep breath. "I used to want to write a cookbook. It was a dream I had for a long time. And I almost did, at one point. But I lost that dream because of you."

Saira looked at her, dark eyes wide. "What?"

So, Reena told her the whole story.

And Saira said nothing. Nothing except sorry.

"You knew I had the blog," Reena said, "and you wrote almost a thousand words about how amateur food writers and their decadent creations were contributing to the downfall of society. It was grossly hyperbolic, and it directly attacked something I cared about," Reena said, strangely annoyed that Saira wasn't more defensive.

"I know." Her sister looked down, fussing with the hummus, swirling a deep groove into it with the back of a spoon. "And it wasn't completely...unintentional." She sighed, looking at Reena through glassy eyes. "I didn't think you would lose your blog or anything, I just...became weirdly obsessed with your popularity...and I guess I wanted to take you down a peg. Living with little Miss Perfect messed me up."

"What? I'm hardly perfect!"

Saira still didn't look at her, and still spoke quietly. "Seriously, Reena? I have a degree in nutrition and food, and all anyone ever talks about is what a great cook you are. Even in your personal life, you've had this best friend for years who is always there when you need her. You and Khizar have a better relationship with each other than you've ever had with me. You had a blog with thousands of readers. Not to mention men...I've had a grand total of three relationships, and you've had, what, eleven boyfriends?"

"Twelve," Reena corrected. Technically, thirteen, but Reena's mind still reeled from what Saira had said. Reena? *Perfect?*

"I was a mess. I shouldn't have taken it out on you." She paused and looked at Reena. "My therapist is helping me learn to stop automatically comparing my life to others and enjoy where I'm at now. It's so hard because I hated myself so much..."

Saira hated herself? Well, join the club. At least Reena didn't resort to ruining family members' dreams when she went through a bout of self-loathing.

"I'm sorry, Reena," Saira said again, finally meeting Reena's eyes. "I didn't know about your cookbook. Maybe you can try for it again? I can ask—"

"No. It's not something I have time for right now. Job search and all."

They were silent for a while before Reena crossed the kitchen and put the lids on the dips. She honestly didn't know how to feel—she'd had some vague idea that if one day she confronted Saira about how much her actions had hurt her, she would gain closure and get over it. It was supposed to feel cathartic. But it turned out this wasn't a Lifetime movie, and it wasn't so simple. Years of sibling rivalry encouraged by their parents and months of resentment couldn't be tied up in a neat bow and put behind them. Maybe with work, the relationship could be saved, and Reena could learn to appreciate how much Saira had grown. But trusting her now was hard—Reena had been burned too many times.

"I should go," Saira said, seeming to understand Reena wasn't ready to move on from this. "You keep the food. I'll try and re-create it all later. Thanks for your help, Reena. I really do appreciate it."

And with that, Saira walked out the door. And Reena was left with a kitchenful of dips, crackers, and a bitter taste in her mouth.

CHAPTER TWENTY-TWO

Saira left Reena with plenty of leftovers from their attempt to perfect homemade crackers and dips, a bonus, because probably for the first time in her life, Reena didn't feel like cooking. She did defrost some lentil soup that she'd stashed last month when she thought some upcoming work projects might mean she'd be too tired to cook in the coming weeks (ha!).

She couldn't stop replaying that conversation with her sister. Should she have let it all go? Just…not brought up the blog and the cookbook? Maybe they could have forged a decent relationship without working through the bitterness.

But she knew it wouldn't be right. Like a perfect loaf of bread without any salt—nice on the surface but tastes off.

For now, all she could do was push past the uneasy feeling and prepare for an evening with her boyfriend and friends.

Boyfriend.

Her heart skipped a bit every time that word passed through her mind. He wanted her to call him that. Already. She wanted it, too. After learning nothing useful from Saira's fact-finding expedition, she was confident that this just-for-fun, only-in-the-present, supportive relationship was worth any fallout that might happen in the future. She'd survived plenty of family implosions, and Nadim was definitely worth risking another.

He came over straight after work, still wearing his suit, a box in one hand and a wrapped plate in the other. He left them on the breakfast bar, then pulled Reena in for a long and leisurely kiss.

"I've been thinking about doing that all day," he whispered into her neck after he had released her lips. Reena hummed with appreciation.

"What did you bring?" she asked as he sucked the soft spot below her ear. She shivered.

He stepped back and grinned, still holding her waist. "We're still trying to finalize the café for the Diamond building. Met with a guy who owns a few franchises of a lunch counter–type place. He may be interested in opening one in the building. He wants us to put up some capital and be silent partners, but his terms seem far from fair to us. Anyway, he gave me some baked goods to sample. I'm sure they're nowhere near as good as yours, but..." He kissed her again, long and deep, tongues tangling and hands clutching. Nadim was an aggressive, all-or-nothing kisser. Reena's favorite kind.

"What was I saying?" he said when they finally broke free.

She giggled. "You were extolling the virtues of my baking."

"Yes. And I'll extol it more when I eat it later. Oh, and this." He pointed to the plastic-bag-wrapped plate he had placed on the counter. "This is proof that your mother likes me. Maybe not as much as you like me, but it's a start."

Well, at least she liked someone. "What is it?

"Keema maani. She gave it to your dad to give me."

Keema maani, or keema paratha, was one of Reena's favorite dishes, and she had never quite mastered the art of making them as well as Mum. Fragrantly spiced ground beef enveloped between layers of flaky flatbread. When Reena attempted it, the paratha dough always broke while she rolled it, or the beef and the paratha melded to a gummy mess.

Mum *knew* her keema maani was Reena's favorite. She always made extras and put them aside for her before anyone else could eat them. At least, she used to. Reena frowned.

"She didn't make me any?"

"Well"—he put his arms back around her—"I have every intention of sharing them with you."

He kissed her again, and she forgot all about this newest parental slight and settled into the kiss. He was smiling when he pulled away. "What smells so good?"

"Just lentil soup. Plus, I have crackers and dips for when Marley and Shayne come over."

He grinned as he walked toward her front door. "Let me change outta this suit. I'll be back. Gotta say, having a girlfriend who lives across the hall is ridiculously convenient."

Reena smiled as she heated up the keema maani in a pan. They'd go great with the lentil soup. He was right. It was amazing to have someone to share her meal with, someone who brought her baked goods and lived right across the hall.

One more tick in the pro column with her new boyfriend. Soon the con column would be a distant memory.

After dinner, Reena found herself herded to the sofa for a short make-out session. But a door knock forced her and Nadim apart. Answering it, she found Marley, Shayne, and an enormous bottle of pink champagne.

"This," Shayne said, holding it up, "is celebratory bubbly because I saw the other videos in the contest. You are so making it to the next round." He grinned before quickly frowning. "Jesus, what have you two been up to? Making out or something? I thought this was a fake relationship?"

Totally transparent. Reena clearly needed acting lessons.

"How did you know?" Reena asked as Nadim took the bottle from Shayne.

Marley laughed as she pointed a perfectly manicured finger at Reena. "You look like you've had a shot of collagen to your lips, and he's wearing your lipstick."

Reena shot a glare at Nadim, who was trying hard not to laugh while wiping his mouth on his sleeve.

"So much for a secret," she muttered, heading into the kitchen to grab the snacks and wineglasses.

After they were settled in the living room, Reena explained: "We're just dating. Casual. Not engaged and not telling our families."

"Sure. Whatever. No problem," Shayne said, dipping one of Saira's crackers into the hummus. "Bang like bunnies, I don't care. Marley and I saw this coming a while ago, though."

They did? They should have done the decent thing and told Reena. "Can we not talk about our personal life right now? What are we going to do for our next video?"

"*Our* video." Shayne smirked. "So now it's *our* video, when before it was just yours...says the girl who didn't want a boy toy."

Marley frowned at Shayne. "Ignore him. Shayne's a little salty today. Anderson dumped him. He said everything was too intense."

"Oh, I'm sorry, Shayne. That sucks."

Shayne glared at Marley. "We are not talking about me right now. What's the theme for the rest of the videos?"

Reena shrugged. "Round two is Farm-to-Table at Home. If we get past that one—"

"*When* we get past that one," Nadim interrupted.

"Fine. When we get past that one, round three is the one at the FoodTV studios. Theme is family picnics. I think we're supposed to be grilling for that. Then the final one, if we're still there, is back at our home—but they send a professional camera crew. Theme is Celebrations at Home. I think with the timing they want us to do a Thanksgiving meal, but really any celebration meal would work."

Nadim frowned. "Isn't Thanksgiving in November?"

"That's American Thanksgiving," Marley explained. "In Canada, Thanksgiving is early October."

Nadim shook his head. "You Canadians are always doing things your own way."

Shayne nodded, clearly deep in thought. "Okay, farm-to-table...hmmm...oh, I have an idea! We could film you at a big farmers' market or something. I hear they have them in the city now. You could pick up ingredients and bring them home and make a meal with them. We can even speak to a farmer." He beamed with pride.

Reena raised one brow. "A farmers' market? Really?"

"Sure! It's original."

Marley laughed. "Farmers' markets are hardly original these days."

Reena nodded. "I can pretty much guarantee that everyone will do the farmers' market, then cook-at-home thing."

"We need to wow them," Nadim said, inching even closer to Reena. "What if we made your table look like a farm. You know, scarecrows and hay bales and stuff."

"That's terrible," Marley said, looking around Reena's knock-off modern furniture. "I am not putting Reena in overalls. She's way too city."

Reena grinned, the start of an idea forming. "What if we take this city girl to a real farm?"

Shayne cringed. "What farm? You going to drag us all to one of those U-pick places with the big MDF pumpkins with holes to stick your head in for pictures?"

Reena smirked. "Hell no. Amira's boyfriend's parents have a hobby farm about an hour and a half away."

"And they'd let us film there?"

"Yeah, I think they would. They just offered me some fresh eggs and goat milk. I've seen pictures of the place on Amira's social, wait."

She queued up some pictures from Instagram of her friend feeding the chickens and goats. The spot looked utterly adorable and perfectly hipster-chic, with weathered wood animal pens, rolling hills, and straw-colored fields in the distance. Amira was, of course, feeding the chickens in a pencil skirt. A denim one, but still.

Shayne grinned. "It's perfect. Set it up, Reena."

Reena immediately called Amira, who promptly agreed to call the Galahads and get back to them. They didn't have to wait long. Her phone rang a scant ten minutes later with enthusiastic affirmatives that they could borrow the farm on Saturday, a list of the vegetables in season, and a warm offer to use whatever they needed.

"Not sure any of these will work," Reena said, looking over the list she had jotted down: potatoes, carrots, beets, and acorn squash. We already did a vegetable curry and potato bhajias."

Shayne let out an excited squeal. "Potatoes! Finally! Curried shepherd's pie!"

Reena cringed. "No fusion. We're not colonizing our food." She bit her lip as she racked her mind for a home-style Indian recipe that showcased these ingredients.

"Wait," Nadim said, "didn't you say they had eggs and goat milk, too?"

"Yes. Goats and chickens are the only animals they keep."

He smiled. "My mother came from Zanzibar. After she died, my father used to send me by ferry from Dar es Salaam to spend weeks with her mother, my nani. He said he didn't want me losing touch with that side of the family. Nani used to make this dish all the time—a curry with hard-boiled eggs, potatoes, and local spices. It's a Zanzibar specialty. I've only ever had it there, and it totally reminds me of home." He glanced at Reena, a wistful look in his eyes. "I remember Zanzibar always smelling like spices—it's one of the island's biggest exports. Anyway, Nani died when I was twelve, and I've barely been back there since, but..." He turned away, exhaling. "I'm sure egg curry would be spectacular with farm-fresh eggs and local potatoes."

Reena watched him. The modest space that had been between them on the sofa had dissolved as his leg now pressed against hers. His face had slackened as he talked about his grandmother. Reena had never been to Zanzibar, but visiting the island off the coast of her parents' hometown was on her bucket list. Pictures of spectacular sunsets over the Indian

Ocean and the breathtaking old Arab architecture in Stone Town had called to her, but the way Nadim talked about Zanzibar was not someone talking about a cherished vacation spot. He was talking about home, a place with bittersweet memories and a deep sensation of belonging there.

Nadim suddenly took her hand and squeezed. Reena looked at him, wondering if her eyes betrayed the uncertainty she felt. After another squeeze, he lifted her hand to his mouth and kissed it.

"We should go," Marley said, standing. "We're all set for Saturday. I'll find something agrarian-chic for you two to wear. Let me know if you have any ideas."

Immediately after Shayne and Marley were out the door, Nadim pulled Reena back on his lap and started kissing her neck. If he kept doing things like this, she would never be able to finish a thought about this "relationship," or about her place in his life.

Later while she was in Nadim's bed, waiting for him to finish brushing his teeth, her text tone filled the room with the rousing sound of Highland pipes.

Amira: I have been instructed to invite you and Nadim to our house Friday night to hang out with your best friends before we go to the Galahads on Saturday for your little film shoot.

Reena: I'll have to ask Nadim. Why?

Amira: Duncan insists that he must meet the man away from the chaos at his parents' place. You know how protective he is.

Reena: How charmingly patriarchal.

Amira: I know. His knight of the round table shtick is getting old. But come early anyway. We'll let the boys thump their chests and assert their manliness while we catch up.

Reena smiled. Clearly Duncan wasn't the only one who needed to meet Nadim to make sure Reena's heart was safe. But she felt fine about their meddling. Truly. Friends who cared enough to meddle were hardly something to complain about.

CHAPTER TWENTY-THREE

Reena spent the next few days shopping and researching for their video shoot at the farm. After a few phone calls to her mother and various extended family members, she had a vague recipe that she perfected with Nadim on Wednesday evening. The egg curry was a simple dish, but without any meat or strongly flavored vegetables, the quality of the spices became paramount. And one taste of her sample curry immediately confirmed that the trip to the store that roasted and ground their own spices had been worth it. Nadim proclaimed Reena's curry to be better than his nani's version, probably because of the bread she made to go with it—a large stack of parathas, heavy with ghee between flaky layers.

The next morning, Reena was on her way to a job interview when her phone rang. She hit the hands-free button on her steering wheel.

"Hello?"

"Were you planning to tell me you've acquired a fiancé to make maani with?"

Crap. Her brother. "Hi, Khizar! Great to hear from you! How's Nafissa?"

"That's it? Hi, Khizar? No *'sorry big brother, I meant to tell you about my engagement.'*"

"I'm not really engaged."

"I figured as much. The bio on the FoodTV site says you've been engaged for six months, and I know that guy has only been working for Dad a month or so. What are you playing at, Reena?"

This wasn't good. If her brother knew, who else could have seen the video? "Since when do *you* pay attention to the FoodTV website?"

"Nafissa is nesting. She was looking for freezer meals for after the babies are born."

"Oh, that's not necessary! I'm coming right after the birth—I'll cook for you. What kind of stuff—"

"Don't change the subject—are you and Dad's new project manager *together*? Because Nafissa's comment after seeing the video was 'humina humina, nudge nudge wink wink.' That's exactly what she said."

Reena snorted. She missed her sister-in-law. "No, we're only pretending to be engaged for the contest. Don't tell Mum and Dad."

"Yeah, of course I won't. So you're pretending to be engaged...but you *are* actually nudge nudging, right? Because there was a lot of chemistry in that clip, and you don't lie that well."

It was really impossible to keep anything from Khizar, even with 450 kilometers between them. And she was fine with that—her brother always had her back. She wished he still lived in town.

"Yeah." She sighed. "We're dating. Just casually, though."

"And Mum and Dad don't know?"

"No, of course not. They still want me to marry him." Her

brother would understand. "Look, Khizar. Can we finish this later? I'm about to get on the highway."

"Where you going?"

"Oh…just an off-site meeting. I'll call you tonight."

She disconnected the call before he could ask her about work, because she knew she wouldn't be able to keep her un-employed status from him. Khizar would keep her secret about the contest and fake engagement, no question, but it would be harder to get him to agree not to let the family know she was unemployed. Because he'd want to help her. He was supportive and amazing, and she was always happy to hear from him, but he was still her big brother, and also prone to meddling like the rest of the family.

The whole conversation just increased her anxiety, which was already pretty high, thanks to the job interview. If Khizar, who wasn't at all into food, saw the video, then others could have seen it, too. Would she and Nadim have to take their fake engagement *public*? They hadn't even taken their real relation-ship out in the world yet.

But Reena needed to put it all out of her mind for now. She was on her way to an important interview. This was the secret food-industry job that Abigail had hinted about—and Reena had full-on squealed when she heard more about it. It was for a financial analyst position at the corporate office of Top Crust, a bakery chain. Reena spent the rest of the drive practicing interview answers in her head.

After parking at the building that held a Top Crust bakery on the main floor, and their corporate offices above it, she squared her shoulders and took a cleansing breath. She'd been to the bakery many times—for a chain bakery, they produced a decent crusty loaf, if a bit overproofed. Their soups and sandwiches were tasty, too, with unique and innovative combinations. This job was perfect for her. She needed to nail this interview.

It went well at first. Angie, the director of finance, described the position, the office culture, and the expectations in a no-nonsense professional manner that Reena liked.

"So, tell me, Reena? What will set you apart from the other applicants? Why do you think you'll fit here?"

Reena put on her best professional yet enthusiastic smile, while ignoring her elevating heart rate. This was her chance to stand out in the crowd of other applicants. "Can I be honest with you, Angie?"

"Of course."

She swallowed. "I'm perfect for this job. I know it's in the finance department, but I'm a firm believer that members of a team must be passionate about the product the company sells. And you won't find anyone more passionate about the product you sell than me."

"You're a fan of bakeries?"

"I love bread. More than anything else. I even keep two different sourdough starters at home. Honestly, I'm obsessed. I'd love to work here to do my part in bringing great baked goods to the world."

Angie smiled widely, nodding her head. "Leon's going to love you."

Reena knew Leon Bergeron was the president of Top Crust. He was a third-generation baker who'd taken his father's small neighborhood bakery downtown and grown it to a national chain of over fifty stores. He was described as a little eccentric, but was well respected in the industry and loved by his employees.

"Our president is very involved in hiring at the corporate level. He normally conducts second interviews himself. Do you mind if I see if he's available now? Save us all some time later?"

Reena couldn't hold back her smile. This interview was going well. Very well. "Of course!"

Angie returned a mere minute later, her face betraying exasperation and amusement. "I should have known...He's at the bakery. His favorite club has booked the back room. Leon always finds a reason to be there when the NLBACC are in. Anyway, he'd like us to meet him there. Do you mind?"

"NL...what?"

"Just a book club. Shall we?"

The warm, familiar scent of bread baking as they entered the bakery felt so...perfect that Reena's knees nearly gave out. This could be her workplace. Well, not precisely, but workplace adjacent. She imagined a company discount for bread and soup instead of the practical separates at Railside Clothing. She imagined corporate meetings surrounded by baguettes and brioche. It had never occurred to Reena to work in the food-services industry, but her skin pebbled with longing now.

After warmly greeting the woman behind the counter, Angie told Reena to order whatever she liked, and Reena chose an apricot brioche tart.

"Leon's in the back," the woman at the counter told them as she handed Reena a plate. "He's waiting near the door for them to finish up."

Angie smiled as she led Reena into the rear of the café.

Leon Bergeron looked as expected, a distinguished older gentleman with sharp intelligence behind gray eyes.

"You must be Reena," he said, standing to shake her hand as they approached the table. "Welcome to my little bakery. Angie tells me you impressed her with your finance jargon and that you will impress me with your love of bread." Releasing her hand, he indicated toward a nearby chair. "Have a seat and tell me your thoughts on my shop, here. We've just finished an overhaul and will roll out this new look in other locations in the new year."

The conversation flowed easily as Leon told her about the history of the company, the changes he had made since inheriting it from his father, and the direction he hoped to take the business in the future.

"We're growing faster than I ever intended. I wanted to maintain that feeling of a neighborhood bakery, but these guys"—he nodded toward Angie—"have managed the impossible. I still feel connected to my customers and to my staff. It's supposed to be about the bread, not about the market share, right, Reena?"

That led to a long discussion about the types of bread Top Crust produced and Leon's focus on producing a quality product over cost-cutting or profit margins.

Reena could have talked bread with this man all afternoon. At one point, she forgot he had the power to make or break her prospective career. Well, not really. While the front of her mind talked proofing rooms and dough hydration, the back of her mind set off mental fireworks in celebration. This job was in the bag, and it seemed utterly perfect for her.

"Ooh," Angie said, turning toward the heavy wood door

behind their table. "Looks like the women are done. You couldn't convince them to let you join them today, Leon?"

He chuckled, standing. "I think I'm wearing them down, though. Won't be long before I'm an official member of the NLBACC instead of just their sponsor and travel manager."

What was this NL…whatever group about? Why would a book club need a travel manager? Reena opened her mouth to ask, when Angie smiled at Reena. "We book out the back room here, and this ladies' group has been renting it for almost five years."

"I've been angling for an invite into their club practically since day one," Leon added.

She turned to the door, expecting to see immaculate, desperate housewife-types emerging.

But that's not who exited the back room. The first woman moved slowly, a bright blue wheeled walker supporting her steps. The next woman had a cane.

"Olive!" Leon said, moving to greet the leader. She had to be at least eighty—easily a decade or two older than Leon himself. The other women after Olive ranged in age from fifties to eighties, some with mobility aides, all with wide smiles. Laughing and turning to each other, and joking with Leon, they were clearly a sharp-witted group. And they were completely not what Reena expected.

"And there's Vanna," Leon said, kissing the cheek of a woman with dyed violet hair and round glasses. "Who won?"

Vanna slapped him playfully on the shoulder. "No one wins in a *book club*." She laughed until she noticed Reena. "Reena! Look at you! You girls have grown up so beautiful. Are you here to pick up your mother?"

What? Reena stood, dumbfounded. Did she know this Vanna? But a sharp exhale from the woman behind Vanna took her attention. And sure enough, it was her own mother.

Mum's eyes were as wide as roti, and she held Vanna's arm for support. "Reena! What are you doing here?"

Leon turned to Reena. "You're Roz's Reena?"

Roz?

"Mum?" Reena closed her eyes a moment, but sure enough, after opening them, her mother still stood in front of her.

Leon laughed. "Hey, now I have an *in*. Reena, convince your mother to let me in her poker group."

Reena nearly fell to the floor. Poker? Mum? The hell? Gambling was against Islam—Reena might not be religious, but her parents would never openly go against the tenets of their religion. Or so Reena thought.

Mum smiled at Leon, like it was no big deal to get caught playing poker in the middle of the day. "We've told you, women only. How do you know my daughter?"

Leon beamed, looking at Reena. "She's a lovely young woman. I see why you're proud of her. Angie and I were interviewing her for Ginny's role."

"So, Ginny's gone then? Such a shame, I hoped she'd change her mind. Imagine, enlisting in the army at her age."

"I know. But she said it—"

"Excuse me," Reena interrupted. Mum was talking so casually to Leon, but then again, she'd always had a superb poker face. And...now Reena understood where she practiced it. "Mum, can you please explain what's going on?"

Leon chuckled. "Ah, daughters. I should head back to the office, anyway. It was lovely to meet you, Reena. Angie will be in touch." He shook Reena's hand and winked. "And keep an eye on that one." He nodded toward Mum. "Your mother's game face can turn even a softy like me into stone. You should have seen the Vegas high rollers quiver. Bye Roz, Vanna."

And with that, the strangest job interview Reena had ever experienced ended, and she was left alone, with her mother, a half-eaten apricot brioche tart, and more confusion than she knew what to do with.

Of course, it wasn't possible to avoid her mother now, so she had no choice but to agree to have tea with the woman before she could get out of the bakery. But after Mum got a fresh pot for them to share, she just sat in front of Reena, staring at her.

"So, are you going to explain?" Reena finally asked, narrowing her eyes.

"What about you? Why are you interviewing for a new job?"

"Why are you playing poker and flirting with a bakery owner in the middle of the day?"

"Flirting? Reena! Leon is my friend. I've been coming here for years."

"Yes, almost five, I heard. You told me it's inappropriate for men and women to be friends. Does Dad know?" She cringed. She sounded like Nadim.

"There is nothing inappropriate here. I'm a married woman. But why are you looking for a job? What happened to the clothes store?"

Reena slumped in her seat. May as well go for broke and tell the truth. "I was laid off a couple of weeks ago."

Mum inhaled sharply through her teeth before saying a prayer under her breath. "Why didn't you tell us? I'll call Daddy, and you can work with him—"

Reena put her hand up. "This is why I didn't tell you. I don't want to work with Dad, and I can find something new on my own."

"But, Reena! This is the third time you've lost your job! You need a new—"

"I'll find one! I just had an interview with your poker buddy, remember? And since when do you play high-stakes poker?"

Mum waved her hand at Reena. "It's not high stakes. We play with small change."

"But it's gambling!"

Mum just waved her hand. "Your father doesn't know everything I do."

Reena shook her head, not believing what she was hearing. "It's against Islam." Which, Reena accepted, didn't mean much coming from her.

"I know. But it's small money, and when I win I always donate it to charity. It's just fun, Reena. Giovanna convinced me to come years ago, and I enjoy it."

That's who Vanna was. Giovanna Pelozzi was the little Italian lady across the street from her parents. Reena didn't remember her having purple hair. The realization didn't do much to make this whole situation make sense.

"So Dad doesn't know?"

"No." Mum sighed. "I am not playing to win or lose, only to enjoy time with my friends. It exercises my brain. I'm at peace with my choice to play, but I know your father wouldn't understand."

Reena closed her eyes, blowing her hair out of her face. She'd known her family kept secrets, and she'd known they were a little...well...odd, but this took the cake. Her aging, Muslim mother playing in a ladies' poker league? What would come next, news that her father had secret tattoos?

She peered again at her mother's face. Calm. Stoic. Small purse to her lips and narrowing to her eyes, but no betrayal whatsoever that she was ruffled about getting caught. Reena couldn't help it, she snort-laughed. It was actually perfect. Who would have a better poker face than someone who never revealed her true self, *ever*?

Reena stood. "This has been...educational, but I need to go. Can I assume we have an agreement? I'll keep hush about your secret card shark life, and you let me continue my job search without letting Dad know."

"Reena, I'm your mother. You can't—"

"Mum, please. Just let me try to deal with this. If I need help, I'll come to you. But trust me to live the way I choose."

Unexpectedly, Mum stood and hugged Reena tightly. "Of course I trust you." She released Reena and held her arms. "We love you and want to help you. All we want is for the family to be successful."

The family to be successful. Not happy, *successful*. And not Reena, individually, but the family.

Actual success or the illusion of it?

CHAPTER TWENTY-FOUR

The next day, Nadim left work early for the drive to Amira and Duncan's. On the way, Reena attempted to warn him about them. She adored her friends, but for most other people, they were acquired tastes.

"Just to let you know, Amira and Duncan are...a lot."

He laughed. "A lot what? I'd figured they would be unusual if they are your closest friends."

"Yes, yes." She waved her hand while watching the road in front of her. "I know you think I'm weird, but you're the one who brought a sourdough starter for a weekend in the country."

"You know Al doesn't like to miss feedings. Anyway, what's wrong with your friends?"

She merged into the highway traffic. "Nothing wrong with them, Amira's just a bit...blunt. She's an engineer and kind of...cerebral at times. She won't put up with anyone's crap—*ever*. Watch yourself for anything even remotely sexist or racist."

He chuckled. "What about Duncan?"

"He's her opposite. He's a musician and a little eccentric, but easygoing. He teaches high school music and guitar at a private music school. And he sings in an a cappella group. He looks like a lumberjack. Expect a great deal of plaid flannel."

"Nothing wrong with that," he said, pointing to the flannel he was wearing. Nadim's style had changed so gradually that she barely noticed that he'd almost completely transformed from bougie douche to Brooklyn hipster in the last few weeks.

"And Doug and Shirley, Duncan's parents, may ask you a lot of questions. They are coming to terms with having a Muslim in the family and are...annoyingly curious."

Now Nadim really laughed. "Okay, I cannot wait to meet them. They accept your friend, though?"

"Yeah, actually. Everyone expected the worst because they were so conservative, but they adore Amira. Duncan's brother is a racist dick, though, so it hasn't been a complete cakewalk, but all things considered..."

"I guess it's easier to date within your own culture."

Reena shrugged noncommittally, but she disagreed. Maybe for others dating within their own culture was easier, but for *her*? No. Dating from within meant family expectations were higher. Parents intruded more. Were involved more. After all, here Nadim and Reena were, apparently "dating within their own culture," and neither had the balls to tell their parents about the relationship. This was hardly *easier.*

She finally pulled into the long gravel driveway of Amira and Duncan's country house to see them on their porch couch, both in jeans and flannel shirts. Reena squeezed her lips shut so as not to laugh at how frickin' adorable her best friend had become.

"Watching the sunset over the river," Duncan said, standing as Nadim and Reena approached. Duncan's eyes narrowed as he made his way toward them in his trademark Duncan-strut and gave Nadim a blatant once-over before crossing his arms in front of him with menace. With the low evening light illuminating his angry eyes and red beard, he looked like a fire Djinn appraising his foe. "Duncan Galahad," he drawled. "I gather you're this Nadim we've been hearing about?"

Reena rolled her eyes as she climbed the porch steps and sat on the seat Duncan had just vacated. "Hey, Meer. Want to call off your guard dog?"

Amira smirked as she leaned close to whisper, "Duncan doesn't trust him."

They watched with fascination as Nadim stood taller and puffed his chest out before shooting his hand out for Duncan to shake. It wasn't much use. Even if Nadim stood on his toes, Duncan would be at least three inches taller and a hell of a lot broader than him. Amira's boyfriend was huge. "Nadim Remtulla," Nadim said, his voice weirdly sounding deeper.

Duncan's eyes narrowed even more as he looked at Nadim's outstretched hand as if it were a dead salmon.

"Is this a glimpse of the dance for dominance among male members of the species?" Reena whispered to Amira.

"Both fearsome, both protective," Amira responded. "True, one alpha is clearly a more formidable opponent physically, but in this arena, brawns may not be enough to best cunning wits."

Reena fell over giggling.

Duncan's head snapped around to glare at them. "What are you girls going on about?"

Amira smiled as she stood up. "Nothing, sweets." She walked down the stairs, patted Duncan on the arm briefly before giving Nadim a quick hug. "I'm Amira. Reena's my best friend in the whole world, and she deserves to be happy. Don't fuck this up." She patted Nadim's shoulder reassuringly before turning and heading toward the front door. "C'mon inside. Duncan made venison chili."

After dinner, Duncan looked at Nadim, sizing him up again. "You look like a man who likes sports. I'm meeting some buddies to watch the CFL game at my friend's bar. Come along."

Nadim looked to Reena, clearly needing her to translate CFL.

"CFL is the Canadian Football League. Football like what North Americans call football, not soccer," she explained.

Nadim rolled his eyes. "You know, the rest of the world has another meaning of the word *football* so I don't get—"

"Nadim," Reena said as sweetly as she could. "Go with Duncan. He'll find you good beer and you can get to know each other."

~

"Well?" Reena asked once alone with Amira.

"He's cute in person. Actually, really cute. I love his accent."

"It's already sounding more Canadian. I caught him saying '*for sure*' the other day, and he's been calling kilometers '*clicks*' for a while now." Reena chuckled. "But is that all? Just cute?"

Amira tilted her head a moment. Reena knew her friend—she had a strong opinion about Nadim but, for whatever reason, didn't want to say it. Maybe to spare Reena's feelings? "He's affectionate. And he's really into you."

"I know." Reena smiled.

"And you're into him, aren't you?"

"It's early, but, yeah, I am. More than I have been for

anyone in a long time." She sighed as she put her feet up on Amira's coffee table. "I just wish it wasn't so ridiculously complicated."

"Is it really, though?"

"Of course! I mean, my parents are trying to set me up with him, and his dad's all like...marry this *good girl*, and I'm hardly that. Plus, the secrets—"

"No one can possibly know everything about a person a week into a relationship. And your parents...they seem okay with your choice *not* to marry him. You're not usually one to chase drama, Ree, but are you sure you're not finding problems that aren't really here?"

Reena folded her arms in front of her. First, Amira was all like, *this is complicated, don't date him,* and now she was accusing Reena of seeing drama that wasn't there? "That's a low blow, Meer, considering your rant on Monday morning."

"I know, I know. I'm just...wondering out loud. I hope you aren't using the drama as a scapegoat for why you're keeping him at arm's length."

"What? This isn't arm's length! I brought him here to meet you, didn't I?"

Amira just shrugged. "You admit you're both keeping secrets. My question is, why is that okay for you?"

She bit her lip. Objectively, Reena hated secrets, and in theory, yeah, it would be better if they were honest. But what could she do? They'd agreed to no strings and no past. Eventually, if this continued, Reena had every intention of letting him know about her insecurities and about her past depression. But for now, she just honestly didn't want to talk about it. And if he also had parts of his life he wanted to keep private, that was okay, too. She absently turned away from her friend, focusing on a shelf near the fireplace. A framed picture of a multihued sunset caught her eye. Amira, walking on the riverbank, with shades of orange, purple, and red framing her long, wavy hair.

"Duncan has a thing for sunsets." Amira smiled, noticing Reena's focus. "I didn't know that until we moved here."

"You two looked so cute sitting out there watching it."

The contented smile stayed on Amira's face as she glanced toward the porch. "I've never felt like this. Duncan and I have a lot of complications, too. I mean, now we have a mortgage, and he has two jobs, and I'm still dealing with sexist crap at work. Plus, his racist relatives hate that he's with a loudmouthed Muslim activist, and my Muslim extended family judges me for shacking up with a heathen without being married. But at the end of the day, we just sit out there and watch the sun for hours." She stood, silent for a moment, before walking over and picking up the picture. "I didn't know it could be like this. When all that noise quiets, it's breathtaking. So painfully honest. I'm going to be with him for the rest of my life. I know it."

A small tickle started behind Reena's eyes. A beautiful sentiment, especially from her once cynical friend. She didn't know if she had ever felt that strong a connection with anyone, let alone Nadim. And although she was happy Amira found it, a small part of her couldn't help but be sad that Amira's happiness took her away from Reena. She wouldn't be Amira's best friend anymore, not when Amira had a soul mate now.

She inhaled, straining to stop the torrent of emotions that threatened to pull her out of the warm comfort she'd been wrapped in all day. "Sunsets are fine and all, but how about we go out there and look at the stars? Without the city lights there must be millions visible."

Amira smiled. "Yes, night skies here are spectacular."

Amira and Reena were still sitting on the porch sofa with Reena's head on Amira's shoulder and a large blanket over them when Duncan and Nadim returned.

"Wow, look at that," Duncan said with a grin. "They look like the Golden Girls after they ate the whole cheesecake."

Amira laughed as she scooted over to let Duncan sit next to her. Reena did the same for Nadim, who immediately took her hand. "Well, you know," Amira said, "Reena and I were supposed to grow old together, so in about forty years I'll be kicking your sorry ass out so she can move in."

Duncan chuckled. "Fair enough. Nadim here now understands the basics of Canadian football, so at least I won't be lonely."

Nadim squeezed Reena's hand before lifting it to kiss her fingertips. Why couldn't she just enjoy this? She leaned into him, kissing his cheek before resting her head on his arm, watching thousands of stars light up the dark night.

CHAPTER TWENTY-FIVE

Doug and Shirley Galahad lived in a redbrick farmhouse on the outskirts of the tiny town of Omemee, Ontario, about fifteen minutes away from Amira and Duncan's place. Reena smiled at the scenery unfolding before her.

The brilliant yellows, oranges, and reds of the wooded area behind the old Victorian house, and the pale straw color of the neighboring farmer's fields combined with the azure sky would look frickin' awesome in their video. Shooting it here was the best idea she'd had in months.

Nadim whistled as he got out of the truck. "Bloody hell, this place is really picturesque. You grew up here?" he asked Duncan.

"Nah. We had a house in Omemee proper back then. They bought this place when my brother and I moved out."

The house was small, but cozy. With worn-wood floors and tall baseboards, it was steeped in the quaint country charm that felt so foreign to Reena but still as comforting as warm bread pudding.

"There you are, kids!" A short, plump woman with frizzy red hair and a wide smile greeted them in the kitchen. "I thought you were coming early?"

Duncan kissed his mother on the cheek. "It *is* early, Ma. It's nine o'clock."

"That's not early. I was up at seven to walk the dog. And the princesses were bleating and hopping all morning. Exhausting." Shirley reached up and patted Duncan's shoulder before hugging Amira, then Reena. She looked to Nadim. "Welcome to our home. I'm Shirley Galahad."

"I'm Nadim. Thank you for letting us film here. I'm sure the scenery will be amazing."

"Oh!" Shirley said. "You have an accent! Are you from England?"

"Tanzania originally, but I went to school in the UK."

"You and Reena have such a fascinating background. You know, we were in Turkey recently, and there was a mosque—"

"Ma, give 'em a minute to get in the door before bringing out the vacation pictures. Where's Dad?"

"In the barn, feeding the princesses," she told Duncan. "I'll put another pot of coffee on. Make yourselves at home." She smiled as she headed back into the kitchen.

"Princesses?" Nadim questioned as they made their way back outside.

"The goats," Reena responded. "Careful with your fingers. Apparently they nibble."

They found Doug in the barn. A strapping man with brown hair, he looked like he'd lived his life on this farm. After introducing himself, the princesses, and a Labrador retriever named Whiskey, Doug started chatting with his son about plans for upgrades to the building and the chicken coops, while Nadim scratched the dog behind his ears.

He dropped to his knees to get closer. "I miss my dogs in

Africa. We always had German shepherds. Technically guard dogs, but they were always such sweethearts." Interesting. Reena hadn't been allowed a dog growing up.

A loud voice from outside prevented her from analyzing this new information. "This place is cuter than a Fisher-Price farm."

Reena laughed. "Sounds like Shayne and Marley made it."

After another round of introductions and a round of coffee served with homemade muffins, they were finally able to set up the barn. Doug found a large wooden folding table, which they placed in the middle of the room and covered with a cream linen tablecloth. A single-burner butane stove would suffice for cooking the egg curry, and Reena had brought her enormous wood chopping board for food prep. Marley added a few artfully arranged kitchen tools she snagged from Shirley's kitchen and some cut flowers in old pottery, while Shayne plugged in the studio lights.

"Ready," he said. "Go change, and then we can start initial shots of you two with the chickens and goats before we start cooking."

For Nadim's outfit, they'd picked a cream cable-knit fisherman's sweater and paired it with his well-worn jeans. For Reena, dark skinny jeans and gray boots (thankfully her own this time), paired with a subtly embroidered teal cotton kurta-style top and a worn gray denim jacket. After a quick touch-up of makeup and a de-frizz of her hair, they were ready.

"Action!" Shayne yelled once they were in place.

"Howdy, folks!" Nadim said with a definite country drawl. Reena raised one brow at him.

"What?" he said, clearly hamming a bit for the camera. "When in Rome, right?"

"We're not in Rome," Reena said, looking directly at the camera. "But we are far from home! First, thank you to all the viewers who voted for us in round one. We're excited to be in round two because the theme is farm-to-table!"

"So, we put a big table in the middle of a farm!" Nadim said, cheerily. "My beautiful bride-to-be here is going to teach me how to make a dish my grandmother made for me as a child—Zanzibar egg curry. But first, I'm going to teach her how to collect fresh eggs."

"Wait, you're going to teach me what? I thought the farm people would just…give us eggs." She now questioned Nadim's insistence that they not rehearse this bit. She didn't know she'd have to touch chickens. "How do *you* know how to collect eggs?"

"I'm a renaissance man. C'mon." He picked up a basket and motioned her over to the corner of the barn where the chickens were. Shayne followed, carrying the camera.

"My boarding school in England had a chicken coop. We used to gather eggs all the time. It's easy. Here, I'll bet this pretty lady has an egg or two under her."

Reena frowned, looking at the pretty lady in question. A shiny black bird with angry eyes and a red comb on her head, she was sitting in one of the nest boxes, scowling at them. At least that's what it looked like. Unless she had resting-bitch chicken face.

"There are eggs here. We don't have to bother her," Reena said, indicating the neighboring chicken-less nest box, which had a few eggs nestled in hay in it. She picked up one gingerly and placed it in Nadim's basket.

"Her name's Agatha," Duncan called out from behind Shayne.

"Cut!" Shayne turned and glared at Duncan. "Can you maybe, *not*, speak when I'm filming?"

Amira laughed loudly, pulling Duncan further away from the others.

"I thought you'd need the chicken's name," Duncan said. "Careful, though. Agatha's a bit frisky."

Reena put her hand on her hips and turned to Nadim. "See! That's why you shouldn't stick your hand under her butt."

"Oh, I am absolutely not sticking my hand under her butt. You are."

Before Reena could object again, Shayne yelled, "Action!"

"It's easy," Nadim said. "Just reach under her and take out the egg. She won't bite."

"She probably *will* bite," Duncan yelled from the other end of the barn. Shayne motioned for Duncan to shut it but didn't stop filming.

"If she does bite, it won't hurt. Just a peck. Trust me," Nadim said.

Reena reached in. "Okay. I'm not going to hurt you, Agatha," she murmured, skimming the bird's soft plumage. "I just want your egg…you don't need it. It's not fertilized so I'm not stealing your baby. Just slide over a bit and—"

It was at that moment that Reena began questioning her life's choices. Because being recorded for a national cooking show while getting pecked at with vigor by an angry chicken named Agatha, while her fake fiancé/real boyfriend howled in laughter seemed like a situation that could have been avoided with a bit of forethought.

Shayne finally took some pity on Reena and yelled, "Cut! That was awesome footage! Let's move on to cooking."

Reena rubbed her hand. Nadim had been honest, at least. It didn't really hurt that much. Only her pride was wounded.

"Let me just get the eggs." Nadim reached into Agatha's box and pulled out two eggs. "Thanks, beautiful." He put the eggs in the basket and rubbed the chicken on her back. Agatha practically cooed.

Figured. That irresistible charm even worked on chickens.

He kissed Reena's cheek. "And thanks for being such a good sport, even more beautiful."

And Reena cooed probably more than the damn chicken.

No one was pecked or injured in the cooking segment, much to Reena's relief. Nadim diced the onions, then peeled the potatoes and hard-boiled eggs while Reena explained to the camera the origins of the egg curry they were preparing.

She then dry roasted and pounded the spices, while Nadim talked about spice farms in Zanzibar, and his grandmother's home there.

"I've always wanted to go," Reena said.

"I'd love to take you. The sunsets are incredible. The markets in old town are so charming, and the spice farms! You'd be in heaven. That's it, honeymoon decided. What do you say?" He winked at her.

Reena didn't know if the wink was a reminder to her that this was all fake. If it was, she didn't need it. Nothing that felt this good could really happen to her.

"That would be perfect," she said. "Here, taste." Tearing off a small piece of flaky paratha, she used it to break open the egg and scoop a bite with a little egg, potato, tomato, and fed it into Nadim's willing mouth. He smiled as the flavors hit his tongue.

"Well," she said, bumping her hip on his thigh, "how did I do? Does it taste like your grandmother's back home?"

"No," he said, grinning. "Better. It tastes like my new home." He looked to the camera and hammed it up a bit more. "Local ingredients married perfectly with my beloved African spices. Maybe home is not just one place, but a moving target. Home is where I'm welcomed. And right now, I've never felt more welcomed than right here." He planted a quick kiss on Reena's lips, before turning to face the camera again. "Thank you!"

Reena waved at the camera as she rested her head on Nadim's arm. "Bye!"

"Cut!" Shayne said.

~

A few hours later, Reena sat alone on the bed in the guest room at Amira and Duncan's house. She'd escaped supposedly to change into a more comfortable shirt, but she couldn't muster up enough energy to lift her arms over her head. Amira, Duncan, Nadim, Marley, and Shayne were all downstairs, crowding around Shayne's laptop, watching him do his editing magic with the footage from the farm. The bits Reena saw before she had to leave the room were amazing. Perfect. The food looked divine, the scenery breathtaking, and even Agatha the chicken attacking her was charming. Reena and Nadim looked so happy and so in sync with each other. Aspirational. Everyone would want to be the couple on the screen.

And it disturbed her that she desperately wanted to be them, too.

"Hey. Ree. You okay?" Amira stood in the doorway.

"Yeah." Reena ran her fingers over her hair. "I'm fine."

Amira smiled gently and came into the room. She sat on the bed with Reena.

"You guys looked great on the screen. This one turned out even better than the last one," Amira said.

Reena shrugged. "I know. But man, watching that messed with my mind."

"Hearing him say you feel like home?"

"Yeah." She sighed. "The first one stung to watch because it seemed real, even though we weren't actually together. He's a good actor. This time..." Her voice trailed off.

"This time all that talk might be real."

"Yep."

Amira was silent a moment. "What's next?"

"If we move on, we go to the FoodTV studio."

"You are moving on. Seriously. The Jeffs have nothing on you."

Reena shrugged.

"What, you don't want to go to the studio? You wanted this."

"I know. I do. It's just..." She sighed. "I know we're supposed to be just casually 'dating' and not seriously committed, but this damn contest is making it feel so much more real. And we've only done short videos. If we go to the studio, we'll have to pretend for longer and in front of real people. I'm not sure I can recover from that."

"Do you want to be seriously committed?"

"I don't know. Even if I did, it's impossible. Those two on the screen have a happy, loving relationship with a full life in front of them. They don't have our...crap."

"Everyone has crap. Life is full of piles and piles of shit.

I told you last night about everything Duncan and I still deal with."

"I know."

"But the difference is, we let each other see the shit."

"This metaphor is getting a little gross."

Amira laughed. "Reena, this *could* work for you! Watching you two together, the way he looks at you. It's not like any of your other relationships. And I think you know that. But I can't be the only person in the world who gets to see you...*all* of you. You won't scare him away."

Wouldn't she, though? The Reena she let people see enjoyed drinks at the bar, fresh bread at home, and no drama. Who'd want the real Reena—the neurotic mess with maladaptive coping skills? Who couldn't manage to keep a job she hated? With a family who never, ever let her be free. None of the other twelve guys had been interested in sticking around once her true self began to emerge.

Amira didn't say anything for a while as she looked at Reena with a soft expression. "Reena, are you in love?"

Loaded question. She didn't know if she even knew the answer to that one.

She squeezed her lips together. "I don't know."

"I know your impulse is always to deflect and distract, but I think you need to stop doing that. Give him a chance. Give yourself a chance." Amira took both Reena's hands in her own. "You deserve it. Even though I know you don't think you do."

CHAPTER TWENTY-SIX

One week later Reena was still no closer to gainful employ-ment. She didn't hear about the Top Crust job, but she also didn't hear from her mother about her unemployment or Mum's covert gambling habits, so Reena considered it a draw.

Nadim still came straight to Reena's apartment every day after work to kiss her with knee-weakening intensity, before retreating to his place to change clothes. They ate dinner to-gether every night and cooked together several times. And each night was spent together in his bed. Reena swore she'd lost three pounds thanks to bedroom exertions alone, and her skin had never been clearer. In fact, she'd wondered what she'd been thinking when she'd decided that celibacy was a good idea— her body and her mind were just kinder to her when she was sexually satiated.

But, of course, she and Nadim didn't talk. Not really. Not about the past, or the future. Amira's voice in her ear was persistent in reminding her that all this was wrong. It was wrong to spend so much time with him without ever talking about their future. It was wrong to sleep with him every night without knowing how he really felt about her.

It was wrong to be in love with him without ever telling him. If she was in love, that is. She honestly didn't know.

But if Reena was good at anything, it was ignoring the voices in her head that told her the path she was on was covered with snakes that would bite her in the ass one day.

Late Thursday night they were in bed when a Google Alert told her the standings after the farm-to-table round were live. The video had gone up Monday morning, and there had been three days of voting. She opened the page right away.

Nadim leaned over her, practically blocking her view of the phone in her hand. "What does it say? Are we getting an all-expenses-paid trip to Toronto this weekend?"

"Did you forget we live in Toronto?"

"Shush. We'd still be getting a night in a posh hotel downtown. Did we make it? I want that FoodTV studio tour!" He tried grabbing the phone out of her hand.

She swatted him away. "You're like a toddler sometimes."

"Half hour ago, you said I was all the man you wanted." He crowded up against her, deliberately pressing his hardening penis against her leg.

Yum.

"If you had faster Wi-Fi, this conversation wouldn't be happening and we'd already know if we made it to the next round," she said.

He looked at her with that mischievous grin that was too damn appealing. "You're right," he said, plucking her phone out of her hand. "Which leads me to wonder if this time waiting for it to load would be better spent." He tossed the phone to the other side of the bed and lowered his lips to hers.

It was a good while before Reena managed to actually check the standings. But she wasn't complaining. And she certainly wasn't complaining when she saw they were in second place, only a dozen votes below the Jeffs. They were moving on to the semifinals.

~

Marley dressed Reena simply for the studio, a pink T-shirt and long yellow pleated skirt with platform sneakers. Thankfully, it was still unseasonably warm for late September, and the skies were a perfect blue again. Ideal picnic weather. Reena had been a complete ball of nerves leading up to the day, but Nadim's firm hand on the small of her back gave her the strength she needed as they walked into the low-rise TV studio downtown. After checking in at security, they were led to an outdoor courtyard space behind the building. A handsome man dressed completely in black and wearing an audio headset greeted them.

"Reena and Nadim! Welcome! Wow, you two have the exact same energy you have in your videos. Makes our job easy, to be honest." The man was East Asian and had unbridled enthusiasm along with high cheekbones and full lips. Reena liked him instantly. "I'm Anderson Lin," he said. "So great to finally meet you."

Tic Tac ears! Reena grinned, struggling to resist conspicuously looking at the man's earlobes. Then she remembered that this delightful young thing had dumped Shayne, which meant she had also had to start resisting the urge to outwardly glare at him.

Nadim, thankfully, had no scruples and behaved like a perfect gentleman. "We're thrilled to be here!" He shook Anderson's hand. "I never imagined we would get this far when we made that drunken bhajias video."

"That video was epic," Anderson said. "I can't believe it was unplanned. You two were made for the screen. Let me take you to meet the other contestants. Then we'll get you set up at your station."

The courtyard wasn't huge, but it was full of people and camera equipment. Four small cooking stations had been set up in the middle of the space, each with a two-burner cooktop and a gas grill. Off to the side, big tables were piled high with ingredients for the challenge. Reena peeked and saw pretty much what they'd told her to expect. Fruits, vegetables, and several different cuts of meat.

The other three pairs who had made it to the semifinals were the Jeffs, the front-runners from Winnipeg; Nate and Amanda, a Black couple from a small town north of Vancouver; and Luc and Renée, a white francophone couple from suburban Montréal. Reena had been pleased when she saw who was in the semifinals, although a touch disappointed for Hala and Maya, the Syrian mother-and-daughter team, who were also from Toronto.

The others were as nice and supportive and pleasant as they had been in their videos. After a bit of small talk with them, Anderson brought Reena and Nadim to their station.

"We'll go over the rules for everyone in just a minute, but first Lana will be coming by with a makeup kit. She'll do a quick touch-up—these high-definition cameras can be a little uncharitable, so you'll want powder."

Anderson suddenly stepped closer to Reena and Nadim. "But while we're alone...I know this is a bit awkward...I am not sure you know that I know...actually used to date your friend Shayne."

Shit. This was it. The end of the charade. Anderson, of

course, knew Shayne and knew this engagement was fake. Damnit. Why hadn't she anticipated this? Reena tensed, not sure if it would be better to come clean, or to double down. Nadim put his arm around her waist. It appeared he intended to double down.

"So," Anderson continued, leaning closer to Reena, "this is probably not my place, but..."

She wasn't getting the Asler scholarship. She was going to be disqualified. Humiliated. Sent home with nothing but a security tag with a bad computer printout of her face.

Anderson smiled sadly. "Is Shayne...you know...dating anyone right now? I mean, like, seriously dating?"

Reena blinked. He wasn't going to expose them? All Anderson wanted was to maybe hook up with Shayne again?

She was relieved but knew she couldn't tell Shayne about Anderson's fact-finding here. What would happen if Reena and Nadim won the whole thing, and Shayne and Anderson became a couple again? Anderson would realize his boyfriend's friends weren't actually engaged or married. Reena would have to stop hanging out with Shayne, which would mean seeing less of Marley. A family rift would start, and she wouldn't be able to explain to Mum why she could no longer go to Marley's parents for their annual Eid party, and—

Nadim leaned in and whispered in her ear, "Don't worry, this is fine."

Reena exhaled. Anderson was still watching her with an adorable, hopeful expression. He ran his hand through his hair. "I just...well, I mean, with the contest I need to stay fair, so I won't call him now. But..." He looked away, a slight tremble on his lower lip. "You ever get scared when something fits a little too perfectly? Like maybe it's just not humanly possible for something to work so well, so you look for problems that aren't there?"

Reena blinked at Anderson, not sure she liked this mirror put up in front of her.

"Shayne's really into you," she said. "You should talk to him."

Anderson bit his lip. "I will, I will. Just...do me a favor—don't tell him what I said here. I need to figure out how to fix things. Oh, here's Lana!"

Saved by the makeup artist.

Lana was chatty, too. As she brushed powder on Reena's nose, she said, "You two make a cute couple. How'd you meet?"

"Through my parents," Reena said, relieved she could tell the truth.

"Cute! They set you up?"

"Yep," Nadim answered.

"Have you set a wedding date yet?"

"Not yet. Reena wants a big Indian wedding, so there is a lot to plan."

Reena raised a brow, which elicited a censorious frown from Lana, who had moved on to touching up Reena's eye makeup. "No, I don't," Reena said.

"Sure, you said you wanted a designer salwar and full mehndi."

"Yeah, but that doesn't mean a big wedding. I can wear full mehndi to city hall if I want to. If we have a huge wedding, you'd have to invite all your friends and family from London and Tanzania."

"And why would that be a problem? I'd want to invite them. It's *my* wedding," Nadim said.

"Really? After the way they treated you? And do you really think all your bougie rich-snob friends would even come?" Okay, that wasn't very nice of her, but she was annoyed he thought she'd want a big wedding. Didn't he know her better than that?

"How do you know my friends are bougie rich-snobs? You've never met any of them. I've never even told you about any of them."

She knew they were bougie rich-snobs because she'd seen that picture on a yacht. And she'd seen Jasmine Shah with them—and from everything she knew about Jasmine, the descriptor was accurate.

Reena folded her arms on her chest. "Well, a big giant Indian wedding with hundreds of our fathers' business contacts isn't what I want—and you should have known that."

"How could I know something you've never told me?"

This was a mistake. Reena had been worrying about faking this engagement in person for days, and yet it had never occurred to her that she and Nadim should have their stories straight before bringing this farce to the real world.

What was this makeup artist thinking right now? And, crap, could the cameras be on them? This wasn't supposed to be a drama-heavy reality show, but could this argument cost them the semifinals? That's when Reena noticed Lana wasn't even at their station anymore.

"Where'd she go?" Reena asked.

Nadim scanned the room. "There," he said, chuckling. "Looks like she fled during our spat. Nice job on that, by the way. Only a real couple could argue that well."

Reena squeezed her eyes shut. And they weren't a *real couple*.

"Hello, contestants!" a voice bellowed. It came from an official-looking woman wearing a headset similar to Anderson's. "Welcome to the semifinals of the cook-off! I'm Cindy—you've all been in contact with me over email going over today's events. Just a reminder of the rules: Each team will be able to grab whatever ingredients you need from the front tables. You were all given a list of what would be available, and there are no surprises. And as mentioned, you were allowed to bring your own spices, seasonings, and specialty ingredients. You will then have one hour to create a picnic meal from start to finish at your own station. The camera people will walk around to catch all of you. The show's host, chef Michelle Finlay, will be visiting each station, asking questions. Remember, voting will still be done by home viewers—no one here will judge you. It's about how the food looks and how you present yourself on camera. Are you ready, contestants?"

No, Reena wasn't. After that fake (or was it real?) lovers' spat, Reena's mind was racing again. She took a deep breath. They'd practiced their picnic menu in the backyard of Shayne's house only yesterday. She could do this. It was all comfort food she could make with her eyes closed.

They were making grilled naan, chicken tikka skewers, grilled corn on the cob with chili and lime, and kachumber salad—classic picnic food, as far as she was concerned. The chicken wouldn't be as good as if she'd had more time to marinate it, but when they'd practiced it using the freshest spices available, it was still tasty. And the naan would have less time for the yeast to ferment, which worked fine for a flatbread.

She needed to stay focused. With cameras on them, and the other teams surrounding them, it was no wonder her nerves were so high. Not to mention being severely shaken up by an argument with her boyfriend/fiancé/whatever who just claimed *none of this was real.*

Nadim seemed fine, though. Charming grin, spring in his step. He winked at her the moment headset lady gave the go-ahead to get their ingredients. And he kissed her cheek right before they started cooking.

So, Reena kept going. Pretended this was all real.

But it wasn't easy. Within minutes of starting, Reena cut herself with her chef's knife. She was able to wave down Anderson to get a bandage while Nadim took over duties requiring sharp implements.

She was putting the corn on the grill when the chef and camera crew arrived together.

"And here are our lovebirds! You know, you two have been so popular, I heard someone is creating actual fan-fiction of your wedding! How are you feeling going into the semifinals as crowd favorites? Pressure getting to you?"

Nadim grinned. "It's like any other day cooking with my love."

Michelle grinned. Reena had always liked Michelle Finley and had been excited to learn she would be the chef host for today.

"Tell us, Reena, why have you chosen to grill the corn with the husk off? Won't the kernels get dried out?"

Thankfully, they'd expected this question. "This is how corn is cooked on streets in India and in East Africa. That's where both Nadim and my family are from. The kernels are a little dryer this way, but I think the flavor is more concentrated. And after I sprinkle it with chili and lime, I guarantee, you'll never want to grill corn with the husk on again." She smiled as she turned the cobs using large tongs.

"Indo-East African cuisine seems to be a common thread between you two."

Nadim grinned. "Completely. It feels like a relief to be committed to someone who not only comes from the same corner of the world as me, but who also understands that these recipes, passed down from our mothers and grandmothers, are like the cornerstone of our culture."

"So, you think you two are so great together because of your shared cultural background?"

He laughed. "No! Not only. But we do have that bond. Honestly, I think food is why we work so well. I love being with someone who loves cooking and eating as much as I do. It feels like home, you know?"

"You two are an inspiration. If you win this thing, I'm going to insist the network give you a show dispensing relationship advice while cooking."

Reena managed not to cringe. The thought of her giving anyone relationship advice was so laughable. And them together— the only advice they could give was how to grift others to win free cooking courses.

Because, as Nadim told her, this wasn't *real*.

"Whoops!" Michelle pointed at the grill. "Smells like your corn might be a little too blackened. I'll leave you for now, but I'll be back to see what happens with that chicken!"

Sure enough, the corn was almost completely black on one side. Reena sighed as she turned the cobs around. Nadim's hand landed on her waist.

"I screwed up," Reena said.

"It's okay. We'll serve it blackened side down."

They managed the rest of the hour with no more burned food or broken skin, and Reena felt better about their finished meal. She still worried that her little screwup with the corn might cost them votes, but after peeking at the other contestants' finished picnics, she saw that theirs weren't all picture-perfect, either.

After the filming, all the contestants met up for a giant picnic to taste the food they'd prepared. This was followed by a tour of the FoodTV studios, and finally a five-star tasting meal at a top restaurant. Reena thoroughly enjoyed herself. The other contestants were charmingly supportive of one another and so damn nice that she hoped they would some-how all win. The Jeffs were particularly delightful, and Reena was stoked that Jeff Gryzbowski even shared his recipe for the Polish baked cabbage they'd made in round two. Like good polite Canadians, no one asked intrusive questions, and it didn't feel like she and Nadim were faking anything—because they weren't. They might not actually be engaged, but they felt like a couple.

After dinner, they all went to the cocktail lounge in the hotel lobby to chat some more. All in all, it was a great evening with her boyfriend. She realized then just how much she wanted to keep him.

～

On the way up the elevator to their room after leaving the bar, Reena smiled at Nadim.

"I had fun tonight," she said.

"Yeah, me too. Man, you Canadians, though. I was so ready to throw down and be competitive, but everyone was so...pleasant. Cooperative." He chuckled.

"I think they only picked nice people." She squeezed her hands together. "I mean it, though...I know you're doing all this as a favor for me, but...I'm glad you are. I'm enjoying doing this contest with you."

"I'm having fun, too." He kissed her briefly.

There was more she needed to say, but she didn't know how. She wanted to tell him that hanging out with other people, pretending they had a future, letting others think they were in love, felt right to her. Didn't feel fake. She wanted to ask him how it felt for him.

But when they walked into their room on the twentieth floor, she was speechless. The curtains on the floor-to-ceiling windows were open, and the CN Tower was illuminated brightly like a beacon in a night sky dotted with glimmering lights. As a lifelong city girl, the nonstop cacophony of cars and movement soothed Reena. This was a magical night. She couldn't risk popping this bubble with difficult conversations. She walked to the window and looked out.

Nadim came up behind her. "Quite the view," he murmured. "Toronto is so beautiful at night."

Reena nodded, leaning back against him.

"I love the hum of cities," she said.

Nadim wrapped his arms around her waist. "The honking cars, drunk screams, and sirens are oddly comforting."

She chuckled. "You've pretty much always lived in cities, right?"

He shook his head. "No, not really. Yes, in Dar es Salaam,

and in London, but my private school was in the English countryside. And, of course, I had holidays and such."

"Do you think you always would *want* to live in a city?"

"Not sure. I used to think so." His arms tightened around her. "I wanted the fast life. Wild parties and free-flowing drinks."

And hot women. And yachts. Night and day from his life now. Reena wiggled free of his grip and went to open her bag.

"Why did you want that from your life back then?" she asked slowly. She regretted saying it almost immediately. She looked at him, but his facial expression was closed. He didn't want to talk about the past, not now.

He removed his T-shirt and walked toward her, close enough that she could feel the heat radiating off his bare chest even through her sweater. He grazed a kiss on her neck. He took a step back, and achingly slowly pulled her sweater up and off. "I was looking for home, I think. I wasn't finding it, though." He turned her around and nudged her forward, positioning her so her arms were outstretched above her head and resting on the wall. He kissed the back of her neck as his hand trailed down her spine. "My soul knows when I'm home," he murmured.

His hand trailed lower to unhook her bra strap, guiding her arms down to let her bra fall to the floor.

She shivered as the cool air kissed her naked chest. He finally turned her around and engulfed her body in his, sharing his warmth, and kissing with what felt like every muscle in his body.

The sex felt different that night. Slower. Agonizingly tender. She lost herself in the sensations. The smells, the sounds, the feel of his body around her, under her, in her. Just him.

This man, who had been dropped into her life at the wrong time in the wrong way, but who ended up being everything she needed.

It wasn't until afterward, when they still lay clutched together, still joined and floating back to the world, that she untangled her thoughts and emotions enough to see the truth. This *was* *real*. No matter what he said. And she *was* in love with him.

And it was high time to figure out if he felt the same way.

CHAPTER TWENTY-SEVEN

Reena was feeling weirdly optimistic on the drive back to the apartment Sunday morning. It was early—she hadn't been able to get out of Sunday brunch with her family, but she and Nadim planned to make dinner together later. She was ready to talk to him. To tell him she was in this relationship deep and she didn't want there to be secrets between them anymore. And she wanted to go fully public with it, even bring him to brunch next weekend. It was time to fight past her instinct to deflect and distract, and live her life.

After dropping him back at the building, she drove straight to her parents' house, where she was surprised to see an extra car in the driveway. Strange. Before she made it into the house, the door opened and her sister rushed out in her stocking feet, pulling a confused Ashraf behind her.

"Saira, what's wrong?"

Saira beamed. "Nothing's wrong. Everything is good. Better than good, in fact. Ashraf proposed! I'm getting married, Reena!"

Saira tackle-hugged her, while Reena stood frozen in shock. Saira, engaged? And hugging her?

After a few seconds Reena smiled and hugged her sister back. "You're happy?" she asked in Saira's ear.

"Yes. Very. This is what I want."

Reena grinned, letting go of her sister and hugging Ashraf. "Welcome to the insanity."

"I am happy to be here," he said awkwardly.

Saira beamed and put her arm around his waist. "He asked me last night. Mum was so excited she screamed when we told her."

Reena took her sister's hand to look closer at the ring, a standard white-gold solitaire that looked perfect on Saira's long fingers. After squeezing her hand, she looked into her sister's eyes, surprised to see them glassy with tears. "I'm happy you're happy," Reena assured her.

"So . . ." Saira's gaze shifted down to their locked hands. "Then we're good, right? I want you to be my maid of honor."

Wow. Could she do that? She wanted things to be good with her sister. Wanted to let go of the resentment she'd felt for the last year—longer, if she was honest. But could she just take all that bitterness and resentment and boil it off, leaving nothing behind but the sweet sisterly bond she always wanted? Maybe, with work. Doing this for her sister could be the first step. She could face it, instead of deflecting. She squeezed her sister's hands again before letting it go. "I'd be honored to stand with you. What did Dad say?"

"Not much." Saira shrugged. "He's in a pissy mood about something to do with his project. As usual, business first, family later." She turned toward Ashraf, who was standing quietly behind her. "Don't ever be like that."

He shook his head. "You know I wouldn't."

Saira smiled widely, pulled him back into the house. "Let's go face the wolves."

They went inside to find Mum and Dad at the table.

"Reena! Did you hear your sister's news! Ashraf, sit..." Mum motioned to the seat near hers.

Mum's and Saira's happiness were infectious, and Reena couldn't help but soak it in as Saira told the story of Ashraf surprising her in her favorite sushi restaurant.

Dad sat quietly while the three women in the family gushed over Saira's ring, talked about wedding clothes, and made plans for bridal sari shopping. Finally, Reena looked at her father. She would have thought he would at least be a little happy his youngest daughter was engaged, and to a good Muslim man this time. A nice, sensible, management-type. Really everything Dad wanted in a son-in-law.

"What's going on, Dad?" Reena asked him. "Saira said you have a work issue?"

"Yes. A disaster, really." He sighed. "We can't trust anyone these days. I hate being lied to."

Shit. Had someone swindled Dad again? "Who lied to you?"

"Shiroz, Nadim's father. Seems the rumors I heard about Nadim were true."

Oh, shit. Dad found out about the yacht people.

Reena bit her lip. She needed to minimize this. She decided to tell the truth, or what she knew to be true, at least. She wanted a future with Nadim, and a future should only start with honesty. "Yeah, I know, Dad. He hung out with a bad crowd in London. But it's no big deal. I mean, who cares who his old friends were?"

"What!" Dad yelled. "You knew about his connection to Jasmine Shah and you didn't tell me?"

"It's not my place to tell someone else's business."

"This is *our* business!" Dad said, still extremely agitated. "You know my feelings about that family, and I specifically asked you who he was connected with. I am disappointed that Shiroz kept this from me, but my own daughter?"

"Jesus, Dad." She shook her head. "You need to let go of your obsession with the Shahs. Yeah, he was at a party with Jasmine Shah, but that doesn't mean he can never work for you."

Dad gritted his teeth. "If that's all you think his relationship with the Shahs was, then he's been lying to you, too. Nadim wasn't just at a *party* with the Shahs, he *worked* for Salim Shah. The new Shah project that failed spectacularly? It was because of Nadim. And Nadim Remtulla has been engaged to *marry* Jasmine Shah for a year, at least."

Engaged? *Marry?*

The walls of her parents' dining room closed in on her as all the air seemed to be sucked out of her lungs.

Her Nadim... *engaged*...

"Oh, shit," Saira said.

"Saira! Language!" Mum snapped.

Engaged, engaged, engaged. Planning to wed. Betrothed. To the daughter of her father's rival. The daughter of his previous boss, it seemed. Nadim was a fraud. The worst kind of player. She was nothing to him.

"Reena, you okay?" someone said.

Saira stood over her, hand heavy on Reena's shoulder.

Was she okay?

"Why would Reena be upset?" Mum asked. "You should be worried about your father, not her."

Saira stood up. "Of course Reena's upset! You just told her that her boyfriend is engaged to someone else!"

"What?" Dad bellowed, standing. "Nadim is not your boy-friend! You said you wouldn't marry him!"

"How can he marry Reena if he's engaged to Jasmine Shah?" Mum asked.

She wasn't going to marry him. But she was in love with him. Reena blinked, not sure if any of this was really happening.

"Why the hell are you two ragging on her?" Saira said. "You've been pushing them together since he moved here! You practically demanded she marry the man, and now he turns out to be a wannabe polygamist, and you're blaming Reena?"

Dad looked furious, but Reena didn't care.

Engaged...

"Enough!" Dad slammed his fist on the table, making Ashraf and Mum jump backward. "I can't have a man with Nadim's reputation working for me, which means I will lose Shiroz's investment in the Diamond project. Nadim betrayed my trust, and I will not have him anywhere near my company, or my family."

"We are very disappointed in you, Reena," Mum added. "Why would you take up with the boy behind our back? Why so many secrets? Don't you care about this family?"

What the hell did they want her to say? That she hadn't asked him about his past and instead listened to apparently incomplete gossip? That she hadn't been willing to be honest with him, so she let him keep secrets from her?

That she wasn't surprised that the first time she thought a relationship was *real*, it turned out to be a giant illusion.

Reena was disgusted with herself. He actually gave her a *fake* ring, and he never pretended it was anything more. Only she did. This was all on her.

Bile rose from the bottom of her throat. She dug this pit herself, and she wished she could bury herself in it.

"That's it," Saira snapped. "I'm not listening to one more word of this. Do you even hear yourself, Mum? Reena not caring about the family? Can't you see what she's going through?" Saira put her arm back on Reena's shoulder and clutched tightly. "Do you two remember what happened when I found Joran with that woman? You were going on about what people would say and ordering me not to tell anyone, and you"— she pointed at Dad—"were going on about how this wouldn't have happened if I'd gone with a good Muslim boy. Reena was the only person in this whole screwed-up family who realized I was in pain. For once in your life, have some goddamn compassion." Saira pulled Reena up by the arm and picked up her purse. "I will not stand around and watch this…C'mon, Reena. Ashraf, get us out of here."

Shaking, Reena gave Ashraf the keys to her car once they were outside, well aware that she was in no state to drive. She opened her backseat, sat down, and buckled the seat belt.

Saira sat in the front passenger seat, talking quietly to Ashraf, who gently stroked her arm. "Sorry," Saira said, turning to look at Reena. "I kinda lost it. I'm not sure that helped at all, but I couldn't deal with them anymore. How're you doing?"

How was she doing? She put her hands over her face, rubbing it to reassemble all the pieces that scattered when Dad said Nadim was engaged.

"I'm fine. Not like I've never been dumped." She closed her eyes, willing away the deep throb that had settled between her brows.

"Jesus Christ, Reena, I don't think I'll ever understand you. The asshole was engaged the whole time! Don't say you're fine! Be upset! Feel this stuff!"

Ashraf started the car. "Where am I going?" he asked.

"Just take me home," Reena said.

"Fine," Saira said, nodding to Ashraf. "But we're staying to run interference in case the dickhead shows up."

But Nadim wasn't there when they got to the building. Or at least, his car wasn't there. And Reena wasn't feeling generous enough to wonder where the fuck he had gone.

Ashraf and Saira spoke softly to each other as soon as they were in Reena's apartment. He kissed Saira on the forehead and left, with a sad smile to Reena.

"He has to work," Saira said.

Reena shrugged, lowering herself onto the sofa.

Saira sat next to her. "What a fucking tool. You had no idea? Did you know he worked for Salim Shah at least?"

Reena shook her head. "No." A tear escaped her eye. She rubbed it away. Fuck. She needed a drink.

"Ugh. I hate men. Should I call Amira or Khizar? I'm sure you want someone better than me to talk to."

"Amira." Reena's brain wasn't working right, but Amira would tell her what to do.

Saira opened a video call on her own phone, and Amira answered with a concerned voice. "Saira. What's wrong?"

"Reena's in crisis. She's here, hang on." She passed the phone so Reena could see the worried face of her best friend.

"What happened, Ree? You okay?"

"Yeah. Just…at brunch…" Her voice cracked.

Saira took the phone back and spoke into it. "Nadim is

a lying cheater. He's been engaged to the daughter of Dad's nemesis for a year."

"What. The. Fuck?!"

Reena leaned back and closed her eyes. She'd woken up so happy in Nadim's arms in that hotel room. He had kissed her leisurely at dawn before moving on to rub her feet. That was just a few hours ago. Now, she had no idea if she would ever see him again.

Reena closed her eyes while Saira told Amira everything she knew. Which, admittedly, wasn't a whole lot.

And none of it really mattered except that he was engaged. And that he had lied to her.

"I'm on my way, Ree," Amira said the moment Saira got to the part about Nadim's engagement. "Give me about two hours."

"Amira, don't." She took the phone from Saira. "You have to work tomorrow. By the time you get here you'll have to turn around to go home. I'm fine." She was not fine.

"It's not you I'm coming to see. It's that snake. I'll kill him with my bare hands."

"It's okay, Amira," Saira said, taking the phone back. "I'm already here. I'll pour sugar in his gas tank or something. That's a thing, right? Ashraf offered to disable his phone service remotely. I know it's not the flashiest revenge, but it's the thought that counts."

"Enough, guys," Reena said. She didn't want revenge. She rested her head back and closed her eyes. She didn't even want to think about this right now. All she wanted was to escape to a world where none of it was happening.

"Saira," Amira said. "Make her sleep. She probably got very

little last night, and she's in no state to think clearly right now. Turn her phone off and lock the door until the snake leaves town or falls off a cliff or something. Get some rest, Ree. Don't think about him...we'll talk tonight. We got you."

Don't think about him. Easier said than done. But she nodded and let Saira help her get into bed. And miraculously, once her head hit the pillow, Reena fell into that blissful state of oblivion where everything was fine and her life wasn't a cataclysmic mess.

CHAPTER TWENTY-EIGHT

Reena slept for only about half an hour, then floated through the rest of the day in a blur. Saira stayed, saying it was to run interference in case Nadim appeared. But her sister also curated a list of Bollywood movies for Reena, stating that these specific films would help with heartbreak. They got through two epic tearjerkers before Saira left and Reena went back to bed.

But despite the existential exhaustion, sleep eluded her. She didn't toss and turn, or squirm and yawn, rather she just lay there, staring into the darkness, wondering how her life had gone so spectacularly wrong.

She hadn't had one of these nights in a long time. The type of night she had sworn off years ago when she discovered a few shots of vodka numbed her self-loathing enough to get some sleep.

Somewhere around Reena's fifth or sixth breakup, she'd made a conscious decision not to let her failed relationships get to her anymore. After all, she had enough to fret about in the other areas of her life, so why worry about her love life, too? She didn't even cry after Jamil broke up with her, and they had been together for over eighteen months. She had loved his quirky hobbies and gregarious personality. And nothing over Eddie or Carlos, either.

But nothing about her short relationship with Nadim felt like any of the others. And, of course, this time the betrayal felt worse, too. No one had ever kept something so huge from her.

But Reena didn't get a shot of vodka to help her sleep. Strangely, she didn't want to numb the pain—she wanted to feel it this time. Like she needed penance for getting herself in this mess.

She tossed around and ended up facing her large mirrored closet door. Illuminated only by the faint streetlight through the window, she saw her reflection. And she couldn't help but cringe at it.

She couldn't lie to herself anymore. This wasn't just about losing Nadim. She had been fighting this angst long before she planted herself on his lap to finally kiss the man who she'd grown to need so much. Long before Nadim even turned up in her hallway with a bicycle and a six-pack of beer, Reena had been fighting the deep emptiness that lay just below the surface. And she'd been fighting it in the way she'd dealt with everything: deflect and distract.

Laid off three times in a career she didn't even like. Twelve (now thirteen) failed relationships. Her best friend moving on with a great job and a loving boyfriend. Her brother having twins. Even her sister, engaged again. And here was Reena. Always in the background. There for her friends when they wanted a good time. Cooking dinner for the whole building. Even there for her sister, despite her sister treating her like crap until, well, today. Reena was the nice girl. The go-to girl. The doormat girl?

What did Nadim see? The fun girlfriend always up for a

romp in bed? The one who made dinner every night and didn't make you dig too deep? The one easy to fool. Fake some interest in her cooking and give her some parasitic bugs and she's yours—long enough to cozy up to her powerful father.

She must have fallen asleep at some point, because the next thing she knew the loud blare of her phone woke her. Barely conscious, she grabbed it and glanced at the name on the screen. Abigail.

"Good morning, Reena! I hope you had a fantastic weekend! How are you?"

Of course, Abigail and her unwavering chirpiness would throw boiling water on the burns already stinging her.

"Fine, thank you, Abigail."

"It's a beautiful day. I hope you'll take some time to enjoy it. I have somewhat of a good news–bad news situation for you this morning. I finally heard from Angie at Top Crust. Unfortunately, they went with another applicant. You made a fantastic impression with the president, but ultimately, they chose a candidate who had several years more experience in the field. But here's the amazing news, I got a bite on your résumé from Cadbury Chocolates! Wouldn't that be a spectacular place to work? I'll be speaking to the recruiter later to set up the interview time. Isn't this fabulous?"

Reena blinked, wondering if Abigail used a thesaurus to get all those synonyms for *great*. Of course Top Crust went with another applicant. She closed her eyes, feeling them well up again. There was no way Mum would let her friend Leon hire her daughter. Not if she wanted to keep her poker habit a secret. Goddamn family. Was she too old to emancipate from them?

"Thanks. Yeah, that sounds great," Reena managed to say.

"Are you all right?"

She fell back, letting her down pillow cradle her pounding head. "Yes, just a headache today."

"Okay. Take it easy then. I'll call you when I hear from Cadbury. Keep your chin up, Reena. We'll get there."

Reena disconnected the call and noticed three texts from Nadim, asking to talk to her. She deleted them and tossed her phone back on the nightstand.

She stayed in her apartment for the rest of the day. Mostly in bed, where she got through most of Saira's Bollywood watch list on her laptop. Drinking chai and watching beautiful women in ornate saris sing and cry into ponds or waterfalls helped. Well, maybe not helped so much as distracted, which felt like a victory right now.

She knew she shouldn't have, but she also watched the cooking contest videos a few times each. From that first gin-and-cold-medicine-fueled potato bhajias lesson, to Nadim showing her how to retrieve eggs from surly Agatha. The videos were a wonder to watch. She could see in her eyes and body language how her affections for Nadim grew each week. The way her gaze lingered a bit longer on him. How she found excuses to touch him a bit more. To smile at him more. She could watch herself fall in love.

But Nadim was the same in all the videos. From the first to the latest, he always looked completely smitten with her on camera. Oscar-caliber acting. Which she knew he was capable of from the beginning, and she still let herself believe the hype.

She closed the videos and made a promise to never watch them again.

He'd texted her two more times just saying he needed to talk to her. Not that he missed her. Not that what Dad learned about him was untrue. She ignored the texts. And he stopped texting.

Saira checked in a few times but didn't mention any new news or gossip about Nadim. Mum and Dad didn't contact her at all.

On Tuesday morning her brother called as she was feeding the starters. He knew the basics of what happened, and he had texted Reena a few times the day before, but this was the first time she spoke to him about it. After telling him everything in exact detail, Khizar, with his skill that was so brilliant, and so compassionate, it was almost unreal, managed to make her feel better by doing little more than repeating back what she told him.

Like, "Wow, he bought you a starter jar? He knew you well," and, "It sounds like he was completely under his father's thumb. We know how much that sucks."

Evil big brother.

"I know, but he lied. He's engaged," Reena said.

"Or was engaged. Don't tell me you believe Dad's gossip at face value, do you?"

"Dad doesn't gossip! He hates gossip!"

"Seriously, Reena? All Dad does is gossip. When he and his business cronies get together and talk about who is losing money, or who is partnering with who, or whatever, what do you think that is? He thinks because he's talking about business instead of love lives or clothes it doesn't count as gossip."

Reena frowned. How was it fair that her brother was both wise and perceptive? It was true—Dad usually knew what was going on with everyone, until Nadim came along. Although, Dad didn't appear to know what his own wife was up to, either.

"Khizar, did you know that Mum secretly plays in an underground poker league and went to Vegas last winter for a card tournament?"

He snort-laughed. "No. Really?"

"Yup. She may have sabotaged a job I wanted." Reena lowered her head to her hard dining table with that statement. With everything else going to shit right now, she hadn't really grieved the loss of the Top Crust job. Ugh. She should have a drink. She hadn't had one yet, but bourbon would be welcome right now.

"What job?"

Right. She forgot Khizar didn't know about her employment woes. There was no point in keeping things secret now, so she told him about losing her job at Railside, and about how much she wanted the one at Top Crust.

"Oh, that sucks, Reena. I'm sorry. That bakery job would have been perfect. What are you going to do now?"

A question for eternity: What the hell was she going to do now? She knew what she wanted to do with her life: she wanted to be working at Top Crust, and she wanted to be building a real relationship with the man she thought Nadim was.

There was no chance of winning the scholarship now, even if they did make it to the finals in the contest. There was no way they would make that last video. So, no bread course to fulfill her dreams and help break the monotony of her life, either.

Everything would go back to how it had been before. She would work somewhere dull during the day and bake bread in the evenings. Live in her father's apartment building. Visit

Amira on weekends. Sunday brunches listening to Mum sing the praises of the newest eligible Muslim bachelor. Maybe she'd even find another superficial relationship with a man who didn't buy her a starter jar or rub her feet.

Reena looked at her bare fingers on the hard table. Never in her life had she accepted the magnitude of her loneliness.

She couldn't break down again. She needed to hold herself together.

"I don't know, Khizar. I don't know what to do."

He was silent a while before he spoke again. "What did Nadim say when you confronted him about this?"

"I haven't seen him."

"At all? Did you find out whether he really did work for Salim Shah? You might find that out by googling."

"I haven't looked. And before you say anything, I know. I just—"

"Reena, I know it's a mess, and I get it that it hurts, but you always deal with problems by pretending they're not there. I'm not saying you have to forgive the guy—I certainly wouldn't. But you can't live with your head in the sand all the time. You can't breathe in there, and you know it."

Evil, *evil* big brother.

"I wish you were here, Khizar. When are you coming home next?"

He snorted. "Nafissa can't sit for more than forty minutes without looking for a bathroom, so it'll be after the babies are born. But you're still coming for the birth, right? It's only four months away."

"Of course I am. You're going to be a daddy." She smiled. He was going to be an amazing father.

He laughed. "I know. It's surreal. Things are changing, Reena. We want you and Saira to be in their lives as much as we can swing it. Those girls are insanely lucky to have such kick-ass aunties."

Reena bit her lip. "Yeah, they are. I'll call you tomorrow, Khizar. Give Nafissa a hug from me."

"Okay, Reena. Take care, and call me anytime."

CHAPTER TWENTY-NINE

After getting off the phone, Reena showered, changed into yoga pants and a sweatshirt, and planted herself at her computer to do something she should have done weeks ago. She googled Nadim Remtulla.

She didn't find much. Some mention of him on a football team (his type) in London a few years ago, plus a Twitter handle that he only used three years ago for entering contests. His Facebook account also looked rarely updated. There was a newspaper article from Dar es Salaam mentioning him as one of many volunteers in a girls' education charity, and a few pictures shared by other people from several years ago—pictures with Nadim smiling, at parties and at restaurants. A genuine smile on his bearded face and no popped collar to be seen. No evidence of Jasmine either.

She googled his father, Shiroz Remtulla, and found mentions of him as a partner in a major law firm with several offices in East Africa, and one in London, and many mentions of his generous charity donations.

Finally, Reena googled Salim Shah and Shah Enterprises. She skimmed the information, confirming what she already knew about the man. A real estate developer like her father, he built buildings and hotels before selling them off at a profit, mostly in the UK. Skimming headlines, she found a mention of the failed project on a small business trends news site from London.

The project was a boutique hotel and spa. It had failed for several reasons—first of which was that the high-end facility was completely wrong for a neighborhood that hadn't begun gentrifying yet. There were also some issues of overspending on fixtures and tradesmen. And some speculation about under-handed deals. Bottom line was that the project was unlike all of Shah's other properties—it was over budget, and it didn't sell. If Nadim was responsible for this mess (as much as only one person could be responsible for such a big project), she could see why Dad wouldn't want the man working on the Diamond project.

But nothing here mentioned Nadim or Jasmine. After googling her specifically, she found some hits from D-list socialite gossip sites. Jasmine Shah apparently had some famous friends. Reena kept googling. Finally, she found a short article on some fashion blog. The picture attached was a heavily filtered, full-length shot of Jasmine standing in one of those ubiquitous London city plazas, wearing a floppy suede sun hat and mirrored glasses, and the attached interview with Jasmine was primarily about her influence as an Instagram model on @JazStyle.

Instagram model?

Reena searched for it, but the account no longer existed. She flipped back to the article. Most of it was fluffy praise for her fashion sense and her eye for composition in photos. Finally, she found a paragraph that made her stomach churn. Answering a question about her future, Jasmine waxed poetic about her fiancé.

Oh, I absolutely have a plan for the future! My fiancé and I are in the final stages of construction of a new boutique hotel in London. It's just the beginning of our plans for an international brand synonymous with luxury and style and with real substance behind it. Nadim, that's my fiancé, comes from Africa, and is passionate about increasing access to hidden oases in the far reaches of the world. We're looking at properties in Egypt soon!

Luxury and style with real substance? Reena nearly threw up. Well, this was the confirmation that Nadim was not only involved with this London boutique hotel kerfuffle, but also indeed was engaged to Jasmine.

But wait…Reena remembered something. Egypt. That day Saira came over with her bone soup, she had some gossip that Jasmine Shah had been abandoned by her fiancé in Egypt. Had that been Nadim? She checked the date on this article. It was almost a year old. She grabbed her phone and called her sister.

"Remember when you told me that Jasmine Shah's fiancé left her in Egypt?"

"Yeahhhhh…" Saira paused. "Oh, that could have been Nadim! Did you ask him?"

"No."

"Shouldn't you?"

"I've decided to ignore his messages."

"Reena, you're impossible. I'll call Rish. She can probably find out."

Reena walked around her apartment for a while, waiting for her sister to call. Eventually she sat back on the couch and lowered her head in her hands. She couldn't believe she had resorted to fishing for gossip again. Why couldn't she just ask him? What was she so afraid of?

It was an hour later when a knock sounded at the door. She peeked in the peephole to make sure it wasn't Nadim. It was Saira.

When she opened the door, she saw that her sister was holding a carton of low-sugar frozen yogurt and a selection of organic juices in lurid colors.

"I stopped at the store. I think you'll need this," Saira said as she walked in.

Damn. Saira had more bad news. Hopefully not devastatingly bad, because Reena was pretty sure that nonfat fro-yo and cold-pressed juice wouldn't have the self-medicating properties she'd need.

"What did you learn?"

"Let's dish this out first," Saira said.

Unexpectedly, the ice cream substitute didn't taste terrible, and the dark chocolate flavor went well with the sour cherry juice.

"Okay," Saira started once they were settled on the couch. "I asked Rish to ask her cousin. Apparently, they're not fighting anymore. Remember I said her cousin was obsessed with this socialite?"

"Vaguely." In all honesty, she didn't remember the convoluted tale Saira had told.

"Well, that socialite is Jasmine Shah. And yep. The fiancé who left her in Egypt was Nadim."

Relief spread through Reena's shoulders. If he had dumped her in Egypt it meant they weren't engaged now. But why did he hide this from her?

"So, he wasn't engaged when I met him."

"Not so fast, sis, there's more. As I said, the cousin doesn't really know Jasmine well, but she pretends they're real tight. She was posting screenshots of Jasmine's Instagram on the family WhatsApp. Rish was able to get some of the screenshots." She handed Reena her phone.

Reena scrolled through the pictures. Nothing interesting here, basic Instagram pictures of an immaculately styled Jasmine. She recognized the one in London from that article.

"Read the hashtags, Reena."

Reena did. #engagedlife. #marryingmybestfriend. #travel-withmylove.

Reena exhaled. "So, she is engaged."

Saira shrugged. "The last screenshot is from about a month ago. That seems to be when she deleted her account."

About a month ago was before Reena and Nadim started dating. If the fiancé Jasmine was talking about *was* Nadim, maybe they'd split up since then?

"There's even more," Saira said. She took the phone and cued up another picture.

It was another screenshot—this one from Facebook. From the Ismaili Muslim Business Owner Network. The post was by Salim Shah. It was a family picture—Salim, his wife, his daughter Jasmine, and Nadim, with his swanky beard and precision hair. The caption was something about how much Salim was looking forward to his daughter's up-coming wedding to his former business manager, Nadim Remtulla.

Reena nearly threw up her fake ice cream.

"Look at the date and time. That's London time," Saira said.

She did some calculations in her head. It was posted last Saturday night, Toronto time. She looked at her sister.

"Yeah, I checked, Reena. Dad is in this group."

Three days ago, Salim Shah posted in a Facebook group Jasmine was marrying Nadim. This is how Dad found out. And this was the truth. Fuck.

CHAPTER THIRTY

I t's not a new picture," Saira said.

"Of course it's not. Nadim was with me Saturday night." But that didn't mean he wasn't engaged to Jasmine. Because why would Jasmine's family lie about this? After all, his engagement to Reena was fake. He admitted that himself, the day this picture was posted.

Reena didn't know what to say. Looking at the picture in front of her, she saw a happy, healthy family. She saw a couple well suited for each other. Intelligent. Beautiful. Aspirational. In love. She put the phone down, her vision blurring.

"I'm sorry, Reena. I can't believe he didn't tell you he was engaged. Fucker."

Reena fell back on the couch, staring at the ceiling. "I'm an idiot."

Her sister was on the floor, feet stretched in front of her, wiggling her toes. Which just reminded Reena of Nadim's foot thing. Ugh. How could the man who'd lovingly admired her arches done this to her? He'd even painted her toenails last week. They'd argued about calling it nail polish or nail varnish.

Saira looked at her. "You're not an idiot. You're trusting. He's the idiot for not realizing your value." She smiled sadly. "I know you like to avoid heavy stuff, but I do think you need to speak to him. No doubt he lied to you, but this doesn't add up. It's going to eat away at you forever unless you know the truth."

"You sound like Khizar. Or a therapist."

Saira grinned. "Janeya's amazing. You should get a therapist. Everyone should. All I'm saying is speak to Nadim. Then we can kick him off a cliff."

Reena sat up and drained her glass of juice, remembering the look on Nadim's face when she tried to ask him about his past on Saturday night. "I'm not sure he'll tell me. Although, we caught his lies, so what does he have to lose at this point?"

Saira shrugged. "You. He has you to lose. I think he'll talk."

~

Saira left soon after, letting Reena keep the rest of the frozen yogurt, and promising to check in soon. And Reena was alone again. She's already cried more in the last few days than she had in years. And she was pretty much done with the Bollywood watch list. Reena stood in her living room, more restless than she could ever remember feeling.

After those revelations, what Reena needed was a drink. Actually, *several drinks*. She couldn't believe that she hadn't had a sip of alcohol since she'd found out about Nadim's secret fiancé. Her abstinence was noble, but was it necessary? One drink wouldn't really destroy her. At least not like she assumed it would. She eyed the collection of bottles stacked on her dining room sideboard. There was no need to be a martyr to her own guilt.

She placed her hand on the bottle, mouth watering in anticipation of the burn that would numb this, when she stilled. Sliding her hand down the smooth glass, she rested it on the bottle for about three seconds when she heard a thump outside her door.

Nadim was home.

Without taking a second to think, she rushed out her front door in three long strides.

He was in his regular work clothes and carrying a stack of cardboard. His shoulders fell the second he saw her. "Reena."

Seeing that face again felt like a blow to her chest. She had been in love with that face. She didn't know what to say. After staring for several agonizing seconds, she went with that. "I have no idea what to say to you."

He sighed, dropping the cardboard heavily to the floor. "Then don't say anything. There is nothing you can say that's worse than what your father said to me yesterday. Or my own father."

"So, it's true then?"

"What's true?"

"You're engaged to that woman?" She couldn't say her name. She was frankly amazed she could say anything at all.

"I was. But not anymore. Not for a while."

"I saw a Facebook post that said otherwise."

"I know."

"From her father. And Jasmine said it on Instagram."

He exhaled deeply. "I know that, too. But we're not engaged."

"Who, me and you? Or you and her?"

He sighed. Reena watched his face. Dark puffy eyes. Crease between the brows. Corners of his lips down turned. He looked miserable.

Good.

"You've been lying to me for weeks," Reena said. "You told me you'd always wanted to work in real-estate development, when apparently you already had. Hell, you even told me that Egypt was on your bucket list, when apparently you were there looking at properties for a new development!"

"I said the Pyramids were on my bucket list. I never got to see them when I was there."

"Jesus Christ, you're going with loopholes and caveats now? When we were getting to know each other you never once mentioned a fiancée. Ex, or otherwise."

Eyes cast downward, he answered, "I'm sorry."

"Why would Salim Shah post that he was looking forward to your wedding if you're not getting married?" Fuck. Her voice cracked. She couldn't hide her pain.

"I don't know why he said that." He barely looked at her.

"What was the point of this?" She gestured between them. "Were you here to run business intrigue for Salim Shah? Cozy up to Aziz Manji's daughter to get his trade secrets?"

"Reena, no. This wasn't fake. I—"

She put her hands up to stop him. "Did you forget about the ring? It *was* fake. Pretending to be engaged for the contest. Pretending not to be together to our parents. None of it was real, and I hate myself for thinking it was." Her voice cracked again.

He took a step toward her and reached for her arm, while she took a step back, hitting her back on her door. She couldn't handle physical contact now. His arms dropped to his sides. He looked at her, eyes blank, brows tightly knit together.

"I wish I could defend myself," he said, meeting her eyes.

"But...I'm sorry." He looked down at the stack of cardboard at his feet. "I'll be leaving very soon. You can pretend none of this happened. I really...I didn't want you to get hurt." His eyes were so dejected that it weakened her resolve. He finally resembled the Nadim more familiar to her. The one from the hotel who told her for the second time that his soul knew when he was home.

He'd been playing her the whole time.

She turned and faced her door.

"Wait, Reena, one thing," he said. She stilled but did not turn.

"I wasn't using you. Or your dad. I know you have no reason to believe me, but you were the only real thing in my life for years. I'm sorry I made such a mess of this." His voice trailed to nothing.

She stared at her closed door. He sounded sincere, but what did she know? She'd heard enough in those damn videos to know he could sound convincing. Her eyes welled with tears as her hand touched her doorknob. She didn't move until she heard his door open and his footsteps disappear inside his apartment.

~

Reena stood in the hallway. Part of her wanted to knock on his door and throw herself in his arms, again. Apologize for not believing him and beg him to just go back to the way things were. She wanted to feel him around her, smell his soap in his neck, his hands on her waist. And she probably would have done it, if Marley hadn't come racing down the stairs then.

"What is going on down here?" Marley asked.

"Nothing."

Shayne was close behind Marley. "We heard you yelling. I don't think I've ever heard you yell."

Marley looked at Reena carefully. No doubt taking in Reena's red, puffy eyes. "You okay, Reena? Come upstairs for a drink."

A drink. Her shoulders slumped. "I, um..."

Marley put her hand on Reena's forearm. "Come. Talk to us."

Reena was pretty sure her parents wouldn't want her to mention the business problems outside the immediate family, but she wasn't much in the mood to do what her parents wanted. "Sure. I'd love some of that oolong tea, if you still have it." She followed them upstairs.

The moment she was in her cousin's apartment she fell onto Marley's sofa. "Want to hear some dirt about my former Tanzanian/English boyfriend?"

Marley's eyes widened. "Holy shit, *former*? It's over already? You guys seemed so great together."

"Yeah, well, apparently appearances can be deceiving."

They took their tea out to the back deck, where Reena told them most of the story, skirting over the part where Dad lost money to the phony architect and the part where Mum spent her free time in a poker club. Best not to broadcast all their messy secrets to her mother's brother's daughter.

"Holy crap," Shayne said. "He was engaged to *Jasmine Shah*? I followed her Instagram. *He's* the mystery fiancé she was always talking about?"

Reena nodded. "He says they actually split a while ago."

"And you don't believe him?" Shayne asked.

She shrugged.

"He was really into you, though," Marley said. "You have to believe that."

"I believe he was very good at faking it. A little too good." Reena paused, looking at the setting sun bathing the asphalt lot in an orange glow. "You think I should believe that he's not with her anymore?"

"Why automatically believe the Shahs?" Marley said. "You don't even know them, and hasn't your father always hated them?"

Reena shrugged again.

"I dunno," Shayne said. "I'd be more likely to believe our friend than that *influencer* who claims her hair is real. I could *see* her weave in one of her pictures, for god's sake. And her hazel eyes? Contacts."

"Shayne, don't be catty. Nadim has nothing to gain by lying now. You should talk to him," Marley said.

"I just did talk to him."

"You yelled at him. Talk, Reena," Marley said. "There's more to this, I can feel it."

"You sound like Saira."

Marley chuckled. "Your sister—she's changed a lot, right? I shop at her store, and she somehow manages to say the wisest things while still being eighty percent inappropriate."

"I know. She's Bizarro Saira, now."

"I adore your sister," Shayne said. "She's so delightfully *extra*."

Reena smirked.

Marley sipped her wine, perfect eyebrows furrowed in thought. "I think you should trust him. You know your parents and his are a little manipulative. The Shahs might be, too. I have no reason to believe that the guy who's become our friend in the last month would lie to us. Do you think maybe you're looking for flaws that aren't there?"

That was ridiculous. Absurd. But...Reena bit her lip. "Last week someone said to me, 'You ever get scared when something fits a little too perfectly? You think it's not possible so you look for problems that aren't there?'"

Shayne recoiled. "Wow, I feel sorry for whoever that person dumped. Why run away from perfection? Who said it?"

Reena gave a small smile, thinking of Anderson. "It doesn't matter," Reena said.

"Why don't you ask your dad what he knows?" Marley suggested.

"Why would I do a thing like that?"

"He's been working with Nadim for over a month. Whether he likes the Shahs or not, he does know them better than anyone else here. Maybe it's a good idea to get support from your parents when things are shitty?"

She snorted. Did Dad know how to give support?

It was so unlike her to go to her father of all people...but maybe that was part of the problem. Reena took a long sip of her tea, the mellow, chilled drink cooling her core. If anything, these last few days had taught her that her normal way of dealing with problems wasn't the only way. And definitely not the best way.

"Maybe. Yeah, maybe I should talk to Dad."

CHAPTER THIRTY-ONE

Reena reluctantly agreed to talk to her father, but she wasn't about to do it alone. She'd learned long ago that difficult conversations with parents were easier with the strength of numbers. So she called Saira and made plans to ambush Dad at the Diamond project together the next day.

They found Dad in the site office—a portable unit that the construction management team used for paperwork and meetings. He was at a desk, typing on a computer while Igor, the construction manager, was chatting with a hard hat-wearing woman while looking over huge sheets of paper on a table.

"Girls." Dad looked up. "What are you doing here?"

"We need to talk," Reena said. "Alone."

Dad closed his eyes a moment, then stood. "Let's go to the corner unit. There's a table and chairs in there." He guided them out.

He led them to a large L-shaped space, unfinished with concrete floors and walls, and an open ceiling. A folding table and grouping of chairs had been set up in the back. This was the store Nadim was struggling to find a lease for. It was strange to see it after he'd talked about it so much.

"Nice," Saira said, eyeing the area. "Did you guys secure a

tenant for this yet? You should think about doing a little shop along with a restaurant. Like a bodega-café."

Dad waved his hand. "Everything is in limbo now. Losing a manager while in the middle of negotiations will set me back a long time." He sat at the chair at the head of the table and waited for them to follow before speaking.

This was a bad idea. What was Reena expecting to learn by coming here? She didn't know where to begin.

Saira apparently had no difficulty speaking, and slapped her hands on the table. "Nadim said the Shahs are lying, and that he's not engaged. That true?"

"That is also what he told me, but I have no proof," Dad said.

Saira shook her head. "And you fired him anyway? That's harsh, Dad. You're supposed to be this compassionate and supportive boss, but when push comes to shove, you won't trust your own employee."

Dad didn't say anything. Reena decided to try Saira's blunt strategy on for size. "Did you already know about Nadim's involvement with the Shahs when you made this deal with his dad?"

"Of course not! I wouldn't sully my reputation by bringing on the man who destroyed Salim's hotel project."

"So, you only learned about his involvement with the Shahs through Salim's Facebook post."

"How did you know that post? It is a private group on the Facebook."

Lol, Dad thinking anything on "the Facebook" was private. She made a mental note to teach him the ins and outs of social media after all this was done.

Dad shifted in his seat, crossing one leg over the other. Reena looked at her father. Really looked at him. She'd never been particularly close to the man, and she'd never felt the daddy worship that some daughters felt for their father. Actually, just the opposite. She'd thought of him as shrewd, rigid, and unfailing. Were those dark circles under his eyes merely a sign of his advancing age, or a sign of stress?

"Dad, why do I feel like you're hiding something?" Reena asked.

"Because I am." Dad sighed. "You care about him, don't you?"

"Yeah. A lot." She wouldn't cry again.

Dad watched her for a few more seconds before slumping forward in his seat. "I am truly sorry, Reena. None of this would have happened if I hadn't made a terrible mistake."

"What mistake? Hiring Nadim?" Saira asked.

"No. Before that. But...I can't tell you. I cannot risk your mother discovering."

Reena threw her arms up in frustration. "Don't tell your mother! Don't tell your father! Don't you people get tired of all these secrets?"

Reena knew the answer to that. *No.* No one in this family grew tired of secrets. Secrets were the glue that held them together.

Except, not anymore. Reena was done with them. She took a deep breath. "How about I be honest first? I've been out of work for weeks because I was laid off again. I've been interviewing for several new finance positions, but it's not going well. I didn't tell you because I don't want your help to find a job. And even though I told Nadim I *wouldn't* marry him, we've been dating pretty seriously for a few weeks. Of course, that's been over since you told me he's engaged.

Those are my secrets, now it's your turn. Be honest for a change."

"No," Saira interrupted. "It's my turn. Joran and I used to invite other people into our relationship from time to time. Sometimes men, sometimes women, and Mum found out because one of her...er, friends knew one of the men."

Reena's head snapped around to meet Saira's face. *What?* She understood the symbolism of coming clean with deep dark secrets to urge Dad to be honest, but admitting to one's father that they'd enjoyed the occasional ménage à trois seemed like taking it a little far. Plus... *really?* Saira had a threesome with a friend of one of Mum's poker buddies?

What the hell was her family getting up to while she was busy baking bread?

"Your turn, Dad," Saira said. "Tell us what you're hiding."

"I wish you had told me about your job, Reena. I would have helped you." Good. He wasn't going to mention Saira's crowded bedroom. "I can ask around to my contacts. It's high time you had a management role, anyway. I'll put the word out—"

"No, Dad. I told you, I don't want your help. I want your honesty."

Dad sighed, standing. "I'm going to lock the door so we're not disturbed." He walked to the front of the empty unit.

Reena took the opportunity to ask Saira what planet she resided on. "I can't believe you told Dad you had threesomes," she whispered.

Saira grinned. "Oh, I'm pretty sure he knows. Just like he knows Ashraf and I smoke weed in the garage for anxiety. He's pretending he doesn't hear me."

Reena had been pretty sure before, but this confirmed it: her family was totally bonkers.

Dad returned and sat heavily on his chair.

"So..." Reena said.

"I made a bad business decision and lost money. A lot of money." He took a breath. "I hired an architect for some late modifications. He cheated me and stole from us."

Reena blinked. *This?* This was Dad's big secret? This wasn't a secret at all. "I know that. Mum told us."

Reena had never seen her Dad's eyes so wide. "What?! Your mother doesn't know this!"

Saira snorted. "Of course she does. You didn't know she knew?"

"How in heavens does your mother know about my loss?"

Reena shrugged. "I figured you told her. You are married, after all."

Dad stared, eyes still wide, lips pinched. Clearly her parents had a lot of stuff to work through. She considered evening the score and telling Dad about Mum's poker habit, but decided to get back to the matter at hand.

"What does this have to do with Nadim?"

"I needed the money from his father to finish the project. And Shiroz only offered to invest if his son came with the deal. He was concerned about Nadim's reputation and wanted it...polished a bit. I would not have agreed to hire the man if I had known he bungled the Shah hotel project."

Reena was learning nothing new here. Dad's only intel was information Mum had already told her.

"So, you didn't know about his connection to the Shahs?"

"No. Not until Salim Shah showed that picture on the Facebook."

"Do you believe Nadim?"

Dad didn't answer. He stood up and walked toward the front window of the unit. "You know," he finally said, "so much of what you see here is Nadim's doing. I would have rented to the first coffee shop who put an application in, but he has ideas about prestige. He believes a restaurant can be an anchor tenant and bring people to the development. The work he has done for this project, research, negotiating with suppliers, tenants, subcontractors...I see no sign of the irresponsible and incapable project manager that they claim him to be."

"You don't think the failure of the Shah project was really his fault?"

"Nadim is not the man his father told me he was. I was under the impression I would have to keep a very close eye on him and help him improve irresponsible work habits. Nadim is very sharp. No babysitting necessary."

"But then, Dad," Saira asked, "if you thought he'd be a deadbeat, why did you try to force Reena to marry him?"

"There was no *forcing*. The marriage was his father's idea—to clean up his image. He thinks Jasmine is below his son—apparently she is an Instant model."

"Instagram," Reena corrected.

He waved his hand. "Yes, yes. Anyway. Your mother wasn't happy that I made this deal with Nadim's father, or that I agreed to encourage you to marry him. It happened while she was away at her card tournament in Nevada, or I am sure she would have stopped it all."

Would Mum have stopped it? She'd been the lynchpin behind this matchmaking from the beginning, or so Reena thought. And shady past or not, Nadim looked pretty good on paper as son-in-law material.

Looked pretty good on high-thread-count Egyptian cotton sheets, too.

Hold up... *Card tournament in Nevada?* Dad knew about Mum's poker? "She told you why she went to Vegas?" Reena asked.

He chuckled. "I shouldn't have said that. She doesn't know I know about her card friends. She's not hurting anyone and has raised so much money for charity. Let her have her secret fun."

Reena turned to Saira. "This family is utterly ridiculous."

Saira shrugged. "You're just figuring that out now?"

Reena tried to keep it all straight in her head. While Mum was in Vegas with Leon Bergeron, Mrs. Pelozzi, and the rest of the gambling grannies, Dad and Nadim's father were making a business deal with a bonus marriage tacked on as an appendix. Dad's motivation was to make up the money he lost when he hired a bogus architect so his wife wouldn't find out, even though his wife already knew. Nadim's dad was trying to cover up Nadim's apparent mismanagement of Salim Shah's boutique hotel project and end his engagement to a leggy Instagram model.

All seemed perfectly normal things for parents to do.

Reena remembered Mum's trip, actually. At the time, she had recently split with Jamil and had been experimenting with online dating apps. She had two regular hookups from Tinder then, if she recalled correctly.

Reena frowned. "This isn't the right family for Shiroz to search for a virgin daughter to make his son look good."

Dad said nothing. Which was fine, because that only gave Reena more time to think. "Wait. Dad. Mum's trip was in February."

She remembered things. Nadim not seeing her picture until he moved to Toronto and being surprised she didn't live at home with her parents.

She stilled, briefly looking at her sister. "It wasn't me, was it? February was a month after Saira caught Joran in his love nest with his cousin. You sold *Saira*, not me."

"Me?" Saira looked shocked.

Dad shook his head. "No. I sold nobody. But yes, I was thinking of Saira. She also needed to clean up her image. The gossip about your sister was disgusting—people were saying she had an open relationship. Incest. Cheating...I wanted to connect her with a good family to counteract that filth."

Saira nodded, chuckling. "The gossip wasn't completely wrong, but I appreciate the effort. Anyway, I have Ashraf now."

"I know"—he smiled fondly at Saira—"but you didn't then. I thought I was helping. Your mother didn't agree. This is why she was angry about the deal—she said you were too hurt for a new relationship and needed to heal. She was right, of course. And when the visa came through and Nadim finally arrived, I realized two things. First, even though I agreed to bring him here reluctantly, I was the winner in this arrangement. Nadim has been an asset to the company. And second, it was not a problem that Saira had found Ashraf, because Nadim was much better suited to Reena. That is why I moved him to the building with you. There was a spark in him that your mother and I both saw. Reena and Nadim were a perfect match." He smiled at Reena. "You two are the most food-obsessed people we have ever met. We have a good track record for matches, you know. Your mother was the one who encouraged Nafissa and your brother."

Reena blinked. This was unreal. That wasn't even true, and Dad knew it. Nafissa and Khizar hardly needed anyone's encouragement to fall in love. Plus, her parents set her up with Nadim because they were both foodies? Really?

But it still didn't add up. "If Nadim's telling the truth, why are the Shahs lying about this engagement?" she asked.

Dad shrugged. "I don't know. I don't trust Salim, though. I believe Nadim. I didn't fire him, Reena."

The room was silent for several long seconds until a sound of relief escaped Reena's lips. She had no idea how tense she'd been holding herself until that moment. Dad trusted him.

He shook his head. "But Nadim's father doesn't believe him. He is convinced that Nadim has been in secret contact with Jasmine. And he won't listen to his son." Dad looked straight at Reena. "You should have told us you had taken up with the boy. It's not right, keeping secrets from family."

Reena nearly snorted in outrage. Saira, on the other hand, found no reason to hold in her disbelief and laughed loudly.

"Saira! Be kind to your sister!"

They were all silent for a bit longer, each digesting the fragile honesty they'd shown in this weird space that somehow gave the Manjis an almost normal family dynamic.

Finally, Reena spoke. "If you didn't fire him, maybe that means we can finish the contest?" She couldn't make herself think about saving their relationship now, but maybe she could salvage something of her life?

Dad frowned. "What contest?"

"Nadim and I were pretending to be engaged for a national cooking contest on FoodTV. We find out tomorrow if we made the finals, and they'll film it in two weeks."

Saira raised a brow. "I thought you told us all your secrets?"

Reena shrugged. "I forgot one."

Dad frowned, then shook his head. "I may not have fired him, but his father pulled his investment in the Diamond project and forced Nadim to resign. He has been summoned home to Tanzania."

Reena swallowed a lump in her throat. "When does he leave?"

"His last day working for me will be Friday, and he'll be on a plane next week."

CHAPTER THIRTY-TWO

After the drive home, Saira pulled up in front of Reena's building and grinned widely. "That was actually kind of fun. We should do Mum next."

"Do what to Mum?"

"You know, ambush. Confront. Although let's not do it when we see her tomorrow. I don't want to risk her not paying for my wedding sari."

"We're seeing Mum tomorrow?" The last thing she wanted was a second parent interrogation. Even if she was the one doing the interrogating.

"Reena! We're going shopping, remember? For bridal clothes? We planned it last Sunday! You're still coming, right?"

Of course. With her life falling apart and all, she'd forgotten about the sari-shopping date with Mum. Ugh. Maybe she should try to get out of it?

She looked at her sister's hopeful face. No. it was time for Reena to move past her own self-absorption and be there for her sister. Her sister, who had been there for Reena every day since she'd found out about Nadim's secret maybe-fiancée.

"Of course I'm coming, Saira."

"Great. We'll pick you up in the morning. I'll text you before I leave."

"Okay. Thanks for taking me today."

"You're going to talk to Nadim, right?" Saira asked.

Reena exhaled. "Yes. I'm going to talk to him."

"Good. See you tomorrow."

Reena got out of the car, and Saira drove away.

As she walked up the sidewalk, nerves fluttering her stomach, she resigned herself to a truth that she probably always knew—deflect and distract didn't work. She'd been sweeping things under the rug for so long, but it only left her with a lumpy and treacherous floor. She was going to talk to Nadim, now. They may not have a future, but she needed closure.

Reena looked at the lot next to the building. Nadim's car wasn't there. She took a breath.

She'd talk to him later. This wasn't deflecting, just... postponing. She didn't want to be alone, though, so instead of going to her apartment, she walked to the Sparrow.

She didn't drink. She had two bowls of lentil soup, several ginger ales, and played three rounds of darts with bar regulars. She had a long, almost existential chat with Steve over their shared love of smoked peppers, and she sat in on a hilarious new card game about sushi. No drama, no self-pity.

At a quiet moment, while she was riding the high of trouncing a man bun at darts, she sat at the bar and waited for Steve to refill her glass with more ginger ale and tried to figure out why she felt so... fine.

It had been less than a week since her so-called life fell apart, and during that time she had also lost a job she really wanted. And yeah, she did feel pretty shitty about it all. But along with the moments of abject misery (like when she faced Nadim yesterday), she also had moments of joy. A few laughs with her sister, tea on the back deck with Marley and Shayne, and tonight, a great night at the Sparrow, by herself. She was dealing. Not incapacitated by...misery or lethargy. This was nothing like the last time life threw her in a ditch.

Was it because she had more support? Was it because she hadn't been drinking? Or was it because she was being honest with herself about her problems for the first time in a very long time?

And there was a big question. One that she needed to know the answer to, considering that no matter how *not terrible* she felt at this moment, there was nothing on the horizon that said her life was going to get any better. How could she ensure that these brand-spanking-new coping skills stuck around?

She remembered her sister's suggestion of seeing a therapist. Before she could second-guess herself, she called her doctor and left a message that she needed an appointment soon. It was time for Reena to stop deflecting and distracting, and face this part of her life, too.

She finally left the Sparrow long after the sun set, after excusing herself from another hearty discussion with Steve about the merits of homemade hot sauces. She was exhausted. It had been a long day, and tomorrow might be even longer. She wasn't entirely sure she had the strength to get through a day of sari shopping with her mother and sister, but she was determined to stop avoiding things that she didn't want to do. That included talking to Nadim. His car was in his parking space now. She pulled out her phone and texted him.

Reena: We need to talk. Breakfast tomorrow? My place?

She bit her lip as she saw the three dots flash on her screen telling her he was responding. Finally, the text came through.

Nadim: Okay. Message me when you want me to come over.

Good. That was done. And at least she'd get a night's sleep before she would see him.

Or…not. Because when she went to open her door, she realized she didn't have her keys. Ugh. She'd had a spare made for Nadim last week—it had seemed like such a huge step in their nonrelationship at the time. And she knew Nadim was home, and awake.

Heart pounding heavily in her chest, she summoned some hidden bravery and knocked before she could change her mind.

No answer. No sounds from within. She knocked again. Nothing.

Her shoulders fell.

But then she heard the doorknob. The chain-latch lock was still fastened, restricting the door from opening more than about four inches. And his deep voice spoke with an accent fainter than the day they met, and a weary reluctance that was also new.

"Breakfast is eaten in the morning, Reena."

"I know. I…just need my key. I'm locked out."

"I'll get your spare." Footsteps trailed away from the door.

Her knees weakening, Reena lowered herself to sit on the old tile floor and closed her eyes. That optimism, the feeling of being *okay*, was gone. All she wanted was her key so she could lock herself in her apartment and cry until he left the country. Her bravery strolled right out of there the moment she heard that sexy, weary voice.

"I can't seem to find it," he suddenly said. "I may have put it in a box by mistake. I'm packing."

Reena nodded shakily, pressing her hands against the floor, ready to get up. "It's fine. I'll get Marley's."

When she was halfway to her feet, he spoke again. "Reena, wait."

Her butt fell back to the floor.

"Are you sitting on the floor?"

"Yes."

She heard some movement from within his unit, a shuffling of fabric, then a hollow thump on the wall behind her.

"Sit against the door," he said.

She shifted so her back was leaning against his door, which was being held from opening fully by the chain. She looked into his apartment and saw Nadim, his expression concerned and sad. He was also sitting on his floor, back leaning against the wall near the door.

They were inches apart now, but with a door chained closed between them, the opening just enough to see most of his face. Hair a little longer, though still firmly in the crew-cut category. Still clean-shaven; he'd given up on that douche-beard, thankfully. Without the beard, his one dimple lit her up every time he smiled. No smile now, though. Intense eyes searched hers, almost asking a question.

She took a deep breath, trying to call back the courage that had deserted her. "Maybe we should just talk now," she said quietly.

"Do you want to come in?"

She looked around the tiny, empty hallway, and then back at the gap into his apartment. This would be easier with the door between them. She didn't want to see his whole face, or his apartment...all packed up into boxes. This was her same old avoidance, but she allowed herself this one. "No. Let's do it here."

She wanted this to end on neutral grounds. Nothing was more neutral than the empty hallway between their apartments.

He shifted a bit. "Okay," he said. "Let's talk, Reena."

CHAPTER THIRTY-THREE

I'll go first," he said, his voice reverberating through the wall. "Jasmine and I are not engaged. We broke up a long time ago."

She bit her lip. She was pretty sure she believed him. "In Egypt, right?"

"Yes. I'm really sorry, Reena. I should have told you about her. My father insisted I couldn't disclose my past with Jasmine to you or your father. I never wanted you to get hurt."

"What I don't get is why after working for Salim Shah while engaged to his daughter, you immediately started working for his archenemy and agreed to marry his daughter? Were you some sort of corporate spy?"

"No, of course not. Honestly, until the shit hit the fan on Sunday I didn't know your father even knew the Shahs. My father made me swear never to tell anyone I had worked with Salim because of all the negative attention the Shah hotel project was getting."

"Nadim, tell me your side of the story. From the beginning."

So, he told her the story. As she sat in the tiny hallway on the first floor of her father's building, Nadim told her how hard he worked to please his father and how he usually fell short. He finally moved to London to distance himself and quickly got involved with Jasmine, the free-spirited woman whose purpose, he thought, was to teach him that life could be more than his father's narrow definition.

"I got caught up in a world that didn't really fit. And I knew it didn't fit, but things just kind of got out of hand. Jasmine had these grandiose plans of being an influencer. The London hotel was her idea."

"And the mismanagement?"

"I can't pretend to be innocent there. I wasn't really... invested. I didn't care. I was partying, taking shortcuts, and just *coasting*."

"I saw pictures of you on a yacht."

"There were many yachts. Jasmine wanted the best of everything. In the business, too. High-end fixtures, materials. She was inexperienced, and it was a disaster. I have so many regrets for how I handled things with that hotel."

"Didn't Jasmine care about her father's company?"

He shrugged. "I know what you're thinking. That she's just a superficial, spoiled snob. But... Jasmine is a complicated person. You think you and I have difficult parents? Salim is a good businessman, but an awful father. Not just neglectful, but downright abusive. She honestly tried. She wanted to succeed—she cared about it more than I did. But she didn't see the big picture and focused on insignificant details. I shouldn't have let any of it, the business or the relationship, go so far."

"And then you abandoned her in Egypt?"

He huffed a laugh. "No. *She* abandoned *me*. We were there on holiday and she decided we should open a hotel there, too. I knew we were in over our heads with the London one, and when I tried to dissuade her, we had a huge fight. I put my foot down and quit my position with Shah Enterprises on the spot, and she took off, leaving me alone in Cairo. She took my passport. Dad had to have an emergency one couriered to me so I could get back to Tanzania."

"That sounds awfully dramatic." Like a Bollywood revenge story.

He snorted. "Yeah. We brought out the worst in each other. That's why you scared me."

"What? What's scary about me?"

"Really?" he scoffed, smiling, and for a fleeting moment, the dimple appeared. "You're *terrifying*, Reena Manji, because you did the opposite. You brought out the best in me right from the beginning."

She turned and their eyes met. This was a lot to take in. She needed more answers before getting sucked into his gaze.

"Why didn't you call me this week?" she asked. "If you're not engaged why did you let me think you were?" True, he had texted her, and she'd ignored him, but he could have phoned if he really cared.

"You didn't respond to my texts, so I figured you wanted to be left alone. Plus, my phone service went dead, and they haven't been able to figure out why."

Reena smiled. Ashraf. Her family had her back.

"I took it as a sign from above not to call you," Nadim said. "I should have come by, though. I'm sorry. Avoiding you after everything that happened wasn't fair to either of us. Actually, nothing I've done has been fair to you."

"You regret this? Us?"

"No," he whispered. "Never. But we should have been honest to our families. And to each other."

That only sounded like regret with a coat of paint. Reena looked away, blinking.

It seemed old Nadim was the same as old Reena. Adapting to whatever others were doing, not taking what he really wanted seriously, and avoiding confrontation until he just couldn't do it anymore. This was so different from the Nadim she knew now, the Nadim in the contest videos—caring, sentimental, and passionate about his interests. She'd thought it was an act, but maybe neither iteration of the man was fake. He'd just left that old him behind, come here, and found a home. And the new home brought out the absolute best in him.

"So, you really did want to move here? You weren't forced?"

"I did. I conceded that I have terrible judgment both in business and in women, and my father agreed to help me start over."

"A new job, a new country, and a new wife."

"Yup. Facilitated marriage has worked well for many. If I didn't like who he picked, I would deal with that, but I wanted to give this option a chance." He smiled warmly. "Of course, I ended up liking who he picked a little too much."

Reena couldn't help but snort-laugh.

"What's so funny?" he asked.

"It was supposed to be Saira."

"What?"

"*Saira*. My father offered my *sister* to your father, not me. It happened right after she caught her fiancé banging his Dutch cousin in their condo, so she needed to clean up her image. I was juggling two guys from Tinder back then, so I wasn't the good, pure woman for you, either."

"Um..."

May as well go for broke and tell him the whole story, so she told him about the swindling architect and Mum's gambling habit. "To think, we owe our introduction to an incestuous Dutchman and my mother's stellar poker face," she concluded.

The wall beside her shook with Nadim's attempts not to laugh. "God, I feel like there's a lot I don't know about your family."

"What you don't know about the Manjis could fill a crater on Mars. Dad *definitely* oversold us as a good family. I'm not even going to mention my sister's threesomes." She paused a second, thinking. "Too bad you haven't met Khizar. All the goodness in our family ended up in him."

He finally turned to look at her, laughing openly now. "God, I'll miss you. Whoever they promised, I'm glad I got you." He turned back around, but with that grin still plastered on his face, Reena was gifted with a perfectly framed dimple through the gap. She hated that she couldn't kiss it.

"I still can't figure out why Salim Shah would lie about you being engaged to his daughter," Reena said.

He shrugged. "Maybe he was trying to one-up your dad? That's all those men do."

She opened the screenshot of Salim's post on her phone. Looking at it again told her nothing. Just the picture and some sentimental tripe about welcoming Nadim to their family.

"Let me see," he asked. She handed him her phone.

After a few seconds Nadim gasped. "He was trying to sabotage your father's daughter's wedding!"

Reena frowned. "Saira's?"

"No. *Yours*. Did you read the post? He says 'It wasn't easy to convince him to leave his beloved Africa, but home can be a moving target. We are so proud to welcome him to ours.' It's practically word-for-word of what I said in the farm-to-table video!"

"Holy shit. Salim Shah watches FoodTV Canada online."

Nadim laughed. "He thought you and I were getting married and decided to stir up a little trouble in paradise for his rival's family."

Reena didn't find it very funny. This stupid rivalry between her father and a man she'd never met effectively had cost her the best relationship she'd ever had.

"So, if that's why Salim lied on Facebook, why was Jasmine lying—claiming to be engaged—on Instagram? Was that her father's doing, too?"

He shook his head. "No, that was me. I told her she could."

"What?" He *knew* she was going around saying they were still together?

"She started the Instagram when we were together, and she had all these wedding-type sponsorships lined up. After I finally got out of Egypt, she asked me if she could still say we were engaged, but only on Instagram, and never mention me by name, or show my picture, so she wouldn't lose her sponsorships. I felt bad for her. She was having a rough time—trying to distance herself from her family and all. And my father isn't exactly tuned in to the Instagram influencer scene, so I didn't think he'd find it."

Reena kind of sympathized with her. Actually, Reena was sympathizing with Jasmine Shah a lot right now, more than she thought was possible.

But then a thought made her giggle. "Nadim, are you telling me that I am not your first fake fiancée?"

He laughed. "No, I guess not."

"So why did she delete the Instagram?"

"That was *my* father...somehow, he found out about it. Someone on WhatsApp posted screenshots and he was furious. He insisted she delete it or he was going to ruin her or something. I was so pissed...Dad even threatened that he would back out of the investment here and make me leave Toronto if she didn't delete it."

"OMG...Rish's cousin!"

"What?"

She looked at him, trying hard not to laugh. "My sister's future sister-in-law's cousin was obsessed with your fiancée and posted screenshots of her Insta all over WhatsApp. Your father must have seen them."

"Seriously?" He laughed.

Reena nodded. "Seriously. You know, the moral of this whole story is that our parents really need to stay off social media."

He laughed. "Oh, man. This is actually hilarious. But..."

"But what?"

"The day Dad found Jasmine's Instagram and gave me that ultimatum—that was the day you found me at the Sparrow. I was in a terrible mood. I was so ready to run off to New Zealand and let Dad cut me off, but you were there. You were so cute and cranky and I had so much fun. That's when I decided I was better off staying as close to you as possible."

They were both silent for a while. She wiped her eyes. This was torture. She wanted to see his face. The whole thing at once.

"And now he's barking orders again. Can't you just tell your dad Salim is lying?"

"My father is uncompromising. This is all a taint on the family reputation. He had my name wiped from the controversy surrounding the hotel failure, and here is Salim Shah publicly stating I'm marrying his daughter. Whether it's true or not is beside the point."

So that was it. Because of stubborn parents and idiotic competitiveness, she was losing him.

"Hey, Reena." His hand came through the gap and returned her phone. "Don't be upset."

"How can I not be upset? I wish, just once, something would happen to me, good or bad, that had absolutely nothing to do with my parents."

He smiled. "Well, I wouldn't have even met you if it wasn't for them, so I'm glad for their interference."

He watched her, his face showing that Nadim-mischief, that playful smirk she loved.

Their eyes held for several seconds.

"Reena, I'm sorry. I shouldn't have hidden my past from you. I should have followed my instinct a long time ago and thrown myself at your feet, telling you exactly who I was and what I'd done, and begged you to take me anyway."

She scoffed. "Don't be ridiculous. You weren't *that* into me."

"Wrong." His voice lowered to a bare whisper. "I was into you. Right away. If you'll recall, I asked you out before I knew who you were. I wanted my hot neighbor, not a wholesome bride."

"I'm not hot," she said, immediately regretting the words. But she wasn't, at least not compared to someone like Marley. Or Jasmine, for that matter.

"Are you kidding? Those sexy black curls? That smile? Not

to mention the smell of bread coming out of your apartment for days before we met." He turned away. "And that's why you scared me so much. You checked all my boxes. Even the secret boxes no one knew about. I could barely breathe that night when I found you sitting outside my door barefoot with a bag of bread. You were prickly and so independent, but I finally felt like I belonged somewhere. You feel like home."

She snorted, still not really believing him.

He turned to look at her again. "Reena," he said slowly. "I liked you. A lot. I still do. I should have been honest with you, but I didn't want you to find out how grossly unmatched we are. You are my superior in every way. I didn't deserve you."

He reached down and placed his hand on the floor in the four-inch gap in the door. She placed hers on top. He immediately flipped his hand over and curled his fingers through hers.

They stared at their connected hands together for a time, heat rising between them. If it wasn't for the thick metal chain holding the door, there would be a lot more touching than just their fingers.

She let her mind go there. If that door were open, she'd climb onto his lap, which had become her favorite place to be in the last few weeks. She'd run one hand up his shirt and the other through the back of his hair. No wait, she'd take off her shoes and socks first.

"Reena, my flight to Dar es Salaam is on Monday."

She closed her eyes. The distance was too great. And four more days together would only make the day he left harder.

"My dad can talk to yours," she said quickly. "He can tell him how well you're doing here and—"

"No," he said.

"No?"

"No. I don't want to do that. Don't get me wrong, I love Toronto and would be happy here, but...I can't let him be the puppet master in my life anymore. I wanted to finally make him proud here, but..." He sighed, squeezing her hand. "I'm not sure he'll ever be proud of any decision I make. And I'm not sure why I still care. I'm thirty-two years old, and I still have daddy issues. It's laughable."

"We don't have *daddy issues*. We have Indian parents. That shit runs deep."

He laughed, squeezing again. "I like your father. I respect him. In another situation, I think we'd work amazingly well together. But the deal was my father's investment in exchange for my job. My father pulled his investment, so no more job. And no more work visa, so I can't stay in Canada. I can't impose myself on your father anymore, even though I really wish I could see where things could have gone with his delightfully terrifying daughter. But who knows...maybe one day you'll come to Africa?"

She smiled at that thought. Anything was possible. "What will you do there?"

"I don't know. My old friend Jabari owns some luxury hotels, and he's approached me to work for him before, so maybe that. I don't need anyone buying me opportunities."

She respected that. She couldn't steal his chance to stand on his own two feet.

Long-distance relationships were torture, but a long-distance relationship with someone who lived in freaking Tanzania bordered on impossible. It would be preposterous to try to continue this relationship.

She bit her lip.

The stupid gap in the door that she thought would protect her hadn't done a thing. His eyes were deep. And they held so much hope for a future. But for him to stand on his own feet, they couldn't be together.

"Open the door, Nadim. Let's say goodbye properly."

He grinned, no doubt pleased she seemed to understand him. This was a goodbye, but without regrets. After a final squeeze of her hand, he let her go and she stood. She heard him unlatch the chain, and seconds after the door was opened, she was pulled into the most enveloping, worshiping hug of her life.

He squeezed tightly as she buried her face into his neck, inhaling his clean manly smell for maybe the last time.

His hands rubbed her back for a second before trailing down tantalizingly slowly, until she was completely in his arms.

She inhaled into his chest, and then used one hand to clutch at his shirt while the other pulled his neck down to capture his lips in a deep kiss.

CHAPTER THIRTY-FOUR

Reena had some vague ideas from books and movies of what goodbye sex would be like. She expected it to be bittersweet. Sensual. Lingering looks and worshiping hands, searching over every inch of their bodies, slowing down to memorize every sight, every touch, every sensation to capture the memory, forever. It was supposed to be an intense, transcendent experience.

Instead, Nadim ran away for a second to get a condom before fucking her senseless against his front door. The same door she'd sat against for half an hour, listening to him tell her she felt like home. But just like everything else that had happened with Nadim, their final night together didn't abide by anything as mundane as *expectations*. It was playful. Exuberant. Exactly perfect in every way.

Sweater still on one wrist and bra hanging off her elbow, Reena held on to his shoulders as she caught her breath.

"Wow" was all he could manage, head resting against hers.

"I can't believe you did that," she said. "What's wrong with a bed?"

"Nothing's wrong with a bed. I love beds. Especially pink four-poster beds with 'I heart Spike' carved into the headboard. But we have so many surfaces we haven't made love on."

"How many surfaces are we talking, here?" She lowered herself to the ground and attempted to replace most of her clothes.

Grinning, he pulled her to his sofa before she could put her sweater on. "Hoping you had a good dinner; you'll need the energy." He kissed her again, kneeling in front of her. "No more secrets?" he whispered in her neck.

"None."

He smiled, pulling back to look at her. "Good. Because I've been meaning to ask you...were you really Team Spike? I thought all the girls were into Angel."

She laughed, looping her arms around his neck. "What the hell would I do with a brooding, moody vampire? Even when I was fifteen, I preferred my blood suckers dangerously funny"—she leaned close—"and with sexy British accents." She kissed him. "You were probably into Buffy or Faith, right?"

He laughed. "Nope. Firmly Team Willow. Smart, adorable, and supernaturally talented with ingredients."

She chuckled as she leaned her head on his shoulder. "What's going to happen to my bed when you leave?" she asked.

"Don't know. Guess your parents will take it back. Want me to leave it for you?"

Reena frowned. She'd slept on that bed for probably eleven years but wasn't sure she could anymore.

After wrapping themselves in the throw from his couch, they sat, talking for hours about everything from their favorite books and TV, to places they wanted to visit, to ridiculous things they'd done in college. It was amazing. Their first night together with no fear of secrets coming out. No sidestepping topics. Just honesty.

She finally got the backstory of his foot fetish—he had gone to a classical Indian dance show as a boy and had been forced to sit on the floor right in front of the stage. The dancers' feet had been at eye level, and were adorned with belled anklets, toe rings, and elaborate mehndi. Watching those beautiful feet dance with agility and power had created a fascination with women's feet, and all that they could do. She laughed at his story but still pulled her socks off. Then, using the practiced dexterity she'd mastered the last few weeks, she used her toes to pull down the waistband of his flannel pants and show him exactly how talented her feet were. She loved watching him in that moment of bliss, eyes alternating between wonder and rolling back in his head with boneless pleasure. She finally had a moment she wanted to memorize—Nadim, completely stripped down to his base desires. Just for her.

Finally, they roused themselves from the nest of his couch to make sandwiches. It would be a long, energetic night, and they needed fuel.

She sliced his most recent sourdough (it still seemed a bit flat to her—she regretted that she wouldn't be able to show him her folding technique, which wouldn't deflate the dough so much), and he wrapped his arms around her back and inhaled in her neck. He looked down and chuckled. "Are you putting coriander chutney in my grilled cheese?"

"Yes. It's delicious. Trust me."

"When it comes to food, I always trust you." He released her and headed to the fridge. "You want a beer?"

"Nah, I'm fine. Just water."

He looked at her quizzically for a second before shrugging and pouring a glass of water. He watched her as she flipped over the sandwich. "You know, I'm going to really miss watching you cook." He put his hand on the back of her neck, rubbing her skin softly. "The semifinal results are live tomorrow, right? My dad already bought my ticket, but I can try to change it if we get into the finals. We can still do the last video."

She had assumed if they got into the finals, they'd have to forfeit. And she was okay with that. After all, if they won, then what? They weren't engaged. There'd be no marriage. The winners got a TV special. She didn't want to lie again, and definitely not on national TV.

"I'm okay. I...I don't really need it anymore." She took a deep breath. "I was so unsatisfied with my life, and it may sound weird, but I thought winning this would save me. But...maybe I don't need saving. Or maybe I can save myself. I don't want to lie anymore."

It stung to lose the opportunity for the Asler Institute scholarship. It was another loss to add to the pile. Like her career. And finding this amazing connection with someone, then watching it walk away. But even with all that loss, she still felt confident she would be okay.

She looked at Nadim. She'd been convinced that he was the only reason she was coping with unemployment this time. But maybe that wasn't true. Yes, Nadim had been there—but that's because she'd *let him in*. She'd trusted a man she didn't know, one her parents had set her up with no less, to support her when she knew she needed it. And when Nadim wasn't in her life anymore, she'd relied on other support. Her friends, and (shudder) even her family. She was no longer paralyzed with anxiety about her inability to cope with life. She *could* cope. She did. She didn't actually need him.

She did still want him, though.

Just minutes ago, they agreed on honesty. She knew his past now, the very things he hadn't wanted her to know. She could no longer keep the truths she'd hidden from him.

As they moved to the table with their sandwiches and sat side-by-side, Reena took a deep breath. Now was as good a time as ever.

"It's true, what I said."

"Hm?"

"That I'm okay, I meant it. And that's actually a bit of a surprise." She tried to smile. "This last week, since Sunday, it's been hard on me. But...I was strong. I was okay."

He smiled with such fondness that she thought she might let out a tear or two. Or twenty. She was so sad he was leaving. But she was okay.

He touched her cheek. "I don't know if I should be upset that you were okay about it all, because I was miserable, but Reena, you *are* strong," he said.

"That's just it. I was hiding this from you, but I'm not strong. I'm kind of a wreck." She paused. "I've been in really dark places before. Several times. The last time was when I lost my job a couple of years ago, I stopped doing...anything. I barely left the house for weeks. I drank a lot. Other times before that I didn't drink so much, but I just felt...dead inside. Like I didn't know how to feel anything anymore. They're depressive episodes. I've been on meds before, but haven't been on them for a while."

His head tilted. "Reena, I'm sorry."

"My sister has a diagnosed mental illness, too. But I always felt that my issues weren't as important or as severe as hers.

And, of course, mental illness isn't exactly openly discussed in this culture. I get through the episodes, usually by keeping very busy. That's why I started baking bread."

"So you're okay now?"

She shrugged. "I dunno. I feel okay, but who knows how I'll be tomorrow or next week." She left it unsaid that he was leaving next week. "I called my doctor today. I'm long overdue for a checkup, anyway. I've been pushing this under a rug, and I don't want to do that anymore."

He smiled softly and took her hand in his and squeezed. "See? Strong. I'm glad you told me." He pulled her into a deep, hard hug, and she buried her face into his chest.

He leaned back to look at her and kissed her briefly. "I'm still sorry about the contest. I know how much you wanted that course. It would have been good for you."

She linked her arms around his neck. "It's fine. Honestly." It had to be fine. The perfection of this goodbye, their honesty, she couldn't risk souring it. The memories of the video shoots with him told her one thing loud and clear—she could not, she would not survive another one with this man. His heartfelt speeches about home, food, and belonging. His loving glances at her. The last video's theme was supposed to be family celebrations. She couldn't celebrate family with the man who would never be her family.

~

They had a long, lingering kiss in the hallway in the morning, and Reena finally felt bittersweet about this night. The unfair feeling that the moment couldn't go on forever mingled with her gratitude for right now. He may not love her the way she loved him, but this *meant* something to him. Something huge.

"So..." she said, not sure how to leave it.

He laughed. "So, I wish I could stick around with you all day, but I have two meetings I can't miss. I know it's my last week of work, but—"

She smiled. "Go. Don't piss off my dad." She shoved him gently toward his apartment.

He took two steps backward into his unit. "Will we see each other again?"

She bit her lip. "I don't..." She shook her head. "I don't know if we should." She smiled sadly as tears gathered in the corners of her eyes. She couldn't spend the next few days with him without making the goodbye harder. "This has been perfect. Thank you," she whispered.

He reached out and took her hand. Raising it to his lips, he skimmed the back of her hand with a ghost of a kiss. "No, Reena, thank you. Expect to hear from me soon from Dar es Salaam. Whether you want it or not, you have a new friend in Africa." He let her go, smiled, and closed the door.

It was over.

CHAPTER THIRTY-FIVE

I t seemed unlikely Reena would be able to manage much for the rest of the day but catch up on lost sleep, so she changed into her coziest sweats, brewed a large mug of coffee, and sat on the couch to think. She had made a big decision on the two steps between their goodbye kiss in the hallway and her apartment—no more searching for a finance job. She wasn't sure what she would do instead, and she realized she would probably take a significant pay cut to start a new career, but she was done with taking the easier route, if that easy came with misery. Tomorrow she would call Abigail to talk to her about a career change. Maybe even look into classes to retrain in a new field. And she would talk to her parents about this. She had no intention of working with them, but she would take the support they would no doubt give—on her own terms. She pulled her computer onto her lap. It was time for research.

Reena had barely opened the continuing education site for a local community college when her phone rang. Saira.

"Mum says hurry up because there's always a line at the kebob place. Who goes for kebobs in the morning anyway?"

"Saira, what are you talking about?"

"We're downstairs. You on your way?"

Shit. Wedding clothes shopping. She forgot.

"Ugh, Saira, I had no sleep last night."

"Mum invited Shaila Aunty and Marley. You have to come."

Reena sighed. Great. A whole family thing. She was not in the headspace for this. "Give me a couple minutes."

She was dressed and out the front door in a little under ten minutes. The grungy ripped jeans that were conveniently hanging off the end of her bed weren't the best choice for a day spent at Indian formal wear stores, but she couldn't make herself care about her appearance now.

Shaila Aunty and Marley were in the car when she got to it. She slid in next to Marley. After greeting her mother and aunt, she turned to her cousin. "Hey, Marley, how come you're joining us?"

"I needed her fashion expertise," Saira said, leaning over Marley. "And Shaila Aunty knows the manager of this store."

Shaila Aunty turned to look at Reena. "He gave me a great deal on the sari I wore to my Eid party. Remember, my yellow georgette? It's all about building relationships."

The kebob place was in the same plaza as the sari shop—in a newish, suburban strip mall that catered mostly to the Indian population living in Markham. It still felt strange to Reena to see sari shops and Indian grocers in the suburbs, but the diaspora was all over the greater Toronto area these days, not just in the city.

And the shop was *good*. Over paper plates of spicy kebobs, tender-crisp vegetable samosas, and steaming cups of rich masala chai, they chatted about color schemes and menus for Saira's wedding.

"You're not going to serve this heathy food, are you?" Mum asked. "Ashraf's family will run screaming if you give them tandoori tofu and kale pakoras."

"Tandoori tofu sounds disgusting," Reena said, "but kale pakoras…" She thought about it. "If you added rice flour to the batter, they'd be really crisp."

Saira smiled. "We're thinking we'll have some organic, healthier options, but we'll do the greasy Indian stuff, too. I mean, this is a *wedding*. When I meet caterers, you're coming, Reena."

"Reena, beti, you have to teach Marley to cook better," Shaila Aunty said.

Mum nodded. "I taught both my girls to cook. Reena's biryani is even better than mine. Not her khichro, though."

Reena wasn't about to let that go. "Mum, you use a mix for khichro! At least mine's from scratch."

Shaila laughed and patted Marley's hand. "See! If you don't make biryani, you'll never get married. Although"—she smiled—"maybe you will marry a girl, and she'll know how to cook," Shaila Aunty said.

Mum laughed. "Can you imagine double the bridal clothes? The expense!"

"Mum." Marley rolled her eyes and took her hand out from under her mother's, "I'm not getting married. No one is getting married but Saira."

"Yes, beti, don't remind me," Mum said.

Reena chuckled, dipping a samosa into the ambli chutney.

"You don't want two weddings at once, though," Shaila Aunty said.

"No, of course not." Mum grabbed Shaila Aunty's hand. "Remember how upset Mummy was when you and Amin wanted to get married a month after my wedding? Such drama."

Shaila laughed. "She accused me of being pregnant!"

Marley frowned. "Ew."

Reena agreed. She'd rather not think about her aunties engaging in premarital sex.

"You were so lovey-dovey," Mum said. "Everyone thought it was a love match."

Reena frowned. "It wasn't a love match?"

Shaila Aunty smiled while putting another samosa on her plate. "I was so smitten with him, but technically, we were introduced by the matchmaker in the Jamatkhana."

"I really didn't like that woman," Mum said, stirring her tea. "She used to pinch my stomach and tell me to stop eating mandazi."

Reena knew that her mother and father's match had been arranged, too, but she didn't really have a lot of details. Her parents weren't exactly the sitting-around-the-dining-table-telling-stories-of-when-they-met kind of parents.

"I don't get how you both agreed to arranged marriages," Marley said. Reena was glad she said what Reena was thinking.

Shaila Aunty smiled. "It was normal, then. We were young, and our parents were trying to look out for our happiness." Shaila laughed. "Remember my wedding, Bhabhi? I had a fit because I couldn't get a custom wedding salwar kameez on time in Dar es Salaam. You took me to that shop in Nairobi, the one that did yours in ten days."

"Why'd you need your wedding dress in ten days, Mum?" Saira asked.

"We were engaged for only three weeks. It was the only appointment we could get for the Nikah, and we needed to be married for the visa to come to Canada," Mum explained.

"Also," Shaila Aunty added, laughing, "Aziz was afraid you would change your mind and go with that other boy who wanted to marry you."

Saira looked impressed. "Mum, you had *two* guys wanting to marry you?"

"Your mother was very popular with the boys then." Shaila Aunty chuckled.

Reena looked at her mother, one eyebrow raised.

Mum snorted. "I was never going to marry Salim. My parents didn't like him, so I didn't like him."

Reena dropped her kebob. "Holy Shit! Salim Shah!"

"Reena, language!"

"Salim Shah wanted to marry you, but you picked Dad! This explains everything!" Her father's rivalry with the man now made sense.

Mum just shrugged. "I trusted my parents' judgment. And it was the right choice, we've been very prosperous."

What could she say to that? From everything she'd heard about Salim Shah, Mum's parents were probably right. She understood Mum's subtext, though—that Reena should trust her parents' judgment. But if they didn't really *know* her, how could they pick someone for her?

But maybe they didn't know her because she didn't let them. And, besides, she *did* fall in love with a man they chose for her. She had fallen so hard that she could barely think (or walk) straight today. They saw something in Nadim despite knowing so little about his past. Maybe they knew her better than she thought.

She should give them more credit for that.

But in the end, she was still losing him because of them. If she had met Nadim in any other circumstance, none of their issues would have existed. She closed her eyes, pushing past the tears she felt forming. She needed to change the subject.

"You didn't marry him only because your parents wanted you to, did you? How could you know that would work?" Marley asked.

Mum smiled an unfamiliar smile. "You don't. You take a leap of faith. It's not hard, you know. You just need to find someone who makes you chai when you are tired, and who rubs your feet when they are sore instead of insisting you are wearing the wrong shoes."

Mum made it seem so simple. And perfectly appropriate, considering Nadim's little fetish.

"Now enough of this talk about marriages," Mum said. "Let's get to what's important: weddings."

~

As they walked toward the sari shop, Shaila Aunty clasped her hands together. "They fly in new stock from India every week. Only the latest designs. I asked the manager to put aside the best from this week's shipment for us to look at."

It was a huge shop, but instinctively, Reena went off on her own. Mum and Shaila Aunty seemed to be in some sort of contest for who knew the most about the newest styles coming out of India. And Marley, having more fashion sense in her pinky finger than the rest of them combined, acted as an age-appropriate advocate for Saira.

As Reena wandered toward the jewelry section of the store, she felt her phone vibrate with a text.

Nadim: Results were posted—congratulations. We made it to the finals.

Reena smiled as she texted him back.

Reena: Congratulations to you, too. We were a great team, weren't we?

Nadim: We were perfect. The offer still stands. I'll figure out a way to stay a little longer if you want to do this.

She looked up from her phone at the jewel-toned bangles and glimmering necklaces surrounding her. Her family in the distance, discussing color schemes and the benefits of georgette over silk.

Even if they won the whole thing, then what? He'd still leave after. And she'd still have to lie—to her family, to her friends, and to the FoodTV people. She'd still be pretending and avoiding the truth.

Reena: I don't want to lie anymore. I am sorry I put you in that position at all.

Nadim: I get it. I'm not sorry, though. I had a blast.

Reena: I did too.

The three little dots appeared on her screen again for a few seconds, and then a final text.

Nadim: No pressure. I'm packing and running errands for the next few days, but I would open my door if you knocked on it on Sunday.

Reena closed her eyes. Should she? She could have one more day.

Reena: I'll knock.

Reena put her phone away and looked closely at the jewelry in the display case. Like so many other little Indian girls, she'd always been drawn to the bright, colorful costume jewelry in

velvet boxes. A wave of nostalgia washed over her as she remembered being in so many similar stores all over the world. It
didn't matter where she was: here in the suburbs or in the city.
In London, Vancouver, or even in Dar es Salaam, Indian stores
permeated with the scent of incense, sequins, and silk gave
her that familiar feeling of shared culture. Home. Reena loved
being Indian. Loved the food, the glittery clothes, and today,
she even loved the deep-seated traditions. Like sari shopping
with aunties.

Resisting her parents' *interference* for so long all felt, in a way,
like resisting her culture. Family meant everything to them,
and parents were expected to look out for their children long
after they weren't children anymore. She was an individual, but
an individual who was part of a family.

But there had to be a middle ground—a way to make the
traditions work for her instead of stifling her.

As she approached the counter, a silvery chain in a black
box caught her eye. It was an odd shape—a large bracelet with
dangling bells on it and a big center medallion with a long chain
hanging off it ending with a ring. The whole thing looked huge,
like it had been designed for a basketball player's hands.

"Beautiful, isn't it?" the woman behind the counter said.

"It's gorgeous. Huge, though. Would never fit my wrist."

The woman laughed. "It's an anklet, dear. For your foot.
This one is a bridal one. But we have less ornate ones as well.
Can I show you?"

"Bridal?" Reena asked.

"Yes. It's designed to be worn with a wedding lehenga. Aren't
you here with a bridal party? I believe we pulled some lehengas
in the bride's size."

Reena couldn't be sure exactly what came over her at that moment, but it appeared her mouth had been disconnected from her logical brain.

But maybe this wasn't the time for logic. Maybe it was time for Reena to take her own leap of faith. "Yes, but could you show me some in *my* size?"

CHAPTER THIRTY-SIX

Considering her unemployment and her decision to change careers, Reena should not have spent over three hundred dollars on a turquoise and pink lehenga with matching costume jewelry, but she wasn't in any state to second-guess anything right now. This unhinged plan of hers was risky, but the money spent would be worth it if it worked.

She managed to hide the outfit from her family, who were too preoccupied by the discussion of whether orange or red looked better on Saira to notice Reena trying it on. When they saw her wrapped garment bag, Reena told them it was for Amira, who had no Indian stores nearby and who'd asked her to pick something up for her.

After Saira dropped Reena and Marley off at their apartment building, Reena said goodbye to her cousin and went straight to her bedroom and hung the lehenga in her closet, lightly fingering the subtle embroidery in ethereal silver and gold threads. It was so beautiful. The kind of outfit memories were made in.

Finally, she took a deep cleansing breath and took off her jeans and socks. She dug around her summer clothes to find a long, Indian-print skirt and white T-shirt. She took her hair out of its ponytail and added a bit of antifrizz serum to make sure her curls looked their best. Finally, she dabbed a bit of fragrance to her neck. She carefully removed the silver anklets from the black velvet box and fastened them to her feet, clipping the rings to her second toes. She wished she had time for a pedicure but needed to do this now before she lost her nerve, and her chance.

She closed her eyes, said a silent prayer for strength, and retrieved a single item from her dresser before leaving her apartment barefoot.

Reena knocked on Nadim's door, her heart pounding in her chest. She clutched the item in her hand, leaving it slippery from sweat on her palm. He left the door chain attached again when he opened and peeked out the four-inch gap in the door.

"Reena, it's you. Is everything okay?"

"Everything is fine. Perfect."

"Then … I thought we agreed not to draw this out … say our goodbyes on Sunday."

"I know. But I have something for you. Sit near the door, but don't open the chain."

"Okay …" Of course he was confused, but he did it anyway. She stepped in front of the opening in the door and could see him sitting cross-legged with a perplexed expression. "What are you up to?" he asked.

It was a bit of a squeeze, but she maneuvered one jeweled foot onto his lap.

She clearly heard him gasp, and she couldn't help but giggle. The lightest touch trailed on her foot as his fingers outlined the chain running from her toe to her ankle. And, of course, that made her giggle more. Maybe this was a bad idea—

someone with a foot fetish really shouldn't be with someone so ticklish.

"This is for me?" he asked, reverently.

"Yes. You like?"

"I love it." He chuckled, fingering the chain again. "This is beautiful."

"There's more." She squeezed her foot off his lap and back into the hallway. "Open the door."

Immediately after the door opened, he fell back down to the ground to look at both her feet this time. Running his fingers over the little bells around her ankles, hearing the soft jangling sound as they hit each other. She shivered as she closed the door behind her.

He looked up at her, eyes wide. "Are you trying to torture me?"

She laughed as she lowered herself to the ground as well, sitting in front of him, knees bent, both her feet in his cross-legged lap. He gripped her ankles before running his hands up under her skirt and over her smooth calves, and then back down to the anklets.

He looked into her eyes. "You're beautiful."

"I..." Her voice shook. She closed her eyes a second and then tried to smile. This was hard. Harder than she expected.

"I..." she started again. "You'll probably think I'm nuts, but I just want to put this out there. Whatever you say is fine—we'll still be friends—but I had to ask you before you leave..." She clenched her fist around the ring in her hand. "Nadim. Will you marry me?"

He stared at her for several seconds, his expression betraying shock, but nothing else. His hands around her ankles tightened. "Marry you?"

She smiled. "Yes. I know it's sudden and ridiculous, but hear me out. We can run to Niagara Falls to one of those twenty-four-hour wedding places before you leave. Then I can sponsor you to come back to Canada as my family. It may take a bit, and we'd have to prove to immigration that this relationship is real, but we have those FoodTV videos as proof. And if the immigration doesn't work or if you don't want to live here, I'll come there, wherever you are. London, Dar es Salaam, it doesn't matter." Her voice cracked. "Maybe this isn't about standing on our own feet to defy our families, but instead choosing the family we want. And I want you to be my family. I'm on my way to falling in love with you. I have your thirty-dollar ring..." Her voice trailed off, losing steam as she showed him the swirling emotions in her eyes.

What she said wasn't entirely true, she wasn't *on her way* to falling in love, but had already been swept in a tidal wave so strong she thought she'd drown. She had no doubt she loved him enough to survive oceans of separation and an uphill fight to be together.

But would he be willing to take this leap of faith, too? Not because his father ordered it, or her father encouraged it, but because *he* wanted to be with her forever? She watched his face, seeing no expression. He was silent.

This was a mistake. He didn't want her. Mortified, Reena looked down, feeling her eyes well up. She squeezed them shut.

His hand suddenly left her ankle to gently open the fingers on her right hand, exposing the thirty-dollar cubic zirconia ring he'd bought her. He took it from her hand and smiled. Then, ever so slowly, he placed it on the ring finger of her left hand.

"Yes," he whispered, still holding her hand. "I will marry you. Yes, to all of it. Niagara Falls, you sponsoring me to come back. Living here, or there, wherever. I am *not* on my way to falling in love with you. I am already there. And I want you to be my family, forever."

"Yes?"

He nodded. "Yes. I love you, Reena." And he pulled her by the arms onto his lap completely and kissed her like no one had kissed her ever before.

She finally pulled away, needing a break, even a tiny one, from the intensity. "Are you sure?" she whispered.

He took her hand in his and kissed the finger that held the ring. He smiled—a wide, incandescent smile that she could look at every day of her life.

He nodded. "Absolutely sure. This...you...are my home. But..." He grinned, pulling her even closer. "I should come clean, there is one more thing you don't know." He kissed the ring on her finger again. "This cost me more than thirty dollars."

Reena's eyes widened. A diamond this size would be worth thousands. Thousands she didn't want. She wanted the fake ring to celebrate their real love.

He grinned widely. "It was actually sixty dollars. Plus, I paid extra for the box."

She laughed, wrapping her hands behind his head and pulling him in. Enough of this talking, she just wanted to kiss.

They should have gotten up off the floor to start planning. They had to figure out how to get a marriage license fast, find a wedding place in Niagara Falls and book it, and call Amira. And Reena had another idea brewing for Sunday, but it would also need a lot of planning and pulling some strings. But instead they just kissed until he finally picked her up off his lap and took her to his bedroom.

And Reena got the reverent, intense, sensual sex she expected. Apparently, that wasn't for endings, but for beginnings.

～

They started planning early the next morning. A quick Google search found a Toronto-based wedding officiant who specialized in elopements in the city, so thankfully they could avoid the drive to Niagara Falls. They'd met in Toronto, and Reena wanted to get married here if possible. After taking the subway downtown to get their license at city hall, they called the officiant and arranged for her to come over late in the evening. License in hand, Reena called Amira.

Her best friend was, of course, shocked and appalled that Reena would do such a thing as elope after only a few weeks of dating, and spoke louder and faster than normal voicing her objections. But once she got it off her chest, Amira informed Reena she wouldn't allow her best friend to tie the knot without standing next to her. She assured them that she and Duncan would leave straight after work and arrive at the apartment, hopefully before the officiant.

She called Saira next, who sounded surprised but happy. She said she was glad Reena was doing this, because if Mum disagreed with any of her own wedding plans, she could just threaten to elope like her big sister. Reena wanted to call Marley and Shayne next, but she knew they were both working late shifts at their retail jobs.

And so, on Friday night, under the October stars on the tiny back deck of her father's building still decorated with glowing white balls of light and rainbow-colored patio chairs, Reena Manji and Nadim Remtulla were married. The bride wore a turquoise and pink lehenga with her hair open on her shoulders, silver anklets on her feet, and to the groom's delight, no shoes. The groom wore a gray kurta with turquoise Converse high-tops that he bought to match the bride's lehenga. Standing beside them, the maid of honor wore a black pencil skirt with killer stiletto boots, the bridesmaid (who'd rushed straight from work) wore jeans and a Nourish health-food store T-shirt, and the best man wore jeans and a red plaid flannel shirt, his vibrant red beard reflecting the low light on the deck.

It was the strangest wedding Reena had ever attended, and it was exactly the fairy-tale wedding she didn't know she wanted. In a single word, it felt *perfect*.

CHAPTER THIRTY-SEVEN

After the ceremony the entire wedding party started brainstorming plans for a reception. And Saturday morning they started making phone calls to plan the event. Not too early, though. It was, after all, the day after Reena's wedding night. First, they called Steve at the Sparrow to secure the venue. Then, together, they called Anderson, explaining that Nadim needed to head back to Tanzania this week, so could they please bump up the video shoot for the contest finals. Anderson, thankfully, was easily convinced, once Reena hinted that Shayne would be there. Then they called their family and friends to invite them—and they fully expected a significant portion of those calls to go badly.

Mum and Dad were not happy. In fact, it took Reena a while to get them to believe she was married at all. And once they did, Mum was so furious, she hung up on Reena.

Well…at least it was better than yelling? Hopefully with time their anger would mellow a bit. Reena shrugged as she put her phone down, not really caring too much what her parents thought right now.

"What'd your father say?" she asked Nadim as he walked out of his room. Reena did not see it as a good sign that he had been in there for less than fifteen minutes.

He squeezed his lips together before smiling sadly. "He's not impressed."

Reena didn't know if he wasn't pleased that Nadim eloped, or if it was his choice of bride. Either way, she could see how upset Nadim was about the damage to the relationship with his father. Reena crossed the room and put her arms around her husband. She wouldn't press—if he didn't want to tell her what his father said, it was fine. She wasn't fooling herself—she knew they were building something, and they weren't there yet. But they would be.

They held each other tightly for several seconds. He inhaled deeply into her hair. "Love you," he whispered.

"Love you, too."

Shayne and Marley appeared soon after, squealing with joy over Reena's texts about last night's wedding. Amira and Duncan, who were still across the hall in Reena's apartment, heard the squealing and came to join the party. And it really was a party, because she was still telling Shayne and Marley about their moonlit wedding when there was a loud banging on Nadim's door.

Reena took a deep breath before opening it. She knew who it would be.

"Reena, is this some joke?" Mum said the moment the door was open. Her father was there, too. Both with tight faces and stiff postures. Saira stood behind them, a wide smile on her face. And Ashraf stood behind her, looking bewildered about this family he'd attached himself to. She didn't blame him.

"C'mon in. The more the merrier." She motioned her family into Nadim's apartment. It was a tight squeeze. Ten people in a small apartment covered with boxes and suitcases.

Mum walked in, dropped her purse on the counter, and turned, glaring at Reena. "You really *married* him?"

"Yes. We eloped last night. I'm very happy, Mum."

Mum somehow managed to make her frown bigger. "Without your family? And what is this...eloped! That is not a wedding! You need a Nikah in the Jamatkhana, and mehndi, and a big reception. Maybe at the Toronto Ismaili Centre, or—"

"Wait—so you don't have an issue with who I married, or that I did it so quickly, only that I didn't have a big wedding?"

Amira stepped forward. "It was a lovely ceremony. Outside, under the stars."

Mum glared at Amira for three seconds before turning back to Reena. "*She* was there, but not us? Not your sister?"

"Actually, I was there," Saira interjected. "I was sworn to secrecy, though. It was so romantic! Might think about eloping myself!"

Mum glared at Saira this time. She was really getting good mileage out of her frown today. This must be how Mum made those Vegas high rollers quiver in their seats.

"Um," Marley said, inching awkwardly toward the door. "Hey, Duncan and Amira, why don't we go upstairs to my place. Duncan said he wanted to see my...um...Gucci bag?"

Reena snorted. She couldn't blame her friends for seeking a swift escape from the family drama unfolding. She only wished she could go with them.

The moment Marley, Shayne, Amira, and Duncan were out of the apartment, Dad sighed and sat heavily on that hideous green armchair. Reena looked from one parent to the other, wondering if she should offer them chai or vodka or anything that could cut through the thick tension in the room, but decided against it—Nadim's coffee cups were packed. She motioned for Mum to sit on the couch and took the seat next to her. Ashraf and Saira took the barstools in the dining room, and Nadim sat on the other side of Reena, immediately putting his hand on her knee and squeezing shakily. She squeezed back, giving her husband the strength he was looking for.

She smiled. *Husband, husband, husband.*

She freaking loved that. Her hand covered his.

Dad cleared his throat. "I wanted to come speak to you alone, but all of…them insisted on joining us."

"As they should," Reena said. "This is a family, right?"

Dad gestured to Nadim with his hand. "Your father called me ten minutes after Reena did. But you probably knew that."

"I assumed he would," Nadim said.

"He thinks I forced you to elope so I could get his money back. That's not true, but I had no answer as to the reason why you have done this. He wants you to get the marriage annulled."

"We did this because we want to be married. This wasn't about money," Reena said, teeth clenching.

Nadim squeezed her even tighter. "I married her because I love her, sir. More than I've ever loved anyone. And I will spend the rest of my life showing her that."

Damn. Why weren't they alone? She wondered briefly if she could pull this man to his bedroom to kiss him senseless.

Mum frowned sharply. "So, you're going against your father's wishes?"

Nadim nodded. "He pulled his investment in the Diamond project, so it doesn't matter what he says anymore. My life, and my job, are no longer tied to him. He wanted me to marry

Reena, and I have. I don't care that it's not according to his terms, or that's he's suddenly decided she's not good enough. He's wrong—Reena is everything. More than I deserve."

Dad's face softened just a hint. "This isn't a game. This is my daughter's life."

"Yes, Dad. It's my life," Reena clarified. "And you used us both. Used Nadim because you needed his father's investment and me because his father wanted a good wife for him. So don't pretend you're suddenly concerned—"

Dad put his hands up to prevent her from saying more. "I know, Reena. I wanted you to get to know each other, not run away and get married so fast. If this is some sort of rebellion against us...you cannot gamble your life, or your happiness, because of your family's mistakes."

"Why can't you believe it's real? Why would you think either of us would marry someone as a *rebellion*?"

"I don't know what to think." He looked at Nadim. "First engaged to marry Jasmine Shah, and now eloping with my daughter? So, tell me, how can I trust your loyalty to this family?"

Jesus Christ, Dad needed to stop. "Oh, hell, no." Reena stood up and pointed a finger at him. "Don't you play that *Godfather* intimidation thing the day after I marry the man. *Our* family...you say...well, did you think about *our* family when *you* both lied to all of us? Mum's off hustling cards with her badass seniors club while Saira smokes spliffs in the garage. And worst of all, *you* made a deal with a man you barely knew to bring his *miscreant* son here to marry one of your daughters because your company was swindled, and you won't admit it! You had no idea of Nadim's character or integrity, or his life before moving here, and yet you threw me at him like a prized goat! And now you want to talk about family loyalty?" She frowned and looked at Nadim, realizing this monologue wasn't very generous to him. "Sorry, babe. Love you."

He chuckled. "Love you, too. Please, carry on."

She stared at her father.

"It's medicinal marijuana," Saira clarified.

"Hustling cards?" Ashraf asked.

Reena sat back down and took a deep breath. "Nadim and I are *married*. This is the life we chose, and you have to accept it. He's going to Tanzania on Monday, and I'm planning to sponsor his immigration so he can come back as soon as possible. If that doesn't work, I'll try to move to Tanzania. We know it's going to be a tough couple of months, or longer. So, what I need from you, my *family*, right now, is to please give me space. Support me. I'm going to have enough pain and turmoil..." Her voice cracked. She squeezed her eyes shut a moment. "For the next two days I'm celebrating, because it's going to be torture to live without my husband for the foreseeable future. I am *not* letting you guys and your barrel of secrets ruin these two days. Now if you'll excuse us, we have a wedding reception to plan."

Everyone was silent for a while. Long enough to feel awkward. Reena wiped the tears in her eyes and leaned into Nadim, while he squeezed her hand tightly.

Finally, Mum shifted and looked at Reena. "Reception? You getting biryani, or tandoori and naan?"

CHAPTER THIRTY-EIGHT

Reena's family stayed after her little outburst, and together they planned the menu for tomorrow's party. Mum finally dragged the crew out after chai and cookies, insisting she needed to make the catering order at her favorite Indian restaurant in person, and also had to squeeze time in for a trip to Little India for some emergency sari shopping. Miraculously, no one mentioned anything about the secrets Reena had told when she lost it on them, not the poker, the weed, or even the swindling architect. And that suited her perfectly. She needed to get through these two days—her family was welcome to implode under the weight of all the truths after Nadim left the country.

It was weird, though, interacting with her parents and Saira with no judgments, no forcing of their ideals on her, just healthy unconditional support—even if it was only short-term. If she'd known all she needed to do was elope to get some normal time with her family, she would have done it years ago.

But, no. She didn't know Nadim years ago. And there was no one else in the world she could imagine marrying.

At eight o'clock Saturday night, long after her family had left, an unexpected mehndi artist showed up, telling Reena she'd been hired to do full bridal mehndi. The poor woman had probably never applied mehndi to a bride's feet while the groom sat happily on the floor watching the process, but she did a beautiful job anyway.

Finally, Sunday morning at the regular brunch time, Reena and Nadim met their friends and family in the private functions room at the back of the Sparrow to celebrate their marriage, and to film the final video for the cooking contest. The party was planned with her parents, with collaboration instead of compromise. A traditional Indian meal served in the back room of their favorite pub. Both bride and groom wore the traditional Indian clothing they'd been married in (Reena in strappy sandals instead of barefoot this time), and the guests wore a mixture of formal Indian and Western clothes.

Shaila Aunty and Amin Uncle arrived together with several trays of jalebi, ganthiya, and platters of sweets. Her aunt hugged her tightly before presenting her with a silver wrapped box. Reena guessed it was filled with a bit of bridal gold. "This is wonderful! Look how sneaky you are, not giving us a hint of this when we met last week! And thank you so much for inviting us to celebrate with you."

"Thank you for coming, and for this!" Reena said, taking the box from her aunt.

"Were we supposed to bring presents?" Shayne asked, walking in with Marley.

"I didn't," Amira said. "But I've only been home for three minutes since Friday morning. It's kind of short notice for presents."

"Not for me," Saira added. "I got her the *best* present. I doubt anyone will top it."

Reena laughed. Saira stealing the thunder only felt hilarious today.

Steve came into the room. "An enormously pregnant woman and a man with a lot of curly hair just wandered into the bar looking for you, Reena," he said.

Saira beamed. "That's my present!"

Happy tears and a huge grin erupted on Reena's face as her big brother and his very pregnant wife came into the room. He laughed as he approached Reena and hugged her tightly.

"Khizar, you're here!"

"We woke up at the crack of dawn to catch a flight to get here on time." He hugged her again.

"I didn't think you'd come when we talked yesterday. I can't even believe it! I'm so happy to see you!"

He smiled and kissed her forehead. "My baby sister got married. Where else would I be?"

"I thought I was the baby sister," Saira said.

"You're both my baby sisters." He opened his arms to get Saira into the group hug.

Reena hugged Nafissa next, and rubbed the belly containing her two baby nieces before introducing her new husband to her brother and sister-in-law.

Husband. She could not stop smiling to herself. How could she have possibly been so lucky?

"We have a gift, too," Dad said, "and we'd like to give it to you now, before the party starts," Dad said.

Reena looked around. Most of their guests had arrived, as well as the camera crew. Amira and Marley were helping people find seats. She smiled and looked at Mum and Dad, expecting them to pull out a box of wedding jewelry. Instead, Dad handed Nadim a slim envelope.

With a confused expression, he opened it. Inside, on her father's company letterhead, was an offer of employment.

Reena blinked a few times. Was this real? Dad wanted to rehire Nadim? What about his father's money?

She looked at her husband, who also looked confused. Then she looked at her father, who was smiling.

"Nadim, I hired you to work in my company because of your father's investment. I didn't expect you would end up being one of the best managers we have ever had. And when I wondered if you and Reena might be a good match, I could not have predicted just how right for each other you two are. Now that you are family, I hope you will let me help you the way I would help any of my children." He paused, looking from Reena to Nadim. "I would be honored to have you continue to work for me. It is your decision, but should you choose, you can stay here, employed in the family business as general manager of the Diamond project, with the same ownership stake I agreed on with your father but without his investment. The work visa will continue, and we will all sponsor you to stay here with us. As family."

Nadim's eyes were wide as saucers. "Really?"

"Yes, really. This is a business decision. Half my construction team was in my office on Friday demanding I bring you back. I made some calls, and thanks to your outreach and professionalism, I have easily secured funding from other investors to keep the project going. And I, personally, would love to finally work with my family."

Nadim laughed as he reached out to shake Dad's hand. "Of

course. Yes. I want to be where Reena is. And it would be an honor to continue learning from you, sir."

Dad let go of Nadim's hand and pulled him into a hug. "No more Sir. Dad. Welcome to the family." He shook his head, smiling. "Heaven help you. You'll need it."

Dad then took Reena's hands and recited a series of prayers for their happiness, health, and prosperity before pulling her into a hug. "Congratulations, Reena. I really wish you all the best."

"Thank you, Dad. Seriously. Thank you so much for this."

"No, I feel like we should be thanking you," Dad said as he stepped back to put a hand on Mum's shoulder. "Your mother is going to teach me to play cards. She says poker will help me in my business."

Reena's eyes widened. Her father? Poker?

"It will bring us closer, too," Mum explained. "We must let each other into our lives." Reena clutched Nadim's arm, resting her head on his shoulder. She would never stop letting him into all the parts of her life.

"Imagine." Mum looked at Dad, eyes dancing with joy. "Two children married, and the third engaged. We are very blessed."

Dad seemed uncomfortable with all this familial joy, though, and started searching the room. "Did Saira speak to you?"

"No. About what?"

Dad frowned. "Saira? Come!"

Saira appeared, rolling her eyes. "Steve was just about to tell me what's in the lentil soup..."

"Tell her what we talked about last night," Dad ordered.

"Fine." She turned to Reena. "Dad still hasn't finalized a

lease for the corner unit in the Diamond building. I proposed he rent it to me. To us, actually, if you're willing."

"You want to go into business? With me?"

"Yes. The space is perfect for a store/café. Or bakery/store/café. You're the best cook out there, and we both know a thing or two about retail management. And then the cookbook—who's to say we can't pitch the project together? Hell, I know the food will be better with your help, and the publishers will probably cream themselves to get a name attached to this FoodTV contest of yours. The cookbook could tie into the café, gaining us more exposure."

After cringing at Saira for saying *cream themselves* in front of Mum and Dad, Reena felt an unfamiliar optimism blossom in her core. It was a preposterous idea. A ridiculous, ambitious, wonderful idea. Owning her own café instead of working numbers. Surrounded by bread instead of cubicles.

"How can we afford it?"

"With a partner," Dad said. "Put together a business plan, and maybe I'll invest. I think it might be a good idea to sell your building and focus on the Diamond project completely."

Mum grinned. "I asked Leon if he would help with your business plan, and he's offered to mentor you to help get it off the ground. He wanted to hire you at Top Crust, by the way, but Angie wanted the more *numbers* person. Leon always lets his employees have the final say for staffing their own departments."

Holy shit. Leon Bergeron, the president of Top Crust bakery, offered to mentor her to help start her own bakery?

"Wait, Mum, is Leon doing this so you'll finally let him into your poker club?"

Mum nodded. "Probably. But sometimes we have to make sacrifices for family. And if we let men in, then your father can join, too. We'll have to change the name."

Reena laughed. Oh, lord, to be a fly on the wall in that poker game. Reena thought about it. This venture would mean working with her father, her mother, her sister, and her mother's friend. A terrifying prospect, but...It was just a proposal. She wasn't committing to anything.

"Okay. Let's talk about this and maybe put together a proposal."

"Yay!" Saira squealed, hugging her way too tight. Reena felt so good about this idea. She was ready to build this with her family.

Marley cornered her next. "Love is in the air. Look," she said, pointing to the area where the FoodTV cameraperson was setting up big LED lights on poles. Shayne stood nearby with his arm around Anderson Lin. Shayne was staring fondly at Anderson's earlobe, probably considering taking it in his mouth. And Anderson was an adorable shade of pink.

Reena giggled. Then stilled. If Anderson and Shayne were going to be a thing again, she needed to come clean about everything, no matter what it meant for the contest. She pulled on Nadim's arm and guided him toward them.

"Anderson, before we film the segment, Nadim and I have a confession. We weren't really engaged when we entered the contest." She explained everything, their parents setting them up, their refusal to be married, and the fake engagement to enter the contest.

Anderson frowned. "So, you're not really married?"

"Yeah, we're married now, but we weren't engaged when we made the videos," Nadim said.

"So, you weren't a couple back then?"

"No, we were a couple." Reena said. "Just not *engaged*."

Anderson shrugged. "You guys are making this more complicated than it needs to be. Your parents set you up, you were a couple, and now you're married. Sounds like you were engaged to me. I'd like to start in five minutes. Are you ready?"

Reena and Nadim looked at each other and burst out laughing. Anderson was as wise as he was cute. There had been nothing fake about their engagement, ever.

Reena's face felt like it would split in two as she walked toward the front of the room, holding Nadim's hand. Mum and Dad's gift had changed everything. He wasn't leaving. She didn't think she's ever been so happy in her life. Until a sudden thought occurred to her. She pulled Nadim to the corner behind tables overladen with smoky tandoori chicken, fluffy naan, cucumber-mint raita, saffron-scented rice, and huge bowls of fresh green salads. She put her hands on her husband's forearms and bit her lip.

"You okay with my Dad's job offer?" she asked.

His grin was wide, not a hint of apprehension behind that intense gaze. "I'm ecstatic about it. I can't believe I get to stay here with you. I am so happy right now."

"But"—she tried to smile, but her nerves were going into high alert—"it turns out we didn't *need* to get married to get you a visa...I mean if Dad wants to hire you back anyway, then you have the work permit, and—"

He kissed her. Not too long, or too deep (a great man knew when *not* to mess up a woman's lipstick) but with more love than she'd thought was possible in her life. "It's a good thing I married you because I *wanted* to then, not because I needed to."

She sighed with relief and wrapped her hands around his neck. "I love you."

He kissed her neck before whispering in her ear, "If you open that place with your sister, I'll be your landlord."

She smiled. "I know. We'll play landlord and tenant later for practice."

He chuckled, burying his face in her neck and inhaling deeply. "I don't get it. How do you always smell like...home? Like you belong right here in my arms."

She laughed as she pulled him toward the table at the front. The ylang-ylang. Her mother was a bloody genius.

Finally, they were ready to start filming the video. Guests sat at tables surrounding Reena and Nadim, who stood in front of a long table decorated with cut flowers, her big cutting board, and a little hot plate. They were going to demonstrate how to make samosas and masala chai, but the food itself wasn't as important as the celebration.

"Okay, we're ready. Try not to look at the camera, and look natural," Anderson instructed the brunch guests.

After delivering their practiced on-screen banter while filling samosa wrappers with a mixture of spiced turkey, peas, and potatoes, they boiled chai with lightly crushed spices. Nadim looked at the camera.

"Today's theme is family celebrations. And while so many people across this country are celebrating Thanksgiving, we are celebrating something else. Just two days ago, this beautiful woman and I stood under the stars and said our vows together.

And today, we have invited our friends and family together to celebrate our marriage. We have learned from our pasts and are excited for our future. But more than anything, we are savoring our present." He leaned down and kissed her.

Reena grinned to the camera. "And we are so grateful to all of our family for joining us! Home cooking has connected us to our roots, to our homes, to our families, and to each other." She held up a glass of champagne. "To home cooking!"

After the toast, Nadim put his glass down and looked into Reena's eyes. She couldn't believe how lucky she had been that day to find him in her lobby. She couldn't believe this life was really hers. She bit her lip before linking her arms around his neck and pulling him down. "I love you," she said against his lips.

He smiled widely before kissing her.

"Cut! Amazing. That's a wrap. You're all done," Anderson said once they pulled apart.

But they weren't all done. They had only just begun.

PRESS RELEASE

TORONTO—Sisters Saira Manji and Reena Remtulla announced a June 5 grand opening of REESA's, a high-concept café, bakery, and health food store in Markham, Ontario.

Reena and her husband, Nadim Remtulla, famously won the FoodTV *Home Cooking Showdown* in October, wowing viewers with their homey Indian cooking and playful banter. The couple was recently showcased in a FoodTV special, highlighting Canada's rich culture of home cooking. Reena was previously a successful food blogger whose amateur bread baking won many blogging awards.

Saira's background is in dietary nutrition, and she was a regular blogger on the Nourish food blog, where she demonstrated how to adapt Indian recipes for the health-conscious. The sisters have also penned a cookbook, which will be in stores in September, containing recipes for traditional and modern delicacies, as well as naturally leavened breads from around the world.

Mentored by Leon Bergeron, president of the Top Crust Bakery chain, Saira and Reena promise soups, sandwiches, and lunch fare, along with slow-fermented sourdough breads and delectable pastries at REESA's. They also plan to showcase traditional East African Indian cuisine, and will serve fresh rotis, bhajias, samosas, and kebobs, along with what they call the best masala chai north of the 401 highway. REESA's, with its elegant decor inspired by India and East Africa, promises to be a welcome addition to an up-and-coming Markham neighborhood.

Media inquiries can be addressed to: Nadim Remtulla, General Manager, Diamond Enterprises.

NADIM'S ZANZIBAR EGG CURRY

- 1 large onion, peeled
- 1 400-gram can whole tomatoes (14 oz.)
- 1 tbsp cooking oil or ghee
- 1 cinnamon stick
- 3 cloves
- ½ tsp mustard seeds
- 4 green cardamom pods
- 1 tsp grated ginger (or ginger puree)
- 2 cloves garlic, minced (or 1 tsp garlic puree)
- 1 tsp ground coriander seed
- 1 tsp ground cumin seed
- ½ tsp ground fennel seeds
- ½ tsp Kashmiri chili powder (or cayenne pepper)
- 1 tsp salt
- 2 medium potatoes, peeled, and cut into 1½-inch cubes
- 8 hard-boiled eggs, shelled
- Handful of chopped cilantro for serving

1. In a food processor, chop onion until fine (or dice fine by hand). Rinse food processor bowl, then use it to puree tomatoes.
2. In medium saucepan, heat oil or ghee over medium heat. Add cinnamon stick, cloves, mustard seeds, and cardamom. Cook for 2 minutes, then add onions.
3. Cook the onions over medium heat until brown—almost burned. If onions stick to the bottom of the pot, add a splash of water to deglaze and continue browning. Keep going this way until onions are very brown.

4. Reduce heat to medium low, and add ginger, garlic, remaining spices, and salt. Stir and cook one minute. Add pureed tomatoes. Stir through, then simmer with the lid on for 5 minutes.

5. Add potatoes and whole boiled eggs, stir, and simmer 15 to 20 minutes until the potatoes are soft.

6. Garnish with cilantro, and serve with parathas.

REENA'S PLAIN PARATHAS

- 2 cups durum atta flour (or substitute whole wheat flour)
- ½ tsp salt
- 2 tbsp vegetable oil
- 1-1¼ cup warm water
- ¼ cup vegetable oil or ghee for brushing
- Extra atta flour for rolling out

1. Mix flour and salt in a bowl.
2. Add 2 tbsp oil, and rub between fingers until it looks like coarse meal and holds together when squeezed in hand.
3. Drizzle warm water over it, a little at a time, and mix by hand until a soft dough is formed. It should be quite soft and pliable and a little sticky.
4. Knead dough for about five minutes until no longer sticky. Add more flour if necessary, but dough should be soft.
5. Form into a ball and cover. Rest at least 30 minutes.
6. Knead dough briefly again and divide into 6 equal balls.
7. Coat one ball completely in flour, and roll in plenty of flour to prevent sticking. Roll with a rolling pin to a 7-to-8-inch circle. (Skip to cooking step 11 to make maani/rotis/chapatti instead of parathas.)
8. Brush surface with oil or melted ghee. Sprinkle with a pinch of flour.
9. Perform 2 letter folds with the circle of dough to create layers. To do this, fold the top third of the circle down. Brush folded side with oil and sprinkle with flour. Fold the bottom third up, covering the folded side of the last fold. Brush with oil and sprinkle with flour. You should now

have a narrow strip of dough like a folded letter. Repeat previous two folds, folding the right third toward the left, brushing with oil and sprinkling with flour, then folding the left third to the right, covering the folded side of the last fold.

10. Now you should have a 2-to-3-inch square of dough. Sprinkle with flour and roll out again, pressing evenly and turning often to maintain the square shape. Roll to a 7-to-8-inch square.

11. Place rolled paratha on a dry pan heated on medium. Cook about one minute until you see small bubbles on the surface. Flip and brush with oil/ghee. It should start ballooning up at this point. Press the bubbles with a spatula to encourage layers. Flip again and brush the other side with oil/ghee.

12. Keep cooking, flipping often and pressing the bubbles and edges with the spatula until cooked through, with dark spots on both sides. Keep in a covered container to prevent drying out.

13. Repeat from step 7 with remaining dough balls.

Enjoy with curry, chutney, or jam.

ACKNOWLEDGMENTS

When I was a kid, I used to beg my mother to cook something other than Indian food sometimes.

My parents were married in Tanzania when they were both twenty-two. They moved to Canada a few months later. Eventually they had my sister, then me. We watched hockey or Bollywood most nights, and all we ate was the East African–influenced Indian food they were raised on. They spoke to us in a hybrid English/Kutchi, with a bit of Gujarati and Swahili sprinkled in, and they didn't care that we weren't interested in learning the language or learning how to cook. My parents were supportive and obliging, so Mum agreed to vary our diet. We'd have kuku paka one night, lasagna the next. Kebob jo shaak, followed by meat loaf.

As an adult, I became obsessed with cooking. Bread from scratch, homemade pasta, Chinese, Thai, Caribbean food, plus any baked goods you could imagine. I love learning to cook food from around the world. But when I want to feel connected to the beautiful country of Tanzania, and my own specific culture—East African Indian Muslim Canadian—I turn to our food. That is what this book is about, connecting to your roots through food. Writing a romance between two people finding their place in their culture and falling in love through their love of home cooking was such a joy for me, and I am grateful to everyone who had a part in making this book happen.

Thank you to my wonderful agent, Rachel Brooks, for having faith in me and for always supporting marginalized writers to get our stories told. Thank you to the early readers for this book, Jackie Lau, Laura Heffernan, and Roselle Lim, not only for their feedback on the manuscript, but also for being great friends who are always there for me through this publishing journey. Thank you to Jennifer Lambert, whose editorial advice on this project was invaluable. A huge thank-you to my editor at Forever, Leah Hultenschmidt, for her amazing insight and for knowing exactly how to make this book be the absolute best it could be. Thank you to the rest of the team at Forever/Grand Central Publishing, the acquisition team, production editors, art department, marketing, sales, and publicity.

This book is dedicated to my parents, Nazir and Shahida, and I want to thank them for being who they are. I was worried about how to write a book with unsupportive, meddling, and judgmental parents, and it turned out to be so easy. I just had to write the exact opposite of my own parents.

Thank you to my rock, my best friend, my comrade in arms through life, my husband, Tony. Like the couple in this book, we came together because of an obsession with food. Years ago, when we barely knew each other, we stayed up all night together waiting for a cooking show to come on in the morning. Twenty-three years later, there is still no one else I would rather be in the kitchen with.

And finally, to my kids, Khalil and Anissa. They asked me to write a limerick to celebrate how much I love that I get to raise two amazing humans, but I'm no poet. They are awesome, and I am lucky they're mine. They are the best people I know.

ABOUT THE AUTHOR

After a childhood raised on Bollywood, Monty Python, and Jane Austen, **Farah Heron** wove complicated story arcs and uplifting happily-ever-afters in her daydreams while pursuing careers in human resources and psychology. She started writing those stories down a few years ago and never looked back. She writes romantic comedies and women's fiction full of huge South Asian families, delectable food, and most importantly, brown people falling stupidly in love. She lives in Toronto with her husband, two children, and a rabbit. She is considering getting a cat.

To learn more, visit:
  FarahHeron.com
  Twitter @FarahHeron
  Instagram @FarahHeronAuthor
  Facebook.com/FarahHeronAuthor